Strictly
Seduction

Lisa Renee Jones

First published in Great Britain 2012
Mills & Boon, an imprint of Harlequin (UK) Limited,
Eton House, 18-24 Paradise Road, Richmond, Surrey TW9 1SR

STRICTLY SEDUCTION © Harlequin Enterprises II B.V./S.à.r.l. 2012

Watch Me © Lisa Renee Jones 2012
Follow My Lead © Lisa Renee Jones 2012
Winning Moves © Lisa Renee Jones 2012

ISBN: 978 0 263 90242 6

24-1112

Harlequin (UK) policy is to use papers that are natural, renewable and recyclable products and made from wood grown in sustainable forests. The logging and manufacturing processes conform to the legal environmental regulations of the country of origin.

Printed and bound
by CPI Group (UK) Ltd, Croydon, CR0 4YY

Lisa Renee Jones spends her days writing the dreams playing in her head. Before becoming a writer, Lisa lived the life of a corporate executive, often taking the red-eye flight out of town and flying home for the excitement of a Little League baseball game. Visit Lisa at www.lisareneejones.com.

Watch Me

1

SCREAMS FILLED THE AIR, jolting Meagan Tippan, the producer of the new dance reality show America's Stepping Up, from a dead sleep to a startled, heart-pounding sitting position. That was about two seconds before the sprinkler system in the restored Victorian beachfront mansion kicked into gear. Meagan arched her back against the icy fingers of wetness that seeped through her thin T-shirt.

The very real possibility of a fire pierced the momentary shock of Meagan's abrupt awakening. Quickly, she shoved away her soaked blankets and darted across the room. There were twelve hopeful dancers in the house who'd come here to chase a dream, not to live a nightmare, and she had to get them, and her crew, to safety.

Flinging open her door, Meagan found Ginger Scott, one of the two choreographers for the show and "House Mom," in the hallway, rushing the six female dancers in the competition down the stairs.

"Is anyone hurt?" Meagan shouted loudly, because

the water seemed to be muffling everything but the panicked voices echoing around her.

"Just scared," Ginger said, shoving a wet mop of blond hair from her face, as Meagan did the same to her light brown hair. "And I don't see a fire. DJ says he doesn't see one downstairs, either." DJ being her twin brother and male counterpart in the house.

"I called 9-1-1," DJ shouted, rushing up to meet them. "Could be electrical though. Big trouble for a house this old."

Right, Meagan thought grimly. Wouldn't that be peachy? After ten weeks spent casting across the country, with one mishap after another—enough to prompt whispers of a "curse" that she'd hoped to put to rest—only to discover they'd also managed to move into a place with electrical problems, and have it catch on fire their first night there.

"Is everyone okay?" came the voice of another male dancer at the bottom of the stairs. "Do you need help?"

"No! Stay where you are," Meagan yelled, taking in water as she spoke. "We don't need help up here, and there is no fire." *That they knew about,* but she didn't say that. She didn't want to freak anyone out any more than they already were.

"Get everyone on the lawn where we can get a head-count," Meagan said, shooing Ginger and DJ down the stairs. The sooner they had this situation under control, the better. Control? After thirty-two years, and her own dance career destroyed by a knee injury, she should know control was a facade. Just when you thought you had it, it slipped away.

Eventually, Meagan finally had all her hot-bodied,

dripping-wet dancers on the front lawn, looking as if they were posing for a kinky spread in an X-rated magazine. She could only imagine editing this segment. Their stationary cameras had no doubt caught everything and the studio execs would *want* this mishap included in behind-the-scenes footage. After all, they'd insisted on broadcasting every other disaster—from falling sets and broken-down buses, to a crazed fan who'd set the hotel lobby on fire.

A thought hit Meagan like a huge brick. Oh, God. It was a very *bad* thought.

Meagan whirled around to face the house, as if it were possessed, glaring at the monster that was about to ruin everything, even her own career. The chance to pitch the idea for this show had come after years of working as the producer for a top news show in Dallas, Texas. Leaving that job on the long shot that this could survive the ratings war had been a big risk. She knew the chips would be stacked against her. Tonight that stack had gotten bigger. Not only were the cameras getting wet, but the house, where they'd intended to spend the next twelve weeks, was being destroyed by the water. And she had enough experience with fickle network executives to know that her show, her darn dream-fulfilling show, was turning into a nightmare that might well be called "cancelled."

And although the top dancer among her contestants was set to win a new car, a studio contract and cash, while the other dancers would earn major industry exposure that could change their lives, she wondered if it would all end tonight.

Meagan tried to comfort herself by recalling the

high-powered panel of judges she'd secured for the
live shows—a well-known choreographer, a highly respected casting agent and even a highly acclaimed pop
star. Surely, the studio wouldn't want to pay out their
contracts and see no real return.

Who was she kidding? Studio executives always
leaned toward taking their financial hits and cutting
losses. Meagan had to do something to save the house,
if she expected to save the show.

Meagan leapt to action, darting toward the house,
ignoring shouts of her name. Clearly, there was no fire,
only water—lots and lots of destructive water. She burst
through the door, and headed straight to the basement
through the kitchen. Though she had no real idea how
to turn off the sprinklers, flipping the circuit breaker
seemed logical, and she remembered seeing it by the
washer and dryer.

Sure enough, the breaker was where she thought it
was, but any relief she felt at finding it was doused when
she realized it was ridiculously high off the ground. Oh
yeah, it was high, well above her reach, or any normal
human's, for that matter. Resigned to the climb ahead
of her, she splashed her way closer.

She couldn't help but ask herself if the night could
possibly get any worse, as she heaved herself on top of
the washer.

Footsteps sounded on the stairs, and she yelled over
her shoulder, "I said go to the lawn!" She jerked the
metal panel, but it wouldn't open. "I need everyone outside and safe." There was the sound of more splashing
and she grimaced. "I said—"

"Come down from there before you get hurt," came an order from behind her.

Meagan froze at the deeply resonating voice of Samuel Kellar, the sexy, blond-haired, blue-eyed, irritating, arrogant, six-foot-two—if she had to bet her life on it—head of studio security, who she knew all too well and wished she didn't.

Samuel, or Sam as everyone called him, had directly coordinated much of the show's security over the past few months, especially the open casting calls. She'd had innumerable occasions to know with certainty that few people could rattle her nerves the way Sam could. When Sam said jump, people jumped. He didn't *ask* anyone to do anything, he ordered them. And since that trait irritated her to no end, how was it that the man made her want to both yell at him and strip him naked at the same time—she didn't know.

But shouting wasn't her style, nor was sleeping with a man like Sam. She preferred subtle and submissive, to his demanding and arrogant. Unfortunately, Sam wasn't the least bit dissuaded by her sharp-tongued retorts meant to be off-putting. In fact, he infuriatingly seemed to enjoy sparring with her.

And just when Meagan thought Sam's presence ensured that the night really, truly, couldn't get any worse, it did. With frustration, she yanked at the panel door with an unsuccessful jerk that hiked her butt up in the air. Meagan froze, mortified, in the embarrassing position. Sam, her sexy pain-in-the-backside, now had a view of her backside. Because Meagan was pretty sure her skimpy, wet, hot-pink boxers weren't leaving much to the imagination.

SAM KELLAR MIGHT BE former Special Forces, a man of restraint and discipline who considered himself a gentleman, but he was still a man when it came down to it. And the man in him was standing at attention for Meagan's impossibly sexy, heart-shaped butt, despite the cold shower he was enduring. It said a lot about how much he wanted this "taboo" woman. Taboo because they not only worked together, but she chilled him with her ice-princess routine every time the sparks between them got too hot.

"Get down, Meagan," he ordered, having no doubt he would get an argument—prickly arguments were part of her ice-princess routine.

She yanked ineffectively at the panel door. "Not until I turn off the water."

"I'll do that," he promised. "Come down before you—"

She slipped before the words were out and then tried to right herself. He didn't wait to see if she was going to succeed or fail. Sam wrapped his arms around her long, slender legs to make sure she didn't fall.

"Sam!" she objected, pressing her hands to the ceiling, shifting unsteadily to stare down at him. Their eyes locked. Awareness flashed hot and fast between them, a silent understanding that she was half naked and in his arms, and that this wasn't the first time either one of them had thought about such a moment.

"Let go of me," she said, a hint of panic in her voice, the same panic he heard every time their combustible attraction flared to life.

"And let you break your pretty little neck?" he asked. "Not a chance." Not giving her time to object, he slid his hands to her waist and forcefully lifted her down from the washer. Not an easy task from his lower position, and she ended up plastered against him as intimately as those shorts hugged her backside. And oh yeah, the man in him was alert and present all right. He'd wanted this woman too long not to react to having her lush body pressed to his.

"What do you think you're doing?" she demanded. Her hips were melded to his, her hands pressed against his chest—hands he'd often dreamed of having on his chest and all kinds of other places. Sexual awareness had caught them like the water they couldn't escape.

Her nervous energy escalated, just as her temper did, meaning their same routine as always. "Sam, damn it! The house is being destroyed. My career is being destroyed." She squirmed out of his arms, and reluctantly he let her go. "I have to stop the water." She turned back to the washer.

That, he wasn't letting her do. Sam shackled her arm and pulled her around to face him, and she was close, so close he could kiss her, and damn if he didn't want to in a bad way. He would have, too, if not for the fact that she was right—the water needed to be turned off.

"Stubborn woman," he mumbled. "I'll do it. That's why I came down here in the first place. That and I saw you rush into the house, and knew you were up to no good."

Sirens sounded in the distance, and unintentionally, his gaze brushed her very visible, red, puckered nipples beneath the transparent shirt. He didn't like the idea of the entire fire department getting the same view.

"Sam!" she objected, folding her arms over her chest.

He scrubbed a hand over his face, as if he would ever wipe away the image of those perfect breasts. "Sorry," he said, meaning it. He didn't want to make her feel uncomfortable—no, uncomfortable was the last thing he wanted to make Meagan feel. "That wasn't on purpose. It just…happened." He slid out of the rain jacket he'd put on before coming inside and handed it to her. "Put this on," he told her, "before a gaggle of firemen make the same mistake." The idea of that gnawed away at his gut in an unfamiliar, uncomfortable way.

Sam turned away from her, lifting himself on top of the washer and hitting the button to the panel door that Meagan had missed.

She made a surprised sound. "I loosened the door for you."

His lips quirked, but he didn't reply. He so enjoyed how easily he ruffled her feathers, even when he wasn't trying. He cut the breaker to the sprinklers. The water was off. The sound of firemen's voices and loud, heavy footsteps echoed from the floor above.

He eased to the floor, ankle deep in water. Meagan was thankfully well covered in his way-too-big jacket, but there was something intensely erotic about her in something of his that he couldn't dismiss.

She slicked her hair back, drawing it away from her face, a face incredibly appealing without makeup, au naturel. And then they stood there.

Water clung to her thick, dark lashes, framing grass-green eyes that swept over his wet studio T-shirt and returned to his face.

More of that sexual tension zipped between them.

"We need you folks out of here," came a male voice from the stairs, effectively jolting them from the hot little spell spinning around them.

"We're coming," Sam yelled, and then to Meagan, "Better late than never, but had this been a real fire, people could have been hurt. I'll be talking to them about how this happened. In the meantime, one of my guys is already arranging a hotel for everyone." He motioned for her to head upstairs.

A sudden wave of vulnerability washed across her features. "I ah…considering the firemen and your guys and…well, thanks for the jacket. And for turning off the water." And then, when he thought they'd made some progress, she proved him wrong, pursing her lips and adding, "But I was about to turn off the water myself. I had it. I was getting it."

He couldn't stop the corners of his lips from twitching, despite the certainty that a smile—and most certainly the laugh threatening to escape—would only set him up for a battle. "Of course you would have," he agreed, playing the cat-and-mouse game she seemed to want him to play—though, damn if he knew who was the cat and who was the mouse half the time. "But I'm here, Meagan. Why not use me?"

Her lips parted slightly at the words. Then her brows knit together, and her hands went to her hips, giving him a delectable glimpse of skin below her breasts. "You're impossible," she announced, glowering, before sloshing toward the stairs.

He stood watching her, thinking that the real "impossible" here, was not him, but that either of them believed they were going to be satisfied with this game much longer. She wanted him. He wanted her. And he was going to do something about it. No matter how many washers he had to climb.

2

SEEING SAM AGAIN SO SOON after…well, he'd seen her up close and personal wasn't something Meagan welcomed. Not even after she'd had access to a hotel bed for a few hours, staring at the ceiling, thinking about his body pressed to hers.

Now dressed in her conservative black skirt and blouse, feeling a mess, as she stepped off the elevator and directly into the studio's executive offices, she was pretty darn sure she wasn't going to escape Sam's presence. Because instantly, as if she had some cosmic radar for the man, a flutter of anticipatory butterflies overtook her stomach. The kind a lover felt for a lover.

Meagan didn't want to react like this to Sam. Life had taught her not to date men like Sam, certainly not to invite them into her bed. She stuck with the easy-going types, who'd actually listen to what pleased a woman, rather than assuming they knew and getting it wrong. Men who cared about what a woman wanted, which right now, for her, was to keep her job. Scratch that. This wasn't about a job. It was about a dream, about the career as a dancer never realized. About how she could use that passion in a positive way and help others who loved dance. Exactly like a very special teacher had done for her once when she was a young girl working hard to become a top-class ballerina.

With an intake of breath, she reminded herself she was here to pitch shooting the show from the hotel she and the cast and crew had moved into. As far as ideas went, it was a good one. Meagan approached the secretary, June, who smiled her usual friendly welcome from behind an oversize mahogany desk.

"Morning, Meagan. Or maybe not. I hear you had a rough night."

"What doesn't kill you makes interesting television," Meagan replied lightly, shoving a lock of brown hair behind her ear.

June chuckled at her quip. "I'll let Sabrina know you're here."

A masculine voice rumbled behind Meagan, thick with a sensual taunt. "Good morning, ice princess. How are you feeling today?"

Meagan tensed, hating when he called her that, and he did it often. Hating it even more since Sam's presence most likely meant the studio intended to shut down the show. He'd be called in to plan damage control in case of any trouble that might occur when the contestants heard they were headed home.

Feeling nauseous at the thought, she told herself to hold it together, to give him the sass he expected from her. She turned to face him, but found herself captured by his amused, piercing blue eyes that not only sent a sizzle down her spine, but to other more intimate places. And that made the "sass" come a wee bit easier.

"I'm feeling downright chilly, why thank you," she replied, pivoting on her heels and making a beeline for the lobby chairs. She was all too eager to escape Sam's assessing stare. He would see that she wasn't feeling chilly at all—she was feeling hot enough to fan herself. And stare he did, indeed. Settling into one of the black leather chairs lining the wall, Meagan didn't have to look up to know Sam was watching her. She felt his gaze, hot and heavy, following her movements.

Crossing her legs, she snagged a magazine, and tried to live up to the "ice princess" label, rather than the "wanton vixen," that he made her want to be. Despite her effort to resist, her gaze lifted at his approach, tracking the strut that she could tell came natural to him. Meagan's mouth went dry at the sexy way his jeans molded those really nice, strong legs, and at the memory of another pair of jeans, wet and plastered to lithe muscle.

"You're easily agitated this morning," he commented, claiming the chair directly across from her. "I usually have to work harder to get you this riled up."

"I'll just have to sleep less more often," she replied. "Then you'll have your princess raring to go."

He grinned, his eyes twinkling again. "I'm not even going to take advantage of that poorly worded rebuttal because you *are* tired, and I'm afraid you might hurt me in front of Sabrina."

Her cheeks heated as the double meaning of his statement sank in, but before she could reply, the door to her boss's office opened. Sabrina stepped into view, her long blond hair neatly pinned at the back of her neck, her white suit impeccable. "Come in, you two. So sorry I'm running late. Would either of you like coffee?"

"No coffee for me," Sam answered, as he pushed to his feet.

"I'd love some coffee," she said, mostly to contradict Sam, desperate to feel like she still had some semblance of control. It was silly, ridiculous, immature, and proof that she, in fact, had absolutely no control when it came to this man.

Sam arched an eyebrow at her, a knowing look in his too-blue eyes that said he knew exactly what she was thinking. She grimaced. "I haven't slept. Who doesn't want coffee when they haven't slept?" She lifted her chin, and headed toward the office.

Once inside, Sabrina motioned to a small conference table, and Meagan found herself seated between her boss and Sam. A cup of coffee quickly appeared in front of her.

Sabrina flattened her hands on the table. "Well. Where do we begin? We knew this show would be a bit of a crazy ride, but just how crazy were we thinking? The good news is, a crazy ride will usually translate to high ratings. Several of the big gossip websites not only reported last night's occurrence, they're feeding the rumor of the show's curse. Twitter and Facebook are buzzing. So we'll go with this and feed the curse, so to speak. The plan is that over the next two weeks, we're going to show reruns of the auditions. Which gives you that two weeks as a reprieve to get settled in a new house. We'll also run a series of promotional commercials playing up the curse. You'll be responsible for the promotional footage, Meagan. We want to give the viewers glimpses of contestants talking about what happened last night, laced with some spooky 'what if' kind of paranormal flavor. Then play up the curse during the first two episodes. We'll talk from there based on ratings. Everyone will be paid as if on-air for these two weeks off."

Meagan's head was swimming with a mixture of relief and panic. They weren't cancelled. That was good and she'd been in television long enough to understand about working the ratings. "I'm concerned about fitting the dancing in with the curse footage."

Sabrina smiled. "You get two hours for your first episode. Deliver the ratings, and that's just the beginning. We keep the same standard format we've planned all along. One night of reality television. One night of competition and results, with the three judges choosing who goes home. The final show will still be open to votes from viewers. And those superstar performers you wanted us to deliver for the live episodes? That will be your reward if the curse promotionals deliver the viewer interest we believe they will. We'll keep investing in you, and the show, as long as the ratings justify it."

Meagan could hardly believe it. In the midst of a dark disaster, everything was looking really quite spectacular. "That's amazing, Sabrina. I'm speechless," she said. "I won't let you down."

"I know you won't," she said. "Exactly why I support this venture so completely. But everyone isn't as onboard here at the studio as I am. There are liability issues with the situations we've encountered. That means, we have to take some precautions to protect everyone. You and Sam will work together to locate a new house for the filming, and get the contestants safely settled. And then as a final precaution, we'll have on-site, around-the-clock security."

A sudden rush of anxiety came over Meagan, and her heart galloped. Her gaze met Sam's. "What exactly does that mean? Around-the-clock security?"

"It means," Sabrina said, "that this show has big potential, but as things have progressed, it has also proven to have huge potential liability associated with it. The studio prefers to protect the up side and limit the down side of the show. Sam was nearby when he got the emergency call to go to your aid. Next time, we might not be that lucky. In other words, we've asked Sam to handle the show's security with a personal touch, rather than a distant supervisory one, as he has up to this point."

The corners of his mouth twitched slightly. "I'm your new roommate. I'm moving into the house with you."

Meagan's silent gasp delivered a smile to Sam's face.

"Am I that bad?"

"There is nothing bad about any of this," Sabrina told them, getting to her feet. "You two are going to make great ratings magic together."

3

Meeting over, Sam followed Meagan into the elevator, and the instant the doors shut, she turned to him. "You're the head of studio security. Surely you have better things to do than babysit me and my dancers."

He arched a brow. "That eager to get rid of me, are you?"

"The only thing great we do together is fight."

"I guess it's time we discover what else we do great together," he said, leaning back to study her. "This wasn't my decision, nor was it negotiable. If I hadn't stepped up to the plate and assured the studio I'd contain liability while you focused on ratings, there wouldn't be a show at all. And no matter how big a jerk you think I am, I wasn't going to see you fail, along with everyone else associated with the show, when I could prevent it."

She deflated instantly, her hand pressing to her stomach. "I knew they were going to cancel us."

"But they didn't," he said. "You have a lifeline. We have a lifeline. Which means—" The elevator door opened, and several people were waiting to enter. "Let's talk about this outside."

She inhaled and nodded, and they exited the elevator. The minute Sam was in the lobby, one of his staff rushed into his path.

"Just the man I was looking for," Josh Strong said. A twenty-eight-year-old former navy SEAL who'd gone civilian to care for a sick mother, Josh never missed a beat. Sam was damn lucky to have hired the man. "I've compiled that list of properties you wanted, as potentials for the dance show."

Sam intended to involve Meagan in the conversation, but he was too late. She was already gone, on the move, speeding away from him so fast that she was leaving a trail of smoke.

"Hold on to those for a few minutes," Sam said. "I'll catch up with you." He headed for Meagan with fire in his step. Avoiding him wasn't an option if they were going to make this work, and he was done with the tip-toeing around what was between them anyway.

Sam caught up with Meagan in the parking lot, just in time to press his hand to the door of her Acura, and keep her from opening it. The wind shifted, light brown strands of vanilla-and-honey-scented hair brushing his cheek, his groin tightened uncomfortably.

"We need to talk, Meagan," he insisted.

"Sam," she ground out, tilting her chin up, bringing that kissable mouth inches from his. "Don't hold my door like I'm your captive. And yes, we need to talk, but not now. I have to get back to the hotel and edit film and check on my dancers. And just so we're straight—

you don't get to decide when we talk or do anything. You ask, and we discuss and decide together. Got it?"

Oh yeah, he got it all right. "It" being a rush of pure male need. "Have dinner with me tonight."

"That doesn't sound like a question," she rebutted.

"And if it had been a question, would you have said yes?"

She hesitated, her lashes lowering and then lifting, defiance glinting in her eyes, as she replied, "No."

He didn't miss the hesitation, or the fact that she hadn't complained about his nearness—so close he could lean in and touch her as he had the night before. And he wanted to. Oh yeah, he wanted to in a bad way.

"What if I said I'm bringing the real-estate listings for the housing options?"

"That's bribery," she said. "You could email me the listings."

The truth was, with their limited timeframe, he wanted to review the properties and narrow the list right away, but he didn't tell her that. "Guilty as charged," he agreed and pushed off the car, but he held his position close to her, soaking in the heat of her body, the scent of her hair still teasing his nostrils. "We need to have this talk. Make a truce and set some boundaries, so we can make those great ratings that you want to happen."

"Fine, then," she agreed. "Dinner will include a lesson on the difference between a question and an order."

He laughed. "Fair enough." He loved the way this woman kept him on his toes.

Her expression softened. "I do appreciate you saving the show, Sam."

"Two thank yous in a matter of hours," he said. "I do believe we're making progress."

"Short lived if you forget that I'm in control of my set, Sam, for even one moment. If you want to make changes to procedures, or anything else, you come to me. You talk to me. Then we make changes."

"Understood," he said willingly. "With the exception of anything I see as an immediate threat to someone's safety."

She inclined her head. "I can live with that."

They gazed at each other, electricity sparking in the air. Sam leaned in, lowered his head intimately, to softly say, "I expect you'll be surprised just how much greatness we have between us," he said, and then he pulled back before he did something crazy and kissed her in public. Surely doing so would get him a great big smack in the face. "I'll see you at seven." He turned and sauntered back toward the building, feeling her eyes on him.

"Sam," she called. "Make that seven-fifteen."

He laughed and waved in agreement. She was letting him know nothing with her would come easily. She remained a challenge—but then anything worth having was a challenge. And Meagan was one of the most interesting, impossible-to-resist challenges he'd ever encountered.

He headed back to the offices, only to find Sabrina walking toward him, her purse and her keys in hand.

"I've debated telling you something," she said, "and I don't want it to get out."

"I'm listening."

"When the higher-ups green-lit Meagan's show, they

insisted on attaching a few people to it. One of them was Kiki Reynolds. You might want to keep an eye on her."

"Could she be a real problem?"

"Could be."

Sam nodded, grateful for the tip, and he and Sabrina parted ways.

It seemed Meagan was going to be fighting a whole lot more than her attraction to him in the next few months and Sam vowed he'd be by her side every step of the way.

4

SAM KELLAR WAS MEAGAN'S nemesis, proven once again by the fact that she was thinking about *him* rather than the on-camera contestant interviews she was supervising. She pressed her hands into her temples. She still wore her skirt, though she'd managed to trade her heels for flats, she hadn't made time to change, but she seemed to have plenty of time to think about things she shouldn't be thinking about. Sam and his too-blue eyes and his hard, tempting body.

She didn't want to work with him, and she absolutely didn't want to live with him for the duration of the show. That was too close for comfort. She knew darn good and well that if she had even a moment of weakness, Sam would take over her bed, and her life would follow.

She focused on the lounge area of the show's private hotel floor, now newly converted into their interview set. The studio wanted drama, so she was working on giving them drama. She was the producer and mastermind of the show, and should have had a say in Sam's involvement in the show. Still, they weren't cancelled.

Her dream of this program's success, and these dancers' dreams of exciting careers, were still alive. That was what counted.

Derek Rogers, the show's young, hot host, was busy interviewing one of the last female dancers. They were finally about to wrap for the night, which meant Meagan would soon meet Sam for dinner.

Maybe she'd get the male dancers on set for interviews, instead of tomorrow as planned, and just skip dinner. And she really did need to squeeze in some footage of Ginger and DJ talking about the events of the night before. They were, after all, not only choreographing the contestants' routines, but helping to supervise the contestants.

"What were you thinking when the fire alarm went off?" Derek asked Tabitha Ready, who at twenty-eight, was the oldest female dancer competing. Many of the other contestants looked up to her. She was a pretty brunette with loads of talent. She was also an absolute drama queen who was so paranoid about, well, everything, that she seemed better suited as a cast member of Scream than of a dance show. And she was making some of the girls act the same way.

In response to the question, Tabitha seemed to sink deeper in the leather chair she occupied, crossing her arms in front of her pink sweat jacket. "I just knew we were all going to die. We keep having these things happen on the set and I... Just thank God, Jensen was there." Jensen being the male dancer who clearly had a crush on Tabitha. The public was going to eat this up.

Derek, looking every bit the handsome model even in his jeans and *Stepping Up* T-shirt, cast a discreet glance at Meagan that said he, too, believed, this footage was a ratings grabber.

"Jensen carried you out of the house, I understand," Derek prodded, urging her to continue on this path of conversation.

"Oh yes!" she said. "It was horrible. We didn't see fire, but we could smell smoke. We knew any second everything would just blow up." She lowered her voice. "You know. We have a curse on the set."

Meagan cringed every time the word *curse* came up, despite the studio's explicit instructions to play it up. She'd planned for drama to unfold in the house with the dancers—in fact, that concept had been pitched with the show—so one would think a curse would excite Meagan as much as it did the studio, but it didn't. A curse was something that would mess with the dancers' heads and their performances. And ultimately, the dancing had to win the public's hearts. But "the curse" had been given new life and new breath by the house fire, exciting the executives with the promise of ratings. Sure enough, every single dancer had brought it up in their interview. Tabitha, however, seemed determined to own the curse.

"We're afraid of what will happen next," she said. "None of us are going to sleep tonight. I don't know how we'll dance under such circumstances."

The cameraman zoomed in on Derek's deadpan look before he said, "Then you know what you should do?"

Meagan exchanged a "here it comes" look with Shayla White, the director, who was fast becoming a close friend. Hiring Derek, an ex-pro quarterback and sportscaster, for a dance show had been a risk, especially considering he'd lived up to his reputation for saying whatever came to mind. If *Stepping Up* was to succeed where other dance shows had failed, it meant they needed originality, and Derek was nothing if not that.

Derek continued, "Get a lucky charm like us athletes do. In my case, I'd get a pair of lucky briefs."

"Briefs?" Tabitha asked, skeptically. "Eww."

Derek grinned and held up his hands. "Hey, don't tell me you haven't got a pair of lucky underwear."

It took a second but finally Tabitha, and everyone else on set burst into laughter. "Well, maybe I do," she said, clearly giving it some serious thought.

Derek assured her, "At least five guys on my NFL team had 'game day' lucky boxers. They swore they'd screw up on the field without them. They believed those transformed them into men of steel, and so they did." He tapped his forehead. "It's all in your head. It's what you believe."

Tabitha smiled slyly. "And if I don't wear underwear?"

If Derek caught her flirty remarks, and he was a smart guy so surely he had, he didn't show it, nor did he miss a beat. "Socks. They're the next best thing." The entire crew erupted in laughter, and Meagan could just imagine the audience doing the same thing. "But really, Tabitha, whatever works for you. Just make sure that your lucky charm is something you can always have with you. Heck, I knew a guy who had to kiss his wife right before the game or he messed up every play he was in. When she didn't travel with him, he was worthless."

"So maybe I should kiss Jensen." Tabitha beamed.

"Then what happens when one of you gets sent home?"

The air seemed to crackle, the silence thick. It was a brilliant moment that had evolved from a talk of curse, and shown human vulnerability that every viewer could relate to on some level. Tabitha seemed devastated. But it was short-lived. She recovered promptly, showing herself to be a pro at flirtation. "Then maybe *you* should be my lucky charm."

Derek grinned and gave her his cheek, tapping it with his finger. She kissed him, and the crew all broke out in grins.

A few questions later, the interview ended. And just when Meagan thought she'd wrap the night's shooting with a laugh rather than with the curse, Tabitha walked to the edge of the set and went tumbling forward, smack onto her face.

AT 6:45 P.M., THIRTY MINUTES before his dinner with Meagan, Sam completed his check-in at the hotel, sliding a healthy tip, compliments of the studio, into the doorman's hand to ensure his bag was delivered to his room for him. With way too much eagerness in his step to suit him—considering Sam knew it had nothing to do with duty, and everything to do with seeing Meagan—Sam headed toward the bank of elevators, rather than the restaurant. He knew Meagan wouldn't be there, and he had no intention of sitting around and waiting for her. Not when he'd bet money on her being intentionally late, and then claiming work as an excuse.

It was a control thing to her—her desire to have it and keep it from him. Fine by him. This was her show, and she was in charge and deserved that respect. But as the person in charge of safety, he'd need to ensure he never ran the risk of jeopardizing his authority and ability to do his job in the face of any threat.

So he and Meagan had some hashing out to do. Tonight. Alone. Still, he'd promised himself he wouldn't touch her for all kinds of reasons. Work wasn't the place to play. Smart people knew that bedroom games, and even simple romantic notions, could easily turn emotional and explode, no matter how covertly they began. He didn't do complicated relationships. He did the uncomplicated, casual type. Namely because he'd seen far too many divorces, and tormented, worried spouses like his mother, when he'd been in the army.

Despite all these brilliant assessments about what he had going on, or rather not going on with Meagan, Sam couldn't stop thinking about her. That had never happened to him with a woman before. And as he punched in the code for the private floor the studio had rented for the show, there was no mistaking the thrum of anticipation he felt during the twenty-floor ride, at seeing her again. A thrum he recognized could lead him to trouble. Big damn trouble.

The elevator dinged, and the doors began to slide open. In the same instant, a scream filled the air. Instinct sent Sam into action, darting out of the elevator to draw up short when he found a studio set almost directly off the elevator in the center of a large lounge area. One of the contestants, Tabitha, was lying flat on her face, her mouth bloody. Meagan was squatting next to her. Hovering above her were the twins, Ginger and DJ, who clearly wanted to help the situation, and didn't know how. Kiki, the thirtysomething attractive redhead, stood in the background looking amused.

Sam grimaced at her behavior and headed for Meagan. "Does she need an ambulance?"

"Yes!" Tabitha screamed. "Yes, I need an ambulance. My front tooth is missing! *My tooth* is gone!"

"I called 9-1-1," one of the crew shouted.

Relief washed over Sam. A tooth he could deal with. No one died from a lost tooth. But any relief he felt vanished when the cast of contestants emerged like a pack of wild animals onto the set, as a rumble of questions and panic erupted. The cameras continued to roll, panning the crowded lounge.

Sam's gaze found Meagan's, even as she helped Tabitha to her feet, a silent question in his stare. He didn't want to screw up footage she needed for the show, but they didn't need another injury, either. Fortunately, as usual, he read her easily—the look on her face said *Please get them under control.* The fact that they communicated without words was a testament to the natural connection they shared. That he agreed with her decision, that she confirmed what he knew already—that she wasn't like the studio executives who put ratings above all else—were just more reasons why he wanted to be alone with her.

"Enough," he called out to the group, holding up his hands. "My name is Sam Kellar, and I'm the head of—"

"It's the curse!" Tabitha shouted. "It's the curse."

Screams erupted from the dancers. Sam and Meagan shared an exasperated look before, together, they went into damage control.

The studio wanted footage that fed the curse, and

now, they were sure getting it, but not because he, or Meagan, were trying to deliver it. He and Meagan were just trying to survive and doing so *together*. Oh yeah, staying hands-off with Meagan was going to be about as easy as calming this group down. And that, it appeared, was damn near impossible.

FIFTEEN MINUTES LATER, EMS was gone and Sam and Meagan had agreed that Tabitha should go to the hospital, with one of Sam's men escorting her to avoid the tabloid photographers.

His man, Josh, had just learned he would be that lucky man. "Josh's an ex-SEAL," he explained to Meagan. "If he can't handle Tabitha, nobody can."

Meagan snorted. "Neither of you know Tabitha or you might reconsider that statement. I can't possibly let you take on this job by yourself. Believe me, you'll want backup." Before Sam could object, Meagan flagged Kiki over, and Sam didn't miss the flash of interest across Josh's face.

Sam leaned close to Josh. "I hear she killed her last lover."

Josh, who had a way with the women, said, "I can think of worse ways to die."

Kiki joined them, looking irritated at having been summoned. "I need you to please go with Tabitha to the hospital," Meagan said and pointed at Josh. "This is Josh Strong, one of Sam's men. He'll go along with you for security reasons."

Kiki looked disgusted. "Why is this my job?"

Sam arched a brow at Kiki's blatant disrespect toward Meagan. It heightened his worries about Kiki, but

Meagan responded with remarkable composure. "Because I need to review property options for the show with Sam, and I can't risk any exposure, tabloid or otherwise, that might hurt us. In other words, I need you, my next-in-charge, who has pull and power. Josh here will offer muscle if you run into trouble. You deal with Tabitha and her injury."

"Shouldn't I be included in the property search?" Kiki asked, sounding a bit like a spoiled brat afraid of getting one less cookie from the jar, and not at all concerned about Tabitha.

"When I know where we stand, you will be," Meagan assured her. "But right now, I need you to attend to Tabitha. Go, please."

Kiki frowned and eyed Josh, motioning to her left. "This way."

"Nothing like having a studio exec's niece forced on you," Sam said, imagining that Kiki resented having to work under Meagan.

Meagan turned to him. "How'd you know that?"

"I make it a point to know things," he said. "And I'd watch my back with her. If a curse exists, it's probably down to her. The last three shows she's been on failed."

"Yeah, I know," Meagan said. "I've heard all kinds of rumors about her that I've tried to tune out. I want to give her the benefit of the doubt because I know how gossip grows. And really, it doesn't matter anyway. She's a mandatory part of this show, per my contract with the studio."

Sam wasn't going to tell Meagan everything he knew about Kiki, but he did want to alert her to keep up her guard. "I understand your position, but there is some truth to what you've probably heard. For instance, she did sleep with that producer who ended up fired."

She laughed. "Well, I won't be an easy target in that department, at least. She can't get me into bed to manipulate me. You might want to warn your man, Josh, though."

"I plan to."

She nodded. "Good, because I'd hate to see him hurt when he's just trying to keep us all safe. All I can say is thank God my director is an angel, so I have someone I can truly trust. She was picked for me, too, and she's marvelous."

Meagan could trust him, as well, but he knew she wasn't ready to embrace that concept. Not now. But he intended to change that.

Fifteen minutes later, the contestants had returned to their rooms, and he'd ordered three more security personnel to keep them that way. The crew, who'd been put up in the hotel for ease of filming, headed to the lobby bar to "analyze" the day's events over drinks and food.

Derek lingered with Sam and Meagan. "What about you two? Surely you both need a good, stiff drink or two, after that disaster. And here I thought football players were rowdy. Those kids are crazy."

"You can't say I didn't warn you before you took the job," Meagan reminded him.

Derek scrubbed his jaw. "Yeah, yeah. I thought you were exaggerating." He gave her a pointed look. "You weren't."

"Nope," she said. "I wasn't. So have a drink for me as well because I need one but don't dare indulge. I have work left to do."

Derek eyed Sam and Sam held up a hand. "I never drink on duty, and the next few weeks are all duty for me." Sam liked Derek. Derek had spent his NFL days racking up awards—not scandal—which was exactly why he didn't think Derek would survive beyond season one.

Derek smiled warmly. "All right, then. I'll make an exception to my one drink rule, and have a few for the two of you." He waved goodbye, and trailed after the crew.

Sam's gaze shifted to Meagan to find her frowning. "I so wish this night was over," she pleaded.

"Not yet." He watched her frown, noting the dark smudges under her eyes, half moons on pale perfect skin. "You look exhausted, Meagan."

"Gee thanks, Sam. Just what a girl wants to hear."

"You still look gorgeous," he said, meaning it. "Just tired."

"Compliments delivered after an insult are meaningless and even less effective when followed by 'just tired.'"

"Saying you look tired isn't an insult. It's a concerned observation. I should feed you and review these prospective house locations for you so you can get some rest. My crew will keep an eye on things."

She opened her mouth, clearly intending to argue and then seemed to change her mind. "You and your crew haven't had any rest, either. Last night was hell for us all." She settled her hands to her slim hips and sighed. "I guess we should at least try to eat before someone's screaming about the curse again."

For a split second, he'd seen a softer side of Meagan.

The one he knew she hid behind. He wanted to know more about that part of her.

They stepped into the elevator, neither spoke. Each of them leaned against a wall so that they faced one another. There was no mistaking the way an awareness filled the space. It may be only dinner, but he wasn't leaving that "trouble" he was worried about behind— Meagan *was* trouble. And standing in this car, with the soft female scent of her tickling his nostrils, her green eyes flickering, he wasn't sure it was trouble he could walk away from.

5

Avoiding the hotel's packed restaurant had seemed a smart move at the time, but she wasn't so sure anymore. While sitting in a dark, secluded corner of the hole-in-the-wall Chinese restaurant next door, Meagan had never been so aware of Sam, never so certain she was captive to her desire for this damnable, impossible-to-ignore man.

His gaze met hers over the menu.

"I haven't had good Chinese in forever." He spoke softly, but everything in his voice, said, *I haven't had you and I want you,* instead. Or maybe she was imagining the hidden meaning, maybe some part of her wanted that to be the case. Because as much as she wanted to hate Sam, wanted to believe there was nothing beyond his arrogance, but trouble, there *was* more there, more to him, more to what she felt for him. It had occurred to her during Tabitha's crisis. He'd not only respected her on the set tonight, but also willingly, efficiently, helped her deal with that mini-disaster.

Suddenly, she noticed she was staring at him—

studying the solid square strength of his jaw, the high cheekbones, the full lips—and not discreetly. His face was as chiseled and perfect as his body.

She cut her gaze to the menu, ignoring his keen stare. "I order from a place near my apartment at least once a week," she said, cursing herself for revealing even one small personal detail. There was just something so darn intimate about the quiet setting, about what felt more like a date than a business meeting, that she welcomed the waiter's interruption to take their orders. Why could she not stop thinking about being in the basement the night before—just she and Sam—both of them wet, her nearly naked, and then wearing his coat? But she knew. It wasn't just the attraction between them that had gotten to her. It was the way he'd been protective, the way he'd helped her. He made her want to hand him just a little control, and that frightened her. She'd dared to do that a few times in her life and each time had led her to the wrong place.

They placed their orders, the silent awareness springing back into place the instant they were alone again.

"I have a confession to make," he said, leaning in closer, as if they weren't the only ones in the entire back room of the restaurant. As if he knew what she'd just been thinking, and from everything she'd observed about Sam, he probably did.

"And that would be what?" The question croaked from her dry throat.

"With all the Tabitha chaos, I forgot to grab the property listings from my bag in my hotel room."

His words conjured naughty, inexcusable images in her mind of what might happen if they ended up in his room. And judging from his darkening expression, Sam was thinking the same thing.

Feeling warm all over and desperate to splash some ice on both herself and the situation, Meagan reached for her only defense, her only hope of resisting Sam—words.

Meagan shifted in her seat. "That defeats the purpose of dinner, don't you think?"

"I guess that depends on whose perspective we're using," he said, his blue gaze holding hers.

Meagan's heart skipped a beat.

Sam continued, "In fact—"

The sentenced dissolved on his lips as the waiter set their plate of egg rolls in the center of the table. Sam exchanged a few comments with the man, seemingly in no hurry to finish what he'd been saying to her. Meagan, whose heart was darn near exploding with anticipation, waited anxiously for the rest of whatever he might have said. Men didn't rattle her this way, or rather, no man but Sam rattled her this way, or any way for that matter.

The waiter disappeared and Sam took a bite of his egg roll. Meagan wanted to reach across the table and strangle him for being so casual. Instead, she reached for her soda and took a long sip, forcing herself to think through the haze of arousal Sam had created in her, blaming it on pure exhaustion and no rest. She had to be reading into his words, into the energy swelling between them, or he wouldn't be so nonchalant. He'd moved on from whatever she'd thought he might say, as if it hadn't been worth saying in the first place.

"Aren't you going to eat?" he asked, snapping up a second egg roll.

"You plan on leaving me anything *to* eat?" She scooted the container of hot mustard in front of her, along with a bottle of soy sauce, and mixed them on a plate.

"We can always ask for more, and since I missed lunch, we might have to."

The prickly exterior she'd erected to protect herself slid away. He'd been there last night with her, then worked all day, and without a complaint or at least one she'd heard. He had to be as tired as she was. She put the sauce between them and set an egg roll on her plate. "You can have the last one. I had lunch, and I plan to do my meal plenty of justice when it arrives."

He gave her an appreciative murmur and dipped his egg roll into the sauce. "About the properties. One of our best bets is a beachfront house that has everything we need—privacy, size, functionality—at least on paper, that is. Oh, and not only does it have a mother-in-law house, the owner has a second house a half mile up the beach that just became available. You could use that for the crew and general whatever. Both properties would put us slightly over budget, but they might be worth fighting for."

"Wow," Meagan said. "It sounds too good to be true."

"Well, there's a catch."

"Of course," she said. "There's always a catch." She motioned with her hand. "Let me have the dirt."

"The place has been vacant for months, but now that we're considering it, there's another interested party."

"Are you sure the owner or Realtor isn't trying to manipulate us?"

"I talked with the other party," he said. "He's real

and he's eager. He's even telling the owner the show will destroy the property, referring to the wildness on other reality shows."

"Surely the owner knows the show will push up his long-term property values?"

"He knows, but he isn't willing to risk losing the rental income from the other party while waiting for us. He wants a fast answer. As in tomorrow."

"Sam, that's insane. We can't possibly decide that fast."

The waiter filled their water glasses. "Look. I'm not pressuring you here. I haven't even seen the place. On the other hand, this property has miles of open beach. You get plenty of room to film, and my team will know if anyone so much as thinks about approaching. And believe me, that'll be important." He unrolled his silverware from a napkin. "This damn curse is going to be a problem. We've already had several paranormal groups contact us, not to mention the media snooping around, looking for rumors and gossip."

"'Damn curse' is right," she murmured, sliding her napkin to her lap and picking up her egg roll only to set it back down. "We better be prepared. Once the footage I'm shooting airs, we're likely to have a three-ring circus on our hands. I hate that the studio is pressing this angle."

His brows dipped. "I thought you'd be glad for the ratings boost."

"Not like this," she said. "I mean, don't get me wrong. At first, I was just relieved to find out we didn't get cancelled. As the day has gone on, though, I'm not so sure. I worry we're headed away from the premise of the show and into trouble."

"Meaning what?"

"My father's a preacher in a small Texas town—and I'm talking small town like in the movie *Footloose*."

"So you're worried that the show may become offensive?"

"Yes and no. I want to give dance credibility and I think having real talent evolve will give it longevity, while short-term thrills and chills only give a facade of success that ultimately fizzles. The curse falls into that category in my opinion. If we build ratings on the pretense of a curse, what do we follow that with? Will dancing and the personal journeys of the dancers, who we want the audience to passionately love or hate, be enough?" She shook her head. "This curse really is a nightmare I wish I could make go away."

"I can see that," he agreed.

"Aside from the staying power issue, I've seen how a small group of people can create demons where they don't exist. It makes people irrational, and irrational can be dangerous." She took a bite of her egg roll and made a sound of pleasure. "And either this is really good or I'm just really hungry."

"I wouldn't know," he said. "I'm too hungry to be objective."

"I'm leaning toward thinking it's really good food," she said. "I'm hoping the rest of the meal is, as well."

They ate in surprisingly comfortable silence for a while before he leaned back in his chair. "I'd never have figured you for a small-town girl."

"Yeah, well, I got out of that small town the minute I could."

"And then you ended up in L.A."

"Not immediately," she said. "I went to school and that led to me producing a news program in Waco, Texas. Some random lucky breaks and I ended up in Dallas at a much larger station. A connection there gave me the chance to pitch this show. And now that I'm here, I don't want to blow it."

"Then I say we need to look at this property," he said. "The right location and security might just silence this curse nonsense. We should go check it out early tomorrow."

"That's impossible. I have footage to shoot and get edited."

The waiter appeared with their food, and Sam paused until he left, before adding, "A busy schedule is all the more reason to secure the right location and move on to other things," Sam said. "And I might be pushing a bit on this but—"

"No matter how amazing the location is, I don't have time tomorrow." She shook her head. "Not unless I can be cloned."

"I have a key," he said. "We can go after we finish here if you like. Or I can go check it out and let you know if it's a waste of time, but if it's good, you have to find time tomorrow—"

"No," she said quickly. She wouldn't be able to make the time, but she also knew this couldn't be left to someone else to decide. It was too critical to the show. "Tonight. We'll go tonight."

For several crackling seconds, they stared at one

another, and reality washed over Meagan. She'd just committed to going to a secluded beach house with Sam. She immediately picked up her fork, stabbing a water chestnut.

Sam chuckled and Meagan's eyes lifted to his. "What's so funny?"

"The absolute horror on your face when it occurred to you we'd be alone somewhere private. I can have one of my staff take you. Or you can bring along one of your staff members, if you want."

The offer surprised her. Her reaction surprised her even more, though it shouldn't have. She didn't want a chaperone. "You were some sort of Special Ops guy, right?"

"For fourteen years."

And since he was in his early thirties, that meant he'd gone into the army when he was a late teen. She wondered why, she wondered...damn it. "Then I'd say you're experienced enough to protect me," she said, shoving aside curiosity, refusing to get to know Sam any more than she felt she already did. She knew too much. She liked too much. She didn't want to like Sam.

She ate her chestnut and dabbed her mouth with her napkin. He was watching her. She could feel the warmth of those blue eyes as surely as if she were looking into them. Finally, when he didn't speak, she glanced up at him, his inspection too intense to bear, his unspoken thoughts unnerving. "Why are you looking at me like that?"

He chuckled. "I'm not sure what 'like that' means, but I was just wondering who's going to protect me from you?"

6

HE'D BAITED HER, unable to stop himself—expecting the flash in her eyes, and the fierceness of her expression that he found so sexy. And it had worked. For the first time since they'd sat down in the restaurant, she leaned towards him, her full lips close enough that he could imagine kissing them, as she said, "Don't tick me off and you won't need protection."

"You like being ticked off at me and you know it."

"Why would I *like* being pissed off at you?"

"At some point I think you thought it kept me at a distance. But seems to me that plan has backfired. I'm here to stay, sweetheart. Now what are you going to do with me?"

"For starters," she said, without hesitation, "if you call me 'sweetheart' again, you'll be wishing for that protection."

"I'm willing to take whatever you dish out and then some. In fact, maybe you need to unload on me and get it out of your system." He lowered his voice, all jest gone, a realization taking form. "Maybe there's a lot we need to just get out of our systems. Maybe then we can move past…it." Her eyes went wide, but she didn't lean back, didn't immediately reject the idea, didn't ask what "it" was, because they both knew. "It" was desire, hot and getting hotter by the second.

Sam didn't know what this woman did to him, but while she worried about him stealing her control, she had all but shredded his. There was something about her. Actually, everything about her worked for him, from how her forehead crinkled when she was thinking, to how passionate she was about her show. Being this interested in a woman wasn't a comfortable place to be. It wasn't uncomfortable, either. Just different for him because he couldn't seem to flip the "off" switch.

Long, sizzling seconds passed and she hadn't responded to his proposition. He arched a brow at her silence. "No snappy comeback?"

"Maybe it would just complicate things," she said, clearly talking about sex. "Maybe it would make things worse."

"My thoughts exactly up until a few minutes ago. But we damn near combust every time we're together, and it's only a matter of time before we do. We both like to maintain control, so I say we deal with this on our terms, where we control how it happens." And, he added silently, *I can finally get you alone and try to tear down the walls you've built around yourself.*

"You don't know me." She didn't sound as if she quite believed those words. "You don't know what I like."

"But I want to know. And I've known you a while now. I know things you might think I hadn't paid attention to. Like how you left a small town for a big city and now you're daring to work for a monster studio who'd eat their own young for ratings. That takes courage. On top of all of that, you're sitting here with me, alone, knowing exactly where it could lead. So I'd lay my money on you enjoying danger as long as it's on your terms." He softened his voice. "After tonight, the cameras and crew will be everywhere."

"Sam, I—"

"Meagan!"

She inhaled at the same moment he stiffened. Before he could speak, they were surrounded by a group of the crew, who'd deserted the hotel bar for the nearest restaurant. Chaos followed as tables were shoved next to each other, only a few steps away from their tiny corner. One of the cameramen—a hefty thirtysomething guy from Texas, who they all called "Double Dave" for obvious reasons—pulled a chair to their table to talk to Meagan about his "concerns" for the next day's shots. He then called yet another cameraman over to their table.

Sam listened as Meagan calmed their concerns, and then did enough listening of her own to manage to get her dinner down, while Sam did the same. He was intrigued by her expressions, her mannerisms, her respect for the people who worked for her, and knew it was a sign of just how badly he had it for this woman. She wouldn't look at him though, and he had to wonder if she was calculating a way to escape his proposition. She was good at running from him despite her obvious interest, and he wondered why.

His meal completed, Sam pushed away from the

table. "I'll check out that property, and let you know how it looks."

Meagan quickly shoved her chair back. "I'm going, too," she said. "None of the rest of this matters if we don't have a house to shoot in."

"You're viewing a property tonight?" Double Dave asked.

Sam's expression seemed to be questioning her, so she gave the same right back to him?

"We are," she said in reply to Dave, though, focused on Sam, not the cameraman. "We have to take it or lose it by tomorrow." She glanced at Dave, and the rest of the group, and then announced the exciting prospect of a new house, and that she'd report on it tomorrow.

The next thing Sam knew, he and Meagan were outside. Their eyes collided the same instant the hot, muggy air slammed into them, and their budding sexual tension expanded around them, while the world shrunk to just the two of them.

"Your vehicle or mine?" he asked, willing his body to calm.

She tilted her head, studying him with such scrutiny that it was his turn to say, "What are you looking at me like that for?"

"I just thought you were the 'I'm driving' kind of guy."

"And I thought you were the 'I'm driving' kind of woman."

"I am."

He waved her forward. "Well, then. Lead the way."

She didn't move. Instead, she stared at him intensely,

then said, "You drive. My eyes hurt from editing too much film, and I don't want you backseat driving."

"So, you'll backseat drive."

"Exactly."

Sam laughed and barely resisted the unnerving urge to grab her hand and pull her along with him—telling himself that he only needed to touch her once, that this thing was sex and sex only. He motioned her forward. "If we walk around to the side of the hotel, we can go straight to the garage and avoid another crew ambush."

"Don't you need to get the property listings from your room?"

"I put the address for this one in my GPS earlier. It's about a forty-minute drive, so we better hit the road. It's almost seven now."

Meagan groaned and they fell into step together. "I have a six o'clock shoot in the morning, and I am going to be hating life when it starts."

"Then it's good I'm driving," he said. "You can nap on the way to the property and back, if you want."

She stopped.

"What?" he asked again.

"Stop being nice to me. I liked you better when you were intentionally trying to agitate me."

She meant she felt safer, but he didn't say it, not when she could back out of their private outing before they ever left. "I simply assumed you required more rest than I do."

Her hands went to her hips. "Why would I need more rest than you? Because…" She paused, eyes lighting with understanding. "Wow. You just proved that you can bait me at will, didn't you?"

He nodded. "But you can do the same to me. Don't even think about saying you don't know it because we both know you do. We both know how to punch each other's buttons."

"Yeah," she agreed. "I guess we do."

Damn, he wanted this woman. She didn't even try and play coy with him. He liked that. He liked it a hell of a lot. "Let's get out of here before we're cornered. Or worse, before Tabitha returns."

"True," she said, her face lit with a warm smile.

At his vehicle, he held the passenger door of his Ford F150 open for her, and she gave him an awkward look. "You don't have to do that for me. I can get it."

He pressed his hand to the side of the truck, the distinctly feminine scent of her reaching him. "I'm a soldier at heart. Opening a door for a lady is as natural to me as busting my chops is apparently for you."

A rich, laugh left her lips. "I don't imagine many people 'bust your chops' easily, so I'll take that as a compliment."

"They don't and I'll take your acknowledgement of that fact as a compliment."

A subtle but obvious tension lit between them. "Actually, it is a compliment." She paused. "Sam. I, well, I've given you such a hard time that I think I should tell you how much I really appreciate how you handled the problems on set tonight. Rather than doing what I would have expected—charging in and taking over—you respected my role."

"And unless there's an imminent threat to someone's safety, I always will. My hope would be that if an unfortunate situation like that arises, you'll respect my role, as well."

"Yes. Absolutely."

"That means no running into buildings that could go up in flames any second. You wait for me."

She pursed her lips. "Unless someone is in imminent danger and I can help."

He lowered his voice. "Meagan—"

She held up her hands. "Yes. Okay. I'll wait. Probably. I'll try. And I admit running into the house wasn't one of my more brilliant moves, but I was afraid the show would go up in flames with the house. Like everyone's dreams. Everyone who'd hoped this show would change their life would have lost their dream, too. I just couldn't let that happen."

Tension curled inside Sam. Somehow, every moment he'd ever shared with Meagan, every thought he'd had, every assumption he'd made, merged into this one instant. And there lay the danger of moving forward with his intention to finally sate his hunger for her tonight.

The morning-after might not deliver the complication-free, tension-easing relief they'd both hoped for, because he simply wasn't certain that one night would be enough. And he knew combining romance with work never ended well.

Several voices sounded nearby, interrupting their moment. "Come on. We have to go before it gets any later."

She jumped into the truck, and closed the door behind her. As he rushed to the driver's side, he tried to talk himself back off the ledge, tried to convince himself not to touch Meagan, to reel himself in before it was too late. Too late? Who was he kidding? He wouldn't find the "off" switch if his life depended on it.

MEAGAN LISTENED to the engine roar to life with a fleeting realization that she didn't have her phone or her purse. She'd taken off for their dinner, expecting to stay in the hotel, with nothing in hand. Normally, she'd insist on going back for both.

Instead, she found herself fixated on Sam's powerful forearms, as he maneuvered the truck out of the parking spot. Everything about Sam was strong and powerful. His hands, his face, and his eyes, when they caught her in one of those penetrating stares.

She wanted him with as much passion as she knew he was wrong for her, which was to the point of complete and utter distraction. Worse—to the point that he was now controlling her with anticipation and fantasy.

Still, it was clear to her that avoiding him wasn't the answer, for all kinds of reasons. Sleeping with him— well, he'd offered her one night, to get "it" out of their systems. She just had to be certain there were no strings. Then, maybe he was right.

Sam sparked something inside her, consumed her without even trying. His voice, his eyes, his powerful presence, all resonated with her.

Honestly, her attraction for Sam wasn't going away, nor was he. But would making love with him extinguish the flames between them or cause them to burn brighter? Meagan admitted this had been her concern all along.

So why was she still considering it?

7

MEAGAN STARED AHEAD as the truck exited the garage, resisting the magnetic pull of Sam next to her, of the desire to turn to him, to study him—to slide up next to him and finally, finally, just be with him. The moon dangled low in the sky, like a lamp on an invisible chain, like her unyielding need for this man.

"Rest if you want," he said. "I'll wake you up when we get close."

"Thank you," she murmured, and sank down low in the seat and closed her eyes. She needed to think, she needed to…she didn't know. For the first time in a long time, she didn't know what she needed to do. Her mind raced to the point that she wanted to sit up, wanted to do something, anything. Instead, she pretended to sleep, sensing the shift in shadows as they maneuvered the streets of L.A., her mind playing with images. Sam looking hot. Sam looking hot while he stood in the basement dripping wet.

She forced herself to remember why she needed to concentrate. Sam might misread her, might think he had more claim to power on the set, if they slept together. They'd argue. Everyone would be affected. But then she thought of Sam's eyes when he'd walked right into the chaos earlier, when his eyes had met hers, when he'd silently asked if he could intervene.

They must have been a good thirty minutes into the ride when Sam said, "I can hear you thinking, Meagan."

She didn't pretend she wasn't awake; in fact, not pretending was a relief. She turned to face Sam. "Did you hear anything that made any sense to you, because I sure didn't."

"Want to talk about it?"

"As in—to you?"

He chuckled. It was a low, sexy sound, becoming both familiar and unnervingly likable. "I would be the only person here," he reminded her.

"Yeah, but I can't talk to you. Not about…you."

He laughed louder and cut her a look. "I can assure you with one hundred percent certainty that I know more about me than anyone else on this earth."

Fine, she'd ask him questions, but not the one really on her mind, which would be, should she sleep with him? "How old were you when you went into the army?"

"I entered on my eighteenth birthday," he said, without missing a beat, as if it was exactly what he'd expected her to ask, when they both knew it absolutely was not.

"Why?"

"It's what I was born to do, what I wanted to do. What my father, my brother and my uncles, all did."

"And you weren't scared? I mean you were a kid, Sam."

"I wasn't scared but my mother was. My brother was in Iraq at the time and my father was on active duty. She, like most spouses, found a place to tuck away the fear of losing her husband to combat. But her son, or sons, rather, were another story. She struggled to deal with the potential loss of her boys."

"I can't imagine how hard that must have been for her."

"My father saw her distress and tried to talk me into waiting a few years to enter the army," he said. "He figured that would give my mother time to get used to my brother serving. I didn't think that was the answer. I thought my mother needed to go ahead and get past her fear because the army was going to be my future. Eventually, she and I talked about it, and she gave me her blessing."

"So you went ahead and enlisted."

He nodded. "And then ended up in a fluffy desk job I didn't want. I'm pretty sure my father pulled a lot of rank to make it happen, too, though he never admitted it. Able-bodied young men do not end up at desk jobs in the army."

"I'm surprised," she said. "With him serving himself, I'd have thought he would have supported you."

"He was trying to protect my mother and he really wanted me to finish college to be eligible for officer training, which my brother rejected."

"From what I know of you, a desk job must have been hard for you to deal with."

"Oh yeah. It drove me crazy. I felt guilty for sitting at a desk while my own father and brother, and plenty of others with them, were fighting to protect our country. I would have gotten out of that desk job if I could have and I tried. It worked out though in the end. By twenty-one I'd completed my degree and I entered the officers' program, then Special Forces."

"Why Special Forces?"

"I was in for life," he said. "I wanted to be challenged and contribute everything I could, on every level possible."

Meagan absorbed those words thoughtfully, captured by him in ways she didn't want to be, didn't expect to be when she'd first met him. He was just so much more than she'd expected he'd be. This man had seen war, he'd fought to survive, and fought for the lives of others. "But you weren't in for life," she finally commented, hoping he'd explain why, nervous she might be in choppy waters he didn't want to enter.

"No," he said a bit too softly. "I wasn't in for life." He inhaled and let it out. "A few bullets in my leg took care of that."

"Oh, God, Sam," she said and added, "I'm sorry." She wanted to pull back these last words, knowing from her own injury how much she didn't like hearing them.

"Yeah, me too, because even if I could have gotten a doctor's release, which was doubtful, I knew I wasn't one hundred percent. And I wasn't willing to risk other people's lives by ignoring the reality of what I had to face."

Suddenly, her lost dream, her knee injury, felt tiny, inconsequential. "That was brave, Sam. It was very brave."

He glanced at her, surprise etched on his handsome face. "No. Those men and women out there on the front lines are the brave ones. I refused to let my ego put them at risk."

"Yes," she conceded. "They are." And he'd been one of them, he still wanted to be one of them, and couldn't. She knew how that felt, as well. How it hurt to want things you could no longer have. "Where are your parents? Are they here? Is that how you ended up in L.A.?"

"No," he said. "This is technically my home, but as a military brat, I traveled all over the place. My parents spent a good number of the last ten years in Germany, but managed to end up back in Japan just in time for the recent tsunami. Both me and my brother got a good dose of the kind of worry my mother has for her sons and her husband. We couldn't reach my parents for days. Jake—that's my brother—was on a mission overseas, and he was in rare completely freaked-out mode."

"But they're okay, right?"

He gave a quick nod of his head. "Yes. They're fine. My mother's a nurse. She was working at a Red Cross shelter at the time and refused to leave when the military families were evacuated. My father's still on active duty, and as a high-ranking officer, he had his hands full."

"I think I mentioned that my father's a preacher in a small Texas town and my mother helps with the church's volunteer efforts. We aren't really close, but I am their only child and they love me, just like I love them." She cringed at her confession, one she normally wouldn't have given, not sure why she had, and quickly moved on, "I would have gone crazy, too, not knowing if they were all right during the tsunami, or hurricane or whatever."

He glanced at her. His gaze too knowing, too aware of what she'd shared. She expected him to push her for more detail, but surprisingly, he seemed to sense she was uncomfortable, and let it pass, saying only, "Maybe you'll tell me more about them one day."

His sensitivity really floored her. "Maybe I will," she said, surprised at how much she meant it. "Tell me more about Japan and your parents."

"There's not a lot more to tell," he said. "They're fine and involved in clean-up efforts that will take years and years to complete. I went to see them right after I left the army and spent a few months helping."

There were tiny telling cracks in his voice at several places during his story. Sam wasn't at all what she'd assumed. "How'd you get hired at the studio?"

"My uncle, a retired SEAL, works for the studio. He hounded me for months to take the security job. I didn't want it. I wanted back in the army." He rubbed his right leg a bit too deeply, and she wondered just how bad his injury was, both physically and emotionally.

She opened her mouth to tell him how much she understood, and quickly snapped it shut. She didn't talk about the past. She focused on the future, like what he seemed to be doing. And my gosh, how shallow would she sound anyway? He was talking about war and sacrifice and she was upset she wasn't able to perform anymore.

"We're here," he announced, turning into a long driveway, but trees blocked her view of the house.

The ride was over and she didn't want it to be. She had enjoyed learning about Sam, which defied the idea of sex being a path to getting him out of her system.

Suddenly, she felt confused. She knew Sam was a distraction she didn't need, knew he was the kind of man that took you by storm and took over your life. Yet, on some level he was exactly what she needed. And that absolutely terrified her. She couldn't lose herself again. She couldn't. Been there, done that, didn't like it.

As soon as the truck stopped in the driveway of the two-story, towering mansion of a house, she lunged for the door handle, intending to get out as quickly as possible. She needed some distance from Sam to process her feelings.

Sam gently shackled her arm, the touch of his hand searing her skin, melting her resolve to escape him. "Hey," he said softly. "What just happened?"

He read her too easily, which only rattled her more. "Nothing. Nothing, I just—"

"Got spooked."

She hesitated, and then nodded. "Yes. I did." Somehow, her ability to be honest about her feelings made him more appealing. "I got spooked." And by the time the words were out, he was closer, still holding her arm. Still the powerful, controlling, sexy Sam, who she couldn't seem to resist.

She could smell the spicy maleness of him, warm and taunting, calling her, warming her, burning her inside out. Thank goodness for the shadowy darkness broken only by moonlight splintering through the tree limbs above them, casting their faces in shadows, hiding the damning desire surely in her eyes.

She inhaled, trying to think straight, before she did something like kiss him, instead of getting out of the vehicle. Instead, she filled her nostrils with more of that sultry male scent that made her want to stay right where she was. "Sam, I don't know what—"

"Me, either," he said, and kissed her, oh God, he kissed her, and it was wonderful. She didn't even remember him moving or how he'd become close enough to have his thigh pressed to hers. All that she knew was that his fingers were laced through her hair, his lips pressed to hers, warm and remarkably gentle—a teasing touch, following by a sweeping wash of his tongue against hers.

"Meg—"

"Don't talk," she said, her fingers curled around his neck to pull him back to her, desperate to keep this just sex, knowing deep down it might be too late. "Kiss me again."

And he did. He kissed her. No talking. No demanding things go his way, like she'd expected from him. His mouth slanted over hers, his tongue pressing past her teeth, stroking seductively against her tongue.

She moaned and arched into him, seeking more of the warmth and hardness that was so very Sam, so very right. Yet she'd have sworn he was wrong. And he was wrong for her. He was, in fact. He would be trouble but he didn't feel like trouble. Not now. Not in this moment. Okay, maybe in this very moment, she did, because she needed him. Her hands traced the rippling muscle of his shoulders.

A low growl escaped his lips, and he pulled her closer, one hand sliding up her back, molding her against his chest. His hand caressed her thigh, under her skirt. His tongue delved deeply, caressing hers in another long, lavish tasting that had her feeling it in all the places he wasn't touching, but she wanted him to be.

"You smell good," he murmured, kissing her jaw, and along to her neck. "Like vanilla and flowers. It's driving me crazy. I know we need to go see that house, and this is not the place for *this,* but I'm struggling to let you go."

The words, the gruff aroused tone of his voice, overtook her. She didn't want to let him go, either. She didn't want to think about why they shouldn't do *this.* "Then don't," she whispered, and barely had the words out before they were kissing again. A blur of passion followed, his hands all over her. Hers all over him. She was on her back, her blouse open, with him on top of her, and she barely remembered how it had happened.

Sam's phone started to ring and he tore away from her. He cursed softly, echoing the frustration she felt at the interruption. "I have to answer that."

"I know," she said, her voice breathless even to her own ears. "Especially since I don't have my phone."

"Right," he agreed, but he didn't move. "I need to get it."

She didn't want him to move. She wasn't ready to let go of this time they were sharing.

The phone stopped ringing, still he didn't move. He brushed his lips over hers. "I didn't mean for this to get so out of control. One minute we were—"

"And the next," she finished.

He smiled and pulled back to look at her, and the mood shifted, the air thickened. They stared at one another, and Meagan felt their connection in every part of herself. There was something happening between them, something that she'd never felt before, and didn't understand.

The phone started to ring again and he sighed with the inevitable demand to get up, and then, he did the most unexpected thing. Sam kissed her nose before bringing her with him to sit up.

He reached for his phone on the dash and checked the missed numbers. "It was Josh both times," Sam said. "He left a voice mail."

Meagan nodded, but she was still thinking about Sam kissing her nose. It was silly, but there was something about that small act that had her stomach fluttering.

Light flickered behind them, snapping her out of her reverie. Meagan shifted around to see a car pulling into the driveway. "Someone's here."

Sam set his phone down. "Per Josh's voice mail, Kiki insisted that he drive her out here so—"

Meagan didn't hear the rest. She shoved open the door, desperate to escape their close proximity before Kiki arrived. She tripped, and went tumbling out of the truck.

Sam was there in an instant, but she was already getting up. "Are you okay?"

"No, I am not okay! I'm embarrassed, Sam. I don't want them to know what just happened. I don't want them to think badly of either of us."

"They won't know." His gaze slid top to bottom. "Not if you button your shirt."

Her jaw dropped at the realization. Meagan rushed to fix her gaping shirt, but her fingers were shaking. "I don't do things like this. I know better. I know they backfire. Sam—"

"Easy, sweetheart," he said, wrapping her in his arms. "Take a deep breath and we'll get through this. What happens between us, is between us. No one will know."

Sweetheart. Why did that endearment sound good now, when it had bothered her before? And why did his vow that everything was going to be okay, calm her? For the first time in years, she'd felt she had her life in the palm of her hand. Neither her parents, nor her ex-boyfriends, who'd tried to control everything from her career to her politics, had control. She had control. Only tonight, she'd let this thing, whatever "it" was, with Sam, take it away from her.

"Stop calling me sweetheart, Sam."

He held her tighter and kissed her. "Whatever you say. *Meg.*"

And despite being a nervous wreck over Kiki and Josh's arrival, the familiar banter with Sam made her laugh, and that laugh had a remarkable impact. Meagan felt just a bit more in control.

She was clearly very confused.

8

"Why aren't you answering your phone?" Kiki demanded the minute she stepped from Josh's black SUV. "We've been trying to reach you for over an hour. When you didn't answer, I decided to come on out here. Besides, I didn't want to miss out on the chance to be in on this very important decision."

There was accusation in everything Kiki said to Meagan, and she didn't understand it. She'd tried to break through it, to bond with the other woman over the show and it just didn't seem to be happening.

"She dropped her phone in the hotel parking lot," Sam explained before Meagan could answer. "Someone ran over it before we could get to it. The driver came damn close to running over Meagan, too."

"My God," Kiki said, her tone dripping disdain. "How in the world did you manage that?"

Sam glanced at Josh. "I left you a message to be sure everyone knew to call me if they needed Meagan."

"Sorry, boss," Josh said. The honest guilt on his face meant that either he really hadn't checked his messages, or he was a darn good actor. He inclined his head at Meagan. "My apologies for not listening to my voice mail."

"I'm sure you both had your hands full," Meagan said, repeating her earlier comment, immensely appreciative to both Sam and Josh for covering for her, but angry at herself for needing to be covered. Then to both Josh and Kiki, she asked, "Why aren't you two at the hospital?"

"I left one of the production assistants to supervise Tabitha's medical treatment," Kiki replied.

"Which P.A.?"

"I don't know." Kiki sounded snippy and impositioned. "Debbie, I think."

"Darla?" Meagan asked, hopeful.

"Yes. Darla." Kiki waved a hand. "But it doesn't matter now. I just hung up with *Darla*. She called me because she couldn't reach you. Tabitha is fine. All is well in tooth-fairy land."

Over and over Meagan had asked Kiki to start remembering everyone's names. She treated the cast horribly and tension jumped every time she was around. If Kiki wasn't related to one of the executives that had approved her show, she'd already have talked to Sabrina about firing her.

"What exactly does that mean?" Sam asked.

She shrugged. "You'd have to ask the P.A. What's going on here?"

"I called Darla myself," Josh said. "After the hospital checked her out, a dentist fitted Tabitha for some sort of temporary tooth held in with a mouthpiece, and she's now in her room resting." He glanced at Meagan. "Sam likes answers. I try to have them."

"Thank you," Meagan said, but she felt that announcement like a blow. She couldn't get answers, but Sam could?

"Why don't we head down to the property?" Sam suggested. "Then everyone can get some rest back at the hotel."

"Yes," agreed Meagan, her gaze touching his. "That sounds like a good idea."

Sam motioned her forward, falling into step beside her, while Josh and Kiki followed them. Sam glanced behind them, apparently making sure they had some distance away from the others, before softly saying, "You'll have to tell me who you ticked off to get saddled with Kiki."

It helped to hear she wasn't being overly sensitive about Kiki, and that Sam read Kiki the same way she did. "I didn't make anyone mad, except for you, that I know of. I'm pretty good at that." If there was a God of dance, she'd have said that was who she'd angered. In that case though, she would have thought her knee would have been the ultimate sacrifice, but apparently not.

"I think it's the other way around," he commented. "I'm good at making *you* mad."

"You are a master of that craft."

He laughed and darn it, she felt the sultry male baritone of it in every nerve ending of her body. There was so much about the man that appealed to her, and so many reasons not to act on what she felt for him. Yet he'd been there for her tonight in so many ways.

They cleared the trees, bringing a large shadowy property into view and Meagan paused, drinking in the cool, clean ocean air as it washed over her, calming her, if only slightly. "I already love it here. I love the ocean."

"I sure hope there are lights," Kiki said, stopping next to Meagan.

"There are," Sam answered, motioning Meagan onward, and she had the distinct impression that no matter how attractive Kiki might be, Sam wasn't impressed. The idea pleased her a little more than it should have. Another reaction she wasn't going to try to analyze at present.

Sam ran down the basics of the property as they walked. "The house is 5,000 square feet with a 2,000-square-foot mother-in-law house in the back of the main property."

"That does sound perfect," Meagan replied.

Motion detectors flickered to life, illuminating an impressive contemporary stucco house, with a balcony that wrapped around most of the second floor.

"The water is so close," Kiki exclaimed, rushing forward and calling over her shoulder. "It's amazing."

Sam sighed as Kiki expanded the distance between her and them. "I better catch up with her before she gets hurt and calls it the curse." He headed after her.

Josh fell into step with Meagan. "Kiki seems to like this place so far. Surely that's all you need to know." He grinned to let her know he was teasing her.

Meagan snorted. "That's about as true as me dropping my cell phone. I used horrible judgment by not going back to my room for my phone. It's just that if I'd gone back, I knew I'd get cornered by someone wanting to talk, and it would be even later by the time we made it out here. Still, I should have known better. Thank you for being loyal to your boss and covering for me."

"I spent the entire drive listening to Kiki talk trash about you." They started up the porch stairs, where Sam waited, having already let Kiki inside the house. "She gloated on the drive over here about how she'd saved the studio millions, insisting you'd be a failure. The worst is that she had to have known I might tell you. It's like she wanted you on edge by announcing her intent. I hate saying this because it feeds into her strategy, but Meagan, she's a cobra. Watch for the next strike, because it's coming."

Meagan crossed her arms in front of her chest, tension curling in her stomach. She had confirmation of what she'd hoped wasn't true. Not only was Kiki a true enemy, she wasn't even trying to hide her agenda.

They joined Sam at the door.

Josh glanced at Sam. "Don't worry, boss. I'll go in first, and strategically engage the enemy."

"Good luck with that one," Sam said dryly, stepping aside to let Josh enter, and then moving again to block the entrance. The porch light played on his chiseled features and full, sensual mouth—the mouth she shouldn't be looking at, but couldn't seem to resist.

"Everything okay?" he asked, towering above her, and she was struck again by the way he used his broad shoulders to shield her, this time from Kiki's potentially, most likely, prying eyes. Protective. That was the word that came to mind, rather than dominant and bossy.

"Everything is just peachy," she assured him. "In fact, tonight is just one big bucket of peachy."

Kiki peeked around Sam. "Are you coming in or what?" She disappeared.

"See," Meagan said. "Peachy."

He didn't move, his eyes narrowing a barely perceivable amount. "What's wrong?"

She lowered her voice. "You were right about watching my back with Kiki. Josh said that she bragged about saving the studio millions by getting rid of people like me. It sounds like she doesn't want the show to succeed. But—"

"Now isn't the time to talk about this, but I have your back, Meagan, and I mean that. You do what feels right and you make this as good a show as you can make it. Don't let her get to you."

Her chest tightened at the unexpectedly supportive, and yes, protective words. Right then, she realized that Sam had snuck through her defenses, into her life, and for the first time in a very long time, if only for tonight, it was a relief to not feel alone. She nodded. "I know. You're right."

"I don't think you do." There was nothing accusing in his tone, no taunt, none of their normal word play.

"I do. I know." Her lips lifted ever so slightly. "But it helps to be reminded. Thank you."

He studied her and then gave a small incline of his head, flattening himself against the door to let her pass.

As Meagan moved by Sam, her shoulder brushed his chest. She froze with the impact, her gaze momentarily meeting his, heat glimmering in the depths of his stare. And she didn't look away, or hide from him, or herself. She wanted Sam. She was so very tired of denying herself this man.

But their window to be alone was now gone. Meagan had no doubt that Kiki would notice if they disappeared after this and didn't show up back at the hotel, which was all but a film set, with cameras and people everywhere.

Kiki might not be able to steal her show, but she'd definitely stolen her one night with Sam. While it was probably for Meagan's own good, it didn't feel that way right now. Meagan believed she would regret this lost chance for a very long time.

9

SAM TRAILED MEAGAN INTO the house, more than a little concerned about Kiki. He saw her actions, her using Josh to taunt Meagan, as confirmation that she felt invincible. Sabrina was right, Kiki was dangerous.

In the kitchen, Sam's gaze drifted over Meagan's skirt and the way it hugged her cute, tight backside. He liked that backside, but more so, he *liked* Meagan. This woman was under his skin and going nowhere but deeper fast. When he'd watched her fight through her worries over Kiki, when he'd seen the determination to succeed reignite in her eyes, he'd been blown away. Meagan was sexy, feisty, and passionate about what she believed in. And that made him passionate about her. He wasn't going to let anyone, especially Kiki, tear her down.

"The setup is perfect," Meagan said, descending a few steps to a sunken living room, and turning to face him. She pointed toward the open kitchen, where Kiki leaned on the island counter, and Josh stood stoically next to her.

"The way the kitchen overlooks the main area is terrific for panned shots," Kiki agreed, actually sounding as if she really cared about the show.

"I love it," Meagan said, holding out her arms, as if embracing the room. "I can only pray the upstairs is as terrific as the downstairs."

That's when Sam did a silent "Oh, crap." The buttons of Meagan's blouse were uneven, obviously hurriedly secured. If that blouse didn't scream an announcement about what he and Meagan had been doing in his truck when Josh and Kiki arrived, he didn't think anything would.

Cautious to appear casual, Sam sauntered toward Meagan. He stood so that his big body blocked the others' view of the problem he knew would panic Meagan if she discovered it.

"It's a unique setup," he explained, two fingers pointing to the left of the living room, by the kitchen. "These stairs lead to a section of the top floor." He then indicated the opposite side of the room, where he intended to herd Meagan and quickly. "Stairs on that side lead to a completely separate second level. Since sleeping arrangements are so important, why don't we have a look up there now?"

Meagan's eyes went wide, and she brushed her wind-blown hair from her face. "I searched everywhere for split quarters when the show was starting, and I couldn't find anything. I had to convert a downstairs den to a bedroom in the other house."

"So I was told by the studio," he said. "But I can't take credit. Josh did the legwork." He gestured toward the stairs. The ones nowhere near Kiki. "Shall we head up?"

Meagan frowned, studying him a moment. "Okay." She began climbing the stairs, but the instant they were behind the wall encasing the steps, she turned to him and whispered, "Now it's my turn to ask. What's wrong?"

Sam was shocked that she'd read his discomfort. He was special ops, trained to be unreadable. And he was cautious enough to know better than to risk her freaking out about her blouse if he told her. "Just concerned about the property," he assured her. "If the bedroom situation won't work, even if I approve the security profile, the house is worthless, don't you think?"

Her brows furrowed, and she looked as if she might question him again. Instead though, she gave a little nod. "Yes. You're right, of course." She headed up the stairs.

For a second Sam just stared after her, wondering what this woman was doing to him, and why he was powerless to stop it. Not that he wanted to, but he wasn't on sure footing which was unsettling. Fortunately, before leaving the main room he'd discreetly motioned to Josh to keep Kiki occupied, before he'd headed upstairs after Meagan.

MEAGAN WALKED THROUGH the spacious upstairs bedrooms, her mind on Sam, who'd officially done exactly what men like Sam—strong, dominant types—did to those around them. He had taken control. But even as the thought occurred, as she knew that she was somehow villainizing him, she admitted he didn't deserve that from her. And that made Meagan want to scream, and not at Sam, but at herself. He wasn't trying to be controlling, and in fact, he'd surprised her with how sensitive he was to her own need for control of the show. If he had control, it was because she'd given it to him. She was powerfully affected by everything the man did—or didn't do, for that matter.

There was a part of her that reveled in being so blown away by Sam, and another that was reeling from him knocking her off guard. She wanted to keep her distance, but again, the logic, while smart, didn't appeal in the slightest.

Meagan passed a bathroom and entered the large master suite, which could accommodate three contestants, but would only need to host two. And what a master it was. Huge double windows led onto what appeared to be a balcony. She needed to get Kiki up here and assign her furniture-shopping duty. With cameras rolling, that wasn't an unimportant task.

"Meagan?" Sam's voice and the sound of big feet climbing the stairs echoed nearby.

"In the master," she called, and headed into the bathroom. Wow. If she were selfish, she'd find a way to make this her suite and her bathroom. There was a separate shower in a sort of rock enclave that was envy worthy, and a deep sunken tub equally so, as well as a double vanity and a huge closet. The girls would have to draw straws for the room. It would be the only fair way to manage them choosing.

Footsteps closed in on her, and her stomach fluttered with the awareness of Sam being nearby. Her stomach had actually fluttered. When in the world had that last happened with a man?

She didn't turn, afraid she'd give away what she

was feeling, but she knew the instant Sam entered the bathroom.

Meagan gasped at the daring, impossibly damning action of him shutting the door, and right then she was sure she had been wrong. Sam was bad news; Sam was still the chaos she thought he was.

She reeled at the sight of her hot soldier, all big and tall. "What are you doing? What are you thinking?"

"I'm thinking your shirt is buttoned crooked, and you need to fix it now, before Kiki notices it."

Her jaw dropped, and then her mouth formed a silent "Oh," before she quickly started to right the buttons. "Oh, God. Oh, God. Did they see? Did Kiki see?"

"No," he said. "Why do you think I all but shoved you toward the stairs and then sent them to inspect other parts of the house? But they will be here any minute."

She checked her blouse in the mirror. "Thank you, Sam. Thank you so very much." This time the appreciation came freely and without an ounce of hesitation. Time and Kiki were all that mattered. Task completed, she patted down the wild mess of her dark hair and turned to him, holding out her hands to her sides. "Please tell me I have covered all evidence of our earlier…that nothing else is where it shouldn't be."

"You're perfect," he said softly, his eyes hot, his voice warm. He yanked open the bathroom door, eliminating any chance they would be caught in a compromising position. Or so she thought. Before she knew his intentions, Sam pulled her into the enclave of the shower, melding her body to his.

"I hate that we were interrupted," he confessed, an instant before his mouth closed down over hers. The assault on her senses was instant—a tangled ball of fear of being caught, and intense, nerve-prickling awareness. His tongue touched hers, suckling and licking, until she moaned and melted into his kiss, his body—correction—his hard masculine body.

Meagan grappled for willpower, her hands going to his shoulders, as she tried to convince herself to push away from him. He just tasted too good, and felt so wonderful.

"We shouldn't be doing this," she whispered, forcing her mouth from his.

His voice lowered, became husky. "And aren't you glad we are?"

"Yes," she whispered, her hands sliding around his neck, her breasts melding to his chest, her lips meeting his again. Meagan felt herself drift away, unable to stop it from happening. This man stole her reason, her presence of mind. There was no show, no Kiki, just her and Sam. Until there were footsteps and voices and a dart of adrenaline shot through her bloodstream.

She tried to pull away. Sam held her, and pressed his lips to her ear. "I can't wait to finally have you to myself." His teeth scraped her lobe before he set her away from him. She didn't know how he planned to have her to himself, but if her trembling with need was any indication, she hoped he had a way.

"Hello! Hello!"

It was Kiki, and Meagan shook herself, quickly checking the mirror, about to rush from the bathroom, when Sam yelled, "In here, Kiki."

Meagan turned to him and mouthed, "Are you crazy?"

He arched a brow, as if he had no idea why she would ask such a thing.

Kiki appeared in the doorway, a frown on her pretty face. "What's going on?"

Sam indicated the sink. "Ants. If you two want this place, I'll need to get an exterminator written into the agreement prior to move-in."

"Oh good grief," Kiki exclaimed. "There's a ton of them."

And sure enough, there were a ton of them. Meagan barely bit back a smile. Sam was a phenomenal kisser, and really brilliant to boot.

"You have to see the mother-in-law house," Kiki said. "It has three rooms, so I can stay with you and not have to drive out every day."

Okay, so there went her lusty, Sam-created high. "Let's go check," Meagan said.

She moved forward, toward Sam, and his eyes twinkled with mischief and the promise of more kisses, more touches, more fire. Promises she really wanted him to keep. Besides. She owed him a thank-you for telling her about her buttons.

Meagan exited the bathroom with him on her heels, their shared secrets somehow uniting them beyond the passion they shared. And for the first time in a long time, she admitted to herself that having someone at her back wasn't such a bad thing, not when that someone was Sam, at least so it seemed.

The realization puzzled her. Oh sure, she'd been standing alone for a long while—beating a path through the entertainment industry with a family that didn't approve and hardly spoke to her. And sure, she'd tried a few times to escape into a man's arms, into a relationship with a Beta-type guy, when deep down she knew alphas appealed far more. But she also knew that alphas were demanding and controlling, and she'd seen enough of that in her small town to last a lifetime—they'd sent her running for the hills. Sam was alpha—one hundred percent all-hot alpha male. So why wasn't she running from him?

10

ONLY FIFTEEN MINUTES after the bathroom kiss, they'd looked at the mother-in-law house and were on to the additional house a mile away that was also part of the lease. Meagan was in the backseat of Josh's SUV, all too aware of her leg intimately pressed to Sam's. Kiki was in the front. Kiki, who Meagan couldn't escape, any more than she could the memories of being in Sam's truck, and what they'd done together. It all threatened to suffocate her right here and now.

"I can't get over how perfect the mother-in-law house was," Kiki said, glancing around the seats at Meagan. "We'll be roommates."

"Perfect." Except for the fact that there had been only two bedrooms, one of which Kiki had excitedly claimed. "We haven't seen the second property yet."

"That'll be for security," Kiki said, glancing at Sam. "Surely you can work with whatever you get, right?"

And bless Sam, he simply said, "We'll see," once again, leaving the power in her hands, doing exactly the opposite of what she'd wrongly assumed he would do.

She wanted to crawl into his lap and kiss him. Though she was pretty sure, he could tick her off right now, and she'd still want him just as much.

MEAGAN SOON STOOD ON the back deck of the extra house, hands on a balcony railing overlooking the dark beach. Unseen waves were crashing on the shoreline and Sam was by her side. Kiki, thankfully, was off somewhere on her cell phone.

"It works for you?" she asked him.

"I'd say the setup is about as perfect as you can get on such short notice, with such a small timeframe to move in and start filming."

A soft purr—or more like a meow—sounded close by. "Did I just hear a cat?" Another meow, muffled but nearby. She pushed off the railing, trying to figure out where it was coming from, and Sam did the same. "Could it be trapped, Sam? Here kitty, kitty. Here kitty." More meowing.

Sam walked down the steps that led to the beach, making a motion with his hands for her to keep calling the cat. Meagan followed him, and the sound. "Here kitty, kitty. Here kitty."

Sam kneeled down at the bottom step, and the next thing she knew, he was holding a kitten.

Meagan rushed forward. A cute little ball of white fur in Sam's hands. "Is it okay?"

"Let's go up to the porch where the light is better and check it out."

Meagan rushed up the stairs. Sam's big hand was like a hammock cradling the kitten. "Oh, how sweet," she said, as it curled on top of Sam's palm. "Oh, no." She shifted the animal a bit. "There's a cut, Sam. It looks bad. It's deep."

"Yeah," he agreed. "She needs a vet as soon as possible before infection sets in."

Meagan glanced at him, surprised. "You'd be okay with that? With us taking it to the vet on the way back to the hotel?"

"Oh, my God!" Kiki said. "Is that a rat?"

"It's not a rat." Meagan grimaced. "A kitten, Kiki."

"Well, keep it away from me," she said. "I'm allergic."

The look on Sam's face said he'd had all of Kiki he could take for one night. "We should be leaving anyway," he said. "We all have an early morning, and we need to take the cat by a vet." The kitten meowed loudly, as if in agreement.

"That thing can't ride with us," Kiki said. "Seriously. I'm allergic."

A muscle in Sam's jaw tensed, and he spoke directly to Meagan. "How do you feel about walking back to the truck? It's not quite a mile down the beach. The owner has beach lights we can turn on here and turn off at the other house."

"I don't mind walking at all."

They wrapped the kitten in a jacket that Josh had stashed in his SUV and started toward the first house, the breeze off the ocean chilling the air. "I feel like I keep saying this tonight, but thank you for this, Sam."

"You don't have to thank me. I would have taken the kitten to the vet, with or without you."

Her chest tightened with yet another unfamiliar emotion. "You keep surprising me, Sam."

He stopped abruptly, and faced her. "What…you thought I was mean to children, elderly people and animals?"

"No!" she quickly said. "No, it's just that—"

He started walking again. She trailed after him. "Sam."

"We need to get to the vet," he said. "And we both know that you made a ton of assumptions about me." He cut her a sideways glance. "Bet you didn't realize that Special Forces are also focused on humanitarian missions, did you? That we spend a huge portion of our careers helping people, and yes, animals, who can't help themselves."

Guilt slid into her gut. "No. I thought soldiers were soldiers. They fought wars."

"Unfortunately, we often have to fight to give the aid to those who need it. But there is nothing like seeing hope in the face of someone who—regardless of age, race, sex, religion or nationality—thought the world had forgotten them. It's something worth getting up for every day."

An injury had stolen that from him. More guilt filled her. "I guess there's a lot I didn't know."

"And a lot you assumed."

"Yes."

He glanced her way. "And?"

"And what?"

"And you know exactly what."

"Fine. I'm sorry. But don't tell me you didn't make assumptions about me."

"You're right," he agreed. "I did."

"And?" she prodded right back, seeking her apology. They stopped a few feet from the truck.

"And I'm not apologizing because so far I've been right about every assumption I've made. You're stubborn, controlling—"

"I am not controlling!"

"Determined, hardworking and a great kisser." He handed her the bundle in his arms. "Hold on to her so I can turn off the beach lights and unlock the truck."

"Her?"

"Yeah. Her."

A female. She liked that. "Then I think I'll call her *Sam*antha, because she's so sweet and cuddly—*just like you*." She snorted. He arched a brow, but didn't comment.

Instead he clicked the lock on the truck and opened the door. Meagan slid inside, careful with the meowing kitten that she stroked and talked to.

Then, to her surprise, Sam leaned into the truck and laid a sexy, hot kiss on her, his tongue delving past her lips for a slow, sensual exploration before he said, "We both know that not only am I not sweet and cuddly, you like that about me." And then he was gone, shutting the door behind him.

He was right—he wasn't sweet and cuddly. He was a big, sexy alpha lion, and she couldn't wait to see if she could make him purr for her. And there it was. For the first time in a long, long time, a man was a challenge. It excited her. He excited her.

It was after midnight when Sam stepped off the elevator with Meagan by his side, and headed along the hotel floor, toward her room. Samantha's cut hadn't been nearly as bad as they'd thought, and she'd received a thumbs-up and a follow-up appointment from the vet.

Sam carried several overstuffed bags filled with an assortment of feline supplies, including a pink bed to match the pink bag in which Meagan was carrying Samantha. Long before the trip to the 24-hour Walmart, where she'd purchased half the pet-supplies department and declared Samantha the show's new "good luck charm," he'd known that she was going to be heartbroken if an owner showed up to claim the tiny fur ball. While at the vet, they'd had time to talk, and they'd decided they'd fight for the property, and Sam had promised to investigate where the kitten might have come from.

They stopped at her room door and their eyes met, instant electricity crackling between them, as it had so many times tonight—and well before tonight, too.

Samantha made a soft meow, and Meagan jerked her gaze from Sam's, swiping at the door with the plastic key she'd pulled from her pocket. She held the door open and went inside. He didn't. Several eternal seconds passed before Meagan grabbed his arm and tugged him forward.

"Sam, damn it, hurry up, before someone sees you." She shut the door behind him and locked it—assuming he would stay.

"I wasn't aware I was invited in."

She ignored the comment and sat down on the floor to let a meowing Samantha out of her bag. Sam laughed as the animal rubbed against her leg and purred up a storm.

Meagan and Sam squatted by the pink bed, where Samantha proceeded to plop down next to the catnip-enhanced stuffed animal that Meagan had bought for her, and go to sleep.

Both Sam and Meagan laughed. "She's so cute, Sam. I hope we don't find an owner. I want to keep her."

Their eyes locked and the air around them seemed to thicken and capture them.

"I know you do," he said softly. She'd told him about the pets she'd had growing up. There was something about Meagan. Something about the vulnerability beneath the guard she erected to protect herself, that spoke to him well beyond the desire he had for her. It made him prod her for pieces of her life, to understand her.

"I worked so many crazy hours in the newsroom that I didn't feel I could have a pet," Meagan said, stroking the kitten's back.

"How does dance and the newsroom fit together?" he asked. "I haven't quite figured out the connection."

Her lashes lowered and he could feel the sudden tension in her. "One of my teachers in high school once worked at Julliard before she had a car accident and a back injury she never fully recovered from. Her family owned some property in our community so she took a job teaching English, which was her second major. Anyway, she found out how intrigued I was by ballerinas and she secretly started teaching me to dance."

"Secretly?" he asked, sensing there was a whole lot of pain behind this story, and wanting to understand it, to understand her.

"My parents wouldn't have approved," she said. "When I told you the town I grew up in was like the town in the movie *Footloose,* I wasn't joking. When I started dancing in college my parents were sure the devil had stolen their only child's soul to test their faith. It was…difficult." She waved a hand as if to wave away the problem. "Long story short, when a television station came to a career day at my college, I hit it off with one of their recruiters, and they offered me a job. It wasn't dancing, but the production end of things really struck a chord with me. I like making things come together."

"It seems pretty darn stressful."

"It is, although that only makes it all the more rewarding when everything does come together." The kitten meowed and the shadows in Meagan's eyes disappeared. "She's just too cute. I think I'm in love."

In love. The words hit him hard. He'd never been in love. He'd never before even said the word in the same sentence as he had a woman's name. But Meagan…there was something about her. She made him feel things he'd never felt. One night. Right. That had been a joke. There was no way one night would ever be enough with this woman. These past few hours had proven that to him.

Sam watched her playing with the kitten, digesting what she'd told him, wanting to press for more. And there was more. He knew there was, but he forced himself to take things slow, not to pressure her. He got why this show meant so much to her now though. She has a passion for dance that she'd had to walk away from, and now had a chance to experience again in some way.

"I think your new cat needs a dog pal," Sam said.

"A Lab, right?" she asked. "A cat and a Lab, like you said you had on the military base."

He liked her reference to what he'd shared with her during the vet visit. "Exactly."

"Well, then," she said. "If the show gets renewed for a second season, I'll get Sam a Lab to celebrate."

"Sam? As in me or the cat?"

"I guess you could share." She looked away, as if she realized she'd inferred he'd still be around then, involved in her life. And if she didn't, he sure did.

Sam slid a finger under her chin, lifting her gaze to his. "That sounds like a deal to me."

Suddenly, they both moved into each other's arms and were kissing wildly, passionately, hands roaming, tongues teasing.

"Either tell me to leave now, Meagan," he rasped near her ear, "or tell me to stay and make love to you."

Her fingers stabbed into his short hair, shoving his head back so she could search his face. "I know I should tell you to go. I do. Every piece of me says that work and pleasure are a bad combination but—"

"Stay or go, sweetheart."

Seconds ticked by like hours before she whispered, "Stay, Sam. I want you to stay."

11

SAM CONFUSED HER. He seduced her. And with his big body pressed to hers, her skirt up to her hips, his hot mouth devouring hers, he consumed her. She didn't want to be consumed by Sam, but at the same time, it was *all* she wanted—and she wanted it so badly, wanted *him* so badly, the mere existence of clothing between them was like sandpaper against her skin.

"One night," Meagan panted against his lips. "We do what you said in the restaurant. We get this thing between us out of our systems." But even as she made the declaration, she doubted that possibility. There was something about this man that drew her, that reached insider her and spoke to her.

"We can try," he replied, and before she could question his answer, his mouth slanted over hers. Meagan's resistance to that kiss lasted all of a second. She'd fought this attraction to Sam for so very long, and she had no more fight in her, not where he was concerned.

His tongue caressing hers, and she could taste the hot coffee they'd drank at the vet clinic. It reminded her of how he'd been there for her, both when Kiki jabbed at her, and when she'd wanted to help the kitten.

Meagan didn't resist as Sam pulled her to her feet and picked her up. He was big and strong, and it felt good to just be with him. To just forget everything except for what was happening right now.

They went down on the bed together, him on top of her, the weight of him, the feel of him, as erotic as anything she'd ever felt. As *right* as anything she'd ever felt. Again she thought of him by her side tonight, facing challenges with her, and it had been good. Too good. It scared her. He scared her. She'd never had anyone create this kind of feeling in her. She could lose herself to this man, her identify, and just then, she didn't care.

"I've wanted you since the first time I saw you," he whispered, his lips by her ear, his hand sliding through her hair, down her shoulder, over her breast. "Do you remember when that was?"

"Yes," she said, barely finding her voice as he pressed kisses along her jaw. She could feel his arousal, thick and hard between her legs. She could feel herself shaking with desire. She couldn't believe she was here, like this, with Sam. "You tried to take the Dr. Pepper I'd paid for, that had gotten lodged in the machine."

His eyes found hers. "I paid, too. You knew that. You just wanted to fight with me."

She wrapped her arms around his neck, a smile tugging at her lips. "Maybe."

His lips brushed hers. "Why?"

"Why do you like to fight with me?"

"Call me a sadist, but it turns me on when you throw darts at me with your eyes."

She laughed and said his name, simply because it felt right on her tongue. "Sam."

The mood shifted with that one whispered word. Gone was the playful banter. Sam leaned in and kissed her, a soft, gentle kiss, a short slice of his tongue teasing hers. So light, so simple, but so intense, so completely overwhelming. And when he pulled back to look at her, to study her, his blue eyes simmered like crystals in the sunlight, desire burning deep in their depths. But there was more in his expression, so much more. There was tenderness, and it was so unexpected, it stole her breath away. His fingers teased her breast. Her skin burned wherever his fingers touched, and goose bumps chased the heat.

He reached up and pulled his shirt over his head, tossing it aside. She traced the rippling muscle of his shoulders, his arms. He was beautiful, the kind of man that was sculpted from hard work and sweat, but in his case, from honor and bravery, from serving his country.

He worked the buttons on her blouse, struggling to unhook them. She did it for him, and she didn't shy away when his gaze held hers, and that act held meaning. She wanted him to know that she was willingly undressing for him, not doing it in a moment of complete abandon like in the truck. This was a choice, and one she wasn't going to let herself regret.

They didn't speak, as if they were both afraid some magical spell would be lifted and this would end before it ever began. Once the buttons were unhooked, his lips kissed her collar bone, his fingers traced the top of her black bra, shoving down the silk to tease her nipples. Meagan moaned at the intimate exploration, her thighs aching, her body hot with need that only Sam could answer.

When finally her blouse was off and her bra, too, Sam worked her skirt down her hips, taking the slash of black panties down with it. She'd barely kicked away her shoes before he tugged her to the end of the mattress, and went down on his knees between her legs. He caressed her then, and she trembled with anticipation.

"Just so you know," he said. "I'm going to do everything to make sure one night isn't enough for you." His lips pressed to her stomach, his fingers sliding into the wet heat of her body.

No. One night wasn't enough. Right now, it felt like too much. Too much pleasure, too much desire, too much yearning. But no. Not enough of Sam.

SAM TOOK HIS TIME with Meagan, savoring every blissful second with her. How he'd ever thought sex would work Meagan out of his system, he didn't know. His lips traveled the dip of her flat stomach, the curve of her hip. His nostrils flared with the soft feminine scent of her perfumed skin. He moved lower down her body. His breath teased her clit, and she arched into him, silently asking for more. Her sex tightened around the two fingers inside her, telling him he was pleasing her. And pleasing her was exactly what he burned to do.

Sam's cock thickened, his body pulsing with the need to be inside her, reacting to how readily she responded to him. With any other woman her willingness to give herself to him wouldn't have impacted him with such force. But with Meagan, it did. It did because he knew she didn't give herself easily. It mattered because she meant something to him, because what she felt and needed and wanted mattered to him in a way it had never mattered before.

Sam lapped at the swollen nub, his fingers gently massaging the tight wet heat of her body. Her soft moans driving him crazy, pressing him onward to hear another and another. He lifted her leg over his shoulder, licked her and teased her until he felt her body clench and begin to spasm. Slowly, delicately, he suckled her, easing her through her release.

To his surprise, she covered her face with her hands, as if she were embarrassed. She was one big wonderful surprise after another, this woman. Feisty and confident one minute, and insecure and sensitive the next. Sam kissed her stomach and slid her farther onto the bed. "You're beautiful. I loved doing that to you."

"Sam," she said shyly, her lashes fluttering, her cheeks turning rosy.

He smiled as he watched her blush. "Don't go anywhere," he told her before he moved away from her to finish undressing.

She lifted up on her elbows to watch him, the timidness of moments before sliding away. Her gaze lingered on his body, her expression hot with interest. And when she scraped her teeth over her bottom lip, his cock jerked and hardened. He started for the bed, and then silently cursed his eagerness, grabbing his pants and pulling a condom from his pocket.

And though he was beyond aroused, beyond reason, he didn't miss the distressed look that flashed across her face. "I don't carry condoms with me, sweetheart. I wasn't, however, going to miss a night with you because I didn't have one. I got a few when we stopped at the store." He tossed two extras on the bed.

Her lips curved instantly and she nodded her pleasure at that answer. "Can I?" she asked, scooting to sit at the end of the bed and holding out her hand.

"You don't even have to ask," he assured her. Every muscle in his body was tense with anticipation as he stepped forward.

She took the package from him and opened it, then wrapped her soft hand around his hard cock, the contrast almost too much for him. When he thought she'd slide the condom on him, she instead slid her tongue over his erection.

Sam sucked in a breath, desire rushing through him, tightening his balls. His hand went to her shoulder. "As much as I like that, I'm about as on edge as a man can get."

"I like that you're on edge," she said softly. "I like knowing you feel what I feel."

Her words were like fuel on the fire that was his need for this woman. He took the condom from her and rolled it on, before he moved them both to the middle of the bed. He spread her legs, settling between them, fitting his shaft into the warm V of her body.

He kissed her before she could say anything more, claiming her mouth, just as he pressed inside her.

Sam buried himself to the hilt, the tight feel of her squeezing him, driving him wild. She gasped into his mouth with the impact, whispering his name. He wanted to hear her say his name like that over and over. He could never hear it enough.

He pulled back to look at her, seeking a glimpse of

the passion on her face. When his eyes met hers, he felt the punch in his gut, the connection that defied one night of sex. And when he did start to move, to make love to her, passion expanded that look, that emotion. A gripping sensual rhythm quickly built, until they were crazy with kissing each other, rocking and pumping, both trying to get closer, to get more of each other. And when they eventually collapsed together, Sam pulled her into his arms and held her. They lay like that for a long while, her head on his shoulder, her hand on his chest.

Sam turned to his side to face her, and she did the same, curling her hand under her head like a pillow. "Tell me more about the town you grew up in," he prodded, wanting to learn everything about her.

She laughed. "We're naked and you want to hear about the town I grew up in? They'd be appalled that we're laying here naked and having a conversation, I can tell you that for sure. Apart from that there's really nothing to tell."

"How do your parents feel about you scoring a national television show?"

"I don't talk to them about it," she said. "We decided years ago that it was the only way we could handle my decisions."

"You can't mean they don't approve of the show?"

Immediately, he could sense the tension in her. Sam reached over and brushed her hair out of her eyes. "I'm sorry. I didn't mean to upset you."

She wet her lips and looked at him. "I know you didn't. And every time I tell myself I don't care what they think, that their opinion of me doesn't hurt, something happens and it does again."

"They really think what you're doing is bad?"

She nodded. "Yes. They do."

Sam took her into his arms. "Well, all I see is a beautiful, successful woman, who inspires me with how she charges after her dreams. Albeit, a little bossy, but I apparently like that in a woman."

She smiled and kissed him. "Do you now?"

"Seems that way."

"Maybe I should test you," she said, and pushed him to his back, before climbing on top of him. And all Sam could say was *please* and *more*. He wanted more.

12

MEAGAN SHOT FROM THE DEPTHS of a hard sleep to a sitting position. Her gaze tracked around the hotel room—Sam. Where was Sam? Gone. He was gone, and for reasons she was too groggy and panicked over to fully grasp. The realization twisted her stomach into knots. And, oh God, what time was it? And where was the ringing phone?

She scrambled across the mattress that smelled of musky male sensuality and grabbed for the phone, her legs twisted in a sheet. Under said sheet she was naked. She'd been very naked, and very happy being naked, with Sam. Who, she was reminded again, was gone. And she really didn't want to know what time it was, considering the prospect of being late to set was very real at this point.

She grabbed for the receiver and it fell. She cursed and yanked the cord, bringing the receiver to her ear. "Hello?"

"Wake-up call, sweetheart."

"Sam." His voice did funny things to her knotted

stomach. "What time is it?" She reached for the clock at the same moment that he said, "Five-fifteen. You have forty-five minutes to be on set."

Samantha meowed loudly.

He chuckled. "I hear the cat. She wants to be fed as badly as I'm betting you want to go back to sleep."

"Please tell me no one saw you leave."

"No one saw me leave."

"You're—"

"Absolutely positive, which is why I left when it was still a ghost town, when I honestly wanted to stay in bed with you."

A memory of him curled around her, *spooning,* flashed in her mind. It was the last thing she remembered. She'd told herself she'd only lay there a minute and then she'd get up, she'd send him away, but she hadn't wanted to send him away. She'd wanted him to stay.

"Although," he added, "you do snore."

"I do not snore!" She scooped up the meowing kitten who was trying to climb up onto the bed, and put her on the bedspread.

"You now have forty-one minutes until set, and a hungry, loud kitten on your hands." His voice softened. "And yes. You do snore. I guess I'll have to record you next time to prove it."

Next time? Next time. He'd said next time. "Sam—"

It was too late. He'd hung up.

Four hours later, Meagan still hadn't seen Sam, and she hated how much she pined for when she would. But she'd managed to get enough footage of the contestants and hotel, which the curse had forced them into, to head to the editing room at the rehearsal studio. She'd told everyone to rest. They'd practice at the rehearsal studio again the next morning.

And so it was outside the editing room, after she'd sent her crew to have some dinner, that Meagan entered the tiny break area of the production facility. There, Meagan finally came face-to-face with Sam. She was struggling to get the package of peanuts she'd purchased from one of the two snack machines when it happened. She was actually *facing* the machine when the tingling awareness started—the same tingling awareness she'd felt in the executive offices, a sensation she'd been too flustered then to identify. But she felt it now, and knew what it meant.

"Sam," she said softly, steeling herself for the impact that seeing him again would have. And she'd been right to steel herself because if Sam had stolen her breath before she'd slept with him, he absolutely sucked it straight out of her lungs now.

He stood there, gloriously male, with one broad, perfect shoulder resting on the doorjamb, his jaw shadowed, already fighting the blade of his morning shave.

"Problem?" he asked, his eyes raking over her slim-fitted jeans and studio T-shirt, as if she were naked. And, heaven help her, the real problem was how many times she'd replayed being exactly that way with him today.

She nodded. "The *curse* appears to have targeted my peanuts."

His sexy, wickedly capable mouth curved upward, and he pushed off the wall. "Let me see what I can do."

He sauntered toward her, and she fought the urge to stay right there in front of the machine, right there in his path. She was losing her mind. Sam was making her lose her mind, distracting her from her job, her dream, and the career she had as the only means of supporting herself. And yet, she wanted to touch him, to feel the warmth of him again. She realized then, that on some level, she'd push Sam away. Since she now knew he wasn't just an alpha male who made her tingle when he entered the room. What he made her feel was awareness on a much deeper level. The kind of thing you were lucky to experience, and so you didn't simply shut it off. Lucky. Yes. She couldn't ignore what she felt for him. She didn't want to.

Meagan didn't move. She stood in front of the machine, and he stopped in front of her. They stared at each other, neither speaking. They didn't have to. The air around them all but combusted.

His fingers brushed her cheek. "You look tired, Meg."

"Meagan," she corrected, fighting the shiver of arousal rushing down her spine.

He smiled. "Whatever you say, sweetheart."

Voices sounded somewhere in the distance and her heart raced. The last thing she needed was her crew talking about her affair with Sam, especially with Kiki out for blood. Not that Meagan was having an affair with Sam. She didn't know what she was doing with Sam. Confusion balled up inside her. "Don't call me sweetheart, either. I said one night, Sam." She hated herself for saying that, and she wanted to take the words back. She didn't even know why she'd said them.

He continued to stare at her, his expression unreadable. "Yes," he finally said. "You did."

There was a sharp quality to the two words that cut her deeply. Just as she'd thought, she pushed him away and didn't mean to. It felt bad. Really bad. "I just…we can't…I just don't want people to see so that's why I said no touching and no sweetheart—"

"And no kissing. Got it. I'll stick to rescuing your peanuts." He didn't sound happy and his mood seemed to darken instantly.

She expected him to shake the machine. Instead, he stuck change in the slot and punched a button. Before she knew it, he'd secured two bags of peanuts, and two Dr. Peppers.

He held up one of the sodas. "I believe I owe you this." He claimed a chair and then tossed out bait to get her to sit with him. "I have news about the contestants' house. Join me and I'll tell you all about it."

"More bribery?"

He arched a brow. "Is it working?"

"Apparently very well." She sat down across from him, and truthfully she was relieved to have a few more minutes with him, to be able to fix whatever she'd broken. "What about the house?"

"They agreed to all my requests, including the exterminator. If you're sure you want the place, then I can have it ready for you to move in by the weekend. That should give you time to get settled before you have to *go live* in the house. And frankly, I'd prefer having the contestants there and contained, rather than at a hotel where I can't be sure they're really in their rooms and safe." He popped open his drink.

There was something about the way he said that statement. "What happened that I don't know about?"

"A tabloid reporter tried to sneak onto the floor dressed as a waiter."

She shook her head. "Like I don't have enough to worry about. Now this?"

"You don't have to worry about this. That's what I'm here for. And that's why I would rather get us to the new house now, rather than later."

"Yes," she said. "Please. The sooner the better. I'm all for as much control as I can get, and as quickly as possible."

Their eyes locked, thick silence stretching between them. "I aim to please, Meagan," he said, finally.

Meagan. Not Meg. Not sweetheart. That should please her. It's what she'd always insisted he call her, but it didn't please her. Not with the distance she felt between them that hadn't been there last night.

He pushed to his feet. "I need to get the paperwork to the appropriate parties. I'll call you if anything goes wrong."

"Okay," she said, standing with him, searching his face, but his expression was blank, his jaw set. She wanted to apologize, but wasn't sure what to say, and he was already headed to the door. Maybe he didn't want her to apologize. Maybe...

He hesitated at the exit, and she held her breath, but when she thought he would turn back, he left without another word.

Meagan willed herself not to move, not to go after him. She had a lot of footage to edit, and she needed to check on the contestants herself. She would not go after Sam. She would *not* go after Sam. She sat down again, rested her elbows on her knees and put her hands to her head. Sam was making her crazy.

SAM WAS PISSED, and he wasn't even sure why. He'd left Meagan's room this morning determined to see her again, to find out where this thing with her was going. He'd gone into that break room, with exactly that purpose in mind. Instead, she'd warned him of her vow to keep things between them to one night and that hit him hard.

She had some deep need for control, and from what he could tell, she had her reasons. Her parents had controlled her and were still trying. Apparently, she thought he would want to do the same, and the only way she could control what was happening between them, what was uncontrollable, was to simply shut it down. Maybe that was for the best. He knew better than to mix business with pleasure. He needed to focus on the show, on security, on Kiki. Both he and Sabrina had agreed that Kiki's comments to Josh meant she planned to turn Meagan's show into another bonus opportunity for herself. He just had to prove it before Kiki made it happen.

His mind shifted back to Meagan, to her naked and perfect in his arms the night before, to her rejection today. His stride lengthened, his pace quickened. He was acting like a fool, pursuing a woman who didn't want him. He needed some space, maybe a bar and another woman, only he had too much work to do. And who was he fooling? He was too into Meagan to want anyone else.

He unlocked the door to his truck and slid inside, before pounding the steering wheel. When his cell rang, he said, "Talk to me," noting Josh was the caller. Loud music ripped through the phone. "Where the heck are you?"

"Kiki took a group of the contestants to the eighteen and over club on the corner two blocks south of the hotel," he shouted. "They're performing, Sam."

"Without studio approval or security?" Sam asked, and he could already smell the trouble.

"That's right," he said. "I told her the studio could be sued if anything went wrong. Sam. She said Meagan approved this."

Sam cursed. "Where are they?"

"Club Z and they're filming—"

The line went dead.

Sam punched Meagan's cell number into his phone. She didn't answer. Of course not. She was going to make him come to her. He shoved open his door, and started for the building, angry and feeling as foul as a soldier dodging a sniper—who, in this case, happened to be the woman he couldn't get enough of.

That's when he spotted Meagan running toward him. "Sam!" Apparently, she'd gotten a phone call, too. "Sam." She screeched to a halt in front of him, her chest rising and falling with exertion. "Sam, I—we—"

"I know," he said. "Josh told me. Let's go."

"Josh? What? What's happening? Is something happening with the cast?"

She didn't know? Had she followed him to the truck for personal reasons? Was she here *for him,* not the bar problem? He didn't get to ask. He quickly updated Meagan.

"Sam, this is bad," she said when he'd finished and they'd climbed into his truck. "The studio's liability if someone gets hurt is bad enough. But we have sponsors that expect a family show. If there's the slightest piece of footage of someone doing something they shouldn't, we could lose them. And that could be the end of us."

"And," he said, "it gets worse. Kiki told Josh that you approved this."

"What? No. Please tell me no, Sam."

"I know the truth," he spoke softly. "I have your back, Meagan."

13

THOUGH SHE'D MADE SAM WAIT for her to run inside the production building for her purse and phone, having learned her lesson about leaving them behind, the short ten-minute ride from the studio to the hotel felt like a lifetime to Meagan.

The instant Sam put his foot on the brake, stopping next to the valet stand, they were both already shoving open their doors.

"Which way to Club Z?" he was asking the young kid he'd palmed his keys to, as Meagan came around to his side.

"Two blocks to the right, then another right, you can't miss it," the valet told him.

She and Sam were walking before the kid ever finished speaking. "I can't believe Kiki is there, and brought cameras. How did she even manage that, Sam? I mean there would be release forms and legal issues."

"You know the answer," he said. "She planned this in advance."

"Right. She did. She had to have done just that. I

can't let this go, Sam. I have to let Sabrina know, but Kiki's going to say I'm behind it. I can't believe this is happening."

They approached the club, loud music banging through the door, and a long line of people waiting to enter the building. Sam motioned her toward the door, then chatted with the bouncer, leaning in close to the brawny man guarding the entryway, to say something that was, apparently, worthy of entry.

Sam reached for her hand and pulled her in front of him, into a narrow hallway. His touch sent a shiver of awareness up her arm, and all over her body. Her mind went back to the break room, to the kiss, to his departure. She'd gone after him, and not because of this mess. She hadn't known about any of this. She'd followed him because whatever had made him leave so abruptly, whatever had made him withdraw, she had this horrible feeling, it was going to haunt her in ways she had yet to discover—and didn't want to. Because like it or not, she *liked* him. He mattered.

One of his hands settled on her waist as she pressed her way toward the crowded bar, which appeared to have two levels, and balconies above the dance floor. There were also stairs leading to a lower floor.

Sam pushed in next to her, his body framing hers, branding her with memories of the prior night. He bent down, his lips near her ear. "Let's stay close. I don't want to lose you in this chaos."

She turned instinctively, and suddenly, her mouth was inches from his, his breath warm on her cheek. "Yes. Okay." Their eyes locked, and all the shadows in the world couldn't mask the connection that crackled between them. She was so alive with Sam.

He leaned in closer again, to talk to her, the spicy scent of him rushing over her—she so loved the way the man smelled. "Shall we try upstairs or down first?" he asked.

"Hey!" Someone screamed. "Some television show is filming downstairs. We have to go downstairs." A rush toward the lower level followed, bodies flooding past them.

Meagan and Sam shared a look of inevitability. They knew where they were going now, and clearly, they weren't the only ones headed there. He motioned with his head and drew her hand in his. A lot of maneuvers, bumps, and her feet getting stomped, and soon they made it down the stairs to find a huge area blocked off around a stage. Four of Meagan's dancers were performing, with cameras rolling. No director, no Meagan—just Kiki and everyone who hadn't been busting their butts in the editing room.

Anger rolled inside Meagan and she pulled away from Sam, charging forward. Meagan had been cautious around Kiki and her corporate connection for too long. She and her assistant were going to do a little dancing of their own.

SAM'S MEN HAD STEPPED UP to the plate, which was one piece of good in a lot of bad. He owed Josh a heck of a lot of kudos. The stage was well secured, the safety of the cast ensured as well as it could be, considering the circumstances. But there was no way to get the dancers off the stage, in the middle of a routine, without making matters worse.

Holding his position, Sam stood a few feet from Meagan, watching the heated exchange between her and Kiki, and noting the moment she broke from the argument to speak to Jensen, the show's host, and then to one of the cameramen.

She then stood alone inside the ropes, arms crossed in front of her chest. She all but screamed annoyance, louder in Sam's mind, than the music thrumming against every particle in the place. The dancer's routine ended, and another started, and still Meagan didn't move. Clearly, she'd decided to let this continue.

Sam made his way over to Josh, who'd texted his position. Sam ended up almost directly across from Meagan, who was staring at the stage.

"We breaking this up or what, boss?" Josh shouted over the music.

Sam could see the tension in Meagan's body, despite the distance between them. Whatever had gone down between her and Kiki wasn't good. Not that he'd expected it to be good, but he had a strong feeling that whatever had happened was worse than bad.

Suddenly, Meagan started walking toward the back of the stage. Sam cut Josh a sideways look. "Hold everyone right here. If anyone so much as breathes in another direction, I expect you to be on them."

Josh gave him a two-finger salute, and then Sam was moving toward Meagan. He rounded the back of the stage and found a long hallway with a restroom sign, which was the only place Meagan could have gone.

He found her at the end of the narrow hallway and

to the right, leaning against a wall with her head back, her eyes shut. For a moment, with her unaware of his presence, he took in the sight of her.

Petite and sexy, her long dark hair brushing her shoulders, he was so in tune with Meagan. He'd always had a connection to this woman. They had always been headed toward each other.

Everything male—hot and protective—screamed inside him, and pushed him into action. There was no hesitation, no thought of rejection, of her not needing him right now, because he knew she did.

Sam went to her, and before she knew he'd joined her, his hand gently cupped the side of her face, comforting her, while the other hand rested against the wall near her chin.

Her head lowered, eyes fixed on his, hands settling on his chest. "Sam." She breathed out the word, and there as if relief there, like she was glad to see him.

"Talk to me, sweetheart. What happened? And why are you back here alone?"

"Just needed to think a minute. I'm handling this all wrong. Kiki and I argued. I threatened. She threatened. She won. She swears I signed a release for tonight along with some other forms I signed. She had to have snuck it in and I missed it."

"Is that possible?"

"I don't know. I told her I want to see the forms. But she says that if I go to Sabrina she'll say she warned me about tonight's potential liability ahead of time. I screwed up, Sam. I can't even pull the dancers from the club because she said I can't. Because *she said,* end of story. I okayed things in my contract I shouldn't have.

I can be removed if I'm a detriment to my own show. I can't stop Kiki."

"I can," he said. "I'll—"

She leaned in and pressed her mouth to his, the softness of her lips, the willingness of the connection, making him instantly rock hard.

"Don't," she whispered a moment later. "Don't protect me, Sam. I don't want to drag you into her line of fire. I won't let that happen. Just...just kiss me."

His arm slid around her. "I'll do both." He slanted his mouth over hers. She moaned and leaned into him, her hands gripping his shoulders. Something wild sprung to life around them—the club, the music, the desire so long bubbling between them—igniting in the seclusion of this one tiny spot, their escape in the midst of chaos. And the acknowledgment that they'd lied when they said they'd never kiss like this again.

Sam deepened the kiss, drinking her in. He knew even though she'd said "one night," that she wanted another as badly as he did. His hands were all over her body, her hands were all over his—under his shirt, caressing his skin—scorching him to the point that he was ready to take her right here and now. And he wanted to.

He wanted to forget everything—he had forgotten everything. He should be focused on his job, but he was here, ready to rip her clothes off, damn thankful he could trust Josh to handle things elsewhere.

He stopped and pulled back to look at her. "You accuse me of wanting control," he said. "Yet you steal it from me at every turn."

"You can have it," she panted. "I don't want it."

She reached for his jaw again, and he kissed her,

tasted her, but there was something in her words, in her face, and he pulled back again, tenderness colliding with passion. "You aren't letting her defeat you. I won't let you."

"Stop talking," she ordered, sliding her hand down the front of his pants and stroking his cock. "Why are you always talking?"

Why was he talking? He palmed her backside and melded her to his shaft, claiming her mouth again, running his hand roughly over her breasts, pinching her nipples.

"Sam—" she moaned.

"Oh, yes—*Sam*." The cold female voice that wasn't Meagan's froze both of them in place. Kiki.

"No," Meagan whispered. "No."

"Oh, yes. Yes, yes!" Kiki laughed. "I am here, and boy, what a show."

Sam cursed under his breath, fully intending to handle this mess, so Meagan didn't have to. But he should have known that Meagan's moment of weakness when he'd found her in this hallway, was just that. And it was over now. In true Meagan form, she faced Kiki, obviously refusing to let her get the best of her. But before Meagan could say anything screams bellowed through the air. "Fight! Fight!"

Meagan took off running past Kiki, Sam behind her. They rounded the corner to discover the crowd surrounding the stage, where the dancers had been performing only minutes before. Now, a shoving match appeared to be taking place.

Meagan's family-approved dance show was turning into a version of female fight club and that meant sponsors could be lost. And so could the show.

14

MEAGAN WAS ON the stage in a heartbeat thanks to Sam, who lifted her up and then jumped up behind her. And thanks to Sam's staff, not only were the observers being held at bay, the fight was somewhat under control, as well.

Josh, and a female security person employed by Sam, were holding two contestants apart—Tabitha and a petite brunette dancer named Carrie White. Meagan had thought Carrie was fairly timid, but considering the clear mark down Tabitha's face, she wasn't so sure anymore.

Tabitha was fighting Josh, trying to get to Carrie. "You better watch your back!" Tabitha yelled at Carrie. "I'm going to make you pay for scratching me."

"Enough!" Meagan yelled. "If either of you touches the other one again, you're off the show." She eyed them both. "Understood?"

Carrie quickly nodded. "I was just defending myself. She jumped on me, Meagan. She jumped on me and… I swear I was defending myself."

Jensen, the tall, blond New Yorker, stepped forward. "It's true. Tabitha jumped on Carrie."

It didn't take Meagan long to put two and two together. Tabitha and Jensen had been flirting on set. And since Jensen was defending Carrie, instead of Tabitha, it was a good bet that there was some sort of jealousy thing going on between the girls.

Kiki rushed onto the stage, conveniently after the fight had been derailed. "What happened?"

"They didn't belong here, is what happened," Sam said and motioned to Josh. "There's a back door by the bathrooms. Let's get everyone out that way, and make it snappy. As in yesterday."

Fifteen minutes later, the dancers were heading in the direction of the hotel as Meagan and Sam followed. "You okay?" he asked, touching her arm to draw her to a halt.

"As okay as I can be considering what happened tonight."

"I called Sabrina," he said.

"What? When?"

"A few minutes ago." He held up his hand. "And before you get mad—"

"I'm not," she said. "I'm not. I know you're trying to help, Sam. I know and I appreciate it. But I don't want to drag you into this and endanger your career, and I feel like I already have."

"It's my job to protect the studio," he said. "I'm working on a documentation trail that backs up my concerns about Kiki. I'll handle this, but in the meantime, you have to keep her from doing any irreversible damage to the show."

"I'm trying. I am desperately trying. What was the outcome of the call?"

"Sabrina thinks a lot of you and this show, but she has powerful people she answers to and big money at stake. I have full authority to investigate Kiki but she is well connected and she's been praised for saving the network from several disasters. I'm fairly confident they were manufactured disasters. She's clearly been rewarded for her actions in some way, shape or form, and she's just as clearly after the gold now. We have to tread carefully."

"If she's that powerful then tonight might be the end, Sam. If that fight makes the tabloids then it could already be the death of our sponsors."

"Then get more."

"It's not that easy for a new show, Sam."

"All right. Then let's think this through. You want the cameras rolling in the house because you want to feature the real lives of the contestants while they traveled this journey."

"Yes, but this isn't what I had in mind. I thought it would be kids getting nervous about performances, their dreams and desires. Their inspiration. Not threats, fights and exploding water pipes."

"So, not real life, then."

"Yes, real life."

"You're too close to this show emotionally," he said. "Step back and think of it like you did when you were producing a news program. Surely, you were battling competitors all the time for top stories."

"Yes," she said. "We were."

"Then do that now. Stop thinking about the show

like it's a dream. Save that for the celebration when it's a hit."

She considered him a moment and nodded. "You're right. You are absolutely right."

"Okay, then," he said. "Us Special Ops guys are all about damage control. My first thought is that what happened tonight, despite Kiki's manipulation and mishandling, was raw and very real."

"Not in a good way," Meagan argued.

"Reality means real—and that isn't always pretty. That fight evolved from the pressures of competition, more than anything else. I bet you can do something with that to make it a powerful episode."

His words sparked a few interesting ideas in Meagan's mind. "You know, now that I'm thinking about this with some distance, I think I can. I could even do a press release and frame the fight the way I want it framed. I can send it to the sponsors and promise them some preview footage before I air a show around tonight's events."

"Perfect," he said. "Hell, give Kiki credit. Praise her to your staff. If you spin tonight into something brilliant, you deflate her efforts to make you look bad. Which means tonight becomes a win for the show."

A slow smile slid onto Meagan's lips. "Oh my God, you are the one who's brilliant. I love you, Sam."

The words dropped heavily between them, out before she could stop them. She could barely breathe because…she might actually be falling in love with him.

"And here I thought I'd be lucky just to get you to like me." His voice was soft, his gaze hot.

Meagan didn't know what to say so she did what

she always did with Sam. She picked a fight. "I won't if you do things like tonight. You distracted me from a critical situation and had me making out in the club."

"No, I didn't."

She blinked. "What? That's all you're going to say? No, you didn't."

"You were beating yourself up, and searching for a way to feel something other than defeat. You used me to do that, and I was helpless to resist, though I shouldn't have been. I should have been focused on my job. So *you* distracted *me*."

"You're blaming *me* for distracting *you* from *your* job?"

He smiled. "Exactly."

"You distracted me," she said. "*You* distracted *me,* Sam."

"Seems we have a mutually distracting impact on one another."

"So we can't…we have to stop doing things like tonight."

"I want to kiss you."

"No."

"*Yes.* I do."

"*No.* You can't. We can't, Sam." Her chest tightened because the realization washed over her and she couldn't selfishly ignore it at Sam's expense. "Kiki is going—"

"I don't care about Kiki."

"I do. We have to."

"Let's walk," he said abruptly, turning toward the hotel, clearly not happy with her.

Meagan's stomach clenched. Her chest got even tighter. The same feelings she'd had back in the break room. She wanted him to understand, yet she didn't want him to understand at all. She was more screwed up over Sam than ever.

"That's it?" she asked, falling into step with him. "Let's walk?"

"What do you want me to do besides walk?" he asked. "Pull you against the wall and kiss you again?"

Yes. Oh, yes. Please. She grabbed his arm and brought him to a standstill. "You're making me crazy, Sam. I don't know what to do here."

"Right there with ya, sweetheart."

"Sam. Please. Even Sabrina is cautious about Kiki. Sabrina! She's powerful. She's one of the executives. I'm afraid that I'll drag you to the unemployment line with me if this goes badly."

"No," he said. "That's not the problem. I'm trying to get through this with you. You're trying to find a way to do it without me. There's a difference. A big difference." He started to walk again. She didn't. She stared after him, all that emotion in her chest balled so tightly, she could barely breathe. She wanted to go after him, she wanted to dispute his words, make him understand. But he wouldn't understand. She'd figured that out about Sam.

He wasn't an arrogant jerk. He wasn't a control freak. He had a whole lot of hero in him. He'd tell her it was okay, that he wasn't risking his job, to be with her. And that mattered to her. He mattered to her. She had to let him go.

He was right though. Rather than using her smarts, she'd been letting her emotions get involved when dealing with Kiki, and everything to do with this show. That ended tonight.

EARLY THE NEXT MORNING, Sam was awake and thankful for the coffeemaker in the room. He might be a soldier at heart, but he'd never been a soldier who denied himself thick, black hardcore caffeine when he needed it.

He finished off a cup, with one thing on his mind. Meagan had let him walk away the night before. Again. Damn, he'd never been a glutton for punishment before. This was unfamiliar, uncomfortable territory, and he had to get some space, to get his head clear. Setting the mug aside, dressed in his jeans and a T-shirt, he was ready to finish the deal for the house and get his hands dirty securing the property.

Around the hotel, Meagan was too close for comfort. Where just knowing she was a few doors down had him climbing the walls, and right out of his skin.

He stepped into the deserted hallway, everyone still in bed, when he was surprised to hear a contestant's door open and then quietly shut. Sam frowned and soon came face to face with Carrie.

"Oh, I…I…didn't think anyone would be up yet."

"I see that," he commented, noting the rolling suitcase behind her. The kid couldn't be more than eighteen or nineteen, maybe twenty. "Going somewhere?"

Silent tears started to stream down her cheeks, and Sam knew exactly what he had to do. "Come with me."

A few seconds later, Meagan's door opened. She was still wearing a pair of Mickey Mouse pajamas, with her hair sticking up wildly, and looking more sexy than he could imagine any one woman looking. And when such an appearance could not only get a guy hot, but make him smile, inside out, he was as hooked as a bee on honey. Sam knew right then, he couldn't hide from what this woman was doing to him, no matter how he tried.

The instant Meagan saw Carrie, her eyes widened, all signs of sleep slipping away. She hugged Carrie, her eyes meeting Sam's. She motioned them inside.

The kitten met Sam at the door, meowing loudly. Sam fed the hungry little beast, and then went for the coffeepot, knowing that Meagan was running on limited to no sleep. By the time the pot was brewing, Meagan had Carrie sitting cross-legged across from her on the bed, spilling her story.

"She hates me," Carrie was saying. "Absolutely hates me."

"Competition can be brutal," Meagan said. "But everything worth having is worth fighting for. And you know what? The things you have to work the hardest for, are the ones you appreciate the most. The question is, do you want this bad enough to fight for it? Your packed bag makes me wonder."

"I want to dance," she said. "I don't want to fight with Tabitha."

"So you don't want this."

"That's not what I said!"

"You aren't willing to fight."

"I am."

"Just not Tabitha."

"She's the meanest person I've ever known."

"Until you meet the next one like her," Meagan pointed out. "There are tons of Kikis in this world."

Sam took a seat nearby, across from the bed. Meagan's eyes found his an instant before she added, "Listen, Carrie. Real life isn't always pretty. Everyone isn't going to be nice to you, and everything isn't going to come with a shiny pink bow on top. You can't let people like Tabitha steal your dreams, make you give up."

Sam took in those words, took in what she was telling him indirectly. She had a dream and she was scared of losing it. He knew that, but hearing it again wasn't easy. She had baggage she had to deal with, and there wasn't room for him inside her life until she did—if she ever did.

"I sprained my ankle last night," Carrie announced. "It's bad, Meagan. I hid it but it's getting worse." She laughed bitterly. "I'd rather the curse would have gotten anything but my ankle."

"There is no curse," Meagan said. "And a sprain can be wrapped and medicated. You have ten days before your first performance. Or, you can use that and Tabitha as reason to quit. Your choice."

"I don't want to quit. I don't. But—"

"No buts," Meagan warned. "I'm going to get tough with you now. In or out. Fight or give up. You choose."

"You really think I can do this?"

"It doesn't matter what I think," she said. "It matters what you know. But for the record, you wouldn't be here if I didn't believe in you."

Carrie flung her arms around Meagan's neck and hugged her. The unfinished business between Meagan and him thicker than the coffee he'd made in his room.

"I'm going to fight. I'm going to beat Tabitha and win this competition."

"Good," Meagan said. "I can't wait to watch it happen."

More chatter followed, and some coddling of the kitten, before Carrie returned to her room to sleep as long as she could before rehearsals, which had been pushed back, after the nightclub incident, until noon.

Sam made to leave, as well.

"Sam, wait," Meagan said, her hand touching his arm, heat scorching, his cock thickening as if she'd just invited him to join her in bed.

He held the door open, not about to let rumors fly any more than they probably were. He also wasn't about to tempt himself into kissing her how he'd wanted to ever since he'd walked into the room.

His gaze met hers, and he could read her expression, read the "I can't" in her face. "I met with my crew last night and we did a press release that also went to the sponsors. One of the sponsors called me immediately and expressed how thrilled they were with the buzz the show was getting. After that, Kiki happily took credit, and I was happy to let her."

"Good," he said. "I'm glad it worked out."

"Me, too," she said, and hesitated, as if she wanted to add something else.

Sam continued waiting, wanting to know what that something else was, his heart racing. This woman really was making him crazy.

Finally, she said, "I…I left my phone and purse in your truck."

"Right," he answered flatly, his pulse slowing. "Your phone and your purse. I'll have it dropped off." He didn't wait for a reply. He left with absolutely no question in his mind, that once again, she had purposely let him go. It was a habit she couldn't seem to break.

15

A WEEK LATER, MEAGAN was pacing the stage in the auditorium where the first live show would take place in two days. Two short, too quickly approaching days and too many days away from Sam. Oh, he was around, but he wasn't really around, not for her, that was. It didn't matter that it was for the best, that it was the right thing to do to protect him. She missed him.

She raked her hand through her hair, her stress level at its highest. There was an electronic short in the stage's lighting system, thus sound checks had gone horribly, and the hot band that was set to perform for the big premiere had cancelled. Their lead singer had laryngitis.

The "cursed" and "nightclub" episodes of the show had run two nights in a row with huge ratings, but the live show was the true test. Could the dancing part of the equation pull in ratings? There were plenty inside the studio who doubted that, thus the contestant house had been incorporated into the concept of the show.

"We snagged Mason Montgomery," Kiki announced, rushing down the center aisle. Mason Montgomery being a popular new singer who'd just hit the charts. "He'll be here and he's excited to perform."

Meagan let out a relieved breath. "That's great news." To Kiki's credit, and Sam's for his suggestion, ever since she'd given Kiki credit for the nightclub episode, she'd actually seemed to care about the show.

"Are we moving into the house tomorrow or what?" Kiki asked, drawing to the edge of the stage, next to the judges' table, hands on her hips. "We need to get organized."

"Negotiations are still underway," she said. "But I hope so. I'm expecting word any minute."

Kiki grimaced. "Look. I know you hate the reality, club-fight stuff, but our ratings are off the charts. I want this show to make it as much as you do. We need to do something spectacular to ensure the dancing gets an audience. We don't have time to make that happen in the house this week."

Meagan's cell phone rang, and she eyed the number. "That's Josh now." Josh. Not Sam. She'd barely seen, or talked to Sam since Carrie's visit to her room. She was shocked at just how much she missed that banter.

She flipped open her phone. "Hey, Josh."

"We're a go, but Sam wants you to drive out and give us a final thumbs-up before we get everyone out here."

Meagan ended the call, eager to see the house and move in. And yes. Eager to see Sam.

"I NEED A SCREWDRIVER," Sam yelled to one of his men from under the kitchen cabinet of the contestant's house.

"One screwdriver coming up." The tool landed in his outstretched palm, and Sam went completely still.

Meagan. Meagan, so close her leg was touching his. Slowly, he eased his head out from under the cabinet to find her squatting beside him. Little brown wisps of hair floating over her brow. He loved her hair—how it felt, how it smelled.

"Your man is apparently MIA, since he's nowhere to be found," she said. "And I wasn't aware you did plumbing."

"I don't," he said, sitting up and leaning against the cabinet. "One of the kitchen cameras is acting up, screwing up the entire link to go live. I'll need you to outline where the private areas are besides the obvious ones. There won't be many, still, we don't want any peep shows."

She nodded, then surprised him by sitting down on the floor herself, her back to the island kitchen so that she faced him. "The entire electrical system at the auditorium is out of whack. An electrician is working on it. I think I'm beginning to believe in the curse."

"The ratings don't seem to be cursed. They've been good so far."

"A blessing for sure," she agreed. "Nothing is going as I expected but it still seems to be okay."

He rested his hand on one knee and stretched out the other leg. "Just because it's not how you envisioned it doesn't mean it's not good."

She studied him. "Like you, Sam. You aren't what I expected."

"So you've told me."

"You've been avoiding me."

No one could accuse her of beating around the bush. "I've been busy out here."

"And avoiding me."

"And avoiding you," he conceded. "Yes."

"Why?"

"Isn't that what you wanted?"

"Apparently not."

He arched a brow. "Apparently not?"

"I think I miss arguing with you."

"Think?"

"Okay I do. I miss arguing with you."

"We'll have plenty of opportunity when we both move in here."

"So what's the scoop? Can we be in this place tomorrow?"

"Looks like. I just want to walk you through the camera setups." He started to get up.

"Sam." She spoke softly, his name packed with so much emotion that it might as well have been a shout.

"Yeah, sweetheart?"

"I miss you."

"You made this decision."

"I really was just trying to protect you."

"I don't need to be protected."

"You're sure about that? Because I'm not."

"Completely."

"But—"

"No buts about it."

"Then…about that kiss I said no to…" She crawled toward him and pressed her mouth to his.

SAM WASN'T SURE WHAT screamed louder—his desire for this woman, or the warning to stay away from her. His hand slid to the side of her face, his lips brushing hers. He told himself to tread cautiously, that he was getting emotionally attached to Meagan, and while he had no doubt she was truly into him, he wasn't sure, that emotion had anything to do with him, no matter how much he wanted to be, that he wasn't simply her escape. Whatever she'd been feeling in the hallway of that club a week before, she was feeling now, too.

But things had changed for him—or at least had become more clear. He liked Meagan. He liked her a lot. And even though Sam was on unfamiliar ground, he wasn't one to run from whatever came his way. He damn sure wasn't about to start with Meagan. He had every intention of finding out what was between them, beyond one heck of a lot of smoking-hot attraction.

She pulled back slightly, her breath warm, her mouth still deliciously near and tempting. He knew in his gut that no matter how much he wanted her naked and in his arms, she was hiding—from her true self and from him. He wasn't going to let her do that.

"Why tonight, Meagan?" he asked. "Why tonight and not last night? Or the night before?"

A door slammed. That they'd been alone this long was a miracle. Now there was no time to talk to Meagan, and make his position clear, though he fully intended to. Just like he didn't run from things, he didn't play games, or talk in circles.

"Let's check out the property," he said, before they were interrupted. He quickly brushed his mouth over hers, silently reassuring her that he welcomed their intimacy. He then pushed to his feet and pulled her with him.

"Sam—" she started, looking surprisingly vulnerable, an emotion he hadn't often seen in her.

Josh entered the room. "We're fine in… Oh, hey, Meagan. I bet you're glad to finally be moving in."

"Very," she agreed and exchanged some small talk with him, before Sam had Josh finish up under the cabinet.

A few minutes later, they'd reviewed the in-house cameras, and were standing on the porch. "If we walk up the beach, I can show you where we set up cameras."

"There are cameras on the actual beach?"

"That's right," he said. "It allows us to ensure we don't have any trespassers, and it gives you some extra unscripted footage to weed through."

"That's more than I could have asked for," she said. "I know this must be a huge change from the army for you, Sam, but if it's any consolation, you're good at what you do."

"I aim to please," he said, leaning on the railing. "I'm focused on the future, not the past. I'm simply not one to linger on what I've lost."

"But an injury took your career," she said. "Doesn't that ever make you angry?"

"Sure. I was angry when it happened. I was angry as hell. But it happened, and I can't change history. You climb inside yourself, duke it out, and move on. And is this where I think I'll end up? Only if I decide I have real value, if I feel I'm contributing. And right now, I'm pretty okay with just helping you succeed."

Surprise overtook her expression. "Sam."

"This matters to you on some deep level that I know I don't understand. But I want to. And things that matter to people the way this matters to you, matters to me." He realized something that had been in the back of his mind for a while. "What are you having trouble letting go of, Meagan?"

She inhaled sharply. "Why would you ask me that?"

"Because I can sense there's something you cling to, something that you carry around like a concrete block," he said. "And because I want to know what makes you tick."

He half expected her to withdraw, but she didn't. Instead, still facing him, she pressed her palm against the railing he was leaning on. "This first season is like standing on a rug, certain it's going to be yanked out from underneath you. For me, I feel like this is it. If this show doesn't make it, I need to reevaluate and figure out where I fit, if I fit, in this industry." She paused. "Did you say let's walk? I think walking would be good right now."

They headed down the beach. Dim lights illuminated their path, as they strolled in silence laden with unspoken questions and untouched passion.

"You asked why I kissed you tonight," Meagan blurted, turning to him.

"Tell me," he encouraged, not surprised by her directness, or how much it appealed to him.

"I like you, Sam Kellar."

She couldn't have said anything more perfect. It was exactly what he'd been thinking in the kitchen. "I like you, too, Meagan Tippan." He stepped close to her, wrapping her in his arms. "So where does that leave us?"

The lights around them flickered, and someone shouted, with footsteps running along the beach. "Apparently," she said, "with nowhere to hide."

Good, he thought. Because he wasn't going to let her hide. She'd opened the door to let him inside her life, and he was coming in, armed and ready to get to know every intimate detail.

"Let me finish up here, and then we'll…talk."

She smiled, mischief in her eyes. "Good. I'm up for a good argument."

"Me, too," he assured her. "That is, as long as we get to kiss and make up."

16

MEAGAN WAS NERVOUS. Nervous! How insane was that? But she and Sam had taken their connection to a new level tonight. Meagan had no idea she was going to kiss Sam while they were on the kitchen floor, but she was glad she had. She was so tired of controlling everything around her, and, despite her spent nerves, it was almost a relief to have her wild desire for Sam become a fact.

Her cell phone rang, and she quickly stuck her headset in her ear and hit the answer button without taking her eyes off the road. She was driving back to the hotel with Sam in his vehicle behind her. She'd been trying to reach Kiki or Shayla all evening with no answer, and that worried her.

"Hello."

"Why do you sound like you want to bite my head off?"

She laughed instantly at the sound of Sam's voice, which was a testament to how much she needed the distraction that was this man. To think she'd believed it would be a bad thing. "I didn't know I did. Sorry. I've been trying to reach Kiki and Shayla and I can't. Considering her track record, silence from Kiki still twists me in knots."

"And you want to let her live in the mother-in-law house with you?" he asked, reminding her of the decision she'd shared with him earlier in the evening.

"I need her under thumb, where I can watch her."

"If she's at the second house, she'll be under my thumb and…on second thought, I think she should stay with you."

"Yeah, I bet you do," Meagan said. "I'm not so sure Josh would agree. He seems to get all hot and bothered when she's near."

"Josh's no fool, or he wouldn't work for me. He knows what Kiki's really about," he said.

She sighed and went back to the prior subject. "I can't believe they aren't taking my calls."

"Don't assume the worst," he said. "I think we should get your mind off of it."

"How do you propose we do that?"

"By talking about something else. What's your favorite color?"

"Are you serious?"

"As a heart attack. So—what is it?"

She laughed softly. "Fine. It's red."

"Why?"

"It's bold and daring like I dreamt of being when I was growing up in a small conservative Texas town. What about you?"

"Orange."

"Like the Texas Longhorns?"

"Only a Texan would turn orange into Texas Longhorn burnt orange," he said. "I'm talking California orange—a new day's sun burning over the ocean. I was born here, you know. Those sunrises were one of the things I missed when I was gone. Us soldiers see more dirt and grunge than we do oceans and sunrises."

Sam was a soldier, a Special Forces soldier. Who knew what all he'd seen, what he'd lived. "Your job was risking your life," she said, feeling a heavy dose of perspective. "It makes all my worries about television and ratings so shallow."

"Soldiers fight for right and wrong, and for freedom. This show, and the kids chasing their dreams, is part of that, too. The land of opportunity, where you dare to dream, and make those dreams real." His voice softened, husky and male, and oh so alluring. "Don't start turning yourself into a villain, Meagan. You'll steal all of Kiki's fun. Which is a bad subject, so let's get back to the American dream. It makes me think of apple pie, which I love. Do you know how to make one?"

She laughed. "I know how to buy one at the bakery, which is far better than anything I could ever bake. Though I make a mean pan of Kraft mac'n'cheese, which is, I assume, because I follow instructions well. It's one of my favorite late-night dinners."

"Excellent choice. I'm fond of it myself."

The drive flew by as Sam drilled her with random questions that had her laughing and eagerly waiting for his own answers in return.

It wasn't until she pulled into the hotel parking lot, and found a spot, with Sam whipping in next to her, that she realized two things. She hadn't heard from her staff, or even tried to call them during the drive. And she was suddenly nervous again about being alone with Sam. Which was nuts. She'd already slept with Sam. She'd done naughty things with Sam in his truck. But she'd also convinced herself those adventures were just that. Adventures. Until tonight. Tonight "things" had become a relationship for her and Sam.

She shoved open her door to find Sam already approaching, and before she could let her nervousness get the best of her, he pulled her into his arms and kissed her. A hot, passionate, reassuring kiss.

"I had to do that before we go inside and the insanity of whatever waits for us steals you away from me."

"Do it again," she ordered, and when he did, she decided there really was more to Sam than bossy alpha male. She really liked the way this soldier took orders.

THEY DIDN'T HAVE TO AGREE to be discreet, they simply were, and Meagan liked Sam all the more for intuitively knowing what was necessary. And somehow, riding the elevator from the garage to the lobby, with him beside her, looking straight ahead, not touching her, only stoked her desire. They'd switched elevators and rode to their private floor. The elevator dinged and Meagan found herself casting Sam a sideways smile. He arched a brow at her all-too-obvious "I want you" look, the heat in his expression saying he was feeling exactly what she was.

The doors slid open, and he motioned her forward. Her smile faded fairly fast when she found a large group of her crew and almost every dancer in the competition sitting around on sofas and chairs, with food and beverages, in the common area. Several cameras were rolling, one of which singled out her and Sam.

"Off of me," she told her cameraman. "You know how I feel about that."

"You're no fun, Meagan," the cameraman shouted.

"I'm not supposed to be fun," she commented. "I'm the producer."

"That's why they have me," Kiki said, lifting her glass.

Meagan gestured to her, and Kiki sighed heavily before arriving at her side. "Before you say anything, we had no brilliant footage ideas for tonight, so we *all* decided to just chill out and talk, and hope for something good to happen."

Carrie and Tabitha had Jensen sandwiched between them. The two giggled and hugged him. He was smiling from ear to ear.

Meagan and Sam exchanged a worried look. She sought out her director. Shayla's expression was one of concern, as well.

"From fight to ménage," Shayla whispered. "If that isn't good television, I don't know what is."

"Or another fight, and a lawsuit," Sam said softly, giving the crowd his back.

"Exactly," Meagan echoed. She wasn't about to stand by and let Tabitha and Carrie end up in another argument, but she chose her words cautiously with Kiki. "While I reluctantly appreciate what you're trying to do for ratings, we need to tread cautiously."

"This is darn good footage, Meagan," Kiki said in a low voice. "This little romantic drama will make them crazy-popular."

Meagan bit back her first reaction, which was disapproval. "In that case, we don't want them to get kicked off the show for poor behavior. We need to get them to go relax and go to bed. We're moving to the house early tomorrow."

"Well, that's good," Kiki said. "But I really dislike the dance part of this show."

"That would be the entire show," Meagan responded.

Kiki snorted and addressed the group. "We're moving into the new house tomorrow, everyone," she called out, "so be ready to leave at the crack of dawn. Time for bed." There were lots of moans and groans, and chaos that followed, but the announcement got everyone moving.

Meagan and Kiki chatted with DJ and Ginger to ensure they were prepared for their lead roles in the move, and then in the new house. Sam and several of his staff ended up in a powwow of some sort by the elevator, and as much as she didn't want to notice, she could tell the instant Sam stepped away. Once all the contestants were in their rooms, Sam positioned several of his people on the floor to ensure no one snuck out. Sam then disappeared with Josh in tow.

In her room, Meagan fought the empty, disappointed feeling she had. She was alone. As in, without Sam, and she admitted now just how much that wasn't how she wanted this night to end.

For the first time in three years, Meagan had not only let someone into her life, she'd let another alpha in. That should terrify her, and scream of a mistake. She'd always chosen the wrong men. But Sam didn't seem wrong. Nor was he some alpha control freak. Sam was…

well, he was Sam, who managed to somehow make being tough and strong so darn alluring and perfect. And now that he was in, she wanted him here, with her. She wondered if he was thinking the same thing, if he wanted to be here. And if he did, why wasn't he?

She laughed that off, knowing all too well, it wasn't as if he could just walk up to her door and come in without creating talk. She might have caved to the impossibility of staying away from Sam, but she still didn't want to paint a bulls-eye on his chest for Kiki. Kiki seemed to be into the show though. Meagan had researched the other programs Kiki had been involved in and this was the first with huge ratings out of the gate. Her hope was that Kiki would believe this show's success was a bigger feather in her cap than its demise.

She shoved aside thoughts of a failed show, and headed to the bathroom, for her surefire comfort ritual of a hot bath. She was about to step into the tub, when her cell rang.

She rushed to grab it from her purse, saw Sam's number and smiled. She flipped the cell open.

"And now you know why I kissed you by the car," he said, without a hello.

She returned to the tub and sank down into her favorite jasmine-scented bubbles. "Now I know."

"Where are you?"

"In my room. You?"

"On my way back to the hotel from the property. We had a problem with some reporters who managed to find their way out there, but it's under control. They're gone."

"Wow," Meagan said. "I don't know whether to be

frustrated or excited that the show is getting so much attention."

"I'll handle the frustrated," he said. "You just be excited."

Warmth filled her. "You keep making me want to say thank you, and I'm afraid it will go to your head."

"Sometimes you have to live dangerously."

"Hmm," she said. "I would rather do that in person."

"Alone time isn't going to be easy to come by."

"Yeah, I know. That kind of stinks."

His voice softened. "Do you wish I was there now?"

She was done being cautious with Sam. "Yes. I do."

"I do, too. You want to have phone sex?"

She laughed. "I'm not into phone sex, Sam."

"Have you ever had phone sex?"

"No."

"Then how do you know if you haven't tried?"

"I don't want to try. Though I can certainly imagine all kinds of things I'd do to you if you were here now."

"Like what?"

"Sam, I'm not—"

"Humor me."

"Fine. I'd be in charge. I'd make you undress—as in completely. I wouldn't undress. Then I'd drop to my knees and lick—"

"Stop," he ordered. "Bad idea after all. I'm driving, and you're going to make me crash."

"Or you don't like the idea of me being in charge?"

"You want to play dominatrix, bring on the leather and whips. Just as long as you remember whatever torture you dish out, I plan to return tenfold."

"Promises, promises."

"That is a promise. You can count on it."

She was so counting on it. And when they hung up, after talking about everything from Kiki to the odd *ménage* possibilities between Tabitha, Carrie, and Jensen, Sam's brother and their relationship, and even how much Meagan had often wished for a sibling, she was still counting on it.

She couldn't wait to test Sam, to discover her inner dominatrix and see just what his "tenfold" promise would reveal.

17

THE NEXT DAY CAME and the arguments over who got what room, while impossible to avoid, were easy to predict. When it looked as if Tabitha and Carrie might end up rooming together, Meagan vetoed it, in spite of Kiki's approving the pairing. Ultimately, Carrie would be crushed if she lost this competition, and Meagan saw the writing on the wall—Tabitha would happily manipulate Carrie to ensure that Carrie failed and she succeeded. In the midst of this, Meagan reviewed the locations of cameras, and a list of house rules.

When it was all said and done, what Meagan hadn't predicted was the somber mood that would overtake the group as they settled into the house. One of them would be gone in only a few days, eliminated at the first live show.

Prior to rehearsal at the studio, Meagan and Sam had managed a few steamy stares with, frustratingly, no hope of acting on the crackling energy anytime soon.

Per Sam's instructions, at nearly ten that night, Meagan called him to report their approach to the house. He was determined to greet her, and the contestants, at the house, to personally ensure he prevented any problems for their first night's stay.

The contestants filed up the stairs, with moans of aching bodies, and a need for bed. "I'm going, too," Kiki said from the doorway. "I'm dead to the world."

That left Meagan and Sam in the foyer of the main house, staring at one another. Suddenly, her tired body was alive and alert.

"And here I thought we'd never manage to be alone tonight," he said, for her ears only.

"If only it were so easy." She had this bad feeling about combusting into flames from wanting this man so badly. She motioned to their surroundings. "I have this terrible fear that this is an alternate universe, and once we step outside it, the real world will erupt around us." And just like that—as if she had jinxed them—a female scream came from the top floor.

"You had to say that, didn't you?" Sam asked, even as they charged toward the girls' side of the house.

They found Tabitha and her assigned roommate— a redhead named Jenny Michaels—on top of the bed. "Mouse! We have a mouse."

The hall filled with females, followed by shouts from the guys, who were also charging up the stairs.

Sam used a stern "soldier in charge" voice, and ordered them all to their rooms, and boy, was Meagan glad he did. Truth be told, she didn't have that kind of energy.

And even if she had Sam alone, tonight was not the night for them. She wanted to be everything she could be, when she was with him again.

After they'd calmed everyone down except for Tabitha and Jenny, who were insisting they move to another room, Sam stopped Meagan in the hallway for a private chat. "You know the best answer to catching a mouse, don't you?"

"If you mean a cat," she said. "Samantha's not quite ready for the job. She's as small as a large mouse right now."

"Ah, but we don't need Samantha," he said. "I found an adult cat today."

"Really? Samantha's mother maybe?"

"Maybe. Anyway, I say we put him to the test."

"Bring on the mouser, so we can try and get some sleep."

He motioned to the girls. "I'll leave you to the…fun, while I fetch Mel to help."

"Mel?"

"I didn't have the heart to call *him* Meagan, despite the fierceness so like your own. But a man—even the tomcat version—can be sensitive about a name. And we need him feeling manly right now."

She laughed and waved him off. "Go get Mel, then."

Mel turned out to be a big hit, adored by everyone in the house, and reveling in all the praise. Meagan and Sam promised to adopt a friend for Mel the next day, which Sam vowed he'd name Meg. Eventually, Sam escorted Meagan to the mother-in-law house, where they walked up the wooden steps of the rectangular deck, and were, at least, semi-alone.

"Well," he said, resting his palm on the doorframe above her head as she rested her back on the door. "I guess this is where I say goodnight."

"Yeah," she said. "I guess so."

"I take it goodnight kisses are off limits."

She barely quelled the urge to push to her toes and take that goodnight kiss. "Probably not the most discreet thing to do."

"You do know this is killing me," he said. "I've been thinking about our 'almost' phone sex all day."

She laughed and bit her bottom lip. "Yeah?"

"Yeah." His eyes darkened and he pushed off the door. "I better go before I decide not to. Or do something someone will see, and which you'll hate me for later. And I'm not calling you when I get to the other place, or I might change my mind and come right back here."

He stepped away, as if he couldn't quite get himself to turn. "Night, Meg."

"Mea…gan."

"Okay, sweetheart," he said, his voice low. "Meagan." And then he turned and walked authoritatively away, all broad-shouldered and muscle-defined, and totally confident. She sighed and entered the house to find Kiki leaning on the kitchen counter, sipping from a coffee cup.

"Oh, hi," Meagan said. "What's up?"

Kiki smirked. "Nothing," she said. "Nothing at all."

But her look, her tone, didn't say nothing. It said something.

Knots formed in Meagan's stomach. Had she just put Sam back on Kiki's radar? Meagan said a quick goodnight to Kiki, thankful it was an easy escape. How was she supposed to do a good job if she was always so worried about her assistant. If this show had a season two,

Meagan was negotiating Kiki out of the contract. That would be a deal breaker. In the meantime, it was critical that Meagan decide how best to protect Sam without destroying what felt like a really good thing.

OVERNIGHT, MEAGAN REALIZED that Sam would never back away from the potential threat that Kiki might represent. She had to pull away from him again, and she wasn't sure he'd forgive her for that. Still, she resolved to do what she hadn't. Take action. She started her search for a new agent immediately. As much as she valued the importance of control, she hadn't been embracing it at all. Taking action was the only thing that kept her distance from Sam in place.

It was early evening when she arrived at the house for the night. After changing into jeans and a T-shirt, she headed to the contestant's house, where everyone was having dinner. Meagan made her way to the kitchen to snag a soda right when Sam came in with a small pet carrier, holding a beautiful white cat.

The instant Sam's eyes met hers, she felt that familiar punch of awareness in her chest. "Hey, sweetheart. How was your day?"

"Productive," she said, and a torment, she added silently. Staying away from Sam when she didn't want to was incredibly hard.

"I'd say mine was too, considering what I have here." He set the carrier on the island counter.

"She's gorgeous," Meagan said sliding a finger inside the bars to stroke the friendly animal who purred loudly. "A perfect friend for Mel."

"We had great timing with this one," he said. "She had to be rescued today or—"

"Don't say it," Meagan ordered, stroking the animal through the bars. "I'm just glad we can give her a home."

"Her name is Meg," he said, a teasing glint in his eyes.

She laughed. "I deserve that, now don't I?"

"She's beautiful!" Ginger called from the doorway, "DJ! Come here!"

It wasn't long before Meg was carried to the other room, and smothered with attention, leaving Meagan alone again with Sam. "It appears Meg is a hit," Meagan said.

"Yes," he agreed. "Meg most definitely is a hit."

The air all but crackled around them. She couldn't help but stare into the man's too-blue eyes. Could she be falling in love with him?

She wanted to tell him her concerns about Kiki, but he was stubborn and macho. He'd insist he didn't need protection.

"Sam—"

"Look at Meg go!" Ginger shouted, and before Meagan could find a way out of it, she and Sam were herded into the living room. They joined the group as everyone talked about how excited but scared they were over the live show the next night, but declared Meg and Mel good luck charms and the "curse" officially gone.

Sam escorted her to her door again, and she felt wildly out of control. She had to change the dynamic between them and she didn't know how. She was juggling so much, trying to make everything turn out right for everyone, for him.

"Stop looking at me with those crazy-blue eyes of yours. It makes it impossible to resist you."

His lips twitched slightly. "Good," he whispered, and before she could stop him, his lips were softly touching hers. "Sorry, but it was killing me not to touch you. Now go rest. You look exhausted." Then he was sauntering away again, just as sexy as ever.

"Stop telling me I look exhausted. That's not nice."

Sexy male laughter floated on the beach air. The sound mingled with the scent of his spicy cologne, and wrapped itself around her like a warm blanket of pure lusty need. She was never going to get any sleep. Worse. She was never going to resist Sam. The only way to avoid him would be to tick him off. She really didn't think she had that in her.

"THE STUDIO CALLED," Kiki said, in the kitchen the following morning. "The ratings for last night's pre-live show were off the charts. The cyberworld is buzzing about the Tabitha, Carrie, Jensen triangle."

"That's great news," Meagan said excitedly, filling a coffee mug. "That should ensure great ratings for tonight's show. Did June say anything about how Sabrina reacted?"

"Oh, Sabrina's assistant didn't call," she said. "Sabrina did."

Sabrina. Sabrina had called Kiki. Her stomach knotted. Sabrina didn't make those kinds of calls. June did. So maybe Kiki and Sabrina were tighter than she thought, than even Sam thought. She tried not to let that worry her. Kiki really was behaving. Meagan was meeting with a potential agent today, a big name with a lot of power, who swore he could negotiate her contract for next season now. Things were going to be fine. Things *were fine*.

"And you're right," Kiki agreed. "Last night's ratings should ensure tonight's. That's exactly what Sabrina said, too."

Meagan didn't miss Kiki's gloating. Kiki gloated. Meagan knew this. It meant nothing. Although, it was hard not to be paranoid, considering what she had found out about Kiki.

"Great," Meagan said, hoping she sounded sincere as she dumped some French vanilla creamer in her cup. "I'm going straight to the theater to be sure we're ready for tonight. I'll see you at the rehearsal studio."

With the contestants long gone, and Kiki with them, Meagan opened her car door to find a bag of chocolate and a note that read "someone I know told me that chocolate is the only medicine for nerves, Sam."

She inhaled, emotion welling inside her. She grabbed the bag and opened it, climbed in her car and started eating. Who cared if it was seven in the morning? She needed this chocolate, and a part of her was starting to acknowledge how much she might just need Sam. Sam, who'd somehow managed to be there for her, without ever taking over her life, without once interfering where he wasn't wanted.

Meagan pulled her car onto the highway, telling herself not to eat the entire bag of chocolate. Chocolate was her weakness, and apparently, so was Sam. Neither seemed like a bad thing right now. In fact, both were pretty darn good.

IT WAS EVENING, twenty minutes until *Stepping Up* went live for the first time, complete with an audience. And every time Sam had seen Meagan, she'd seemed more frazzled.

When he eventually located her backstage, she was in conversation with a tech guy, and it wasn't going well.

"You yelled at two of my dancers right before they have to go on stage," she said. "Okay, you're under pressure here, we all are, but that doesn't mean you can be rude."

"I'm trying to fix the lights before the show starts," he said, tapping his watch. "I have eighteen minutes. Seventeen by the time I finish this sentence."

"Meagan," Sam said, joining them. "Can I review a few last-minute security points before the show starts?"

She whirled on him. "Is there a problem? A security issue?"

"Everything is fine," he assured her, promising himself he wouldn't kiss away her fears no matter how tempting the idea. He was crazy about this woman—completely, insanely crazy for her, like he'd never imagined he'd be over a woman. "Walk with me."

"Sam—"

"Walk with me, Meagan," he repeated, adding a bit of push to the words he was sure would get him yelled at, especially when he turned and strolled away, with the assumption she would follow.

She did and he stopped behind a curtained-off area, much like a small room, used to enclose supplies.

He grabbed his phone and dialed one of his men. "Electronics problem on set. We could use your magical touch right about now, Rick." He hung up. "Listen, Meagan." He ran his hands down her arms. "You need to take a deep breath and ease up a little."

"Sam, please don't—"

"Don't what?" he asked. "Worry about you? Ask what I can do to help? Care enough to be here with you, instead of somewhere else?"

She blinked at him and then pressed her hand to her face. "I'm sorry. I'm just…" She looked at him. "I'm a wreck. I swear this show has made me this way. I was never like this in the newsroom. You were right. I'm too close to this."

"In a few minutes, what will happen, is what will happen. Whatever that final product is, embrace it and call it a success, Meg."

She paused, considering his words, and then to his surprise, pushed to her toes and kissed him. She smiled at him and then disappeared back onto the stage.

Sam's lips turned upward, his blood running hot for Meagan, who was driving him to the edge, he wanted her so badly. And though he was certain their time out of bed was working in his favor, helping him to get to know her, keeping her from hiding behind sex, he was damn ready to strip her naked and have his way with her. Or *her* have her way with him. He really didn't care, as long as the end result meant they were together.

Tonight couldn't arrive fast enough as far as he was concerned. In fact, tonight seemed a perfect time for pleasure in celebration of the success he was sure the show was going to have.

It was the prospect of holding Meagan, and making love to her, that led him through the next several hours of the show—including the tight security needs of a Pop star—with that smile remaining on his face. That was, until the last fifteen minutes of the show, when the bottom three dancers were announced.

Sam stood across the stage from Meagan, his eyes locked intently with hers. Derek, the host, called the first name. A dancer named Rena took her place next to Derek. The second name… Tabitha. Sam couldn't say he'd be sorry to see her leave. But it was the next name that set the place into a purr of shocked "ohhhhs." The final name was Carrie.

Sam watched as Meagan's face paled. Yes, he knew she had a soft spot for Carrie, but beyond that, Meagan was a smart cookie. She was bound to be thinking the same thing he was. What were the chances that both Carrie and Tabitha would end up in the bottom three without some manipulation of the results?

18

Meagan felt sick when Carrie's name was called. She did see Carrie as the underdog, which she'd always felt a bit herself. But then there was the coincidence factor. Had the judges been persuaded formally or informally to put Carrie's and Tabitha's names on the bottom three?

Kiki stepped to Meagan's side, digging her fingers into Meagan's arm. "We can't lose Carrie or Tabitha. Please tell me we aren't about to lose Carrie or Tabitha. We need them for ratings."

Relief washed over Meagan. Kiki hadn't played with the outcome of the judging. This second guessing Kiki thing was distracting her more than she thought.

"The first contestant that's safe is…" Derek said, "Tabitha."

Tabitha squealed and rushed to the bleacher-style seating where the other nine safe contestants were sitting. She flung her arms around Jensen's neck. Carrie looked sad and disappointed, and suddenly Meagan felt as if she were on that stage with Carrie, about to hear her fate. She felt guilty for that, knowing this was emotional for the other candidate, Rena, as well, but it was Carrie whose moment Meagan was in.

"And the final contestant who is safe tonight is… Carrie!" Carrie burst into tears right along with the girl who'd just found out she would be the first to leave the show. Instead of rushing to safety, Carrie turned to her and hugged Rena. Meagan watched Carrie walk with the ousted dancer, talking to her, comforting her, and knew she was right about Carrie being a nice person.

Derek wrapped up the broadcast and the aftermath followed, the celebration and tears backstage. Meagan spoke to the celebrity judges and put fears of contestant tampering aside. These were people who took their roles seriously. The performances had been the deciding factor, and Carrie and Tabitha had spent too much time focused on Jensen, rather than on practicing, to come out on top.

When Meagan's team, with Sam and his men following closely, arrived at the contestants' house, they'd all vowed there would be a midnight swim. By the time they'd all quickly changed, a delivery of gourmet strawberry cupcakes arrived, donated by a famous chef who hosted a show on the same network. Everyone dug into the treats, even Rena, who seemed to find the indulgence welcome.

Meagan stood in the kitchen, watching the crowd, feeling sad that Rena was leaving, but relieved that the girl had been offered a Broadway audition before they'd ever left the theater. Meagan wanted to create dreams that came true, not crush them.

"It could have been me saying goodbye tonight," Carrie said as she joined Meagan in the kitchen.

"You're right," Meagan agreed. "It could have been you. Stop focusing on Tabitha and Jensen, and focus on dancing."

Carrie leaned on the island counter. "I know. Believe me, I know. Dancing is everything to me, and not only did I almost quit the show, I almost let silly distractions ruin it for me, too. I've lost track of my priorities."

Distractions. Priorities. Meagan had allowed herself to be distracted by Sam, but somehow, he'd helped her move forward, not held her back. It was this Kiki distraction that was destroying her. She was at the point where she needed to just let the cards fall where they would with the show. She was working hard. She'd landed her new agent today. She had to learn that some things were out of her control. Like her strategy for Sam. She didn't want to let down her guard and be with Sam, only to find him the true loser by associating with her.

She shoved aside the worry, at least, for now, and challenged Carrie to succeed. "So what are you going to do to make sure tonight doesn't happen again?"

"Practice and focus." Her voice tightened with emotion. "Thank you for talking me out of leaving. I've gotten several lifelines now. I'm not foolish enough to think I'll get another."

"Good," she said, picking up a cupcake to take to Rena. "I'll hold you to that."

"Carrie!" came a shout.

Meagan shooed her away. "Go enjoy tonight. Tomorrow it's back to work, harder than ever."

Carrie grinned and took off to the other room.

Meagan sighed, and with a growling stomach that

had been treated to nothing but chocolate that day, she snatched a cupcake from a tray for herself and scooped decadent icing onto her finger. In the next moment, Sam showed up, his heated gaze zeroing in on her finger in her mouth. "I see I've been missing more than I realized."

Meagan laughed, wondering how it was that Sam always had such interesting timing.

"Tabitha!" Carrie screeched abruptly from the other room. "That was so mean."

Meagan and Sam both raced toward the girls, but it was too late. Rena grabbed a cupcake, and smashed it into Tabitha's face. A snowball effect ensued, and before Meagan knew what hit her—as in a cupcake or two or three—there was icing flying everywhere.

"Enough!" Meagan shouted, standing in the middle of it all. Another cupcake bounced off her chest.

Sam echoed her order. "Enough!" he yelled. A cupcake bounced off hit him in the forehead.

Meagan burst out laughing. Seeing rough and tough Sam plopped in the head with a strawberry cupcake was just too much on too little sleep.

He cast her a grumpy look in reaction to her amusement. Meagan liberated one of the last cupcakes from a contestant's hand and scooped some icing. She wasn't even going to think about the furniture or the floors. She'd be damned if she was wasting a gourmet cupcake, when she hadn't eaten today.

Once she'd finished her cupcake, and was starting on a second, the frenzy died down, and Meagan's cell phone, tucked in her pocket, began to ring. With sticky fingers, she pulled out her cell and eyed caller ID.

Meagan's gut clenched. This wasn't about cupcakes. It was about ratings, and since the call wasn't going to Kiki, but to her, her stomach clenched tighter. Maybe she only got the bad news calls, and Kiki got the good? She answered, listening to Sabrina deliver the verdict. And it wasn't bad news, not bad news at all.

Meagan grabbed Sam's arm and had him boost her up on top of the coffee table to shout out. "Top show of the night, people! Top show of the night!" At least in preliminary ratings, and that was fine by Meagan. Joy ensued, and Kiki of all people jumped on top of the table and hugged her. Sparkling grape juice sprayed Meagan and Kiki's already strawberry-flavored skin.

"Midnight swim!" someone hollered. "Midnight swim!" A mad rush for the door followed.

Meagan stood where she was and tried to revel in the moment. But next week's ratings would be the real test, and next week's booted contestant might not get a Broadway audition.

"Whatever you're thinking, stop," Sam ordered, standing beside the table. "Tonight is about success."

"What about the contestants?" she asked. "I have to watch out for them."

He grabbed his phone and made a call, in which he asked someone to see to her gang. "Josh will keep an eye on them," he told her and held out his hand. "Tonight, you're mine."

She glanced down at Sam from on top of the table. at his hot-and-hungry stare, she felt certain he was prepared to clean the icing from her entire body. And boy did she believe she could do the job on him. For days now she'd wanted this man, for days she'd wondered if it was unquenched desire for him or something more. For days now she'd been stressed, worried, confused. She'd felt as if the world were spinning out of control.

For tonight, what was wrong with being on top of the world? Okay, she was on top of a coffee table, but with a cake-covered, gorgeous army guy about to carry her away to a private place, she believed she could do anything. She had a hot show and a hot man. If that was a curse, bring it on.

She slid her hand into his.

SAM HAD PLANS FOR Meagan, a celebration of her success, that led them down the beach, off the grid of the cameras, to a secluded area where he'd pitched a tent and set up a lantern inside.

Meagan laughed the minute she saw the tent.

"I thought I'd show you how a soldier roughs it on the beach." He motioned her inside, and she disappeared through the open zipper. "And you and I get privacy we wouldn't get at either of the houses."

"Champagne?" she asked, as he joined her on the inflatable mattress.

"Unless you prefer the sparking grape juice you're wearing as perfume? Derek was right when he said those kids are crazy."

She laughed. "They're excited."

"As they should be," he said, and popped the top on the bottle and filled her glass. "Congrats on your ratings." His mouth brushed hers. "You taste like strawberries. I think I just decided I love strawberries." And yes, he'd said love. He was falling in love with Meagan. He'd never been in love, thought it wasn't in his cards.

And he was probably a fool to choose a woman sure to kick his ass a hundred times over, but then, Sam never ran from a challenge. And Meagan was more his kind of challenge than any he'd known in a very long time.

She inhaled on his words, as if she'd understood the discreet message. Softly, she breathed out his name. "Sam." Her fingers curled on his cheek, and for long seconds stayed there. The air was thick around them, electric and hot, until she pressed her lips to his. "You... taste like strawberries, too."

"I taste like you," he told her, leaning back so she could see his expression. Then he slipped a glass into her hand. "Drink up. You deserve to celebrate."

She crinkled her nose and downed the drink. "Always the bossy one, aren't you?"

"Hmm," he said, emptying his glass and scooting to her side. "You seem to like me being bossy, like I do you, at least sometimes."

"Only because it hasn't gone to your head," she said, letting him ease her to the mattress. "The minute it does—"

"You'll put me in my place," he said, framing her face with his hands. "I know. Believe me, I know. I like that about you, too. But do you know why you keep letting me take control?"

"I'm sure you'll tell me," she commented dryly, but not without a rasp of desire in her voice.

"Aside from trusting me," he began.

"When did this become about trust?"

"Are you saying you don't trust me?" he asked, sliding her shirt up to her stomach and kissing the delicate skin he'd revealed.

"I didn't say that."

He caressed her narrow waist, her hips. "So you do trust me?"

Her expression softened. "I do," she whispered. "I trust you, Sam. Very much."

The confession took him off guard, warmed him. "I'm glad," he said, resting his hand on her belly. "Not so long ago, I wasn't so sure you ever would."

A smile tugged on her lips. "You kind of blasted into my life like a bolt of lightening. The minute you arrived, I felt your presence."

"I know the feeling."

He would have lowered his head to kiss her then, but her fingers slid into his hair. "Do you ever feel out of control, Sam?"

"When I'm not with you."

"I'm serious," she said.

"So am I, sweetheart. I've never had a woman twist me in knots like you can."

"I don't mean to do that to you."

"Then stop pushing me away. Let me inside, Meg. Really let me in."

"I don't want to push you away," she said. "But—"

He kissed her. "Then don't. Just don't. Be with me, Meagan."

"I am, but—"

He kissed her again, a long stroke of his tongue against hers, before repeating, "Let me in, Meagan. Let go of just enough control to give me room inside your life. Everyone has to let go sometimes."

"If everyone has to let go of control sometimes, when do you let go?"

"Whenever you say you want me to."

She searched his face. "That easily? Just like that."

"Sweetheart, your definition of control and mine are two different things. You don't think I've given it up, but I have."

"What does that mean?"

"It means I not only can't stop thinking about you or wanting you," he admitted. "I don't even want to try."

"I feel the same way," she said. "I do. I—"

His mouth came down on hers, hungry to claim her. Finally, she'd stopping fighting him, stopped pushing him away. This had never been about the chase with Meagan. It had been about this, about how good she felt in his arms, how good they felt together. He knew now that all those years that he'd sworn he wasn't a relationship man, had been because he hadn't met Meagan.

She moaned, her tongue meeting his, caressing his. Sam rolled on top of Meagan, feeling her delicate curves beneath him, his hand sliding down her hip, beneath her backside, to arch her against the thick ridge of his erection.

She murmured his name, pleading with him. He pulled back to stare down at her, to search her face. "I never believed one night was enough. Or two, or three, or—"

She leaned up and captured his lips with hers. "Me, either," she said.

A wild frenzy of touches, kisses, and undressing followed. Until she was beneath him, naked and perfect. Until he was buried inside her, memorizing every inch of her beautiful, heavy-lidded stare. He saw the trust there, in her, but he knew instinctively, it was still fragile, still far too easily shattered.

19

MEAGAN HAD DONE just what Sam had suggested. She'd let go of control, let herself say what she felt, let herself just be with Sam. Even now, after they'd dressed again, her in her bikini and Sam in a pair of swim trucks he'd worn under his jeans, she sensed the newfound intimacy between them. A closeness that had nothing to do with sex, and everything to do with making love.

Meagan sipped from her glass. "Thank goodness I told everyone to sleep in tomorrow," Meagan said, the bubbles tickling her nose. "I have a feeling my head is going to pay for the sugar and champagne in the morning."

"There's a twenty-four-hour diner a mile up the road," he said. "We could walk it."

"With cheeseburgers?"

"I'm pretty sure any diner has a cheeseburger."

"Then count me in," she said, agreeably, reaching for her sandals and T-shirt as Sam did the same. That was when her eyes caught on the scar above his knee.

Her hand went to it, and he froze a moment, his shirt

half over his head, the action telling her the injury was more of a sensitive spot than it was a physical injury.

"Does it bother you often?" she asked, as he pulled his shirt on. She remembered the way he'd rubbed it when they'd been in his truck the week before.

"I deal with it," he said, repeating what he'd already told her.

She knew that all too well, thanks to a knee injury of her own that flared often. It hurt. "Will you tell me about it?"

"I was on a covert mission in enemy territory," he said. "It wasn't the bullets that got me, but the days without treatment. By the time I was back at camp it was a mess. I almost lost it."

She could barely breathe thinking of how bad his leg must have been, and how devastating the outcome. "You can't tell me that doesn't mess with your head, Sam. You act like it's nothing, but it is."

"I had months of rehab to get my head right."

No one just got their head right that quickly. A horrible thought hit her. He hadn't dealt with his leg. He was going to eventually wake up and reject this new easy life, and her with it. She pulled her hand back from his leg, suddenly feeling burned, certain this thing with Sam was going nowhere good and not sure why that upset her so much. Why couldn't this just be about sex anymore? She began to move away from him.

He grabbed her hand, gently holding her beside him, when she wanted to dart away. "Whatever you're thinking, I can tell it's not good. We're talking about *my* leg, and you're the one withdrawing and I don't get it." His eyes narrowed. "Am I damaged goods, Meg? Is that the problem?"

Her eyes riveted to his. "No. Oh God, no, Sam. It's not like that. Your leg—if anything the scar is sexy and you're more man than any I've ever known. And that's exactly why I must seem silly to you, worried about dancing and ratings, when you've been off saving lives and protecting our country. Coddling me must be—"

He slid his hand into her hair. "I never coddle you. How could anyone ever coddle you? You're way too tough for that. And there's nothing silly about a dream." He stroked her cheek with his thumb. "We've had this conversation. Dreams are what soldiers fight for. And your dream is personal to me now. You're personal to me."

"I believe you mean that. I do. I see nothing but honesty and directness in you, Sam, and that matters to me. It's been part of what has made you so hard to ignore. Probably why I didn't want you to talk to me and show me what I already sensed was there. But you had your life stripped away by an injury." She looked away, unable to keep her eyes on him. "I know from things you've said to me that you weren't ready to leave the army. You planned on that life being a career for you. And here you are, in the middle of all this superficial glamour."

"And with a woman I really care about."

"Sam," she chastened. "I can't…you have to understand that I…" Her voice broke.

"Don't want to count on me if I'm not going to be here," he said, accurately filling in the blanks. "Who let you down, Meagan? Who did you count on who let you down?"

Her lashes lowered, the confessions on her tongue, unspoken—of a dream of dancing, of a family who'd said her injured knee was proof she'd been on the wrong path.

"You don't have to tell me," he said gently. "Not now, but I hope sometime soon you will. You're right. The network isn't for me long term."

Her gaze lifted sharply, a knife jabbing her right in the chest. "I didn't think so."

"I have a plan. And that plan is probably why I'm okay with where I'm at now and will be in the future. I'll be opening a private security business next year, when several of my former Special Force team opt out of re-enlistment. And my uncle, the one who works for the studio, is our primary investor. He fully intends to pull some of the Hollywood crowd as clientele and even move studio business."

Relief washed through her. Sam wasn't going to run off. Sam was invested in this world, in her world. Sam was Sam, and she liked everything that meant.

"Why are you smiling?"

"I don't know," she replied honestly, but she really couldn't hold it back. She kissed him, and it was a good thing that the diner was open twenty-four-hours because they'd managed to undress again.

Meagan and Sam shifted comfortably on the mattress. "You've been so polite lately," he said. "We haven't fought at all. You've been full of thank-yous."

"You complaining?" she challenged.

"Not at all," he assured her. "In fact, I like the way

you say thank you. So much so that I wonder if I can make you say it now?" He trailed kisses down her jaw, over her neck, until he suckled her nipples, teased them with his tongue and his teeth.

"No thank you yet?" he asked, lapping at a hard peak.

"Not yet," she confirmed. "Right now, you're just driving me crazy."

"Hmm," he said. He suckled again. "I like that."

"I don't."

He raised his head. "No? I'll see what else I can come up with." He palmed her breasts and kissed a path down her stomach, until he was licking her, teasing her, in the most intimate of ways. And just before he pushed her over the blissful edge, before she happily said thank you, she made a vow.

"Just remember. One thank-you deserves another. Your time is coming."

And the low masculine laughter that radiated against her clit, sent her tumbling into release. She'd never had a man bring her to orgasm in the midst of laughter, but then, there were a lot of firsts with Sam. And that made letting go feel a whole lot less scary.

AN HOUR LATER, SAM reluctantly allowed Meagan to dress, but only because of her threat that she'd collapse if he didn't feed her. He had this nagging feeling that as soon as they exited the tent, she'd run from him emotionally. He'd pushed her tonight, taken her from "don't talk so I won't like you" to someplace much more intense, much more long term, and he could see that she was wrestling with that wall of hers—which meant *he* was wrestling with that wall of hers.

They were just stepping out of the tent, into the cool air rising off the ocean, a high moon overhead, and he was looking forward to the diner, when his cell beeped with a text.

Displeased with the news and knowing she would be too, Sam glanced from the message to Meagan.

"I'm not going to get any food, am I?" she asked.

"Depends," he said. "How do you feel about contestants getting to know each other in, shall we say, an intimate fashion?"

Meagan's eyes went wide and she started walking toward the house. Sam immediately caught up with her. "I take it the answer is, you don't like it. So the good news is that Josh broke them up. They weren't happy but he stopped things before they got too out of hand."

"Jensen and Tabitha?"

He cleared his throat. "And Rena."

"Oh my God," Meagan said, stomping through the sand. "This is forbidden in their contracts. Rena has nothing to lose, but the other two do. And Kiki knows it, but I can bet you she's counting on those cameras we have rolling to tell all. How can I convince her that some facade of good ratings based on scandal will plunge within a few episodes and is not security, without turning her against me? *American Idol* and *Dancing with the Stars* didn't build ratings off of who slept with who and who was fighting who."

"Meagan, sweetheart—"

"I believe so strongly that we can't go in this direction, even if the ratings please the sponsors. I shouldn't have been away. I—"

"Oh no." He shackled her wrist and pulled her to face him. "I see where this is going. Don't even start coming up with reasons to make *us* wrong. We are not wrong, Meagan. You are not wrong by taking a few hours off. And you didn't count on Kiki. You counted on Josh— *on me, Meagan*. Josh contained the problem, and he called us the instant there was trouble."

She let out a breath. "I know and I appreciate it. I do. I really, really do." She tugged on him. "But please come on. We have to hurry. I don't want to lose someone I don't have to lose over this."

They took off towards the contestant house and with the beach lights on, it was lit up well enough to rival the Christmas Vacation house. Soon it was easy to see Carrie sat on the porch with Josh by her side, and Mel in her lap.

"Where are they?" Meagan asked anxiously.

"Beach," Josh said, pointing to the water. "They took off when I told them they couldn't share a bedroom."

Carrie nodded.

"I've got this," Meagan told Sam, and she sprinted away.

Sam watched her depart, and leaned on the railing to the steps. He eyed Carrie. "Good thing you entertained yourself with Mel and not Jensen."

"That's what I told her, too," Josh said. "Life is way too short to bury yourself in a popularity contest."

"The show makes it feel like a popularity contest," Carrie said.

"No," Sam said. "The show is about dancing and

so is your future. Don't let anyone convince you otherwise."

She nodded. "You're right. That became crystal clear
to me tonight when I almost got kicked off the show.
Jensen and Tabitha have families with money. They can
go live in New York and try to make it with a dance
company. I have a single mom who's a secretary who
I want to take care of one day. I can't believe I ever
tried to leave because of them. This is it for me. I'm
not blowing it."

No wonder Meagan had taken to Carrie. The kid had
character. "Good. That's real good, Carrie."

They talked a few minutes about her mom, her life
back in Washington, and the mess in the house that
needed to be cleaned up before they saw Meagan and
the three dancers approaching the house. Looking
guilty as heck, Jensen and Tabitha rushed up the stairs
without a word.

Meagan stopped beside Sam. "I threatened to send
them both home. Hopefully I gave them a reality check.
Neither of them wants to get kicked off the show."

The door swung open and Kiki joined them on the
porch. "Talk about some great footage for next week.
The 'almost sex' incident is going to be gold."

Meagan eyed Carrie. "Can you please go inside and
give us a minute?"

"Yes, of course," Carrie said, and toted Mel up the
stairs and past Kiki.

The instant the door was shut, Meagan said, "We
can't air this or the studio could make the kids leave
the show. I told them that won't happen."

Kiki crossed her arms, attitude rolling off her. "They

chose to ignore their contracts. Besides. They didn't break the rules. They almost broke the rules."

"I doubt they thought we would put this on air."

"Why would you say that?" Kiki asked. "Oh wait." She lifted her chin at Sam. "I suppose you did set a bad example by shoving your tongue down Sam's throat. Maybe we should include some footage of you two instead? We're here for the good of the show and the network."

Kiki's claws were officially back out and Sam wasn't waiting for Meagan's reply. He was close to having the evidence he needed to end Kiki's career as a troublemaker.

He held his hands up. "Sorry, ladies, but I have to throw up a stop sign. Since this is a contractual issue, there are legalities involved. If this footage is used and ends those kids' runs on the show, they could potentially sue. I can't release the film without studio approval. If I do, you two can figure out what to do with it." He glanced between them. "You're both welcome to curse me out over a cheeseburger at the diner down the road."

"I'm going to stay here," Kiki huffed. "I have some phone calls to make." She turned and headed back into the house.

Meagan asked, "How about that burger?"

He arched a brow. "I'm surprised you're willing to leave."

"A very sexy man once told me that sometimes you just have to let go."

20

IMAGES PLAYED IN Meagan's sleepy haze. Of sitting at the table across from Sam, of sharing a strawberry milkshake, as if the strawberry cupcake icing hadn't been enough. Of celebrating. Of telling Kiki where she stood. And of kissing Sam goodnight in the shadows behind the house. Then she fell asleep with her own hands on her body, wishing they had been his.

"Wake up, sweetheart."

"Hmm." Meagan snuggled into the warmth of the blanket. She was so tired. So very, very tired. And there was this sweet, warm touch she didn't want to end. The scent of Sam lingered around her.

"Meg, honey, wake up."

"Can't wake up. Not yet."

"Please." Light touches tickled. Warmth trickled along her neck, a nibble of teeth on her earlobe. Wow. This felt real. She sat straight up. The blanket fell to her waist, exposing the skimpy tank top and matching boxers to the hungry blue eyes taking her in without one bit of reserve.

"Sam?"

He sat next to her bed, fully dressed, the sun beaming through the window.

"What happened? Did I oversleep? What's wrong?"

"You let everyone have the morning off, so no, you didn't oversleep, but you weren't answering your phone and I started to worry."

Samantha pounced into her lap and purred. Meagan replied with a long stroke of her back. "Oh yes." She remembered letting everyone sleep, but not her phone ringing. She reached for it and noted that Sam had called her at least a dozen times. "I can't believe I didn't hear it." She set Samantha aside. "What's going on? Why are you here?"

"Kiki took Jensen, Rena, Tabitha and some other dancer named Susie to breakfast. After last night, I didn't think you'd like that."

"Oh no." She started to get up. "That can't be good." Sam leaned in and kissed her, his big hand on her shoulder, and her nipples went instantly stiff and achy.

"I sent Josh along for the ride," he told her. "Kiki wasn't pleased. Neither was Josh."

Relief washed over her. "I seem to owe Josh big favors."

"I owe Josh," he said, setting the kitten on the floor and climbing in bed with her. "He's calling me when they head this way. We're alone. In a real bed."

She bit her lip and curled her arms around his neck, no hesitation. She'd been dreaming about Sam all night. "This feels so very naughty, Sam. We might get caught."

"Naughty, which means hot and fast, if we don't want to get interrupted."

"I like hot and fast," she assured him, splaying her fingers over his crotch, and caressing the thick bulge. "And it seems you like hot and fast too." She unzipped him, and slid her hand inside. "You like it a lot."

His fingers wound around her neck. "Not nearly as much as I'm going to enjoy taking my time with you, someplace secluded and private and soon."

"Promises, promises," she said, gently gripping his cock.

He moaned softly.

"You like?"

"Yeah," he said. "I like."

"I'll tell you a little story," she said, caressing the slick, wet tip of his erection, and then nibbling his neck, then his ear.

"A story?"

"Hmm. You'll like this story, but you have to take your pants off first." She tugged them downward, helping him get as gloriously naked as she wanted him, even as he tugged his shirt over his head. Meagan settled between his legs, hand wrapping around his shaft. "Now for the story. This is the story of how I make you say thank you."

And she drew him into her mouth. His hips lifted, he inhaled deeply, and she smiled at the reaction. She suckled and licked and played with him, until he tried to pull away, before he couldn't. She teased him unmercifully. Before long, he was shaking, all that power that was Sam was radiating through him to her. His release came and she took it all, took him to the moment when he sighed in complete satisfaction, when he relaxed.

She climbed on top of him and kissed him, delivering the promise, "The next time you sneak into my bed-room, the punishment will be a hundred times worse."

His hands closed down on her hips, but she pressed away. "One second." She pushed off him and he let her, not suspecting her departure. "I have to go shower be-fore they get here." And she dashed into the hallway, bare naked. Sam had teased her. This time, she was teasing him.

When he poked his head around the shower curtain, he gave her an intense up-and-down inspection. "I dare you to find out what happens when you sneak into my bedroom tonight."

And then he was gone.

NOT EVEN WORRY OVER a battle with Kiki could keep Meagan from being all smiles as she walked into the contestant house to find everyone, Kiki included, clean-ing up the strawberry mess from the night before.

Meagan went in search of Carrie. She found her in the kitchen, sweeping up cake crumbs. "I hear you missed the big breakfast meeting this morning."

Carrie snorted. "I'm happy to be part of my own ménage."

"I wasn't aware you had a ménage," Meagan said, trying for a casual tone.

"All I need is Mel and Josh," she said. "They make fine company. Neither of them are overly friendly, and both give a pretty good comfort pet when needed."

Meagan straightened. "What? Josh's been petting you?"

Carrie giggled. "No. Not like that." She patted Mea-gan's head. "Like that. Like a big brother kind of petting." She wiggled her hips and brows. "Though bring on more, baby. He's gorgeous."

Meagan shook her head and poured coffee into a mug. "You stay away from Josh. He's too old for you."

"I'm mature for my age," Carrie said. "I'm like a twenty-seven-year-old trapped in a nineteen-year-old's body."

"Oh, Carrie, honey, you just hang on to the nineteen-year-old body," she said. "Take care of it and treat it right so you have a long career, with zero injuries." She lowered her voice. "Any idea what this breakfast was all about?"

"Tabitha said Kiki lectured them about getting into trouble, and warned them she was cracking down before they got her fired."

Meagan's brows dipped at the behavior so contrary to how Kiki had acted the night before.

"Yeah," Carrie said, seeming to read her mind. "Sounds odd to me, too." She leaned in closer. "Last night, Kiki was the one encouraging them to, you know, get down and dirty. So now they want me to believe she was scolding them, telling them they were lucky not to get kicked off the show?"

"That part is true."

Carrie shrugged. "Yeah, well, she didn't seem worried about that last night."

The back door opened and Sam walked in looking like sin and satisfaction—her satisfaction. "Speaking of lucky," Carrie said. "I think I've become a soldier kind of girl."

"Carrie," Meagan warned.

"Sorry. Sorry. I'm leaving." She grinned at Sam. "Hi, Sam." Then she took off into the living room.

Sam sauntered over to the coffeepot, real close to Meagan, and filled a cup for himself. "Morning, Meg."

She smiled. "Morning, Sam."

"It is," he said. "Very good. It started when some-one told me a story."

She smiled. "Really?"

"Oh, yeah," he said, whispering in her ear. "I plan to rewrite the ending. You'll like it."

"I liked the original version," she assured him.

"You'll like this one better. Wait and see." He winked. "Tonight."

Kiki appeared in the doorway. "How about seven o'clock tonight, okay?"

Meagan about swallowed her tongue considering what Sam had just said, and she didn't dare glance at him for fear of completely giving away their conversa-tion. "Tonight?"

"For the group movie night you wanted to organize."

"Oh, yes. In-house movie night. Sure. Excellent." She ignored the mischief in Sam's eyes that said there was way more than a movie night on his mind. "I need to watch what we've filmed in the main. I'm hoping for some really good footage for next week's show."

"If you come down to the security house later this evening," Sam suggested, "I can let you view what we have so far."

Meagan tried not to react to the invitation that had nothing to do with film, and everything to do with get-ting her to his bedroom. "Perfect. I'd like to get to the editing booth early tomorrow."

"Hopefully they deliver some fun viewing minus the scandal," Kiki said. "Don't worry, Meagan. I got the message. No more scandal. You want the show to have mass appeal. I get it." She was being so sweet it was downright sticky. "But if the ratings falter even one week, all bets are off. I'm not going down with the ship." She smiled brightly as if she hadn't just issued a threat. "Meanwhile, dinner's being prepared." She eyed Sam. "So, try and stay out of the kitchen, okay, Sam?"

"Absolutely," he confirmed.

Kiki said, still way too brightly, "And they want to watch Freddy Krueger, Meg. I figured I'd pick up some Jason action, too." She disappeared and Meagan really hoped she was talking about the fictional Jason Meyers, not the Jason who was one of the judges on the show.

"Meg," Sam chuckled. "She just called you Meg, and we both know how dangerous that can be."

"I don't know what scares me more," Meagan agreed. "That woman or having to watch those movies tonight which will ensure I don't sleep for a week. I don't do scary."

"I'll protect you from all the scary bumps in the night," he promised softly, his eyes glistening with something deeper than the jest behind his words.

And oh, how easy it would be to buy into the fantasy that he could protect her, and fix everything that might be scary in life. How easy it would be to be the damsel in distress, and Sam, her knight in shining armor. The idea absolutely made her shake inside. She was falling, too hard and too fast, for Sam. What if she lost her show and him in one fell swoop? What if she started relying on him and then he was gone? Suddenly, she was shaking inside as surely as she had shaken in his arms. She had to get a grip on both herself and her situation.

"Alas," she said, trying to sound lighthearted, to hide the wave of emotion consuming her. She'd told him she wasn't. "Movie night is one nightmare I must face alone, though I know it will break your heart to be left out."

His eyes narrowed, his intelligent stare all too aware of her sudden withdrawal, which was why she did what any intelligent woman would do.

She darted away.

IT WAS A DARK AND STORMY night. Literally. As in, lightening, thunder and pouring rain. A night made for scary movies, though Sam and three of his crew, Josh included, had opted for watching sports and the live security feed.

Sam sat on the couch of the security house, one booted foot crossed over the other on top of the coffee table. Josh and two other guys had taken spots in various locales around the room. The game in question was playing on the big screen, the security footage, on a table lined with monitors that Josh had expertly wired days before.

Sam's gaze kept drifting toward the security footage, toward Meagan, replaying her words as he had in the hours since she'd spoken them. He was no fool. She'd run away the instant she could, and he didn't know what to do about it. It was exactly what she'd promised not to do again. How to handle it was the question. Did he give her some space? Did he press her so that she knew he was serious about where this was going? And he was. Every moment drove that point home. He'd never fallen in love, but he knew he was in love now. He knew months ago with their first sparring words.

Meagan screamed at the movie, and Sam found himself grinning.

He wasn't sure if she, or Carrie, would win the award for loudest scream of the night. Suddenly, lightning struck outside and thunder roared. The entire group of movie watchers screamed, and Sam and his men chuckled. Another blast of lightning and thunder, and the lights went out, including the security feed.

"Damn," came several voices in unison a second before the backup generator, hooked directly to the feed, purred to life.

Sam was already on his feet, dialing Meagan, his eyes adjusting to the darkness. The security feed was useless, nothing but darkness and the mumbles of scared contestants. Sam could hear Meagan's phone ringing, but she was too busy trying to calm everyone down to answer.

One of his men passed out flashlights, and Sam turned his on. "I'm headed over there," Sam said.

Josh groaned. "I'll go with you. Sounds like Freddy Krueger and the storm has them in a total panic."

Ever prepared, they grabbed rain jackets from the supply closet, and extra flashlights. They were about to leave when one of his men shouted. "Hold up, Sam man! We have a tornado warning in effect for the next thirty minutes."

Sam cursed and motioned to Josh. "Let's go now."

The instant they were out the door, they were slammed in a downpour that made it seem like the ocean was raining down on them, not the clouds. Sam ran faster, pushing through the wind and over the sand.

Sam was in sight of the porch stairs to the main house in minutes that felt like hours. His cell was ringing, but he didn't dare stop to answer it. The front door burst open, and Meagan appeared as Sam rushed up the stairs with Josh on his heels.

"Tornado warning," Sam said, wishing they weren't too close to the coast to have a basement, like they'd had in the other house. "Get everyone into the bathrooms now."

Screams followed, and to Meagan's credit, she went into action, calm and collected, moving everyone where they needed to be. Kiki, Ginger, and DJ were calm under pressure, herding the cast and crew to safety.

"Funnel cloud on the ground nearby," Josh shouted behind him.

"What's happening?" Meagan yelled, rushing down the stairs toward him in the beam of his flashlight.

He charged toward her. "Bathroom, sweetheart. Go to the bathroom."

Terror flashed in her eyes, the kind that spoke of panic not calm, but she'd shown it to none of the people in her care. He rushed her to the master shower where several other people were huddled, and pulled her into a corner, wrapping his arms around her.

"Sam?" she whispered.

"I got you, Meg," he said, tightening his hold on her. "I got you, and I won't let anything happen to you."

She stared up at him and then hugged him, her cheek to his chest. "I got you too, Sam."

He buried his face in her hair, and he knew in that instant, he wasn't letting her face this storm, or any other, without him, ever again. Now, he just had to figure out how to convince her of that.

21

THE TORNADO BRUSHED past them, but it was enough to shake the walls, terrifying Meagan and everyone else in the house. The minute it was gone, Meagan kissed Sam as she'd never kissed a man in her life. He was officially her hero, and she didn't care who knew. To heck with fears of "what if" things didn't work out with Sam. Life was short and that's why she'd chased her dreams, even when doing so was difficult.

She clung to him and then stared into his eyes. "I am so glad you're here, for so many reasons."

"Me, too, baby. Me, too." He ran his hand down her hair.

"Meagan! Meagan!" Carrie rushed in and bent down to hug her. "I can't believe it. I can't believe this really happened."

"We're okay. That's what counts. I need to make sure everyone else is, as well."

Sam pushed to his feet. "Keep everyone inside until I can make sure it's safe, and assess any damage."

"I'm coming," Meagan said. "Carrie, you stay." She got to her feet.

Sam pressed a flashlight into her hand. "I need you to stay. Let me do what I do. Let me get everyone out of this safely."

She inhaled. Damn, he was hot when he was in soldier mode. She couldn't believe she was thinking that, even under the circumstances. She nodded. "Okay."

He started to turn, but she grabbed his arm, unable to help herself, and she kissed him. "Be careful."

"Always" he said before departing.

"It's the curse," Carrie murmured, drawing Meagan's attention. "There really is a curse."

"If everyone is alive and well, this is a blessing, not a curse."

It was only a few short minutes before Sam shouted all was clear. Meg came running up the stairs and into Carrie's arms, and Meagan's stomach lurched. "Samantha! Sam! Samantha! I have to find Samantha."

Meagan took off toward the front door and didn't stop when splatters of rain hit her face. She dashed over to her own house and, in seconds, was yanking open the door. She dropped her flashlight, and darkness overtook her. Meagan knelt down, fumbling for the flashlight. "Samantha! Here kitty, kitty."

Behind her, someone switched on a flashlight. The scent of Sam was unmistakable. "Do you see her?"

"No." Her heart twisted. "What if something happened to her?"

"She's okay. Just scared and hiding, I'm sure. Here, little girl. Come on, kitty." He moved through the house, calling her in various ways. "There she is."

Meagan heard the cat's meow and just like that, Sam became Samantha's hero, too. He scooped her up in his arms and brought her to Meagan.

"Now that my two girls are safe and united, I need to go deal with this mess." He kissed Meagan's forehead and headed toward the door.

And Meagan was pretty sure in that moment, she had fallen in love with Sam. She was scared, she felt exposed. But tonight in that bathroom, she'd made a decision to put herself out there with Sam, to be willing to get hurt.

JUST BEFORE SUNRISE, having spent the past few hours juggling the after-tornado crisis, Sam found Meagan at her house. She was still dressed in shorts and a T-shirt, asleep on the couch with Samantha curled next to her. The remote control lay by her head, and the weather channel was on mute.

The house was quiet, and he assumed Kiki was asleep. Either way, it didn't matter. Kiki knew that he and Meagan were seeing each other. Probably everyone did, at this point. They hadn't been exactly discreet in the bathroom during the storm.

Sam debated moving Meagan to the bedroom, but feared he'd wake her up and then she wouldn't go back to sleep, especially considering Samantha had a way of getting noisy. And Meagan needed rest. She'd already told him she would have to go to the studio that day to edit this week's show. He turned off the television and then settled onto the floor in front of her, back against the couch, stretching his legs out, exhausted and happy to rest his eyes.

He figured he'd steal Meagan away for breakfast when she woke up. Or just make breakfast. With that delicious thought on his mind, he dosed off, able to sleep in the most awkward of positions.

How long he slept he didn't know, but the sun was up when he woke, and he could hear Kiki talking on her phone as she passed by in the hall behind the sunken living area, the setup blocking Meagan and Sam from her view.

"She's asleep in her room," Kiki said. "Right. I knew I had to call. It's a wonder the kids weren't hurt, Sabrina. No. No. Yes. I'm on my way now." The door opened and shut, and she was gone.

Sam frowned. What was that? What the hell was that? He replayed the conversation, and though there was nothing that screamed foul play in the words, the very fact that Kiki was speaking with Sabrina set him on edge. And the tone of the conversation, something about it.

Sam quickly got to his feet, intending to call Sabrina, who he was still briefing about the Kiki issue. He'd interviewed ex-employees who'd worked with Kiki, and found more than a few who might not have spoken up before, afraid they'd never work again if they did, but they would now. A few key people he'd located had since moved on with their careers with enough confidence to help him. He'd been compiling quite the damning file, but for the kind of connections Kiki had, Sabrina kept pressing for more.

"Sam?" Meagan sat up, her hair a wild, sexy mess of light brown silk, her lids heavy, her voice groggy. "What's wrong?"

Even when she was sleepy and barely awake, she worried, Sam thought. "Why do you always ask me that when you wake up?"

She blinked several times, as if trying to clear her head. "Well. Let's see." She was already sounding a bit feisty, he noted with amusement as she continued, "While I'm not beyond admitting that I tend to worry obsessively about almost everything, I think I have ample reason to do so under the circumstances. A tornado, an electrical fire, a knocked-out tooth, and a long list of other problems—all pretty good reasons to worry. In fact, when I list them, I can buy into the curse a lot easier than I'd like to."

He bent down on one knee in front of her. "There's no curse to a show that brought us together, and I'm going to prove that to you before this season is over."

She visibly relaxed, her expression softening. "Promise?"

He brushed a wild lock of sleek brown hair off her brow. "Promise."

"You're making a lot of promises. I hope you intend to pay up."

"Well now," he said, his hand sliding up her leg. "Since Kiki just left, we are alone."

Her brows dipped. "Kiki left? This early? That's odd."

He kissed her, not about to put her on edge about Kiki when it wasn't necessary. He would have the answer to the problem very soon. "It's all fine, Meg. And did I mention…"

A slow devilish grin slid onto her incredibly sexy mouth. "What do you have in mind?"

He set Samantha down on the floor and scooped Meagan up into his arms, Tarzan-style. "I have a story to tell you."

He carried her to the bathroom, stripped them both naked and pulled her with him under the hot water of the shower. They both sighed with relief, and their bodies melded together, tension melting into attraction, into desire.

Sam leaned against the wall, molding her close, kissing her, taking his time to savor her. She was soft in his arms, her breasts full and tempting, her nipples hard peaks against his chest. And he wanted inside her, wanted to lose himself in her, wanted to claim this woman as his own, and wished it were that easy. But he didn't want to lose her, he didn't want to pressure her. And he darn sure didn't want the sex to be her escape rather than an extension of what he felt for her, what he hoped she felt for him.

"I was thinking about a story I want you to tell me," he said, caressing the wet hair from her face. "Are you ever going to tell me *your* story? All of it, Meg. I know there's something you haven't told me. Something that got you here where you are today."

Her fingers trailed over his jaw, his lips, a moment before her mouth brushed his. "Yes. Yes I am."

"Yes?"

Her fingers stroked his chest, his ribs, between their bodies. "Yes." She smiled against his mouth, wrapped her hand around the thickness of his erection. "I'm most definitely going to let you in."

Desire pumped through his body, but he forced himself to slow down his lust, and his need to just lose himself in Meagan. He reached down, and covered her hand with his. "That's not what I mean."

"I know what you mean, Sam. And the answer is still yes. Yes, I'm going to tell you my story. Yes, I want you in my life. And yes, I still really want you inside me right now." She stroked his cock, and he let her this time.

He'd held weapons while being fired at, and he didn't so much as tremble. But then, he'd never wanted a woman the way he wanted Meagan, never felt what he felt now, with her, always with her.

He sheathed himself, his gaze sweeping her breasts, water droplets clinging to her tight rosy nipples. "You're spectacular."

Her hands slid down his shoulders. "Remember that the next time we disagree."

"Have I told you how much I love your ass?" he asked, palming one cheek, and angling her hip as he settled his shaft between her thighs.

One of her hands slid to his backside. "Have I told you how much I like yours?"

He entered her and she gasped. "Sam," she moaned.

"Yeah, sweetheart?" His forehead settled against hers, his hand skimmed her breast, fingers teasing her nipple.

"About last night." Her hand pressed to his cheek.

He moved his hips, fitting himself deeper inside her. "What about it?"

She panted and then breathlessly replied, "I'm pretty sure when we huddled together and kissed in the shower, everyone figured out we're together."

Together. He liked that word. He liked her using it as

a given. "Yeah," he agreed, his cock swelling inside her, need building within him. "I'm pretty sure they did."

"I don't regret it. I don't care that they know." He pulled back to look at her, and she quickly added, "I know we have to be discreet. I need to be discreet, and I'm sure you want to be discreet. But…but, Sam, in that shower, in the worst of situations, when I was completely out of control, you made me feel…safe. You made me feel safe, Sam."

Sam swallowed her confession in a hungry kiss, knowing the trust that it had cost her, how difficult trust was for her to give. And as for the regret she'd mentioned, he was feeling absolutely none, and he intended to demonstrate that fact in a number of creative ways.

AT THE STOVE, SAM FILLED plates with omelets he'd made and toast, before joining Meagan at the small white kitchen table, where she was listening to a message on her cell phone.

She'd dressed in black jeans and a red T-shirt with a V neckline that displayed ample creamy white skin in a tantalizing way. But then, he had a good imagination where Meagan was concerned, and it wouldn't take much to encourage him to drag her back to the bedroom, if he thought she'd let him.

Meagan sighed and set her phone on the table. "Kiki left me a message that she's meeting me at the studio. Something is just strange about her taking off this morning when we had the tornado last night." She waved away her worry. "I don't have the energy to think about what it might be." Her gaze lit on her plate. "Wow. No one told me you're a chef. I'm starving and this looks so incredibly good. Honestly, Sam. I can't believe you can cook. You don't strike me as the domestic type."

"I still have a lot of surprises for you," he assured her, looking forward to showing her just how many. "You'll find us soldiers are a resourceful bunch."

She took a bite of her eggs and swallowed. "So good, Sam. At least one of us can cook. Don't be expecting anything but microwave from me."

"So you've told me," he said. "But I'm not interested in you for your cooking, I assure you." He poured sugar in his coffee.

She set her fork down as if the subject turned her stomach. "I fired my agent and hired a new one who says next season I can pick my own crew. Michael Beckwith, that's his name, said that I could have gotten that to start with if I'd been with him. He seems to think he can negotiate for next season now, not later, based on the ratings. That's good news, right?"

"Yes," Sam agreed. "It's very good news."

But it also meant Sam needed to step up what he was doing about Kiki. If in future she wasn't going to running the show—Meagan's new agent seemed to be all but guaranteeing that—would Kiki go so far as to ruin it and make herself look good by having jumped from a sinking ship?

22

In a whirlwind of ratings, chaos and two more live shows, one of which was going on at that very moment, Sam had become a quiet, strong, passionate force in Meagan's life.

She stood backstage, watching yet another megasuperstar perform and awaiting the bottom three results. The cupcake footage had turned out to be a really fun episode that they'd used to contrast with the tornado footage. That had been last night's broadcast. And boy, had it been a show, with massive ratings that had already stirred talks of renewal for another season. Her agent was sure that would happen and he'd insisted they hold off on further contract talks because ratings were the king of cash, not to mention leverage.

Soon, Derek took center stage to read out the names of the bottom three dancers. Meagan held her breath, waiting for the results.

"Tabitha," Derek called for the first time since the debut show, and the audience wailed, some with boos and some with celebration. Tabitha was, by far, a fan favorite. She seemed equally loved and hated.

"Next up," Derek said. "Kevin." Kevin, tall and brunette, rushed forward—a quiet guy not overly well known because he didn't draw much attention to himself.

"And finally," Derek said, "Carrie."

Meagan's heart stammered instantly. Carrie, like Sam, had surprised her, finding a way into her life that was as powerful as Sam's presence, though different. Carrie was the kid sister Meagan had never had. They cut to commercials on the tense moment of the last name, and Shayla's voice came through Meagan's headset, "I really, really hope she doesn't go."

"Me, too," Meagan whispered. "Me, too."

Sam stepped into view across the stage, out of audience viewing range. It was the perfect place; exactly where she needed him to be. She sometimes worried she was becoming too dependent on him, that she was forgetting how to be alone, how to be strong without him. Then there were times like this, when just knowing he was in this with her made her stronger, not the opposite.

Someone grabbed Meagan's arm and asked her a question and she had to turn away, and when she refocused on the stage she noticed Sam had gone. He'd been concerned about Carrie, too. She'd seen it on his face.

When they were live again, it was time for the reveal. Derek called out the first safe contestant. "Tabitha." The crowd went crazy.

Carrie and Kevin joined hands, and Meagan could see Carrie's hand shaking. In that instant, Meagan knew that although this was her vision, her show, but she just wasn't sure she had it in her to get to know the contestants and see their hearts broken. She wasn't sure she could be this close to it all next season. Next season. If there even was a next season.

"And the other dancer who is safe tonight is…Carrie. Kevin you will be going home." Meagan's breath rushed past her lips, guilt twisting inside her at the relief she felt that Carrie would continue on for another week.

Poor Kevin. What did she say to him? How did she make this better? Sure, he'd been picked out of hundreds of thousands of wannabes, but the result was the same—he was still chasing a dream, and still going home. Meagan watched as Carrie, Ginger and DJ surrounded Kevin, to comfort him.

Tabitha signed audience autographs, ignoring Kevin. Meagan realized then that she didn't want Tabitha to win. She was definitely way too close to this to be objective, and she was frustrated at herself for allowing that to happen.

Hours after the broadcast had ended, Meagan was just finishing some paperwork backstage, when her cell rang. She smiled at Sam's number, knowing he, too, was probably finishing security matters for the evening.

"Hey."

"Hey, sweetheart," he said. "Listen I'm going to be a while. We've had a few complications here tonight—*nothing to worry about*. At least, not related to security. But I thought you might want to know that Carrie is still at the rehearsal studio."

"What? What's she doing there?"

"Dancing in the dark and crying."

Meagan sucked in a breath. "Oh," she expelled. "I'm going to her now."

As Meagan arrived at the dim rehearsal studio, the sound of music touched her ears. She found Carrie in the middle of the hardwood floor, in front of the shadowy mirrors, dancing her heart out. Meagan set her purse down and opened her bag, where she kept her old ballet shoes as a reminder of how easily dreams could be lost. She stared down at the worn black shoes, her throat tight as she slipped off her street shoes, and slipped on the dance shoes.

"Want some company?" Meagan asked, flipping on the light.

"Meagan," Carrie rasped, her throat thick with tears and exertion. "I just needed—"

"To rehearse and feel like you have some control of your destiny," she said. "I know. I get it." Meagan went to the sound system and switched the music. "Why don't I teach you a routine that once got me into Juilliard."

"You got into Juilliard? I thought you went to a Texas college?"

"After Juilliard," she said, confessing the small part of her life she spoke of so infrequently that sometimes, *sometimes,* she almost convinced herself it had never happened. "How about I teach you my audition piece?"

"Yes," Carrie said excitedly. "Yes, please."

And so they danced, and danced, and danced some more. And Meagan's leg hurt, and hurt some more, but she didn't stop, until they were both ready to collapse. Until Carrie broke down in tears, and Meagan with her, and they hugged.

"I don't want to go home, Meagan. I don't want to go home."

"I know, sweetie," she said. "But this show is one opportunity, just one. There are so many more. Look at Rena. She joined a Broadway show. You don't have to win to have doors open. Focus on one week at a time."

"I'm trying. I'm trying so hard. To focus, to do well. I want to do well."

"You are. You will."

The sound of a male voice clearing his throat echoed at the door, and Josh appeared in the entryway. "I'd like to offer to take Carrie to get something to eat on the way back to the house." The light in Carrie's eyes was almost instant. Josh was at least seven years older than Carrie, but Sam thought a lot of Josh, and that held weight with Meagan.

And Meagan was in pain, and afraid she wouldn't hide it well if she didn't get some distance from Carrie fairly quickly.

"I'd like that," Carrie said, before casting Meagan a hopeful, cautious look. "Unless that breaks any of my contractual rules?"

"You're safe with Josh," Meagan said, casting him a warning look. "Right, Josh?"

"Without question," Josh assured her. Carrie hugged Meagan and gathered her things.

"Turn the light out behind you," Meagan called as she switched off the music. The lights went out, and she dropped to the floor, against the mirror, pulling her knee to her chest and squeezing her eyes shut.

She knew long before he was kneeling in front of her

that Sam was there. Felt that prickling, tingling wonderful sensation, that only he could create.

"How bad?" he asked.

She bit her lip and forced her eyes open, and that was her mistake, looking into his eyes, knowing he saw everything—her pain, her defeat, her loss of a dream. Suddenly, she felt completely vulnerable. This man knew her in ways no one else did. This man could hurt her with the same deep cut that the loss of her dancing had.

He massaged her leg, like he'd done his own any number of times, and it helped the pain but somehow made her feel all the more exposed.

"How bad, sweetheart?" he prodded.

"I deal with it." It had been what he'd said to her, when she'd asked about his leg. "And don't call me that. You call me that all the time. My name is Meagan, Sam. Meagan. I need to go back to my place." She tried to get up and moaned.

"Meagan, sit." It was an order.

"No. Damn it, Sam. I'm fine. And you don't get to tell me what to do."

His broad, damnably perfect chest of his rose and fell as long, tense moments passed. "I don't deal with it. I said that because it's what guys say. Otherwise, it makes me feel weak, and it reminds me that my life changed without my permission. But it brought me here to you. And you made this place a place I want to be. I hope that maybe, just maybe, I can do that for you."

She dropped her head back, fighting tears. "I need to leave, Sam. I need to be alone."

"If you think for one minute that I'm going to let you walk out of here alone—not that I even think you can—

you're wrong. When we're back at the house, if you want me to go, I will. But not until I know you're okay."

She forced herself to stand, forced herself past the throbbing pain that grew with each passing second. "I'm fine. It comes and then it's gone."

Sam's phone beeped, and he eyed the number, then cursed. "I have to run to the office for a few minutes. Wait for me, Meagan. If this wasn't important I wouldn't even think about leaving you. Don't be stubborn and try to take off. Okay?" His phone stopped ringing.

"It's not like I'm doing any marathons," she bit out between her teeth, and he cursed, knowing she wasn't listening.

His phone started ringing again. "I have to go. Please." He slid his hand to her neck. "Wait for me." He kissed her and then took off at a fast trot to the door.

She didn't wait. She gathered her things as quickly as she could and headed for her car, and to the E.R. where she knew she had to go for that cortisone shot.

Over the course of the next three hours, Sam called her over and over, and she refused to answer. She was exhausted and it was midnight when she left the E.R. and the painkillers had kicked in.

And she knew Sam was going to know the instant she arrived. She knew he was going to be upset, that he was going to demand answers, demand to know why she didn't wait for him. Fine, then. She was going to see him. She was going to walk right into the security house and right into his bed. She was going to take charge of what happened, she was going to make sure there was no talking. Sam had too much control, and she was taking it back.

SAM PACED, CURSING THE TIMING of Sabrina's phone call. Though the call was important to Meagan in ways he was hoping to share with her very soon, it had allowed her to escape him. And he was kicking himself for not being honest with Meagan about his leg in the first place. Maybe, if he had, she'd have felt more willing to tell him about her own.

"You're wearing out the carpet," Josh said from the couch. "Seriously, man. You haven't slept in like two days. Go rest and I'll call you the minute she shows up at her place."

Sam forced himself to stop moving and scrubbed his jaw. He needed a shave, he needed sleep. Josh was right. He couldn't even think straight.

"I'll call you," Josh said, "the absolute instant she appears. We know she's okay. She answered her phone when Carrie called her."

Right. She'd answered Carrie, but not Sam, and made some excuse about visiting a friend. "Okay. Call me." He turned away. He had to face facts. Meagan had shoved him away again. Everything male inside him wanted to throw her over his shoulder, carry her off someplace, and hold her captive until she came to her senses, until she understood how much she meant to him. Until he could erase her pain.

He hit the shower and changed into shorts and a T-shirt, and was somewhat clearer headed. As long as he knew she was safe, that would have to be enough even though he wanted to go after her, he wanted to demand they talk now. To see with his own eyes that she was okay. But every logical instinct he owned told him that was a mistake. To back off, to let her come to him. Fear that she never would, though—that was killing him.

He remembered a saying his mother had always told him. "If you love something, set it free. If it comes back to you, it's yours. If it doesn't, it was never yours." He had to let go. He had to know if she'd come to him. Sam crashed on his bed and forced himself to close his eyes.

And that was when the door to his room opened and shut again.

23

Sam scooted up the headboard, but he didn't dare move any farther, and instinctively, he knew if he said anything, it could set off a firestorm of…he didn't know what, but it wouldn't be good.

"Undress," she ordered. And Sam knew then that this was the Meagan from the first night in the truck, the one who'd planned to use sex to put him in his place, to control him. He wondered if she even realized what she was doing. But he did. He did, and he knew he was treading some rough terrain, because he couldn't let her do that. He reached for his shirt and pulled it over his head, then made quick work of sliding his shorts and boxers down.

He lay back down against the headboard, his shaft hard and jutting forward. Her gaze raked over him, her teeth digging into her bottom lip, and it was all he could do not to reach down and wrap his hand around his cock. But it was so clear though, that she wanted complete control.

"Here I am, *Meagan.* Now what are you going to do with me?"

Her eyes lifted to his, glinted with a hint of anger. She'd told him not to call her sweetheart, and he hadn't. Though having her tell him not to had definitely hurt, once he would have laughed it off and just called her sweetheart again.

"Don't talk." She dropped her purse to the floor, and began undressing. In a matter of seconds she would be in his arms, and he would make love to her. And he'd make damn sure she knew it wasn't just sex.

He held his breath, watching as she revealed the pink sheer bra he loved so much. Her nipples, plump and rosy and beautiful, puckered at the combination of the cool air-conditioning and his hot inspection. Next came her slacks and then her thong—also pink and sexy as hell. His eyes traced her long, toned legs and settled on the tiny V he fully intended to explore with his tongue before this night was over. His cock throbbed, pulsed, demanded to be touched.

"Don't move," she said.

His gaze lifted to hers, lingering a moment on those beautiful breasts, before he said, "Whatever you say swe—Meagan."

She inhaled, her expression flickering with an instant of emotion. She didn't like that correction, and that pleased him. She sashayed toward him, but he didn't miss the slight limp. She paused at the window beside him and yanked two curtain straps free, and instantly he knew she was after total control.

He let her climb on top of him, straddle him, teasing him by settling her perfect little backside against his erection. She held up the straps. "I know you don't mind giving me control." She leaned forward, pressing her hands on the headboard, her nipples so close he could almost taste them, her breath warm near his lips. And then for just an instant, pain flickered over her features, and she turned her head, discreetly shifting her knee before turning back to him. "Isn't that right, *sweetheart?*"

The pain, her pain, did him in, and he acted on pure instinct. Sam wrapped his arms around her and slid his hand up her back to her neck. "Meagan," he whispered, the feel of her in his arms removing any reserve he'd pretended to have. "I'll let you tie me up. I'll let you do anything to me. But not if you're trying to hide from me. Not if you're using it to hide from what's real. And that's us. Us, Meagan. We're real."

"I'm not hiding," she rasped.

"Yes, you are. You are and we both know it. What happened to telling me your story?" He leaned back and looked at her. "Or creating one together?"

"Sam," she whispered, relaxing into him. "I've just dealt with this alone for so long. It's attached to a lot of pain."

He slid his hand down her arm. "That I'll share with you if you let me."

She shifted slightly, and he felt the tension ripple through her body. Sam rolled her over beneath him, settling between her legs, elbows resting beside her head. "You're in no shape to be on top or to tie me up tonight. I expect a full dominatrix routine when you're okay— including leather." His voice softened. "Sometimes you have to let someone else carry some of the burden."

She reached up and trailed her fingers along his jaw. "I'm afraid I'll forget how to be without you."

"I've already forgotten how to be without you."

Her eyes teared up. "Sam."

He kissed his name from her lips, a slow sensual kiss that deepened slowly, before becoming something far more passionate, far more wild and emotional. They clung together, tongue against tongue, body against body.

Sam slid inside her, and he felt her fear disappear, felt it fade with every touch, every kiss. He buried himself deep within her, felt the warm wet heat of her body consume him, just as she had him in every possible way. He loved this woman, he loved her with all that he was.

A slow, sweet rhythm formed. Neither of them wanted it to end, but neither could resist the build up of sensation that was leading them into a frenzy of thrusts. Their need beckoned them to get closer and closer, yet they never seemed close enough. To touch each other everywhere, yet they were never touching enough. Until finally, finally they couldn't take anymore. She held tight to him, tensing with release, her body contracting around his cock, demanding his satisfaction as she had his heart.

When they stilled, sated and relaxed, he pulled her against him, and didn't speak, finding he was holding his breath, afraid she would withdraw.

Long seconds ticked by and then she said, "I was at Juilliard. The teacher I told you about helped me get in."

Sam kept silent, afraid he'd ruin her confidence their intimacy had brought her.

"I was one of the few students to get a full scholarship, which I needed since my parents disapproved. One day during practice, I was doing a lift with another dancer, and we fell. He tripped and I tumbled and...well, my knee went in the wrong direction. I tried to recover and return to school, but I just couldn't compete at that level. So I transferred home, and gave it a whirl at the University of Texas, still dancing, still struggling with the injury. But they had a film school there, and I gravitated in that direction and ended up in news, like I told you." She laughed, but not with humor. "My parents, at least, found that choice acceptable, if far from perfect."

"That must have been hard."

"It still is," she said. "Every time I tell myself it can't hurt me anymore, it does."

"But you never stopped loving dance," he stated. "That's true passion, if I've ever seen it."

She leaned up on one elbow. "No. I never stopped loving dance which was why in Texas, it was painful to be around it and not be able to truly live it. I needed to step away from it, but nothing else interested me."

"Until that recruiter came to your school."

"It took a while," she said, "but I needed to get excited about something to keep pushing forward. And truthfully, the connections I made there allowed this show to happen. I thought I was beyond the emotions of my own failed career enough to pursue this without it affecting me, but tonight with Carrie—that tore me up. I don't know if I can come back to the show next season if I'm this close to it."

They analyzed her options, where she thought she might go. They talked. And talked. One thing kept bugging Sam, and he had to have an answer. "Why didn't you tell me about your knee before now?" he asked. "You knew about my leg."

"That's *why* I didn't tell you," she said. "You were hurt while fighting to save people's lives. I was hurt in a pair of ballerina slippers. Who am I to complain? You're a hero, Sam. You might not still be in the army, but I'm proud that you were, and that your family is."

If Sam wasn't already in love with her, it would have happened right then. His heart softened and he wrapped her in his arms and kissed her. They made love then, no hang-ups, no barriers. And Sam had no doubt that when she curled by his side and fell asleep, her walls were still down, and he intended to keep it that way. And no one, most especially Kiki, was going to take her dream from her. He would make sure of it.

SAM WOKE TO THE BEEP of a text arriving on his cell, The message was from Sabrina. Tapes that he'd gotten from an ex-studio had been given to Kiki's uncle, the network executive. The content of the tapes, which included everything from bribery to seduction, were impossible to dismiss as misunderstandings. Sam had the thumbs-up to escort Kiki off the property.

He kissed Meagan, who was so dead to the world, she didn't even move when he got up. He'd wake her with the news that she no longer had to be worried about, at least, one problem. He quickly showered and left her a note saying that he had security detail. And then Sam went to track down Kiki.

Sam knocked on the door of the mother-in-law property, and then knocked again louder. Eventually, Kiki, dressed to the hilt with model-perfect makeup, yanked open the door. Sam should have thought her sexy as hell, but there was nothing about this woman even remotely appealing to him.

Sam stepped forward, crowding her. "We need to talk. Alone."

She rolled her eyes. "Can't this wait?"

"No," he said, leaving the screen door open and following her to the kitchen. On the counter he dropped the file he'd been carrying. "Open it."

She frowned and seemed increasingly uncomfortable. After a pregnant minute of silence as she scanned the photos and documents, which held a history of her becoming a snitch for the studio.

"So. There's nothing wrong with what I do. I help separate the losers from the winners. Of course I should get paid for it."

"You mean you sabotage programs to avoid actually having to work, while still collecting the bonus your uncle offers you."

"That's insane," Kiki said. "That's enough. You can't prove anything of the sort. I'm completely innocent." She started to turn. "I'm going to call my uncle."

"He knows everything," Sam said. "There are tapes, we made a transcript. The content makes it clear that you manufacture problems to destroy people, and get paid anyway. And if that's not enough for you, I managed to catch you on tape myself. One particular call really caught my attention. You were telling your friend Jenna about how you'd decided to stay on with this show and get rid of Meagan. You'd be amazed at the places I have audio hooked up." He motioned to the room. "Like right here in your favorite place to chat on the phone when Meagan's gone. And yes—it's legally recorded. You agreed to it in your contract for the show."

She burst into tears and before Sam knew her intention, she'd flung her arms around him. "Please. Please don't do this. I'll do anything. My uncle will disown me. He's my only family, he's—"

Sam tried to pry her off him. The woman must think he was a fool, that he hadn't fully investigated her. "You have three brothers, a sister and a living mother and father."

That's when he heard the footsteps on the porch, a trip, and a soft murmur of pain. Meagan. Meagan was on the porch and Kiki was plastered all over him.

MEAGAN CRINGED AT THE weakness in her knee and forced herself up the last of the porch stairs, seeking a shower and clean clothes, wondering at the screen door.

She hated so much that she'd missed Sam this morning. She'd heard him leave, and had scrambled for clothes, but couldn't catch him before as he drove away. Somehow the idea of seeing him after the intense experience of the night before, made her feel a little shy and nervous. She was never shy and nervous.

Voices sounded in the house just as she was about to push open the door. Kiki and— Meagan frowned. "Sam?"

Ridiculous butterflies fluttered in her stomach at the prospect of seeing him yet she desperately wanted to reaffirm how right last night had been, how right they were. Her steps quickened, and she froze; in fact, she was pretty sure her heart completely stopped beating. Kiki was pressed against Sam, intimately, and…

Shock came hard and fast, with the force of a concrete block. Meagan gasped and rushed away, instinct sending her into flight. She couldn't catch her breath.

She stumbled down the stairs and almost fell, but she pushed past it, righted herself and hit the beach at a limping run—forgetting her car, forgetting anything but the fastest escape. Air came in salty gulps, as she bit back a sob.

Sam's shouts followed almost instantly. "Meagan! Meagan!"

She heard him, she did, but she wanted distance, she wanted freedom. She wanted to get away. Had to get away. She ran toward the water. She had no idea why.

Suddenly, his hand gripped her arm, and he turned her toward him.

"Go away, Sam."

"Meagan." His chest rose and fell from his fast sprint. "Sweetheart."

"Don't call me that. I told you not to call me that."

"I know you don't mean that, any more than you think I want that woman. You know I don't."

She searched his face, but didn't have to look too hard. She knew there would be sincerity in his eyes, knew it in her heart. She even knew she was being silly and irrational. "I do. I do. I just…" The ache inside her wouldn't ease. This man could so easily tear her heart to shreds. How did she say that and not put herself even more at his mercy? "It's just…" She jerked away from him and stumbled backwards, her feet, shoes and all, sloshing into the water.

He followed her right into the water, boots plunging into the ocean.

"Sam, back off. Just back off. Give me time to process what I'm feeling."

He stepped closer, but she took off running.

But Sam had her arm again, forcing her to face him. "I'm not letting this go. I'm not letting *you* go."

"You have to!" she yelled, jerking away from him and stumbling backwards again. She tumbled, arms flaying as she reached for Sam and he reached for her, but it was too late. She landed on her butt, with water splashing all around her, her hair totally drenched. She glared up at Sam. "You didn't have to choose that moment to listen to me."

"I wasn't trying to." He extended a hand and pulled her to her feet. She tugged him forward, intending to stand and throw him into the water but she wasn't fast enough. He fell into the water and on top of her.

His hands braced the sand at her sides. "I'm not letting you go. Last night—"

She shoved at him. "People are watching. You're going to get me in trouble. I can't focus like this. I can't focus on the show and the ratings and—"

"Because of me."

She couldn't say yes. She tried. On some basic level, she knew he would walk away if she pushed hard enough. So why wasn't she pushing?

"You know, Meagan," he said, "I thought I could get you to open up to me. I thought after last night you had. Clearly, I was wrong. You're looking for a reason to get away from me." He shoved off of her, left her in the water, which spoke volumes to Meagan. He wasn't helping her get up. He was showing her that she was on her own now from here on out.

He stood, looking down at her, ocean slashing around his feet, around her face. "Chase your dreams, Meg. Kiki is gone, as in terminated. That's why I left you last night, to meet with Sabrina, and compile the evidence for executive approval. Kiki wanted your job and was plotting to get you fired. And I'll stop distracting you. I'll ask to be removed from the show." He turned away and headed down the beach.

Kiki was gone—but that barely registered. Sam was leaving, Sam was all but gone already. "Sam! Sam, please." She struggled to get up and damn, her knee buckled. "Sam!" Desperation rose inside her. And she knew then and there that losing Sam was far more frightening than was the fear of being hurt. She already hurt. She hurt because he was leaving, she hurt just thinking about never touching him again, never just being with him again. She couldn't let him go. "Sam." She swallowed hard, and then with resolve firmly in place, shouted, "Sam! I love you. I love you. Please don't walk away."

She couldn't go after Sam and she couldn't watch him go. She let her chin drop to her chest, staring at the water splashing around her.

But then, he was there, in the water, on his knees, too, his hands framing her face. "I love you too, sweetheart. I thought I should wait to tell you until you were ready to hear the words, until I bought you a ring and... until I thought you'd agree to marry me."

Slowly, he got to his feet and brought her up with him. He kissed her. Ahh, how he kissed her, salty and sweet, and wicked and wonderful. And when they finally stopped, and trudged through the water, his arm around her to help her walk, there was an audience, a group of cast and crew, to watch them. Neither Meagan nor Sam cared.

Sam stopped and stared into her eyes. "So? Will you marry me, Meagan Tippan?"

"Do I get to tie you up and have my way with you, if I do?"

"Only if you promise to wear leather."

"Then, yes!" she said. "I'll marry you, Samuel Kellar."

He picked her up and carried her toward the house, carrying her because he knew she was injured. And Meagan knew, she was never going to walk alone again.

Epilogue

WEEKS LATER, CENTER STAGE, Derek waited with the last
two contestants—Tabitha of all people, and ironically,
Jensen. The final show had arrived on the announcement that there would be a second season. They were
on a ratings high, even with the curse being weaned
slowly into the background. A strategy Meagan had
proposed to Sabrina to ensure the ratings would hold
for the next season and it had paid off.

Meagan stood backstage with Carrie by her side, now
her intern, after being eliminated from the competition several weeks back. Carrie was learning the ropes
amazingly well, and Meagan was pretty darn certain
she'd be able to justify a staff position for her next season. And since she and Josh had become a hot commod-
ity, Carrie had an extra incentive beyond her career to
make L.A. her home.

As for Meagan, this was her baby, and Sam had convinced her to stay on as well. He'd helped her see how
many opportunities the show had created for all kinds
of people associated with the program, even beyond the
dancers. Besides, by the end of season two, he'd have

his business up and running, and she could reevaluate what she wanted to do if there was a season three. She was thinking about a reality show called *Men of Kellar Security,* but Sam wasn't buying it. She'd work on that, though.

Derek opened the envelope and drew out the results, "The winner of a new Ford Mustang, a check for one hundred thousand dollars, and a two year contract with the network as featured talent is…Jensen!" Screams erupted, and Tabitha, bless her sweet little heart, stormed off the stage in true Tabitha style.

Hours after the broadcast and debut season had ended, Meagan walked onto the empty stage, smiling at the empty auditorium. Her dream had come true, in so many more ways than she'd ever believed possible.

"I thought I might find you here."

She turned with a smile to find Sam, looking gorgeously masculine, dressed in black slacks and a blue button-down that matched his sky-blue eyes to perfection.

"We have a flight to catch."

Excitement filled her. "I know. I can't wait. Italy, here we come." They'd been planning it for weeks.

He wrapped her in his arms and held out a velvet box. "Sure you don't want to see it now?"

"Not until we get there," she said, with absolute certainty. This was one area she was more than willing to give him full control over. "What if you don't like it? I really want you to have a ring you love."

"I can guarantee that I'll love it," she said. "I'll love it because I love you, and because you always surprise me in such a perfect way." She couldn't stop smiling.

"But I have a surprise for you, too." She unbuttoned the top of her blouse to reveal a glimpse of a black leather strap. His eyes glimmered with instant heat, which she planned to flame for the rest of her life.

* * * * *

Follow My Lead

1

DARLA JAMES STOOD IN THE WINDING security line at JFK airport trying not to think about the moment the plane would take off with her inside it. That moment when the massive steel cage, otherwise known as "the plane," would lift into the air with nothing she perceived as logical to keep it from falling to the ground. She pressed her hand to her throat, mentally reprimanding herself. She had to get past this fear of flying if she was going to travel to the various audition cities. Darla had been hired as the new judge on season two of the smash hit *Stepping Up*. The studio was even allowing her to film her morning show on the road, despite it being on a competing network. She wasn't about to blow this opportunity over some dumb fear of flying. She *would* pass through the security gates. She *would not* turn away and run back to her car. This was too big an opportunity for her to mess up, even more so for her parents' struggling ranch and animal shelter.

Darla blew a wayward strand of long blond hair from

her face and noted the televisions hanging from the ceiling. A perky cooking channel goddess was muted, but it was clear that she was describing how to make a strawberry cake. Darla welcomed the distraction the show offered, telling herself that she might recreate that perfect masterpiece in her own kitchen. Although she was better known for burning a grilled cheese sandwich or two.

By the time Darla made it past the metal detectors, she was eager to double-check her stock of necessities for the flight. She should have a package of Hershey's kisses, her favorite romance author's latest book and her headphones. Anything not easily spotted per a quick inspection would be purchased at the gift shop. Those items represented her best hope that she wouldn't embarrass herself on the plane. Anything to avoid wayward yelps during takeoff or panicked questions about the sounds the plane might make. She'd been there, done that, and received the dirty looks of those who were not afraid to fly. She hated those looks.

The plastic bin containing her things slid to a halt in front of her and with her plan in place and fifteen minutes to spare before boarding, Darla whirled toward departures. That was when she was hit with her first wave of turbulence. Coming face-to-face with Blake Nelson—her show nemesis—or rather, face-to-chest with him, considering the man was a good foot taller than her measly five foot two inches, was bad news. She swallowed hard, not having to look beyond the navy T-shirt stretching across an impressive chest to be convinced of Blake's good looks. She already got his appeal thanks to another up-close-and-personal occasion she wished she could forget.

Darla tore her gaze from his impressive set of pecs. She wondered what her weakness for a man who had been downright mean to her a few months before said about her. Sadly, she concluded that her producer, Kayla—two years her senior at twenty-nine and happily married to a gorgeous veterinarian—was right. Darla must really have a secret, self-defeating mechanism when it came to relationships. She was attracted to all the wrong men.

Blake's brilliant blue gaze captured hers and twinkled in a moment of mischief before he glanced down at her socked feet peeking beneath her blue jeans. He arched a dark brow. "I always seem to catch you with your shoes off."

She grimaced at the reference to their "incident" as she thought of it, in which they'd been working a red carpet event, side by side, when her heel had broken off her shoe. She'd proceeded to stumble happily against that hard body of his. He'd reciprocated by catching her and flirting outrageously. Unfortunately, his camera crew had captured the entire embarrassing event on film.

"I'd have thought you'd gotten the shoe jokes out of your system when you made fun of me on your show the next morning," she muttered, and then marched toward the line of chairs just past security and sat down.

He followed, stopping in front of her—or rather, towering over her. She refused to look up at him and instead, infuriatingly, noticed his powerful thighs flex beneath his jeans. Not that his muscles—or that sexy cleft in his chin mattered. He was not the man for her.

"My guest made fun of you," he said, as if that gave him some form of defense. "Not me."

Her gaze jerked to his, anger brought her back to her senses. "You played the footage of our exchange on *your* show. *Your* guest—Rick—was the host of *Stepping Up* not *The Blake Nelson Show*. He didn't have the power to make that happen."

"Rick plotted with my producer who was fishing for ratings. I told him off and my producer. And I called you to apologize."

She laced one of her boots, seeing no reason to deny that he'd called. "I didn't want to talk to you any more than I want to work with Rick. But we don't always get what we want."

Surprise registered on his chiseled, too-handsome, arrogant face. "Are you always so honest?"

She stood up. "With appropriate discretion—which means not at the risk of hurting someone. What you and Rick did to me could have hurt my career and my livelihood. You made me look like I wasn't focused on my job, like I was playing games on the red carpet. And, no, it didn't get me fired, but had my ratings dipped, it would have been brought up again, and you know it." It certainly had made her doubt her desire to be in the public eye. She threw the strap of her bag over her shoulder. "And for the record, I didn't take your call because I was afraid our conversation would later become

a part of your show. I have to run to catch my flight."
She started walking.

He fell into step beside her a bit too easily, as if he'd
anticipated the move. She glared up at him, quickly turning away before those blue eyes captured hers, sending
a flutter to her stomach. "Why are you following me?"

He ignored the question. "If it's any consolation, not
only did that show's content not hurt your career, your
fans—and mine, for that matter—were furious with me.
I got hate mail and the phones rang off the hook for
weeks after. My viewers thought the incident was just
as inappropriate as you did."

She knew that because she'd gotten her share of mail,
as well. And that mail had been what had kept her from
quitting. That—and her family who, as always, loved
and supported her. "What you did was inappropriate."
She cut him a look. "But I assume your ratings softened the blow of the outcry." They'd been huge—off
the charts.

He threw up his hands. "I didn't have anything to do
with what happened. I swear to you, Darla. I would never
have done something so callous. If you replay the footage
of my show you'll see the shock on my face. And you'll
see I tried to salvage the situation while I was on air."

Dang. He sounded sincere. So sincere that… *Don't
do it,* she silently warned herself. Don't fall victim to the
wrong guy saying the right things. She wanted to do it,
too, she wanted to believe him, to stop and tell him that
it was okay, that it was old history, because that is what

she did. She made people feel better, she forgave them. She lay down and let them walk all over her.

Knowing how close she was to making a huge mistake with this man, Darla all but shouted with joy at the sight of a ladies' room. She had her escape from Mr. Wrong.

Darla stopped abruptly. "Excuse me, but I have to run in here."

"Wait, Darla. There's something—"

"Sorry," she said, knowing if he talked one minute more or kept looking at her with those damnable gorgeous eyes, she'd start caving in again. She motioned behind her. "No men allowed." Cringing at the silly statement—like he didn't know no men were allowed?—she rushed down the narrow, tiled hallway.

The instant Darla was out of Blake's sight, she slumped against the wall, unaware that she'd been holding her breath. He was just one heck of a lot of man. And there was no question that it would be easy for her to forget why she had to be on guard around him, forget he was her enemy.

She pushed off the wall and plopped her bag down on the corner of a long counter running beneath a mirror. She'd vowed to lay off the Easter chocolate, which always meant an extra five pounds, and the wrong men, which usually amounted to an extra seven. The camera was pretty darn unforgiving, which helped strengthen her otherwise weak promise. There was no Blake Nelson anywhere in her future but as a competitor for ratings.

There was, however, something to look forward to.

Though her show wasn't a money-maker, not yet, she still sent every dime she could home. *Stepping Up* could solve all her problems by giving her enough to pay off her parents' debt and get them ahead. *If* Darla made it through the first four episodes. That's when the reality show's executives either had to call her a one-season wonder or take up the option, guaranteeing her one more season with a big fat bonus. Even if they didn't option her, she hoped she'd have enough of a ratings boost on her morning show to increase her pay there.

Darla shoved Blake and worries over the future out of her mind and focused on the urgent matter at hand. She did an inventory of her bag for the flight to Denver, the first audition city. Chocolate—check. Book—check. *Oh, no.* Where were her headphones? She had to have her headphones so she wouldn't hear the sounds the plane made. A frantic search proved they weren't there and she cringed when she remembered reminding herself to grab them off the kitchen table.

She snatched up her bag and headed for the exit, intending to search out the gift shop, not even thinking about Blake. That was until she was out the door and felt a rush of disappointment that he was gone. Clearly, she was so not over her Mr. Wrong guy syndrome. Nor, she realized five minutes later, was she going to have a headset for the flight. Darla charged down the walkway, and just that one chink in her travel armor had her fear soaring. What if they crashed? What if the engine stopped working? What about birds?

She halted at the gangway to the plane and handed

the stewardess her boarding pass. The woman scanned it and smiled. "Welcome, Ms. James. You'll be in a window seat on the fourth row and I'll be by to check on you momentarily."

"Thank you," she said, and wondered if the reality show had put her in first class because it was safer. That had to be it. Why else would they spend such a ridiculous amount of money on a seat not so unlike the others a few rows behind? She inhaled, and fought the urge to ask the stewardess the millions of questions rushing through her mind—like how experienced the pilot was and how much rest he'd had.

Forcefully, she sent a command to her legs to move, to walk through the entry and down the aisle. And that's when the second wave of turbulence hit her, because Blake Nelson was sitting in the seat next to hers.

2

"I TRIED TO WARN YOU," Blake said, doing his best not to smile at the adorably distressed expression on Darla James's face. He could see why the Colorado country girl gone big city had charmed her audience into a top ratings slot. He was as taken with her as her viewers were, something no woman had done to him in a very long time, he realized.

"Warn me?" she asked, blinking in confusion and shoving a lock of blond hair from her eyes to see him more clearly.

"Right," he said, unable to keep himself from teasing her. "When you tucked tail and ran into the bathroom." And it became abundantly clear that she didn't know he was taking the trip with her.

"I did not tuck…" Understanding slid across her lovely heart-shaped face. "You were going to warn me that we were traveling together?" He gave a slow nod and her pale green eyes glinted with yellow flecks, then narrowed on him suspiciously as she, no doubt, began to put two and two together. "How would you have known we were on the same flight, next to each other, unless…"

The same person made our reservations, he finished silently for her. Noting the flight attendant approaching her from behind, he suggested, "I think you need to sit down." He stood up to let her by and reached for her bag. "Do you want me to put that overhead?"

"I'll keep it and I don't need to sit. I need you to tell me what is going on."

"Hello, Ms. James," the flight attendant said, drawing her attention. "Is there a problem? I need to clear the aisle for boarding. I can help you with your bag if you need help?"

"I… No. No problem." She turned a perplexed look on Blake, her ivory cheeks now flushed a pretty pink. "I guess I need to sit down."

His lips twitched and he motioned her forward. "Probably a good idea."

She scooted into the seat by the window and Blake quickly took his seat, the soft scent of her floral perfume hung in the air—sweet like the woman. He was really ready for sweet, and someone with her own career, her own dreams, instead of the women who chased his success or his money.

She whirled on him, her tartness doing nothing to sour her sweetness. "What's going on?"

"I work for the same network as *Stepping Up,*" he said, stating the obvious. "I'm filming a special segment on the first audition stop."

She inhaled and exhaled, her fingers curling around

her bag, which she clutched in her lap. "I'd have thought someone would have warned me."

"Well," he said. "I did the same thing last year. They probably assumed you knew that since we have competing morning shows. I guess I should warn you that I'll be back the first week the finalists move into the contestant house to film the reality portion of the show. Then again when the winner is announced and gets the studio contract and the two hundred and fifty thousand dollar prize. And, for the record, I doubt the studio thought you'd react quite so…shall we say *intensely* to my presence, since you're the one with the new cable contract."

"I was surprised, not *intense,*" she countered. "Whatever intense is supposed to mean."

He glanced down at her bag. "You're holding on to that bag like you either plan to hit me with it or make a run for the door."

"Hitting you with my bag would bring me a lot of joy after what you did to me a few months ago," she said. "Unfortunately, it would also bring unwanted attention and trouble, so I'll settle for simply fantasizing about it. It'll distract me from the run to the door. And I'll just tell you right now that I don't like to fly. You might want to consider changing seats with someone. I'm going to drive you bonkers. Then again, maybe you should stay. This trip will be my revenge for your past sins."

"Ah," he said. "You're a control freak."

"I'm not a control freak."

"People who don't like to fly are control freaks."

"I'm *not* a control freak. And by the way, before I

forget and you think I didn't catch what you said—you wouldn't have felt the need to 'warn me' if you didn't think I was going to react intensely to you being here."

"I thought you said you didn't react intensely?"

"Your word, not mine."

"Can I get you two something to drink?" the flight attendant asked, stopping beside them.

"A glass of champagne," Darla said quickly.

Blake frowned. "It's ten in the morning."

"Then make it a mimosa," she told the attendant, then to Blake, "That has orange juice in it. I wasn't joking when I said I was a bad flyer and, honestly, I'm not a good drinker, either, but it's better than a sedative." She glanced back at the attendant. "In fact, you better bring him one, too. Actually, you might want to have one yourself because you were unlucky enough to have me on this flight."

Blake laughed along with the attendant and nodded his approval. "Bring me one, thanks."

The attendant glanced at Darla's bag. "It needs to go under your seat for takeoff."

Darla unzipped it and handed Blake a bag of chocolate. "Hold this, please." Next she handed him a book. "And this."

He glanced at the romance novel and read the title. "*Dangerous Passion* by Lisa Renee Jones?"

She shoved her bag under her seat and buckled her seat belt. "Paranormal with a hot military hero who is going to save the world and his woman." She grabbed the candy and the book. "It's for the book club on my show. You got a problem with romance?"

"Not at all," he chuckled. "In fact, maybe I need to send a few to my sister. She falls for losers and then wonders why they walk all over her. I'd rather she find a hero in a book than try and turn someone into one that isn't."

"Your sister and I should talk," she murmured. He would have asked about that loaded comment, but she quickly added, "And on that note, not one word we exchange on this flight better end up on your show. If you turn my fear into a joke, I swear to you—"

"I won't," he said, capturing her gaze, trying to let her see the truth in his. "I wouldn't do something like that."

"Mimosas have arrived," the attendant said. "But drink up quickly. We'll be getting underway soon."

Blake accepted the drinks and handed one to Darla. She reached for the glass, their fingers touched, and damn if he didn't know that touch. She felt it, too, that connection they'd had on the red carpet. A connection that he'd fully intended to act upon, if not for the disaster on his show the following morning. He'd been hot for this woman then, and time hadn't changed that. Hot and hard, and remarkably getting harder from nothing more than the idea of touching her, holding her as he had when she'd fallen against him. He was going to hold her again, all right, and this time without an audience. There was something about this woman that made him want to know her and that was something he hadn't felt in a very long time.

He lifted his glass. "To new beginnings."

She studied him a moment and clinked her glass to his. "To new beginnings." And suddenly, the plane's engines started.

"Oh, God," Darla exclaimed. All the heat and fire in her stare turned into panic.

"I promise you," he said, strongly contemplating the likelihood that kissing her right now as a means of distraction would end with him getting punched. "Everything's fine. If it makes you feel any better, my father's a retired commercial pilot, so I've flown a lot." He glanced down at her drink, but not before he noticed, and not for the first time, the small, sexy mole just above her lip. Damn, he liked that mole. "This might be a good time to drink that mimosa."

She downed it. "Can I have another?"

He handed her his. "I thought you said you weren't a good drinker?"

She downed his drink. "I'm not. I need to eat something." She tore open the chocolate.

"Chocolate isn't food."

"Chocolate absolutely is food." She laughed. "Oh, boy. I'm already feeling a buzz." She sank in her seat and cut him a look. "Did I mention that you should probably find another seat?" The stewardess came by and took the empty glasses while another began the standard instructional chatter.

"You did," he assured her. "And I refused." The plane started to move and she sat bolt upright to look out of the window.

"Oh, no," he said, easing her back. "Don't watch. That's the worst thing you can do."

"I have to watch," she said, glowering at him. "And how would you know that's the worst thing I can do?"

"Because my mother was afraid of flying," he said, trying to distract her. "And she is one hundred percent a control freak. I bet you balance your checkbook every day." He shoved down the window shade.

"Doesn't everyone?"

"I don't."

"Well, that's a mistake." She glowered. "Let go of the window shade."

"If you don't look out of the window you won't know whether or not to question if it's normal or not."

"I told you. I have to look."

"That's what my mother said, too, and then she tried it with the shade down and it worked. She relaxed instead of spending the entire flight in a tense ball of nerves. Now she's a travel writer."

"I'm not your mother."

"No," he said softly, his hand dropping from the window, and settling on her leg. "You are most definitely *not* my mother. And believe me, I am very aware of that fact." Sexual tension crackled between them, as good a distraction as he could ever hope for. Then the damnable wheels growled beneath the plane, retracting.

"Oh, my God," she whispered, "did we just take off?"

He flipped up the armrest between them. "Yes," he answered, turning so that he faced her fully. "See how fast things happen when you aren't watching every little movement? How about opening that chocolate?"

"I need to look—"

He ran his hand down her arm, keeping her toward him. "Look at me."

Her eyes met his and the connection was instant. He didn't remember the last time a woman made his blood boil with nothing more than a look. But this one sure did. "You need another strategy to deal with your fear, other than mimosas and chocolate, if you're going to make the twenty-city audition schedule."

"Thirty," she corrected.

"Thirty," he repeated. "That's a lot of cities. It's going to be hard to keep up that pace if you stay this uptight. Try it my way. Stay away from the window and focus on other things. *Like me.*"

"I think focusing on you is a bad idea."

"And why is that?"

"Because I've been drinking and I might forget how much I don't like you."

"Or alternatively," he suggested, "you might remember that you actually *do* like me."

THAT'S EXACTLY WHAT SHE WAS worried about. Liking him. Forgetting why she shouldn't. Forgetting he was just another one of the power-hungry, driven men who attracted her, but later left her emotions bruised. He'd proven that by using her for better ratings. Blake was far more the wrong guy than any of the wrong guys before him, because he could impact her career. She'd been clipped by his potential power already and survived. Next time she might not. So, knowing all of this, why, why, *why* was she staring at his mouth, wishing he'd kiss her and distract her from the window? Didn't she care that they were in a semipublic place?

"You might even decide that you want to kiss me," he said, as if reading her mind. He leaned in closer, so that the spicy male scent of him teased her nostrils.

There was no "might" about wanting to kiss him. It was all she could do not to press her lips to his, which was a clear indication that a mimosa was not the way to cope with travel—or Blake Nelson.

"I'm not going to look at you or out the window." She shifted in her seat and put her tray table down, setting the bag of chocolate on top and grabbing her book. "I'll read." She opened up her romance novel and began reading from where she'd left off.

She shoved him to his back, straddled him. Kissed him. Wild didn't begin to describe what kissing Lara unleashed inside Damion. One minute they were kissing, the next they were touching, licking, tasting. Her naked backside rubbing against his cock drove him insane with need. He couldn't get enough of her. Couldn't make himself stop kissing her, caressing her, couldn't resist molding her breasts in his hands and swallowing the moan that slid from her lips to his. They melted into one another, the play of tongue against tongue, and wildness turned into an unfamiliar desperation

*like nothing he had ever experienced with another
woman, a need to escape into each other, a need
not to speak, not to think.*

*Damion's hand slid up her back, into her hair,
angling her mouth to deepen the kiss, to take more.
Whatever happened beyond this moment, beyond
the desire, didn't matter. There was no right or
wrong, no enemies or even friends—there was just
feeling, needing, taking.*

Darla set the book down. *No enemies or even friends.*
That passage was just a little too close to what she
wanted to happen with Blake. This was so not the answer
to resisting Blake Nelson. She reached for the bag of
chocolate and unwrapped a piece, not looking at Blake,
but she could feel him looking at her. She was about to
stick the first Hershey's kiss into her mouth when the
plane jolted. She yelped and the candy—the piece in her
hand, and the entire bag—went flying.

Blake captured the bag and pushed her tray up, turning her toward him again. "Turbulence is nothing to
worry about. Once you've been on a few really bad
flights you realize just how much a plane can take."

The attendant rushed over to them. "Everything
okay?"

"Is it?" Darla asked.

"Of course, honey," she said. "Bumps are normal.
It's August. This time of year, hot air pockets create
turbulence."

"You're sure?" Darla asked, watching her expression

closely for signs she, indeed, was not sure but didn't want to say as much.

"I'm positive."

"Two more mimosas when you can, please," Blake said, his focus on Darla. "If you get drunk, I promise to get you to your room, and I won't take advantage of you, no matter how much I want to."

3

HE WOULDN'T TAKE ADVANTAGE of her, no matter how much he wanted to. That was the statement Blake had made that had opened the door of possibility for Darla, the one that spoke of honor, of a good man. Maybe she really had misjudged him. Maybe she was so conditioned to believe she always chose the wrong men that she was looking for flaws in Blake unfairly.

"Here you go," the flight attendant said. "Two more mimosas."

Blake passed Darla her drink and kept one for himself.

"Actually," Darla said. "I think we need to even the stakes here. I've had two. These two are yours."

He arched a brow and then eased his shoulder back into the seat, still facing her, his voice low and intimate. "I really will take care of you if you want to drink that."

"I believe you. How old is your sister? Younger or older?"

"Younger by five years," he said. "She's twenty-seven."

"And here I thought the wrong man syndrome was a curse for show business types. Maybe it's the curse of the twenty-seven-year-olds."

"I love the hell out of my sister, but she has issues way beyond age. Namely, she needs to act hers—but that's a long story that would require a few extra mimosas. And you and I, well, we aren't exactly in an industry that's relationship friendly. It's populated with a lot of people who are out for number one. That has to be different from the life you were living as the Colorado rancher's daughter."

"I still live life as a Colorado rancher's daughter," she said. "And the minute this business makes me something else, I'm out."

"You might not know when it happens," he suggested. "Most people don't."

"My family will know and they'll knock some sense into me."

He smiled. "Same with mine."

"You're close to your family?"

"Very. It was my father's investment strategies that got me here to begin with. I started doing YouTube investment segments about the stock market while I was in college, which began with too much tequila and a dare." He lifted his glass and took a sip. "Luckily I handle my alcohol better at thirty-two than I did at twenty-one. The first video was such a hit that I kept doing them, and somehow, someone who mattered saw them and the rest is history. That's how I ended up writing that handbook for investing in the stock market and why it's a regular feature on my show."

"You highlight stocks on your show and I highlight romance novels," she observed. "Like night and day."

"Which is why there's an audience for both of us," he said. "Sometimes people want business advice and sometimes they just need to escape. Sometimes the same person might want one thing one day and the other the next."

She'd thought the same thing many times. "You'll never convince my network of that. They want me to take you down."

His eyes—so brilliantly blue—twinkled with mischief. "And what about you? Do you want to take me down?"

"After you made a fool of me on your show, I did," she admitted.

"I didn't—"

"I'm willing to accept that maybe—just maybe—you weren't responsible for what happened," she conceded.

"Maybe?"

"That's all you're getting from me right now."

"It's better than the outright hatred I got from you earlier, so I'll take the maybe." He downed the drink. "You know, this is a three-hour flight. You can drink another mimosa and still not have to worry about what happens when we get off the plane."

She was more worried about what wouldn't happen if she drank. Meaning, she wanted him to know that if their flirtation went beyond this flight, she was clear-headed. Not that she was planning to do anything with this man. Still…options were good.

She took his empty glass from him and handed him her full one. "I'll consider another drink when you're one up on me."

He hit the attendant button. "Then I better get busy." He downed her drink.

She laughed. "I thought you weren't going to get me drunk and take advantage of me?"

"That's exactly why I need to get you drunk," he assured her. "So you'll be safe. But just in case you're wondering, I'm okay with you getting *me* drunk and taking advantage of me."

She laughed again but right at that moment, the plane jolted back and forth. Her heart lurched and she grabbed his leg. "Easy," he murmured, his hand closing over hers. "Just the heat—remember?" He eased closer so that their knees were touching. "You're perfectly safe right now."

Heat. Oh, yes. There was heat—plenty of heat screaming a path through her body, making every nerve ending she had tingle with awareness.

"Hi," the flight attendant said.

Blake glanced at Darla. "Another drink?"

"Only if I eat first."

"We're actually about to serve brunch," the attendant said, and proceeded to give them their meal choices.

Once they'd ordered, Blake turned back to Darla, still holding her hand. She stared down at his. He had big, strong hands. Hands that made her think of him touching her.

"Now where were we?" he asked, drawing her gaze. "Oh, yes. Talking about you getting me drunk and taking advantage of me. But since I'm barely above getting beaten with your bag, I'm pretty sure that's not going to happen. So why don't you tell me how your show got started?"

The plane shook and she inhaled, quickly diving into her reply to keep herself from diving for the window shade instead. "I was at the University of Colorado with my sights set on a journalism degree. I took a drama class thinking it would be a fun, easy elective that would allow me time for the college paper. The next thing I knew I was writing scripts and producing a school play. Long story short, I ended up working for a casting director in New York and met with a producer looking for a new morning-show host."

"And the producer decided it should be you."

"Yes, but I said no at first. I was terrified to be in front of the camera. I still am half the time. I have silly things happen, like when I spilled water all over Miss Universe, who'd come on the show to support a children's charity." She cringed. "I suppose if they didn't fire me over that I shouldn't have thought they'd fire me over my broken shoe. I just keep worrying they'll realize I'm not meant to be on camera."

"Those things make your audience love you, you know," he said softly. "It's part of that country-girl-gone-big-city charm."

She felt her cheeks flush red. "Thank you. But seriously, my show is less than a year old. It's hard to feel like I belong here. It's all just so…surreal."

"Well, you do, and clearly the powers that be for *Stepping Up* see that, too."

"Yeah, well, did I mention that I was the assistant casting director who found Rick the job as host for *Stepping Up?* And yes, I mean Rick—as in the guest who used my broken shoe as fodder on your show."

His eyes went wide. "You're freaking kidding me."

"Nope," she said. "I got him the job, and still he used me. That's what really got to me about the whole thing, I think."

"Funny," he said. "I kind of thought it had something to do with you maybe thinking that we had a connection that you then questioned. I know I thought we had a connection."

She inhaled, taken off guard. She had. God, had she ever. She liked him. Too much. She still did.

"Food's here," the attendant said, sparing her from a reply.

Darla sat up, quick to break eye contact with Blake, not sure what she was feeling right now. Alcohol, an empty stomach and an airplane. She was not in a position to be making decisions about men, especially this one.

It wasn't as if her track record was stellar even on her best day, and this wasn't one of them. She'd dated one player after another since moving to New York, even before her show, until she was so afraid of becoming jaded, she'd simply stopped dating. There was just something about Blake, something that made her want to try again, and that scared her because it had hurt when she'd thought he'd used her for ratings. Hurt more than it should have, which told her that he could possibly break her heart. Which was why she had to get control of the situation, and of herself.

So as soon as she and Blake had plates in front of them, she quickly picked up the conversation in comfortable territory. "Back to *Stepping Up*," she said. "I not only helped them find Rick, I also did some pre-screening of the dancers for the first season, including three that made the top ten. That's how this came about, how I got the job offer to be a judge."

"And now you're going to be working with Rick."

"Yeah," she said. "Now I get to work with that jerk."

He laughed. "I agree. He's a jerk. And I told him so after my show."

"So did I," she admitted with a smile.

"So you took his call but not mine?"

"He didn't call," she said, stabbing an egg with her fork. "I called him."

"But you wouldn't talk to me?"

"No," she said. "I wouldn't talk to you."

"I would have gladly let you call me a jerk to have the chance to explain what had happened."

And she would have let him explain, and would have forgiven him. Like she was now. The conversation continued, and more and more she laughed and relaxed. When finally their plates were gone, she had changed her tune about Blake, about where this was—or was not—going. They had one night and then she'd be flying from city to city, absorbed in filming the reality show. It wasn't as if this attraction could become anything more serious. There were really only two ways this flight could end: Darla in her room alone, or Darla in her room with Blake.

Tomorrow would be the same no matter what—they would be hundreds of miles apart. She wanted him. She wanted him like no other that she could ever remember. And she wasn't letting anything—including too many mimosas—get in her way. He might be a mirage, the wrong man once again hidden beneath hot, sexy perfection. But tonight, she decided right then and there, she was going to make him hers.

4

NEAR SEVEN IN THE EVENING, Blake and Darla stood in front of the arrivals terminal, waiting for their car, battling the chilly gusting Denver wind.

Blake inhaled the delicate floral scent of Darla's perfume, the feminine sweetness like whiskey warming his limbs. He rarely noticed a woman's perfume. But then, Darla wasn't just any other woman. He wasn't sure of the exact moment, sometime after she'd traded in her mimosas for coffee and before the bumpy landing, when she'd desperately clung to her seat and then momentarily to him, he'd realized she had, and still was, effortlessly seducing him.

"I can't believe I forgot it would be this cold already," Darla said, fighting an obvious shiver. "And I darn sure can't believe there isn't a cab to be found. This is an international airport. It's just strange."

"Mountain country gets cold at night by most standards, even during the summer. Will you be seeing your parents on this trip?"

"I wish," she added. "But they're tied up with the ranch and hours away. We're here and gone so fast I won't have the time." She motioned to a line of cabs rounding the corner.

"Looks like someone opened the flood gates," he commented.

A four-door black sedan pulled up at the curb in front of them and the driver quickly exited and spoke over the roof. "So sorry, Ms. James and Mr. Nelson. There's a traffic accident on the highway leading into the airport." He popped the trunk. "I'll put your bags in the back."

Blake reached for Darla's large suitcase—large as in the size of Texas. "You better let me get that for you." He rolled it to the rear of the vehicle and hefted it into the compartment. "Good gosh, woman. This thing weighs a ton. You might want to rethink such a huge bag for so much travel. Next time I won't be here."

She scoffed. "Only a man would suggest such a thing. I'm going to thirty cities and a girl needs good shoes to be on television." She grimaced. "There's a way to bring up bad memories."

Somehow, he was going to live down the past. "One of many reasons I'm glad I'm a man. Shoe choices are simple." He opened the back door for her and waved her in. "Ladies first."

She slid inside and Blake joined her. Again in close quarters with Darla, his blood thrummed with anticipation. Darla definitely gave him another reason to be happy he was a man right now.

"Might as well get comfortable, folks," the driver suggested. "We're a good forty-five minutes from down-town."

"Yikes," Darla said, glancing at her watch. "I was supposed to meet my producer for drinks at 8:30 p.m."

"Meagan Kellar?" Blake asked, confirming they were both talking about the show's creator, and whose husband was the studio's head of security.

"Yes," she said. "You, too?"

He nodded. "I doubt it will matter if we're late. It's probably a large group."

"Still," Darla said, clearly concerned, "maybe I should call her."

"Sorry to interrupt," the driver said. "But I did send a text message to Ms. Kellar when I arrived at the airport, per her request."

"Oh, excellent," Darla said. "Thank you so much."

Blake found her quick, polite response sincere and refreshing. She was like a cool drink of water in the midst of what had become the murky water of people with agendas, whether they be work-related or personal. He wasn't sure most people separated the two. Darla was who Darla was, untouched by success, free of airs and a big ego, and thankfully without fake niceties.

"You know," he said, "I'm glad you got mad at me when you first saw me in the airport."

She gave him an inquisitive look. "You're glad I got mad at you?"

"That's right," he said. "Nothing like someone who hates you smiling to your face and cursing you behind your back."

"Well, I don't hate you," she said, and then smiled, "Not since my second mimosa."

"And did that feeling remain intact after coffee number two?"

"Shockingly," she teased, "it did."

Darla's cell phone started to ring. "If we were at one of the Denver casinos, I'd bet you this is my mother calling." She glanced at the number and held up the screen. "My mother. She knows I hate to fly but then so does everyone after today, right?" Darla shook her head. "I have to get over that." She answered the call and he could hear her mother asking about her trip, how she was doing, what happened next. Darla glanced at Blake, a cute, playful expression on her face. And sexy. Damn, the woman was adorably sexy, which was not a combination he'd often come across. "Would you believe Blake Nelson is here?" she asked, continuing her conversation with her mother.

"What?" Blake heard her mother through the phone. "That jerk that made fun of you on cable television?"

Blake arched a brow and Darla laughed, her eyes dancing with mischief. "I don't know if I'd call him a jerk."

"You did call him a jerk," her mother said. "And with good reason."

"Yeah," she admitted. "I did call him a jerk but I was upset at the time." They talked a bit more and Darla hung up. "She's protective. So is my dad."

"I kind of gathered that." He settled against the door

to face her. "Have you revised your thoughts on me being a jerk?"

"I've decided not to judge the host by his guest," she teased, leaning on her door as well and studying him. "With caution, that is."

"What if I buy you dinner as a peace offering?"

She frowned. "My dinners are paid for by the show."

He laughed. "Okay, so that wasn't my best foot forward. What did you have in mind?"

Her brows furrowed. "My mom says she never wants anything that she doesn't come by honestly, and I live by that. I'm not suggesting anything."

"And my mother would say bring chocolate or don't come at all," he quipped. "But you brought your own."

"What would your father say?"

"Have you seen any of my father's visits on my show?"

She shook her head. "No. I didn't know your father visits your show. That's actually really amazing that you are close enough to him to have him on."

"Yeah, well, the audience loves him. He's an ex-rodeo bull rider who now runs a chain of rodeo-themed bars. My mother used to do promotional work for the rodeo. Now she does damage control for his big mouth. You'd never guess the man has a golden stock portfolio he handles himself, which he talks about on my show in a colorful way. *Which* is part of what makes my viewers love him. But we have to bleep him at least once every time he visits. In other words, if we're looking for advice on peace offerings, my father's suggestions would probably get me in hot water. Maybe we should stick with your mother's wise words."

"Well," she said, laughing, "I think your father sounds wonderful, but my mother does have one other piece of wisdom that seems fairly appropriate." Her eyes dazzled with a combination of mischief, mayhem and enough sizzling heat to set his seat—and him—on fire.

He was intrigued. "What would that be?"

She leaned closer, her red-tinged lush lips curved slightly upward. "You get what you give." He smiled at the suggestive words. She smiled back. "You'll have to use your imagination from there."

His imagination was well into overdrive, not needing a nudge one bit—in fact, it went as wild as he wanted to with her. "I should warn you that my imagination is about as active as my father's colorful words."

"Well then," she said approvingly, "I guess I better have big expectations." His cell phone chose that inopportune moment, when his blood was pumping hot, to ring. He grabbed it from his belt, intending to shut it up so he could get back to working his imagination, but no such luck. It was his producer.

"My producer," he told her, "who isn't happy that the studio brought me here without my crew." He answered the call and listened to a laundry list of notes for the next day's interviews. Then a long list of questions followed, one of which had him glancing at Darla and smiling. "What are my chances of getting an interview with Darla James? I'll get back to you on that."

He would most definitely regret letting what might be

a once-in-a-lifetime opportunity with Darla slip away—
but not the on-camera kind. The up-close-and-personal
and absolutely private kind.

"I'LL GIVE YOU AN INTERVIEW on one condition," Darla
said when Blake ended his call.

"Let me guess," he said, his blue eyes glinting humor
and intelligence. "You want to interview *me* for your
show? The whole 'you get what you give' concept,
right?"

"Now you're getting the idea," Darla said with approval. She still couldn't believe she had flirted so
openly with Blake. But to her surprise, she was incredibly comfortable with her now-past nemesis. "Besides,
I think it would be fun. Our audiences would eat it up."

"Here we are," the driver said, pulling into a hotel
parking lot.

Darla frowned. "I thought we were staying at the
Rocky Mountain Tower?"

"My apologies, ma'am," the driver said, glancing
in the mirror at her. "I thought you knew about the
change of plans. Apparently, the paparazzi are all over
the Tower, looking for the new judges. The studio felt
you'd have more privacy here, at least for the time being,
away from where the auditions are happening and where
the press won't be on your back."

"Oh," she said, not sure what to make of that. "Paparazzi?"

"You seem surprised," Blake said curiously. "The

ratings for *Stepping Up* were huge last season. You're about to walk into the middle of a hurricane."

"Yes, of course," she agreed, trying to sound calm. She didn't feel calm. The magnitude of this endeavor hit her like a ton of bricks. It could change her life, her family's life. She didn't want to blow this. She wasn't going to let them sell everything, or allow the ranch to be taken over by the bank, whichever came first. "That makes sense."

"'That makes sense'?" Blake repeated, nudging her. "Your choice of words says this isn't what you expected. And why do you now look like you want to be sick? What's wrong?"

She jerked her gaze to Blake's, realizing she'd been staring at the back of the driver's seat. "That obvious?"

"You're pretty transparent," Blake said as the driver parked the car.

Darla crinkled her nose. "I really need to work on that."

The driver opened her door. "Home sweet hotel," he said, waving her outside.

She glanced at Blake, trying to shake off her panic over the show, and gravely joked, "See you on the outside." She scooted out of the car and headed for the trunk, where Blake met her. And oh, was the man sexy, a handsome blend of rough-edged good looks and charming grace. If anyone could keep her mind off tomorrow's first day on camera, this man could.

"I'll get your bags to your rooms," the driver offered and handed them both small packets. She noted a number on the front of each. "These are your room keys, which work the elevator, as well. Your room numbers are on the envelopes. You'll both be going to floor eighteen. That's a private floor. And drinks with Ms. Kellar and her party will be in the lounge area of eighteen, as well."

Darla blinked at that. "Thank you. That's wonderful." Blake slid the man a tip and the driver gave them a quick formal bow before departing.

They entered the hotel and went directly to the bank of elevators. Blake punched the elevator button and checked an incoming text, quickly sending back a reply and then another, before putting away his phone. "You're not afraid of heights, are you? Eighteen is a fairly high floor."

She pursed her lips. "Not when there are windows and walls."

He chuckled. "No skydiving for you then?"

"Uh," she said, "No. No skydiving for me."

"Hmm," he murmured, giving her a thoughtful inspection that did nothing to diminish the heat in his gaze. "I think we should make a bet and if I win you go skydiving with me. There's plenty of gorgeous jump locations in Colorado."

"You did see me inside that plane, right?" she asked, giving him an appalled look. "I was the white-knuckled one who dug her fingernails into your hand, I held on so tight." The elevator doors opened.

He smiled. "I do seem to have a vague memory of fingernail-induced pain, but that's just all the more reason to face fear and conquer it. I promise you, once you skydive you'll be over the flying phobia."

She entered the empty car and he followed. "By jumping out of a plane? Are you now going to tell me that's how your mother got over her fear? What happened to the window shade theory?"

"I plead the fifth," he said, slipping his key card into a slot on the wall and punching the button for the eighteenth floor.

"There you go," she said decisively. "You didn't talk her into it and you won't talk me into it. No skydiving."

"You'll have a parachute in place. Besides, you don't even know what the bet is. You might win."

"I never make a bet I'm afraid to lose."

"You do know you get to pick the prize if you win."

The prize. Oh, yeah, she could think of some really interesting prizes. Like a thousand orgasms. She laughed mischievously, unable to stop herself. This was her opening, her way to make him hers for the night, if she could find the courage to be daring.

He shrugged. "Care to let me in on whatever that secret is? It looks worth knowing, based on your reaction."

"I was just thinking of what that prize might be." She'd almost been daring, but not quite. The butterflies in her stomach got the best of her.

"I'm guessing from your pleased little giggle that your prize most likely involves my embarrassment as payback for your shoe."

"I'm over the shoe," she assured him. "And I am not looking to embarrass you." But unbidden, an image of herself falling off her shoe and into Blake flashed in her mind. What if she was letting their short time together make her too trusting, too naive? The butt of a shoe joke was one thing. The butt of a bedroom joke could be truly career ending.

"The longer you're silent, the more curious I am," Blake said, prodding her to confess her naughty thoughts. And judging from the glint in his eyes, he had already guessed they were naughty.

"It really isn't important," she said, swallowing the lump forming in her throat. "Because I'm not making a bet that includes me jumping out of a plane. Besides, we have drinks with Meagan and the crew. There's no time for bets or anything else." Really? Had she really just said "or anything else"? The elevator doors opened. "Home sweet hotel," she said. "I want to change before we meet the others for drinks."

They stepped out into an elegant lobby area of red oriental carpets and impressive artwork. Her nerves tingled just thinking being in a hotel room she'd been fantasizing about for hours—or rather, a hotel room with Blake in it.

She glanced down at her key. "1835."

"I'm next door." He motioned toward the hallway that led to their rooms. "If you want to change, we better get moving."

They started down the hallway, her gaze traveling the luxurious corridor. "Hopefully our bags will arrive quickly." There was a nervous hitch in her voice that Blake couldn't ignore.

"You looked really stunned over the paparazzi issue. You do realize you're about to be a big star, don't you?"

"Don't say that," she chided quickly. "It's bad luck to assume success. And I don't care how popular season one was, season two could tank. Or I could tank. They could decide I'm too young or too old or too fat or too tall. Or I don't resonate with the audience or—"

"Worry much?" he asked her.

She let out a breath. "I excel at it, yes."

"You can't survive this business like that," he said. "You'll drive yourself insane." They stopped in front of her door and he motioned to it. "Just as I promised. I got you to your room safely, without being seen, and without taking advantage of you." He leaned against the door. "But no one said you can't take advantage of me."

Her desire burned a little brighter. "I'm not drunk."

"Are you giving me permission to take advantage of you?"

Blake's words *you can't live like that* resonated with her. She truly was a worrier, and she was about to let that worry cheat her out of a night with Blake. It was now or never.

A hallway door opened and Darla turned away, feeling like a child caught with her hand in the cookie jar. A bellman wheeled their bags forward from what appeared to be a service entrance.

"Saved by the bellman," Blake said, pushing off the wall.

Darla turned back to him, determined to salvage her "now or never" moment. "Who said I wanted to be saved?"

5

DARLA WATCHED HIS DARK EYES, full of understanding and desire. For her. This wasn't about television ratings or competition. It was just about a man and a woman, and she didn't remember the last time she'd let herself experience such a thing. Actually, she wasn't into strangers and casual sex, so she'd never done something like this. But then, Blake wasn't a stranger. Not really.

"Ms. James?" the bellman asked from behind her.

"Yes," she said, turning to greet the young man. "That's me. Thanks for being so quick." She stuck her key in her door.

"I'll just grab my bag myself," Blake told the kid, his attention capturing Darla's for a moment. She thought she might combust from heat if he spent the next few hours looking at her like that. Everyone was bound to notice, too. She gave him a warning glare.

Blake's lips hinted at a lift and his eyes danced with amusement. "Thanks for the promptness," he said to the kid, passing him a tip before he retrieved his bag.

He gestured toward the elevator. "I'll meet you here in twenty minutes, if that works?"

She swallowed hard. "Ah, yes. Sure." Was he serious or…?

He rolled his bag to his door.

Feeling more than a little out of sorts, she forced her attention from Blake and opened her door. The bellman carried her bag inside and she added to his tip. When all was said and done, the kid departed and Darla poked her head into the hallway. Blake was in his room, it appeared, his door firmly shut. She shut her own door and fell back against it. Was he being discreet or…*no!* She refused to believe Blake was playing her. She felt a connection with him, a level of comfort she never felt with another man so quickly, if ever. A knock sounded on the door and she jumped. The knock sounded again. Darla grabbed the door and pulled it open.

Blake stood there, tall and broad, still wearing his faded jeans and T-shirt, looking too sexy for her own good. "You gonna invite me in or leave me out here where someone might see me?"

"I have to get ready for drinks." She looked at her watch. "We have fifteen minutes."

"It was canceled," he said. "Now can I come inside?"

She backed up and let him in, fearful he would be seen and eager for an explanation. "What do you mean drinks are canceled? I didn't get a call."

He stepped inside and shut the door, sliding her lock into place and turning to face her. A mixture of hot man scent and some deliciously right cologne washed over her, overpowering her with a spike in awareness. Of the man. Of the bed behind her—that she wasn't going anywhere near until she knew what was going on.

"Meagan tried to call and text you, but apparently you don't have good reception in the mountains. They've had some security issues at the audition site." He leaned on the door as she had just moments before. "She had to cancel."

"Oh, no," Darla said, obviously alert, concerned. "What kind of security issues? We have to go and help out."

"Wait. There's more." He read from his cell phone. "Blake. When Darla offers to come over and help us— and since I know Darla well, she will—tell her I said no. Sam gets cranky when too many people get involved with his things. I suggest both of you just get some rest and we'll see you in the morning." He glanced up at her.

"My God, she typed you a full memo in text message."

"Yeah, she did," he agreed. "But our bottom line here is that there is no meeting and no drinks with Meagan." He reached for her and pulled her against him, his hand sliding down her back, molding her to his long, hard body. Her thighs pressed to his, her hips melded to his, making the thick ridge of his erection more than evident. "So, instead of a bet," he murmured, "how about we negotiate more of a deal?"

"I'm not sure why that's different but I'm not skydiving." Her hands settled on his chest, his impressively hard chest, and warmth seeped into her palms. She couldn't believe she was doing this, that this was really happening, that she wasn't even trying to talk herself out of it. "Just for the record, if at any point before you leave this room and I tell you I will skydive, don't believe me. I won't be responsible for saying it. If you can live with that, then I want to know what your 'deal' is."

"The idea that I might get you to agree, even if you change your mind later, isn't a bad one." He laughed. "But no skydiving. This is the 'deal.' For the rest of the night, if I can't make you forget to worry about tomorrow morning, then my father will go on your show. I'll give him the thumbs-up to embarrass the hell out of me, and believe me, not only will he do so and do it well, he'll enjoy every second. My father revels in that kind of stuff. But if I succeed, then you give me my interview and we talk about the shoe incident and clear the air in the same public way this war started."

"That's big Texas talk and big Texas demands, if I ever heard them."

His hand traveled a path up her back, to her neck, under her hair. "Sweetheart, talking isn't what I have on my mind." His bent toward her, his mouth a breath from hers, tickling her lips and so much more with promise. "Do we have a deal?"

If it was going to get him to kiss her, and sooner rather than later, oh, yeah, they did. "Sure," she said. "We have a dea—" His mouth closed down on hers before she ever got the final word out.

BLAKE HAD INTENDED TO START slowly with Darla, to start with tender, seductive kisses, before exploring every inch of her sleek, sexy body. Intended but failed. She wrapped her arms around his waist, her lush breasts pressing against his chest. And once again, when he'd have sworn it was no longer possible for a woman to do so, Darla seduced him, not the other way around. The instant Blake had set eyes on her again in the New York airport, and ten times over since, she controlled him without even trying. He was charmed by her, intrigued by her, and he was lost in the touch of her soft, yielding lips beneath his.

He deepened the kiss, his hand caressing her heart-shaped backside, which he'd admired more than a few times during this trip. A delicate, erotic little sound of her pleasure unraveled him, ripping through him like rocket fuel. Fuel for a simmering desire he'd been holding back, since the moment she'd fallen off her broken shoe and into his arms. Hell, he'd not touched another woman since, and now he knew why. He was tired of settling for sating a male urge, rather than truly feeling something beyond simple, short-lived lust. Finally, someone had made him feel something real, something worth staying for, something worth experiencing.

He turned her so that she was against the wall, his legs framing hers, his hands gliding over her waist to her breasts. His teeth scraped her bottom lip. "What are you thinking about?"

"You," she added in a teasing voice, "and tomorrow morning when I begin the biggest career move of my life. So I'd say you still have some work to do to uphold your end of our 'deal.'"

"Now you're just being bad." But dang, he liked it. His gaze held hers, his thumbs brushing over her nipples pebbled against her thin T-shirt. She bit her lip, her face etched with pleasure. "And I'm clearly not doing this bet service if you can mock me so easily."

"I thought it was a deal," she said, "not a bet."

"Deal," he conceded, shoving her shirt upward, then pulling it over her head and tossing it behind him. His gaze fell to her breasts, to the bra that, somehow, so fit her. "I knew it would be pink."

She crinkled her nose at him. "You did not. And if you did, you shouldn't have been thinking of my bra in the first place."

"No?" he asked, pulling it down to tease her pretty rose-colored nipples. "I'll be better next time."

"There won't be a next time," she said breathlessly, her teeth scraping over her bottom lip. "We're competitors. We don't belong in bed together and this is against my better judgment."

He glanced at her. "Yet I'm here."

"We have one night and then we're worlds apart," she agreed. She leaned into him, her hand sliding down his crotch, caressing the hard ridge of his erection. "I wasn't going to let that pass me by, but we better make this count. There's no do-over."

They weren't competitors. Her career was going places he'd long ago decided he didn't want to go, but to tell her that would only remind her of the pressure she was under, and that would defeat the entire purpose of their "deal." "I plan on making it count," he said and placed his hand over hers, over his pulsing erection. "Just as I plan on making you forget anything but how *bad* I can be." He turned her around to face the wall.

"Blake—" The objection died on her tongue as she tried to turn and he stopped her.

"Stay where you're at," he ordered. His hands settled on her waist, his cock against her backside.

"I want—"

"To be in control," he finished for her, leaning into her. He pressed his lips to her ear, even as one hand popped her bra clasp. "And sweetheart, if that's what you want, I'm all yours. But you know what I think?" He slid the bra straps forward until she shrugged out of them, then filled his palms with her breasts, his teeth nibbling her lobe. "You'll overthink what that means. You'll worry that you aren't doing it right. You'll worry that I'm like the studio and wonder if I think you're too young or too old, or too something, when all I'm thinking—" he turned her back around, wanting her to see the truth in his eyes "—is how damn perfect you are and how damn lucky I am to be with you tonight." And he meant that. This wasn't just about their obvious physical attraction. Somehow he had to show her that.

"Blake." This time his name was a whisper rather than a command, her voice and her lovely features etched with vulnerability.

"Believe me," he said, brushing a silky strand of hair behind her ear, knowing he had to earn her trust. "And, Darla. What happens here stays here. I just want to make sure you know that. This is our time, our experience and our secret." He dipped his head, brushed his mouth over hers. "You have my word." His fingers trailed over her jaw, her neck, over one of her nipples. His gaze swept over her body, then lifted. Their eyes collided, the air sexually charged. One minute they were staring at one another, the next, they were kissing, touching, her soft hands sliding under his shirt, pushing it upward.

Blake tugged it over his head and before he even tossed it away, her mouth was on his chest, her teeth grazing his nipple, her fingers working the button on his jeans. Had any woman ever felt this good? Every inch of his body was aware of her. He wondered what she was thinking, what she was feeling beyond desire.

"No, sweetheart," he groaned, capturing her hand before she worked the zipper down. "Not yet. I want you way too much to rush this, and I'll be damned if I let you get away from me without making sure you remember tonight." And that she would give him a chance for another night, which he was pretty damn sure wasn't going to come easy and he already knew he wanted. She might justify their bedroom adventure as here and gone, but he wouldn't be here if that's what this was, if there wasn't more to this. She pushed to her toes and kissed him, and the instant her tongue touched his, he was a goner. He lost himself in the honey-sweet taste of her, the feel of her skin against his. Quickly, she unzipped his jeans and pressed her hand inside his boxers, her slender fingers wrapping around his shaft. Blake moaned and pulled away from her, squatting to help her take off her boots. He had to slow things down, otherwise it would be a "wham, bam, thank you ma'am" experience that he was certain as Sunday would haunt him the rest of his life.

"Now, where were we?" he said, her boots gone now, and his, too. He ran his hands up her legs as he stood, to settle on her hips. "Oh, yeah. We were talking about how you'd agreed that I'm in control so you can just relax and let me take you away."

"We didn't agree to anything of the sort," she said, swallowing hard as he worked the front of her jeans.

"Pretend." He tugged her jeans down and noticed the blond triangle of neatly trimmed curls that came into view. He glanced down and then up, and playfully tried to put her at ease. "No underwear?"

"I don't like panty lines," she said, stepping out of her pants without hesitation.

"Of course," he said, wrapping his arm around her to comfort her. "I hate panty lines." He gently tweaked her nipples, then soothed them with his thumbs.

"Aren't you the funny man?" There was a breathless quality to her voice that told him he was getting to her, and he liked it. He liked it a lot.

"It's not my intention to be funny," he assured her, kicking her jeans aside. "In fact, why don't I show you just how seriously I'm taking your pleasure right now?" He dropped to one knee, settling his hands on her hips. "Do I seem like I'm trying to be funny?"

She wet her lips. "No. *Funny* isn't the word that comes to mind."

He pressed his lips to her stomach. "Then what word comes to mind?" He kissed her again then ran his tongue around her belly button. Her belly quivered. The vulnerability it showed made his chest expand, tighten. She was like a delicate flower, and a sense of protectiveness toward her surprised him. He didn't want to keep her at a distance, which defied everything he'd taught himself about self-preservation. He glanced up at her, aware she'd yet to reply. "What are you thinking?"

"Am I supposed to be thinking right now?"

He smiled against her stomach, pleased with that answer. If she wasn't thinking, she was letting go; she was trusting. "Not if I can help it." He slid his fingers into the slick heat of her sex, his cock pulsing at the intimate touch.

She made a soft sound, squeezing her thighs around his hand. "We really should move to the bed before I fall down."

"I won't let you fall," he promised, his lips traveling over her soft, silky skin, his teeth grazing her sexy hip bone, the curve of her waist.

"If you keep doing what you're doing," she whispered, "I'm not sure you can stop me."

His fingers delved past the slick folds of her sex. He sought the sweet spot he knew would drive her wild. And he wanted to drive her wild. He wanted to see her let go of her control, to relinquish her prim and proper persona fully—for him, with him. "I want to taste you, Darla." He lifted one of her legs over his shoulder, his fingers explored her more intimately, his thumb flickering over her clit. "Any objection?" He leaned in and licked her clit, glancing up at her, arching a brow.

"You don't really expect me to say 'no,' do you?"

He chuckled, licking her again and again until she gasped and her head fell back against the wall, her dark lashes sweeping her ivory cheeks. Blake suckled her swollen nub, stroking her with his fingers, still seeking that sweet spot that would drive her wild. He knew he'd found it when she moaned deeply and laced her fingers into his hair. The more he licked, the more he delved and stroked and teased, the firmer her fingers tightened on his hair. She rocked her hips, pumping against his fingers. He felt her stiffen, heard her suck in a breath. She went still—and he knew she was on the edge ready to tumble, one lick away from orgasm. He suckled her instead, drawing out her pleasure, then swirled his tongue around her nub. Her hands flattened on the wall a moment before her body jerked, hips lifting against him. Spasms spiraled around his fingers. His body reacted instantly, his cock a hard ridge against his stomach, ready for her the next time she came.

His cell phone started to vibrate on his belt, but he didn't think he'd care if the fire alarm was going off right now. He was too into Darla, too into her honeysuckle-sweet taste, her scent, her perfect ivory body. Her satisfaction. That was the ultimate turn-on, the ultimate goal, and Blake went after it with the fierceness of a wild animal. He wanted it, he had to have it. Nothing but her complete, utter satisfaction would do. And so he licked and caressed her to a simmering slow down until she inhaled deeply, as if she'd forgotten to breathe, and that breath brought her back to reality.

She blinked down at him, her cheeks flushed red, her bottom lip swollen from his kisses. "That was…" she started, her voice trailing off, her teeth working her bottom lip.

"A warm-up," he promised, kissing the inside of her thigh and easing her leg over his shoulder and her foot back to the ground. "We're only just getting started." He pushed to his feet, palming her backside and lifting her.

She made a surprised sound and hung on to him, her arms holding tight around his neck and her legs around his waist. He went down on the bed on top of her, the feel of her beneath him a tiny piece of heaven. "I have to warn you," he confessed, "you've got me right on the edge, sweetheart, and my slow romancing is about to explode into fast and hard if we aren't careful."

"Fast and hard sounds good right now," she said, again proving she wasn't all about prim and proper. "But you said it yourself. Talk is cheap and you're still wearing your pants."

His cell phone vibrated on his belt again and her eyes went wide. "Is that your phone?"

"Yes," he said. "And whoever it is can wait." He slanted his mouth over hers, claiming her. She whimpered, her tongue searching for his, her hands gripping his back. One of her legs entangled his as if she feared he'd get away. He wasn't going anywhere. His phone vibrated again. Ignoring it with Darla underneath him and her hands all over his body wasn't hard. Hell. He couldn't even manage to pull himself away from her long enough to fully undress. She tasted of honey, felt like sunshine.

He spread her legs wider and sank deeper between them. Arching against her sex, his hands explored her body.

"Please," she whispered. "Take off those damn pants before I scream in frustration."

"One more kiss," he said. Just then, the hotel phone started to ring. Blake went still. He burned to kiss her into oblivion and ignore the call, but he couldn't. Not when his phone had been going off and hers wasn't getting a good mountain signal. He was so frustrated, the last thing he wanted was to make her feel second to anybody in that moment. "As much as I don't want you to, you have to get that. It could be the studio." He rolled off her and grabbed his phone, checking his text messages. "It's Meagan. She wants us to meet her for drinks after all."

Darla scrabbled for the nightstand. Blake turned to find her grabbing the phone and giving him an alluring view of her creamy white backside. The one he'd had pressing into his palms a few minutes ago. The one he had a feeling wasn't going to be pressed into his palms again tonight.

"Yes, hi, Meagan," Darla said, sitting up and looking over her shoulder at him. "I'm not sure about Blake. His phone must be having signal issues, too." She frowned. "I'll go knock on his door. Sure. Yes. I'll meet you in twenty minutes." She hung up the phone. "I can't believe this is happening."

Blake grabbed her and pulled her back into his arms. Damn, she felt good, and he didn't want to let her go. "And I can't believe I had you naked and never even managed to get my pants off. You're going to regret this as soon as we leave this room, aren't you?"

"Of course I am," she said, her words giving him an unexpected jab in his chest until she added, "What kind of woman can't get a man's pants off?" She pressed her lips to his. "And now I'm going to be thinking of how to do it the entire time we're with Meagan."

"And even if I buy that, which I don't, I know where this is headed. Our one night just ended."

"Well," she said, barely giving him a pebble of hope. "It could be fast and everyone says good-night."

"More likely," he said unhappily, "it'll stretch into hours when everyone should be in bed resting. Except you. You should be in bed with me."

She laughed. "That was my plan, in case you hadn't noticed." She ran her fingers over his jaw. "Thank you for making sure I didn't miss that call when you could have easily distracted me from it."

He drew her fingers to his lips. "I better leave or I won't let you get dressed." He started to get up.

"Wait." She grabbed his arm. "What if you're seen leaving my room? Sounds like there's show personnel already going. We're competitors, Blake. If my station finds out that we, ah... Well, it could jeopardize my show. The studio might think I have your interests, not theirs, in mind."

"Things would have to go horribly bad for you in all kinds of nearly impossible ways for that to happen, and they won't." She started to object and he held up a hand. "But I understand you're worried and I'll be discreet. Complain about your phone service and tell everyone I stopped by to make sure Meagan was able to reach you. That way, if anyone sees me leave, you have an explanation."

"Right," she said. "Good thinking."

He glanced down at her bare breasts and back up. "I wasn't kidding about not letting you get dressed."

She tugged up the comforter and slid underneath, then smiled. "Go, before I don't let you, and that would be very bad."

"Or very good, depending on how you look at it." She started to object and he leaned in and kissed her. "I'm leaving."

He pushed to his feet and searched for his shirt, finding it in the hallway. He tugged it over his head and quickly put on his boots before hesitating at the door. He didn't want to leave and that said a lot, when he normally couldn't run from a woman's door fast enough. Of course, they'd had a premature finish, but still... he wasn't ready to walk away from Darla. Not until he understood what she was doing to him. He resisted the urge to back up and tell her exactly that, or at least frame a plan to end up here after tonight. Dang it, Darla was making him feel every bit the primal man. Some part of him wanted to declare her "mine." That thought rattled him to the core, and he reached for the door. A cold shower and some stern self-reprimanding were in order—and fast.

6

DARLA SAT ON THE MATTRESS, unsure of what had just happened. He'd left. He'd had no choice. He'd even said he didn't want to leave. But yet, he had, and they'd made no plans for what came next. Did anything come next? Probably it shouldn't. Darla liked Blake. She liked him a lot—too much, in fact. History told her that was trouble, especially with a man who'd been trouble in the past. She shook herself, realizing that she should be showering and dressing, but was thinking about Blake when she should be thinking about her job. Grimacing at the man's ability to distract her, she shoved away the comforter and rushed to the bathroom.

Fifteen minutes later, she'd managed a superfast shower, changed into a clean, dressier pair of jeans and a pale pink blouse. Her hair had been a wild mess, compliments of Blake's hands. But thanks to a hot iron, her hair was now smooth and orderly. Her makeup had been reapplied, the whisker burns covered. His whisker burns—Blake Nelson's whiskers. They had felt really good on about every part of her body. How in the heck was she going to face him in a group of people and act like he hadn't just rocked her world? She didn't want Meagan or anyone else to think she wasn't focused on her job.

She grabbed the small pink beaded purse she'd unpacked, filled it and crossed the strap over her head and shoulder, before making her way to the hallway. Darla glanced at Blake's door. Should she knock? What would she do if the man hadn't just been half-naked with her? That was pretty hard to think through when being naked with him was pretty darn heavy on her mind—so was every flirtatious second leading up to her being naked. But prior to tonight she'd considered him her competitor—even her enemy. Yet she'd bonded with him on the plane and they had become friends. She didn't give herself time to reconsider. Darla rushed to his door and knocked, then nervously looked around. Which was absolutely crazy. They'd flown into town together. They could walk to drinks together. She knocked again, more confidently this time, but he didn't answer. He wasn't in his room. He'd left *without* knocking on her door. Okay. So she wasn't sure what to make of that. The worrier in her could conjure all kinds of trouble that she didn't need right now.

Darla started walking toward the lounge area, her stomach suddenly fluttering with renewed nerves, which she tried to squash. The process of said squashing wasn't going well, and by the time she stood at the door of the lounge, she was worse, not better. But when she entered the room, she realized the show was on. A group of about twelve, maybe even fifteen, of the show's staff sat around a group of tables shoved together in the center of an oval-shaped room. Her gaze moved past the tables, drawn to the ceiling-to-floor windows and the view beyond that, which mesmerized, even calmed, her. The sun and mountains had faded into a pitch-black sky decorated with twinkling stars and city lights.

"Darla!" Meagan called, waving her forward. Her light brown hair fell haphazardly from a pile on top of her head, her jeans and T-shirt were casual and comfortable. The big burly blond man next to Meagan stood, as well, and Darla assumed him to be Meagan's new husband. Evidently, he'd used his role as head of studio security to ensure he was the man watching over his wife and her show. Darla found this endearing and romantic.

Seeing Meagan again dissolved what was left of Darla's nerves. Meagan wasn't a big bad studio person. She might be Darla's new boss, but she was also one of the nicest people she'd ever met. Someone she knew could blossom into a close friend.

Darla rushed forward, and was soon trapped in Meagan's warm hug. "I can't believe you're here." She leaned back. "Isn't it crazy how both of our lives have changed in such a short time?" They'd met during the casting of the first season of the show and quickly bonded. Like Darla, who'd started out in casting and become a camera personality, Meagan had taken an unexpected path, from injured dancer to producer of a reality dance show.

Affection filled Darla and she paused to look at Meagan. "I can't tell you how much it means that you made this happen for me. I'm not going to let you down."

"I know that or you wouldn't be here," Meagan assured her. "I really wanted to make drinks happen so you could meet your fellow judges before the first audition. But before I introduce you to everyone, I have to warn you, Darla, last season, we didn't have anyone but our own crew and a few local press people on hand for the auditions. We couldn't even get a good showing for the contestants. There are people who have been camped out for a full day already. This season is already chaotic but we have plenty of talent this time."

Darla grinned. "I'll be the judge of that." Auditions had gone so poorly last season that Darla had personally set up some additional New York tryouts, where a bulk of the cast had been found.

Meagan grinned back at her. "Exactly why you're here. But consider yourself warned. It's going to be a wild ride the next few weeks."

"She's not kidding," Sam said, offering Darla his hand. "Sam Kellar. Nice to finally meet you, and good thing we did it tonight. Something tells me I'm going to be on duty around the clock from here on out."

"So nice to finally meet you, too," Darla said, accepting his hand. "I guess the security threat is over now?"

He scrubbed his jaw. "We had some contestants get into a fight outside the hotel."

"Needless to say," Meagan added, "those individuals won't be auditioning. I don't like trouble or scandal. I'm trying to keep this show more *American Idol* than

Jersey Shore. After last season, I know all too well that once we start filming the reality portion of the show that's incorporating the contestant house, it'll be a pipe dream to avoid."

Meagan motioned to the chair in front of Darla. "I saved you a seat so we could chat. Let's eat, drink and drink some more—God, don't I wish I could do that, but morning will be here soon enough." Meagan and Sam sat down, and Darla grabbed her chair, looking across the table for the first time. That's when her gaze froze, her eyes colliding with the wicked heat of Blake's sexy blue stare.

"Glad you made it," he said, a twinkle of mischief in his eyes.

"We were starting to worry you might have fallen asleep," Meagan teased. "But Blake said you drank a pot of coffee on the plane."

"I did," Darla said, easing into her chair and wondering what else Blake had said exactly, and from the look on his face he not only knew it, he was enjoying it. "And since I fly horribly, Blake felt the full wrath of me on a caffeine and fear high. But then, he's my competitor, so who better to torture but him?"

Meagan laughed and waved a finger between the two of them. "That's right. You two have a little baggage of your own, don't you?"

"We did," Blake said. "But she forgave me."

Darla crinkled her nose, wondering why she was looking at his mouth. Oh, yeah, she knew why. It had been all over her body, which was a very bad thing to think about right now. "I didn't actually forgive you." Okay, maybe. Almost. If they'd had just a bit longer alone.

"We made a deal, though, Darla, remember?" Blake asked.

Her mouth gaped. "What?" He wouldn't. He couldn't. She'd trusted him, and that meant he probably would.

"Hi, Darla. So good to see you again."

Darla cringed at the greeting and not just because of the timing. She'd already noticed who was sitting on Blake's left and it was all Darla could do to force her gaze from Blake to the source of the greeting. Lana Taylor was the gorgeous, twentysomething Broadway star with trademark long red hair and pale, perfect skin, who was a second season judge. She'd also acted like a mean diva to Darla's staff during a guest spot on her show, post *Stepping Up* season one. Darla wondered if she regretted her behavior now. The world was always smaller than people thought. Then again, Lana was the mean judge on the show—mean just seemed to be a part of her character.

"Hi, Lana," Darla said, leaving off the "nice to see you again" because Darla tried really hard to stay sincere in a business that tended toward the opposite direction. Her gaze drifted back to Blake's, to his clean-shaven jaw. The skin of her stomach and leg tingled where that stubble had grazed her earlier, taunting her with how intimately exposed she was to this man, and this table, if he chose to betray her.

"Nice to meet you, Darla."

Darla inhaled and greeted another judge sitting to Lana's left. Jason Alright was a sexy thirtysomething Vegas producer who'd been a favorite of the viewers' last season, especially with the female audience.

The fourth and final judge was Ellie Campbell, who was about Darla's age and one of the hottest choreographers in the business. Ellie, who had pink hair tonight, was known for frequent, unique hair color choices and hip street-style clothing. She sat at the far end of the table, but quickly appeared at Darla's side to offer a friendly introduction. Darla liked Ellie instantly and as Jason joined the conversation, she found him quite likable, as well. Everyone got along with Blake, she noticed.

A number of crew members chimed their greetings to Darla. There were some friendly, familiar faces Darla was glad to see. And she told herself this distraction was good. There was no time, or room, for Blake to fit in more about their "deal." But she'd fit it in all right. She and Blake were going to have a good heart-to-heart, sooner rather than later.

"I'm so excited to see you again," Lana continued after everyone settled back into their own conversations. "You went from casting to your own show. Impressive, Darla. You're rocking showbiz."

It was a sticky-sweet compliment lacking sincerity and laced with a chill. "And on that note," Darla said, feeling the ball and chain of performance pressure tugging at her, she lifted her hand to flag a waiter. "Can I get a dessert menu?"

"What about dinner?" Blake asked.

She gave him a pointed look. "I have a sudden urge to go straight to the heavy stuff."

"The camera adds ten pounds," Lana sweetly reminded them.

"Good thing tonight will only be worth about a pound of that ten," Darla said, accepting a menu from the waiter. "Because I fully intend to indulge."

"I said it earlier," Blake chimed in. "And I'll say it again. I'm so glad I'm a man. We really don't give a damn about a pound or ten."

He'd changed his shirt to a dark blue collar tee with a studio logo and he wore it like he wore the room— casual and comfortable. He had this cool air of confidence about him that screamed of being comfortable in his own skin, never rattled or out of his element, and she envied him that.

"What did I say that merited an urgent request for dessert?" Lana asked, laughing. "Surely, you aren't nervous. You have a show and an audience of your own."

Darla could play coy and cool with Lana, but that just wasn't her style. "I have a show and an audience," she agreed. "But not a prime time show with millions and millions of viewers. That audience is going to expect this season to be better than the last, and with me being the newbie, I'll be under the microscope."

"And hearing you talk about the viewers wanting this season to be better than the last makes me want a big fat dessert, too," Meagan said, nudging Darla's menu closer so that she could see what was on offer. "I keep thinking that what goes up must come down and we have to get off the ride before it does. Go out gracefully, with style, and on our own terms. And with some reality show kind of twist."

"Hearing you talk about the program ending is only making me more worried," Darla said. "At least your job is secure."

"Oh, please," Meagan pleaded. "You'll be great and everyone will love you."

"We hope," Darla replied. "We both know there is no certainty in this business."

"You two are not good for each other," Blake said, moving a finger between Meagan and Darla and then lifting his chin at Sam. "I just spent hours on a plane with Darla from New York and she freaks herself out enough. Together, it's clear that they are dangerous to each other's sanity."

"And everyone around them," Sam readily agreed.

"We need to have Darla and Lana change seats," Blake suggested, "so there's some distance between Darla and Meagan."

Was he really trying to jockey for her to sit next to him? And did he really think that wasn't obvious? Darla gave Blake an incredulous look and kicked him under the table.

"Ouch!" Lana screamed. "Someone just kicked me." She rubbed her leg. "Who did that?"

Darla's eyes went wide. Blake burst out laughing. Meagan looked between Darla and Blake, then to Lana, and immediately turned to her husband. "Sam," Meagan scolded. "I told you to be careful with those big, long legs of yours."

Oh, thank you, Meagan! But Blake barked more laughter, and the rest of the group was looking their way. Darla considered kicking him again, only she hadn't kicked him in the first place, so for safety's sake, she settled for a glower and a silent promise that she was going to kill him. He laughed louder. "Stop laughing!" Lana ordered Blake. "It hurts."

"I'm so sorry, Lana," Meagan said, squeezing Darla's leg under the table, telling her she knew darn well who had kicked Lana. Meagan eyed her husband. "Sam. Apologize."

"I didn't—" Sam grunted, and Darla had a feeling Sam had just gotten pinched or kicked himself "—mean to," Sam finished. "I didn't mean to kick you, Lana. I'll be more careful. Sorry about that."

Lana scowled at poor Sam. "Remind me not to sit next to you. I'm going to have a giant bruise."

"Yeah," Sam said. "Sorry again." His gaze slid curiously between Blake and Darla. "I think I want to hear about this deal—*ouch*." He grimaced at Meagan. "Would you stop that?"

Darla's heart leaped. She couldn't speak and couldn't breathe for that matter.

The deal was about to be exposed.

7

"DEAL?" BLAKE ASKED IN REPLY to Sam, but his attention stayed on Darla a moment before flickering to the other man. "Did I say deal? I meant truce. Darla has agreed to forgive me for our past 'incident' for the good of the show. Rick is on his own, though. Where is he, by the way?"

"I don't remember saying that I forgave you," Darla said and eyed Meagan. "And yes. Where is Rick? I'm looking forward to giving him a nice warm greeting."

"He's doing a charity baseball game and won't arrive until late tonight," Meagan said and pursed her lips. "And you better behave when he arrives. You promised me you two would play nice."

"Of course," Darla assured her. "I just want to have a little one-on-one chat with him to make sure I don't become the brunt of any more of his attention-grabbing schemes."

"I already tackled that," Meagan promised, lowering her voice. "Rick knows I'm trying to keep this a top-quality talent show, not an extension of a tabloid."

"Which, as Meagan mentioned," Sam added, "is a tough task once you get six young men and women in a contestant house for eight weeks. The cameras are rolling, the hormones are high, and the weekly live competitions and eliminations are always hanging in the air. But Meagan and I learned from last season. We're determined to run things better this year."

"Even if the studio doesn't believe they're better," Meagan commented. "They love scandal because they think it equals ratings when, in reality, it's our ability to appeal to families that gets us powerful advertisers we'd lose in the long run if we tainted our image. It amazes me that the suits are so blinded by short spikes in numbers, rather than the big picture. Yet, they'll cut us in a heartbeat if I let their strategy dominate the show and it fails."

"Back to the topic of Darla and Rick," Blake said. "The press is absolutely going to try and stir up their past conflict. It's what they do—stir the pot. So even if you talked to Rick, they're going to bait him and Darla, and they'll likely make stuff up if that doesn't work."

Meagan sighed. "I assumed as much."

"Yeah, I know, which is why I say I interview Darla and Rick together tomorrow and address the past then, where I can control the outcome. We'll be able to shut down all speculation and rumor because all three of us will be together." Blake gave Darla a quick nod. "I'll cut extra footage that you can use exclusively on your show and some on mine. Then we both win. Everyone wins."

"It's a good plan," Sam agreed quickly. "We then head off at least one story the press will be chasing and maybe stop one headache."

It *was* a good plan, Darla thought, and she actually found herself wondering if she'd wanted an excuse to see him again all along, that tonight had never been about just one night. Good grief, she was so clearly not good at handling men. "How do you feel about the idea?" Meagan asked, studying Darla.

"How do *you* feel about it?" Darla asked.

"I think it's a good idea," Meagan said. "If you're okay with it."

Darla nodded and glanced at Blake. "But I want us to talk to Rick in advance. I want to know what's going to come out of his big mouth before he says it."

"Expected and understood," Blake agreed, gaze raking her face. "Now I just have to convince you to do a full interview on my show before I have to head back to New York."

It felt as if her stomach had done a somersault, which set off all kinds of warning bells. She couldn't risk a bad judgment call—a misstep tonight that might hurt her contract over something that was going nowhere. He clearly had an agenda and she was part of that agenda. His deal had conveniently been made when she'd been distracted. By his hands. His mouth. His body.

She shook off those thoughts, focused on her own agenda—saving her parents' ranch. "You come on my show."

"I'll come on your show, if you come on mine."

"So now we're back to deals, are we?" she challenged without thinking—a behavior he seemed to incite in her—and cringed for what she might have given away.

His lips twitched and he leaned forward, elbows on the table, his voice soft. "Why don't we call it a 'truce with benefits'?"

"Oh, how funny," Lana said. "That's a play on that movie *Friends with Benefits* where Justin Timberlake and Mila Kunis try to keep friendship and sex separate. Never works, by the way. I've tried." She wiggled an eyebrow. "But sounds like fun anyway. How do I sign up?"

This was so turning into a disaster, Darla chided herself. "Fine," she said to Blake, leaving Lana out of the equation. "We'll show-swap, but let's figure out the details later. I'm having trouble thinking past tomorrow right now."

"Maybe talking out the details will get your mind *off* tomorrow," he suggested smoothly, and she knew he wasn't talking about "talking" at all.

"I don't think so." She shook her head. "The night is short and morning is coming early."

"You sure about that?"

"Absolutely." *Not.* But she should be.

The waiter appeared. "Ready to order?"

Meagan wrapped her arm around Darla's shoulders. "You know what I'm thinking? Let's get room service in your room where Sam won't be so we can do the girl-talk thing before the season starts. I've spent time with everyone else. I want to spend some time with you."

Regret filled Darla as "absolutely not" became an

instant "absolutely yes." She was now absolutely certain that there would be no her and Blake tonight. She wanted to finish what they had started—wanted it maybe a little too much.

AN HOUR LATER, DARLA AND Meagan sat in their sweats and sock feet on Darla's bed with a selection of desserts spread out before them.

"I can't believe we have this many to choose from," Darla said, scooping a bite of a brownie covered with hot fudge. She moaned with pleasure. "This might be a ten camera-pound splurge."

"Hmm," Meagan said, digging her fork into a piece of cheesecake. "While I'm never gonna be the diva *some* people associated with the show have become, I do enjoy a splurge here and there." She took a bite and then added, "So…what was up with you and Blake tonight?"

Darla's heart raced and she busied herself with the carrot cake. "What do you mean?"

Meagan gaped. "You tried to kick the man." She snorted. "I died when you kicked Lana. That was hilarious. Lana plays that villainous role well and she eats it up. We all, audience included, love to hate her. If only we could have gotten that on camera."

Darla started laughing. She and Meagan had talked about Lana way back during the casting of season one. "That kick did work out pretty well, but poor Sam. You made him take the rap for me."

Meagan shrugged. "I'll make it up to him later. But

seriously. What's up with you and Blake? I might be married but I'm not blind. The man is easy on the eyes."

Darla stabbed the brownie. "And infuriating, and arrogant, and just so— The man made me want to kick him under the table. That should say it all. He makes me crazy."

"Uh-oh," Meagan said, and grinned. "That's what Sam did to me."

"Oh, no," Darla said quickly. "No. Blake and I are nothing like you and Sam."

Meagan just smiled.

"You don't understand," Darla objected. "I attract all the wrong men. That makes Blake another one of the wrong men."

"Or you choose all the wrong men, like I did," Meagan said, "until the right man steps into your path, like Sam did mine. Then, like Sam also did to me, that right man infuriates you right into love."

Darla shook her head. "I'm not you. Blake is not Sam. And besides, Blake leaves tomorrow." So he wouldn't be infuriating her into bed or into love. *Love.* That was a silly word for her or Meagan to use, one of fairy tales women created over too many drinks or, in this case, too much sugar. She and Blake were oil and water, and people who were oil and water had sex. They did not fall in love.

Meagan just sat there, smiling coyly.

Darla tried again. "Blake and I are not happening. We're competitors. He upsets me. He leaves tomorrow."

Meagan grinned. "Okay."

Frustrated, Darla stabbed the brownie again and took a bite, but she didn't want the brownie. She wanted Blake—which infuriated her all the more. She ate the entire brownie, half the cheesecake and a few bites of several other desserts. And then she blamed Blake for the ten camera-pounds she was going to imagine she had in the morning.

BLAKE DIDN'T THINK MEAGAN would ever leave, but the instant he heard Darla's door open and shut and he knew she'd gone, he dialed Darla's room. Sitting at that lounge table with Darla tonight, he'd done nothing but fall deeper for her. And no, he wasn't going to her room tonight, he knew that. Not because he doubted she would let him, but because he wanted to so damn bad. Because that meant something, and he'd decided she interested him far more than would last one night.

"Hello?" she said in that soft, ever-feminine voice, her tone making it more of a question than a greeting.

"How was dessert?" he asked, lying back on his pillow.

"Better without dodging your bullets at the table," she said. "What's with the 'deal' talk and the 'truce with benefits'?"

"If I'd have known it would have gotten me kicked," he said, chuckling, "I would have controlled myself."

"So not true," she accused. "The 'truce with benefits' comment came after I tried to kick you."

"So you admit you tried to kick me then?"

"Absolutely."

"You're big on the 'absolutely' statements tonight."

"You bet I am. You do remember Meagan saying she didn't like scandal, right?"

"It's only a scandal if someone else knows about it, and they won't."

"We could have been seen," she said. "I shouldn't have taken a risk that we might be seen together."

"Translation. I'm absolutely not coming over tonight, am I?"

"Not a chance."

"Ouch," he said. "I wasn't coming over anyway."

"Good."

"Good, huh?"

"Yeah. Good."

"You aren't going to ask why I wasn't planning to come over?"

"No."

"First of all, you have a big show tomorrow and you need sleep. If I come over, you won't sleep, and then if things go wrong tomorrow you'll blame me. They won't go badly, by the way. You're going to rock the house. But the bottom line is that you doing well matters to me, which brings me to the second reason why I wasn't planning to come over. I *want* to come over. And by that I mean I want to come over more than I should. Too much, Darla."

Silence, until she said, "I don't know what that means."

His voice lowered to meet hers. "Yes. You do." More silence. Okay. That wasn't good. Or maybe it was.

"I have no interest in being in tabloid headlines,"

she said. "That's not how you build a lasting career. At least, not the kind of career I'm building. Not the kind of career I want."

"It's not the kind of career I want, either, and my actions both past and present support that as accurate."

"Tonight, you—"

"Got carried away. You're adorable when you're feisty and I couldn't resist teasing you. But I would never have gone too far. What happens between us, Darla, is between us. I told you that earlier and I meant it."

"Blake—"

"Go to sleep. You have an early morning. I'll see you then." He hung up and then sat there, half expecting the phone to ring again, *wanting* it to ring again. But it didn't. She didn't call back and he had a bad feeling she was far more happy he was leaving tomorrow than he was. Which was exactly why he should go home and not look back. He wouldn't, though. This was new territory for him, that his younger, very happily married brother would find amusing. Blake wasn't laughing but he wasn't running, either. And he had to figure out why, even if that meant taking a few darts from Darla in the process. Hopefully, he could convince her to lick the wounds.

8

YOU KNOW WHAT I MEAN. MORNING came with Blake's words repeating in Darla's head. *And no.* No, she did not *know what he meant,* but she'd darn sure spent the entire night trying to figure it out. No wonder she didn't have one-night stands. Apparently, she was really really bad at them—hauntingly so. She managed to spend the night in bed with the man and he wasn't even there. Darla just hoped she didn't fail the awkward morning greeting as bad, because she was about to see him again.

With that thought in mind, dressed again in sweats, with no makeup on, and her hair freshly washed for a stylist to work magic on, she dragged herself to her door. She'd see *him* on the 6:00 a.m. shuttle to the audition site and she looked like crap—and why, *why* did she care about seeing him, or that she was seeing him premakeup artist? She supposed her distraction meant that Blake had actually achieved success with his "deal" because she wasn't thinking about camera nerves anymore. She'd been thinking of him then, as she was now.

Darla shoved open the door and tugged her roller bag filled with clothing and a variety of other items behind her. The door slammed on the bag and she turned to free it. That was when the door to her left—Blake's door—opened and she stopped.

"Trouble already?" he asked, rushing forward to shove her door open and free her suitcase.

"Yes," she whispered furiously. "And you're it. If you were going to keep me up all night you could have at least done it in person." She wasn't sure who was more stunned by those words—her or him. She froze. He froze. Silence expanded until she finally said, "I can't believe I just said that. More proof that you are making me crazy."

He pulled her suitcase into the hallway and let her door fall shut. He was wearing faded jeans and a T-shirt with *Stepping Up* written on it in a deep blue that matched his eyes. He looked good. So very good.

"*I'm* making you crazy?" he asked, turning the full force of those eyes—those wickedly beautiful eyes—on her.

Darla silently declared it official. Every time he was near, without any effort he got her hot. "Yes. My God. Yes. You are making me crazy. You already know I'm a worrier, a fretter and an overthinker." She'd come this far, she might as well go all the way. "Did you really think you could make a statement like 'you know what I mean' when I didn't know what you meant, and I'd actually sleep?"

"You knew—*you know*—what I meant."

"I *do not* know what you meant and I don't—"

He leaned in and brushed his lips over hers. "Now do you know what I meant?"

Heat spiraled through the center of her body and spread like a wildfire. "Are you insane? Someone could have seen you." But she didn't pull away from him. She should have. She told herself to, but he smelled so darn good—all freshly showered and masculine.

"If that's your only concern about me kissing you then you definitely know what I meant last night. And if you spent the night thinking about it—you definitely knew what I meant. My question is—how do you feel about it?"

Out of control. "We can't do this."

"But you want to?"

"We *can't* do this," she repeated.

"Why not?"

Why not? There were reasons. Lots of reasons. None of them seemed to come to mind. "You like questions, don't you?"

"I'm a television host. Of course, I do. Talk to me, Darla."

A million replies flew through her mind at once, things she'd said already, things she hadn't. *Because you're my competitor. Because you scare the heck out of me for reasons I don't want to think about right now. Because you'll make me care about you and then you'll hurt me.* Finally she said, "You leave today."

"We both live in New York."

"I won't be there for months."

"You'll be back, and I'm not afraid of flying, not to mention you'll have several weeks off when the filming moves to the contestants' house."

"Only for two weeks and not for two months. Which doesn't matter anyway. This was supposed to be…" *A one-night stand.* She couldn't say it out loud despite the wild hair that had made her bold a few moments before.

"I know what it was supposed to be, but it wasn't and it's not. It was never going to be, if we're both honest with ourselves."

She suddenly knew what he'd meant when he said he wanted to come to her room "too much." She liked him too much. Too much for all kinds of reasons. Namely, that no matter how much she didn't want him to be her competitor, or the wrong guy she made the right guy, she really had no control over either thing. No control was bad when she was headed to the first day of a big career move that not only terrified her as much as he did, but meant as much to her family as it did to her.

"No. No. This is bad. This—" she waved a finger between them "—is not smart." She grabbed her bag and tried to move around him. It caught on something, her own foot probably. She stumbled and fell forward and, once again, smack into Blake, just as she had done on the red carpet. His strong hands went to her elbows, his long, hard body catching hers. The concern in his blue eyes stirred a tidal wave inside her. She wanted this man in a bad way, but it was so much more than that. There was this warm feeling in her chest that seemed to expand and do funny things to her stomach.

"It appears the universe is conspiring to throw you into my arms," he suggested. "Maybe you should listen."

The door across from them opened. "I guess I know what 'truce with benefits' means," came a female voice.

Lana. The warm spot in Darla's chest turned to ice. "It appears," Darla said, replying to Blake, "that the universe has a wicked sense of humor."

Darla pushed out of Blake's arms, and with no plan, turned to face Lana. She wore a black sweatsuit, her red hair falling in contrasting silky waves around her shoulders. She wore no makeup and she looked fabulous. Darla wilted, unable to find her voice.

Blake came to the rescue, quickly explaining away their behavior. "The only 'benefits' being received this early in the morning are my personal baggage boy services." He grabbed Darla's suitcase and walked toward Lana, who had one as well, and motioned to her to hand it over. "I'll take yours, too. You can both thank me by not giving me a hard time on camera later."

Lana's lips lifted, and Darla couldn't help but envy how pink and perfect they were. "There's nothing wrong with a scandal," she said. "It's good for ratings. In fact, it's job security."

"Meagan hates scandal," Darla warned. "You have to know that."

"And the studio likes ratings," Lana assured her, making Darla's argument irrelevant. She scooted her bag in Blake's direction. "I do love a man with muscle and manners."

Ratings. Darla heard that familiar bad word with shattering clarity. Lana was going to turn this into ratings, and say to hell with Meagan. Darla knew Meagan trusted her to help maintain a certain image for the show. She didn't want to be the ratings boost—at least, not like this. She had to say something, do something. Fix this.

"My father," Blake said, speaking up in what Darla hoped might be that "fix" because she really had nothing of her own, "raised a scandal-free gentleman. He taught me that a good man carries a lady's bag, holds doors and generally uses good manners. Most importantly, he taught me that a gentleman keeps his private life private. Exactly why I keep my attention, and camera, keenly focused accordingly."

In other words, Darla thought, reading between the lines, Blake wouldn't be giving Lana any feature on his show if she burned him. Darla was thrilled. This was a perfect "fix."

Blake turned to Darla, his eyes lighting on hers as he added, "And a gentleman always catches a lady when she falls."

"I'm pretty sure you're to blame for both of my falls," Darla accused in jest, trying to play off his comment so that Lana wouldn't pick up on the obvious deeper meaning. "The only two times I've stood close to this man, I've tripped over his big feet."

"Oh, I see," Blake said, motioning them all forward. "Is that how it is? It's my big feet, not your clumsiness?"

Darla fell into step with him at the same time that Lana did. "I'm only clumsy when your big feet are in the way." Her shoe caught on the carpet in that instant

and she tripped, stumbling and barely catching her footing. She righted herself and ignored Lana, who most
certainly was laughing. Her attention flashed to Blake
and her gaze found his, they both burst into laughter at
the same time.

"Okay fine," she admitted. "I'm not the most grace-
ful person on the planet, but that only makes standing
next to those big feet of yours all the more dangerous."
There was a lot about him that was dangerous.

Lana punched the elevator button. "Big feet, big—"

"Lana!" Darla objected, appalled she was going there.

"I guess I do have big feet," Blake agreed.

"Neither of you are funny," Darla said, heading into
the elevator. Blake joined her, standing beside her, the
suitcases parked in front of him. When his arm pressed
against hers, Darla felt that one small connection like an
electric charge that spread through her entire body. Lana
stepped to Blake's other side. Darla turned to rest against
the side wall, facing them both. Blake's lips twitched and
she knew he knew why she'd moved.

Lana settled against the wall across from Darla. Her
gaze slid to Blake and then back to Darla and her lips
twisted in an evil little smile. "You really are going to
have to lighten up to be on this show. Actually. No.
Maybe you don't. I think you might amuse the viewers."

"Amuse the viewers?" Darla asked, feeling like she'd
just been insulted. "What exactly does that mean?"

"Your response defines what I mean," Lana replied
in an amused tone.

Darla never got the chance to respond. The elevator

doors opened and Jimmy Davis, one of Meagan's production assistants, stood waiting for them.

He flipped his cell phone shut and threw his arms in the air. "Thank goodness." He hit the mic peeking from his mop of blond hair. "They're here." He focused on Darla, Blake and Lana as they exited the elevator. Tall and thin, he was dressed in jeans and a tee that looked like they'd been crumpled by his suitcase. "Damnable mountains in combination with the hotel tower is making cell service impossible. We're doing makeup here. It's just too much of a madhouse at the audition locale." He motioned them forward and Darla and Lana scrambled toward him. Behind her, Darla heard him add, "Blake, stay. You're going down to the garage. We'll take the suitcases, which I assume are the ladies'. Meagan has a situation. She needs you over there with her, as in yesterday. We have a car waiting."

Darla turned to find another crew member retrieving the bags from Blake. "What situation?" Darla asked. "What's happening?"

Jimmy made a shooing motion. "What's happening is you're going that way to makeup. Go, go, go!" Another crew member appeared, a young girl Darla had never met. "Follow Allison."

Darla drew in a breath. Lana shrugged and fell into step behind Allison. The elevator doors shut and Blake was gone with so much unsaid between them, so much unclear.

Jimmy grimaced at Darla. "Please, Darla. I need you out of the main lobby, where we might draw attention."

Darla quickly tried to catch up with Lana and Allison. To say that she was frazzled was an understatement. She was pretty sure Lana believed that she and Blake had a thing going on. But even if she didn't, Darla's gut warned her that Lana would use the possibility as a publicity stunt. Maybe not now, but at some point. Darla had put herself in this spot, starting something with Blake, against her usual good sense. Worse, though, was the out-of-character fact that where Blake was concerned, Darla wasn't sure she had any good sense left to draw on. If she had the chance to hop right back in his arms, regardless of outcome, she all but knew she'd do it. Which made the fact that he was leaving tonight very good. Right. It was a good thing. Her insurance that she would stay out of trouble—the sexy, tempting, really wonderful trouble also known as Blake Nelson.

THE DRIVE TO THE AUDITION location should have been short, but a road was shut off to accommodate the mixture of contestants waiting to perform and fans hoping to see the celebrity judges. The delay gave Blake time to replay that moment when Darla had stumbled in the hallway, then laughed at herself with him. She'd charmed him then—and ten times over. Charmed him, and taken her sex appeal up yet another notch. That every single thing she did was sexy to him told him this wasn't about sex at all. He was pretty sure she could have the flu and be red-nosed and he'd think she was sexy.

The car rounded a corner and Blake couldn't believe his eyes. He sat up, taking in the sight before him. "Holy smokes," he murmured. There were people and cars everywhere. It was pure mayhem, just as Meagan had said it had been the prior day. He was about to be out there in that mess, interviewing people. Adrenaline pumped through him. He loved everything about the scene— the wild crowds, the energy. That's why he enjoyed red carpet events. It wasn't about the stars. It was about the people who came to see them. His studio audiences were important to him. They were what was real, what made him enjoy his work—not the cameras. Like Darla, he thought. She was real. No fluff and stuff. Ambitious, but determined to build a strong career with talent and hard work. Not some get-rich-and-famous publicity scheme. That was rare in this biz. Rare indeed.

A few minutes later, Blake stepped out of the car in the private garage to find Meagan waiting for him. "We have a problem. Or I have a problem. Rick broke his arm in the charity baseball game."

"And?"

"As in broke it to the point of emergency surgery that didn't go well."

"That's awful."

"He'll be all right, but in the meantime we want you to fill in for Rick on the next few shows, until we figure out what comes next. Do this for me, and I'll make sure the job is yours, if you want it."

Blake was stunned. "My agent—"

"Is waiting for your call. I faxed him the contract. I know this is short notice. We'll accommodate footage for your show now and as needed, and we'll get you a flight home in between this audition show and the one we film Wednesday to take care of whatever you need to take care of."

Blake had always believed that things that fell in your lap were meant to be—just as he was beginning to believe that the lady who had fallen into his arms was meant to be, as well.

A slow smile slid onto Blake's lips. "Count me in."

9

ALL THREE OF THE FEMALE JUDGES, Darla included, sat in chairs lined up inside a small changing room. And all three female judges were receiving the same beautifying treatment. Jason leaned against the wall, one boot pressed to the wall, looking biker bad-boy hot in a way that assured him female audience approval. He'd proven that as a season one judge, but she doubted he cared. He was a famous director. This show wouldn't make or break him. But it could her. Which only made Darla worry about her own audience approval. She forced the thought away and went back to thinking about Blake, which was better than thinking about how important her performance was today. She didn't know where they stood. What if Blake left before she got a chance to say goodbye? Alone, that was. If that happened, would that mean that they were officially "off" or that they were still maybe "on"? She'd told him they were off, so surely that would mean they were off. The entire thing between them felt in limbo and incomplete. "Okay, folks," Jimmy said, rushing into the room. "Let's review our schedule."

While Jimmy paced and talked, Darla's nerves preyed on her. This was it. This was really happening. She was really about to be on one of the hottest shows on television.

"When we get to the hotel," Jimmy said, pausing to look at the four of them, "you'll be taking publicity shots as a group. We'll have the first gang of auditions already inside the building, being prescreened. Once you finish pictures, you'll head straight into the audition room. We're beginning at exactly nine, with cameras rolling. We'll end at precisely seven tonight."

"What exactly was the crisis Meagan had that required Blake's help?" Darla asked. "Is this something that we need to know about before we get there?"

"My job is to worry," Jimmy said. "*Your* job is to be a star and pick stars." He touched his headset. "Yes. Right. Coming now." He glanced at Darla, then his watch, and then, already headed to the door, called over his shoulder, "We leave in fifteen minutes."

"That man gets so hyper," Ellie said from the chair where she sat next to Darla, whose pink hair now glistened with the same kind of tiny purple stones she wore on her jeans.

"That might be the only thing we agree on today," Lana said, standing up to run her hand over her slim-fitting red dress that hit above the knee, her black boots accentuated her long legs. She looked every bit the acclaimed Broadway star. How would Darla live up to that?

"All done," the stylist said, tearing away the cover over Darla's own attire—black jeans with cool floral stitching down the sides and a turquoise V-neck tank. She'd loved this outfit days ago when she'd picked it, but not so much now. Now, she felt like the boring school-teacher in the midst of rock stars. She felt comfortable on her show and her audience was warm and responsive, her staff, too. They all made her feel like she belonged. Now, though, she wondered how she'd ever gotten here. How she'd ever gotten her own show. She was nothing like these people. She was just Darla from Colorado. How was she ever going to impress viewers and keep her place on the show?

TWENTY MINUTES LATER, they were loaded into a limo—Darla and Ellie on one side and Jason and Lana on the other—about to make a grand front-door entrance to the auditions for the crowd with cameras rolling.

"Isn't it exciting?" Ellie asked, grabbing Darla's arm, clearly thrilled about the lines of people they were passing. "We've come a long way, baby, from last year."

"She's excitable," Lana said, rolling her eyes at Ellie. "Everything is 'exciting.' You'll get use to it."

"Lana's a bitch," Jason said drily. "You'll get use to it." He glanced at Darla. "She'll eat you alive if you let her. Don't."

That statement had Darla stiffening her spine and questioning how she was coming off. "I'm nervous," Darla admitted. "Extremely so. But I'm not a pushover—

especially when it comes to making people's dreams come true."

"We can see you're nervous," Jason said. "You look a little like you might be sick." He motioned toward Lana. "Aim to my right."

"Yes, please," Ellie agreed. "Right before we get out of the limo." She grabbed her phone and seemed to be setting her camera. "I want personal pictures."

"Oh, aren't you funny, Ellie," Lana said, wrapping her arm around Jason and peering up at him. "I guess I better stay nice and close to you so you're in the target range, too." She cut a look at Darla. "And we'll see about that pushover comment. We'll see today, in fact. This should be fun."

Oh, great. Darla, aka the new fish in the pond, had just managed to taunt the resident shark. If things were different, if this job weren't so important to her, she wouldn't care. She'd focus on casting, which she knew she was good at. But things were different, and this was going to be an interesting day. One of many, it was beginning to seem.

"We're here!" Ellie announced. "Lights, camera, action. The new season has arrived."

The car stopped in front of the hotel entrance and Darla could indeed see flashing camera lights. Adrenaline rushed through her. She inhaled and closed her eyes, forcing herself into performance mode, into the place she didn't let the rest of the world bleed into. Where she was a talk show host and no fears could touch her.

But everything happened so fast. The car stopped

and then she was outside, the crowds shouting and calling to her. Darla waved and smiled, blinking against
the camera flashes.

Almost the very instant that she and the other judges
cleared the front door, they were herded into a room with
a big *Stepping Up* panel set up as a backdrop for photos. Blake was there, speaking into the camera, doing
an intro about the judges arriving.

Darla's eyes met his for an unintentional instant that
both made her heart flutter and made it clear that he
was asking several silent questions. Did she want him
to stop her, to interview her? She gave a discreet shake
of her head. She didn't want to create more speculation
about the two of them or risk Lana getting jealous over
the camera time.

Blake gave an equally discreet nod and stepped toward Ellie. "Ellie, can you give me a quick sixty-second
remark for the camera?"

Darla took a spot in front of the panel that Lana and
Jason were already standing in front of, thinking that
only a day ago, she would never have thought Blake
would be so considerate of her wishes.

"Ellie!" the photographer, a young, spiky-haired,
punk-rocker-looking dude, shouted. "I need you in front
of my camera, not his." Clearly, the photographer either
knew Ellie, or he was just plain cranky in general. Ellie
ignored him and kept talking to Blake, which escalated
the photographer's demand. "Ellie! I only have a few
minutes and I'm good, honey, but even I need everyone
in front of the camera."

Ellie grimaced and turned toward him. "Take a chill pill, Frankie, will ya? We're filming and we'll be here all day."

"You might be, but I won't," he assured her. "I have another shoot I'm flying out to in two hours. So unless you want to be excluded from these promo shots, get your butt over here."

"Well, why didn't you say something?" Ellie objected, making fast tracks to join them.

Frankie threw his hands in the air and muttered, "Right. Why didn't I say something?" He flagged Jimmy. "I need Meagan and Rick in ten minutes." He turned back to the group and spoke to one of his assistants, who arranged Darla and the other judges like flowers in a vase. Darla, then Ellie, then Lana, with Jason positioned behind them to offset his six foot-plus height. Frankie fired off a good two dozen camera shots, and then glanced around the room, waving a hand in Jimmy's direction. "We need Meagan and Rick here now."

"Meagan," Jimmy said, rushing forward as he punched his headset and spoke into it. "You're late. We need you here now or we can't get the—"

"I'm here!" Meagan yelled, rushing into the room, clearly flustered. Darla noted Meagan's white jeans and white *Stepping Up* shirt. Meagan's casual attire was a reality check for Darla. She was making herself insane, obsessing over the craziest things, like clothing, when the rest of the judges weren't even dressed up. Evidently, the pressure was getting to her more than she'd realized.

"We have one of two," the photographer complained. "Where's Rick?"

Rick. Darla heard the name and was glad for it. She was really ready to get on with the auditions and the kids with their dreams. She loved casting. She loved that this show let her toe that water again.

"Rick isn't coming," Meagan announced. "He had an emergency and he won't be here today at all." She turned and called out, "Blake! We need you for photos. Hop on over here."

Blake? Darla thought. Why would Blake be in the photos?

"Why is Blake in the photos?" Lana asked, thinking the same thing.

"I'm supposed to have Rick in the shots," the photographer corrected quickly. "I don't see anything about Blake."

"Blake is filling in for Rick," Meagan explained. "I need promo shots for the first show. I want Blake in these shots." She glanced at the group. "And before you ask, I have ideas to spin this Blake and Rick switch-up for ratings. That's all I'm at liberty to say now."

Blake stepped to the side of the set, to Darla's direct right. "You sure about this, Meagan?" he asked, looking as puzzled as the rest of the group.

"Absolutely," Meagan said, using the same word Darla had earlier with Blake. "Details will be discussed when I don't have a thousand people waiting on us outside a hotel." Blake glanced at Darla and then back to Meagan. "The women on this show sure like that word." He shrugged. "I'm easy. I can go with the flow. Where do you want me?"

Frankie motioned to Blake, "Next to Jason."

Blake headed toward the group. Darla quickly turned away, afraid her desire for this man was written all over her face. He stepped behind her and her nostrils flared with the scent of him, warm and spicy, so richly male, so familiar. His hand slid discreetly to her waist and she barely contained a gasp of surprise at what most would consider a casual touch, a posing stance. No different from the way Jason had his arm draped over Ellie's shoulders. Darla knew, though, that Blake's touch wasn't any more casual than the desire sizzling through her.

Meagan rushed forward and squeezed in between Darla and Ellie. She leaned into Darla and touched her head to hers. The camera flashed. "How you doing, sweetie?" Meagan whispered.

"I'm good," she replied softly as more flashes went off. "What's going on with Rick?"

"Surgery for a broken arm," she explained. "He hasn't even made it to Colorado yet."

"You're kidding?" Darla asked Meagan. "Will he make the next show?"

"Face the camera!" the photographer yelled.

"Oh, ah, sorry," Darla said and quickly posed.

The photo shoot wrapped and Darla and the judges headed to the audition room. "Darla," Blake said, gently touching her arm to get her attention before she could get away. She swallowed hard at the impact of those piercing blue eyes that never seemed to lessen. "Don't think about the camera or pleasing an audience," he said, his voice a caress for her ears only. "This isn't live and the auditions won't even be shown for another six weeks. Think about the contestants, about doing what you did last season, and picking the best contestants. Forget everything else or you're going to make yourself crazy."

Darla softened inside, surprised by his words. So very right. "That was *absolutely* what I needed to hear right now." Someone called her name, and she backed away, hesitating to leave, wanting him to know… There seemed to be something she needed to say. She heard her name shouted again.

"Thank you, Blake." Darla rushed away, but silently vowed not to let him leave tonight without a proper goodbye. She was smiling, rather than fretting, when she walked into the audition room.

FOUR HOURS AFTER THE AUDITIONS started, Blake finished an interview with a joyful, crying seventeen-year-old girl who was chosen for the finals. She was the last candidate for now. During the next hour and a half, there'd be prescreening of candidates while the judges were given a chance to eat and take a break.

Beaming at the excitement of the girl and her family, Blake decided he loved this job, and he planned to tell his agent just how much.

Seeking Meagan, Blake stepped inside a small room where the cameras were recording the action in the audition room. Meagan stood in front of a row of monitors, watching the live feed from the judges as it played on the screens.

"Why must you ask every contestant about their dreams and goals?" Lana demanded of Darla. "We simply need them to dance well."

"We're looking for stars," Darla said. "People who have drive and ambition. There's a reason why Jason is so respected in the industry, why Ellie is in demand by big-named stars to choreograph. They're special."

"She's right," Ellie said. "I like hearing people's stories. I've worked with a lot of talent. The ones who make it have certain qualities."

"Hear them after we see them dance, and once they make it to Vegas," Lana argued. "We have a huge line of people out there and not enough time to see them all."

"That's why Meagan has a team of screeners making sure we only see the best," Ellie argued. "The ones we see can dance. But can they become success stories? That's up to us to decide."

"If we send them to Vegas and they have no personality or career potential," Darla added, "then we've wasted time and money. The top twelve are going to be living in the contestant house with a live camera on them. We have to pick people who can become reality television stars or people won't tune in."

"We did fine last season," Lana said tightly. "You need to respect what worked."

Darla drew in a long breath and Blake could see her biting back words. "Tell her," he said softly, stepping to

Meagan's side. "Tell her you cast the winner of last season and most of the top twelve."

Meagan glanced at him, then back at the screen, seemingly waiting right along with him. But Darla didn't tell her. She stood up and said, "We'll have to continue this argument later. I need to check in with my producer back home and make arrangements for filming my show."

Blake scrubbed his jaw. "I don't get it. She'd never let me get away with that. Why didn't she tell her she was the primary casting agent last season?"

"I don't know," Meagan said, still watching the screen. "Her confidence isn't where it normally is. Something is up with her." She glanced at him. "You got anything to do with that?"

"Me?" he asked. "How would I have anything to do with it?"

"You tell me."

He opened his mouth to deny his guilt but shut it again, remembering the incident with Lana in the hallway. Surely, Darla wasn't so worried about a scandal created by Lana's big mouth that she was afraid to stand her ground with her. Then again, he wasn't sure what was behind it, but Darla was almost irrationally worried about losing this job before she even got started. Especially so, considering her own show's success. He wanted to know why. He wanted to know a lot of things about Darla—and not just what made her moan and sigh. Those things were high on his list, but so was discovering what made her happy and sad, what made her afraid of flying. Hell. He wanted to know what her favorite food was. Actually, he was pretty sure that would be chocolate.

Blake watched the screen as Darla walked toward a door that led to a private hallway, and he felt himself stir inside. This woman got to him in a big way and the last thing he wanted to do was create turmoil for her. But he couldn't step back from her without knowing what she was doing to him.

"What's her cell number?" he asked, grabbing his phone from his belt.

Meagan considered him a moment and then recited the number by heart. He was already turning away and hitting the call button by the time she said the last digit. Darla answered almost instantly. "We need to talk and we haven't got long," Blake said. "It's important. I'm about to be at the other hotel waiting on you. *By your door.*" He hung up before she could decline, cringing as he thought of just how mad he'd probably just made her.

He was going to have to do some fast talking to get on her good side.

10

BLAKE QUICKLY LEARNED THAT *MAD* wasn't quite a strong enough word to describe Darla's reaction to his maneuvering her to meet him. She rounded the corner of the bank of elevators, found him by her door, and hit him with a look that could have flattened the entire building. Her cheeks were flushed, her spine stiff, and her eyes as sharp as knives. She stormed towards him, her room key in hand, and she didn't say a word as she stepped next to him to swipe it. He could smell the floral scent of her perfume—jasmine, he thought—and taste her anger. He could feel his desire building at a fairly inappropriate time, for a completely inappropriate reason. She turned him on when she was hot and fiery. She *was* hot and fiery, and she'd shown none of that in that audition room with Lana.

She rushed inside and grabbed his shirt, pulling him with her. His body reacted to the touch, his cock pressing against his zipper. Damn, when had he ever wanted a woman this badly?

"Are you freaking nuts? What kind of stunt are you trying to pull? I didn't sign up for this, Blake. Someone could have seen you. Someone *might have* seen you!"

Blake's plans to talk went right out the proverbial window, his desire for Darla getting the best of him. "Yes," he said, backing her against the door, his legs framing hers and his hands twining into her hair. "I am nuts. Nuts about you."

"Blake," she hissed, splaying her delicate fingers over his chest, scorching him with heat that set his heart to pumping. "I'm furious with you. Don't you understand?"

"I get that," he murmured, lowering his lips to a whisper above hers. "It appears it turns me on. So much so that I'm quickly forgetting I came here to talk." His mouth met hers, claiming the kiss he wanted. She didn't respond immediately—her body was rigid and her hand still flat on the solid wall of his chest. But she didn't push him away and there was just a hint of a moan sliding from her mouth to his.

Blake caressed a palm over her backside. His tongue gently coaxed hers into responding, just a little kiss, a little moment of escape.

"Damn it, Blake," she said gently. Then her tiny moan became a full-out sound of pleasure and her body relaxed into his. The hand resting on his chest traveled upward and wrapped around his neck, the other around his waist. Her tongue caught his, hot and sweet, and eager. He melded her closer, absorbing all her soft curves into his hard body. And he was hard. So hard it hurt to even think about leaving this room without finding his way inside her. She moaned again, her arms wrapping around him, as if she couldn't get close enough. And she couldn't. Not in his book. "This doesn't mean I'm not furious with you," she promised. "It just means that—"

"I know," he said, his cock pulsing thickly against his zipper. "I want you, too." He kissed her and, this time, he didn't even try to hold back. His tongue plunged into her mouth, taking it, claiming it. Claiming her. A taste of honey among the bitterness he hadn't even realized had been eating him alive. This business had gotten to him—the people, the wants, the demands of money and fame. Darla had broken through all of that and she hadn't even tried. She was just herself—and that was unique in his world.

He reached under the silk of her tank, pulled down her bra and fingered her nipples. She shuddered with pleasure, her nails digging into his shoulders. He pushed the shirt upward. "Take it off before I get impatient and ruin it."

She tugged it over her head, leaving her with only her pale pink bra and rose-tipped nipples peeking out. "We can't be late back to set."

"We won't be," he promised, unhooking the front clasp of her bra. "Hard and fast." He teased her nipples, sucking them lightly. "But next time we're going slow and hot. You have my word."

Her hand went to his zipper, tracing his throbbing erection. "Who says there's going to be a next time?" She unsnapped his jeans and the next thing he knew she had her hand on his cock.

He groaned, both from her touch and the way she challenged him. Lust jolted him. He pressed his hand to the wall above her head. "There's going to be a next time. You can count on me doing whatever is necessary to convince you of that fact."

She massaged his shaft, her fingers trailing along the top, spreading the dampness gathering there. "Not if you manipulate me to get me to my room, or anywhere else, ever again."

"We needed to talk," he defended. "And you wouldn't have come any other way."

"Your talking isn't a good idea," she warned, pressing his boxers out of the way and freeing his cock. It jutted forward, thick and pulsing, and she lowered her lashes, inspecting him, stroking him, driving him freaking wild, before her gaze lifted. "Talking is just going to make me mad again. And before you say you like me mad, you should know that mad may or may not include me kicking you out of my room." She slowed her movements, then sped up again.

He barely contained a groan. It felt as if liquid fire was burning through his veins. "Though I do think you're insanely hot when you're mad, I sure as hell don't want to get kicked out of the room right now." He closed his hand around hers. "Keep touching me just like that and I'll shut up." He moved against their joined hands. Her lashes lowered again, her attention on his cock, her tongue biting her bottom lip. It was official. She still hated him and was tormenting him to death. Death by lust. She stroked him harder, faster, and he quickly real-

ized he was further gone than he thought. Too far gone
to have her touching him like this if he was going to
last—and that sure wouldn't get him a take two. And
he wanted a take two, three and four—and whatever
and wherever that led. He *wanted* this woman in his
life. But he couldn't convince her by pushing her. Not
now, at least.

He brought her to the foot of the bed and held her
tight, pressing his lips to hers, her bare breasts teasing
his chest. He would convince her with pleasure. The kind
two people who felt something special for each other
could make. "You have on too many clothes."

"So do you," she murmured just before his mouth
came down on hers in a searing kiss that burned with a
possessiveness so new to him, it threatened to unravel
any control he still possessed.

She lifted his shirt upward, scraped her teeth across
his nipple, then tongued it softly. "Take this off before
I get impatient and ruin it," she ordered, repeating his
command. "This time you're not getting away with leaving anything on."

"Believe me," he assured her. "I want nothing more
than to be naked with you, sweetheart." *Naked and tearing down your walls,* he added silently. He kissed her
and then set her away from him, immediately tossing
his shirt aside.

They stared at each other a moment, stared at the
clock, then back at each other. One hour left. One hour
would never be enough. In silent agreement, there was a
frenzied rush of undressing. Blake made it to his socks

and then forgot everything but Darla—standing before him gloriously naked. Her breasts were high, full, with pebble-tight cherry nipples. Her hips were slender, her skin ivory perfection. Every second he was with her, she seemed to grow more beautiful. He stepped toward her.

"Wait," she said, holding up a hand then pointing at this feet. "I said everything off this time."

He didn't argue. He was too hot and too ready for her. He had his socks off in seconds and pulled her into his arms, lifting her. Her legs wrapped around his waist, the wet heat of her core warming his stomach. Lust tore through him, the desire to bury himself inside her and get lost was almost too much to resist.

"Tell me you have a condom," she panted, apparently feeling what he was.

"A half dozen," he said, carrying her to the dresser.

She pulled back and gave him an incredulous look. "Pretty sure of yourself, aren't you?"

"It was one or six. I chose six. But yeah, I'm hoping you'll let me convince you we need all six sometime in the near future." He settled her on top of the dresser and slid his fingers into her hair. "What do I have to do to make that happen?"

She pulled back and stared at him, more of that raw innocence he found so appealing swirling in the depths of her stare. "I don't know… I…"

He leaned in and gently kissed her neck. "We'll talk about that later."

He inched her knees farther apart, skimming his

palms up her thighs, taking in the blond curls and pretty pink flesh, glistening wet with desire.

"You're beautiful," he said, his gaze lifting to hers. "Perfect."

Her cheeks flushed. "Blake," she whispered shyly. He loved that about her. The way she ordered him around one minute, and then turned sweetly vulnerable the next.

It was the vulnerability in her in that moment that got to him, that had him cradling her face and lifting her face to his. "Whatever you're doing to me, keep doing it. I like it."

The way she seemed to have no idea how much she affected him, no intent to use it against him. It only made him want to please her more.

Confusion knitted her brow. "I've pretty much been mad at you the entire time we've known each other."

"Are you mad now?"

"Yes."

"Why?" He caressed her breasts, pressed her backward, her weight on her hands behind her. He licked one pretty pink bud and then the next.

"We never made up," she claimed breathlessly.

"We seem to be getting along pretty well to me," he said, licking her nipple again.

"If you don't get that condom—"

He kissed her. "I don't have to be told twice."

Blake grabbed his jeans, digging out his wallet. He fumbled for the condom. He wanted her so bad he was trembling. That was a first. There were a lot of firsts with Darla. That seemed good. He hoped. He didn't know. He didn't know much of anything right now, except how badly he wanted to be inside her.

She leaned back on the dresser, her breasts thrust high. For a moment, he went still, his throat dry. His cock got impossibly hard. He sheathed himself in seconds as she watched, and then wasted no time returning to her. Wrapping his arm around her slender waist, he slid his fingers in the wet heat of her body to ready her for him. He wanted to be in her, he wanted to feel the wet wonder of her body clenching him tight and holding on. But he wanted this to be good for her. He wanted there to be a reason to use those five other condoms.

"I'm way beyond waiting," she said hoarsely, closing her hand around his shaft and guiding the blunt head of his erection to where she wanted it—telling him she was ready. She was driving him out of his mind with desire. She was hitting all the right marks.

He parted her with his fingers and entered her. She was tight and hot, and he groaned with the pleasure of her muscles contracting around him. An intense urgency built inside him. He thrust deeper inside her and swallowed her gasp with his kiss, a wild, ravenous kiss. Too wild for the dresser—he struggled to fully reach her.

Blake lifted her again and carried her to the mattress. He placed her on the bed beneath him, and she opened for him like a flower—a jasmine-scented flower that he couldn't get enough of. He raised one of her legs over his shoulder and pressed his palm under her perfect ass. He swiveled his hips and drove into her, right where he wanted to be. She had him all now.

He lingered a moment, his eyes searching the depths of hers. He wasn't quite sure what she might see in his eyes, but he couldn't look away. Her fingers traced his lips and he kissed them, then kissed her. He lost himself in the seductive bliss that was her taste, her body. He started to move, to pump into her. What started as slow and cautious quickly became fast and confident. And she met that uncontrollable need—her hands were all over him, her body rocking with his.

He palmed her sweet ass and thrust again and again. Her hips lifted on a moan, her body stiffened. "Blake I…" Her body clenched around him, pulling the pleasure from him, taking it from him. Blake shuddered with his release until his muscles relaxed. He eased her leg down and buried his face in her neck. Long seconds passed and he forced himself to consider time, and work and things he'd rather forget. He had to talk to Darla about why he was here—why they were here—in the first place. He would upset her and he could think of a lot of things that he wanted to do and with the soft and willing female beneath him, and upsetting her wasn't on the list.

11

BLAKE LIFTED UP ON HIS ARMS, his elbows framing Darla's face. "What time is it?" she asked urgently.

He checked the clock. "We have half an hour. We should get dressed." He didn't move.

"Yes," she said, but she didn't move, either. "We should get dressed."

"For the record, I could stay in bed the rest of the day with you and be a happy man."

She reached up and touched his face, her small fingers gentle. The touch sent a rush of renewed heat down his spine. "I'm still mad," she said.

He smiled. He couldn't help himself. He loved the way she dueled with him, the way he knew he had to work to earn her. He loved that she didn't want him just because of who he was or what he could give her.

"In case you missed basic emotion 101," Darla scolded, "anger is not a reason to smile."

"Be angry. Be whatever." His voice sounded gravelly, affected. "Just tell me you don't regret this."

"Blake, I… No. No, I don't." Her tone shifted from a mix of sultry innocence to a stronger one. "Not yet, that is. Not unless you make me late to the set."

Darla scooted to the edge of the bed and he resisted the urge to reach across and shackle her wrist in a gentle hold. He turned to face her, unconcerned about his nakedness. He liked being naked with her. But she wasn't in such a receptive mood. She kept her back to him, as if debating a run for the bathroom.

"Just tell me this," he said, baiting her to turn around, to talk to him. "Why are you so damn feisty, and in my face, but you let Lana run all over you in that audition room?"

She whirled around, her breasts bouncing in a way that he couldn't help but admire. She yanked the sheet up around her, obviously noticing. "Lana isn't running over me."

"Says who?"

"Blake—"

"Meagan noticed. She said you weren't acting like yourself. She's the one who gave me your phone number."

She paled instantly. "What?"

He shook his head. "I was standing at the monitors when you argued with Lana and then walked out of the room for the break. Meagan heard the entire exchange and she commented about you backing down." She ran her hand through her hair, her bottom lip quivering as if she were fighting tears.

He softened his voice. "If this is about us, about Lana's threat—"

"It's not." She swallowed hard. "Not really. I mean, yes, I'm worried about her causing trouble for us, but I'm not sure I'm rational about it, either."

Us. He didn't miss the choice of words, and it pleased him.

Darla continued, "I know I'm not myself and I certainly wasn't myself in that audition room. I hate that Meagan noticed. I hate that I'm letting her down."

"Don't be so hard on yourself. You aren't letting Meagan down." He was both surprised and impressed that she was self-aware enough to know when she wasn't in the right mind-set, that she was open enough with him to say so and to share her fears. "Meagan just wants the real you in that room and on the show. The same you who came storming down the hallway not so long ago, ready to lay into me."

She studied him a long moment, her green eyes glistening with a story he wanted her to tell, but he had a good feeling she wouldn't. Not now, not yet. "Most people in competing time slots wouldn't have told me about this," she finally said. "They'd hope I would fail."

She was right. "I live in this world, Darla. I don't *live* this world." He drew her hand into his. "Talk to me, Darla. Is there something going on with your studio? Did they put some condition on you doing *Stepping Up* that you're struggling with?"

"No." She shook her head, her fingers curling beneath his, telling him he'd hit some sort of nerve. "It's just that…it's complicated." She glanced at the clock. "Oh, God. It's later than I thought. I have to go. We have to go." She dropped the sheet, making a mad dash for the bathroom. Blake tried to catch her, but his damn feet got stuck in the sheet. He had no chance to stop her. No chance to talk to her about the show, about him hosting it or about the next time they could be alone together.

The bathroom door shut with a decisive thud. Blake was shut out. Of everything. She was running from something and he had somehow become a part of that that. Which meant he had to find a way to help her if he wanted a chance with her. And he did. In fact, for a man who hadn't been looking for a woman, he was remarkably ready to do some fighting of his own for that chance—*for her.*

Blake considered his options. Pushing Darla now, when she had to go in front of a camera to face whatever personal demons she was battling wasn't going to earn him points. She wanted space and he had to give it to her. He had to respect what she had ahead of her the rest of the day. He darn sure wasn't throwing her the bombshell that he was going to be around a whole lot more than she thought from outside a bathroom door. No. She wanted him gone now, so he'd be gone. He just wasn't going to like it.

12

DARLA STOOD IN the hotel bathroom with her back against the door and her eyes squeezed shut. She'd run from Blake, run because she was afraid of the emotion he was making her feel. She just had to get away from him before she did something crazy, like fall for him. He felt too right, too good, and her track record—even with him— was proof of the trouble that always followed. And so she stood, naked, with her clothes and her purse on the other side of the door—where he was. Which was where she wanted to be, and knew she had no place being.

She inhaled and, against all reason, willed Blake to knock on the door, to talk her off the ledge. Still, she'd be better off if he didn't and left the room. If he left without a word, in fact, and proved to her that this was about a half dozen condoms and not a half dozen emotions.

Time stretched by and there was no knock. She heard movement, though. He was dressing. Of course, he was dressing. He had to get to the set, just like she did. He'd knock when he was done. He'd say goodbye. He'd ask to see her again and make some sexy remark that referenced using condom number two. That would prove he only wanted sex. That would make this easy. They were supposed to be just about sex. That's why she'd stepped out on this ledge in the first place. It had seemed simple, uncomplicated. An escape she'd desperately needed.

The hotel room door opened and shut. He'd left? She listened, waited. No sound. Nothing. He'd left and had said nothing before doing so. No request for a sex date. No anything. Not even a goodbye. What did that mean? It had to mean he'd read between the lines when she darted away, that he knew she was running scared and he wasn't up for the chase—not that she wanted him to chase her. It wasn't like that. She wasn't sure what she wanted. The knots in her stomach said it wasn't this, though. It wasn't him gone and her in here.

Darla slumped against the bathroom door. She had her answers to the burning questions in her mind, of the possibilities that might exist between her and Blake. This meant there was nothing of substance between them. She should be happy. She wasn't happy.

Darla yanked open the door and raced around the room, gathered her clothing, pulling items on, trying not to think about taking them off while Blake watched. While Blake stood naked in front of her—tall, broad, ripped, gorgeous Blake. She hadn't even had time to fully enjoy just how gorgeous.

She shook away the image and rushed to the door to find her purse where she'd tossed it earlier. She stopped dead in her tracks at the piece of paper sitting on top of it.

Her heart skipped a beat and she barely managed to breathe as she darted for it, a bit too eager. She picked it up and five condoms tumbled to the floor. Her throat went dry. She wasn't sure she wanted to read the note after all.

It wasn't just sex. I figure I can't prove that to you while these puppies are taunting me with the many ways we might use them. And speaking of taunting, don't let Lana win. Show her who is really the boss.
Blake

Emotion welled in Darla's chest. She was so falling for this man. She was falling and falling and falling. Hard. She liked him, plain and simple. Too much. Yes— "too much" was a theme for her with Blake. She didn't think it was possible to ignore him, to walk away from this thing between them until she knew where it might lead. *You have to,* a voice in her head said.

Granted, there was more on the line than just her needs and her feelings for Blake. Making this show work wasn't only about her. It was about the parents who'd always been there for her, who'd supported her dreams and her life choices.

She had to go back to the same thing she'd told herself in the bathroom. Her track record with men wasn't one she thought supported a gamble on Blake, not when she owed her parents everything, and they deserved the world.

Darla arrived at a room set up with tables and chairs,

with various wardrobe and toiletries. Allison, who Darla now knew would be her makeup and hair person, was there alone, eating a sandwich. She glanced up at Darla, right as she was about to take a bite, and froze. She set down her food and pushed to her feet. "Finally, you're here! You look like crap."

Darla exhaled. So much for believing she'd doctored her hair and makeup in an acceptable manner. "Well. No one can say you're not honest."

"What the heck did you do on your break?" Allison complained, motioning Darla to a chair. "Sit down— and fast. You're due on set in minutes. The other judges have come and gone."

"Sorry," Darla said, settling into the chair. "I have a case of nerves and lunch didn't sit well. I've been, uh, lying down."

"Oh," Allison said, her brows dipping. "Why are you nervous? You have a show of your own and I love it. Did I mention I'm a fan? Huge, huge fan."

Darla gave her an appreciative smile. "Now you're just saying all the right things, and I prefer the honest, 'you look like crap' kind of communication."

"I said I was a fan. I didn't say you don't look like crap."

Darla laughed. "Okay, then," she conceded. "I stand corrected. Thank you for the compliment and, ah, insult."

"All meant in the most loving of ways," Allison assured her. "I'll fix you all up on one condition."

"Okay," Darla said cautiously, thinking everyone was all about conditions today. "I'll bite. What condition?"

She lowered her voice. "That you put that diva Lana in her place every chance you get this season." She dropped to a whisper. "We're all looking forward to watching it."

Darla absorbed the words, taking them in with surprise. "Who is 'we all'?"

"All the crew," she said, rolling a cart of makeup and hair supplies to Darla's side. "No one likes her. She's just so mean to the contestants. We know you'll stick up for them, like you do for all kinds of people on your show—and the animals. We all love the animal rescue special you do on Fridays."

The comment made her think of her parents, how she had to focus on her agenda to save their ranch. It had suffered from a virus that attacked cattle. Her mother and father hadn't told her how bad it had gotten until it was almost too late and they'd taken on debt they couldn't afford to pay back.

Darla's chest expanded with warmth and understanding as her father's frequently spoken words replayed in her head. Words he'd repeated about their financial struggles. *Honey, things happen for reasons. You have to have faith. Sometimes we just don't know what those reasons are until later.* Darla's fear that Blake was a distraction lifted like a cloud of worry and paranoia. Blake had heard Meagan's concern. Blake had warned her so she could fix what was broken. Blake had made her late enough to the set to have Allison share this piece of information with her. And, most importantly, Blake had given her good advice. She had to be herself in the audition room or she would disappoint everyone, not just Meagan. She'd disappoint herself. She'd disappoint her parents. She had to go into that room and forget about the pressure, about her parents' predicament. If she did that, everything would be okay. She had to come through for them the way they'd always come through for her.

After Allison made up an excuse of burning Darla's hair with a flat iron to buy more time, Darla managed to inhale two chocolate bars—Allison agreed chocolate was safe, even for a sick stomach—and she was ready for work. She was ready for Lana. She wasn't, however, ready to see Blake. Or to say goodbye. But she had to.

THE AUDITIONS HAD BEEN TAKING place for a good three hours when Blake wished a young male dancer good luck in Vegas, and then found himself being flagged down by Meagan. She lifted her hand and motioned for him to follow her.

Blake froze in an "uh-oh" moment. He'd been hoping for a break to check on Meagan and hoping, even more so, to find out if she'd shaken off her morning. He now prayed he wasn't about to find out the opposite, a fear easily conceived considering Meagan had made her suspicions about him and Darla obvious. She'd also made it clear she suspected that Blake was negatively influencing Darla. Hell, Darla thought he was, too—or at least, that was what he'd now surmised about the bathroom incident. And maybe he was. Maybe he needed to keep his distance, no matter how much he wanted to have

Darla up close and personal. Not forever, but for now, until she found her footing on the show.

Blake followed Meagan to an empty event room that had been cleared as a contestant holding room. "What did you say to Darla at break?" she asked immediately, going right for the gut.

Blake felt the blow, and while he wasn't one to be at a loss for words, it took him a minute to recover. "Not anything different than I imagine you would have," he replied cautiously.

She studied him, as she had earlier and then waved off his words. "Details aren't important. Whatever you said, it worked and that's all that counts. She's back to her normal self in there and I couldn't be happier. Now, I feel free to actually talk to both of you about an idea my team has been bouncing around since early this morning when we found out about Rick."

"Talk to us?" he asked, a warning alarm going off in his head.

"Meagan," Darla said, appearing in the doorway and going white as a sheet as soon as she spotted Blake. She was as worried as he was that this was about them.

"You needed me?" she asked Meagan.

"Come in," Meagan encouraged. "And pull the door shut."

"I'll get it," Blake offered quickly. He closed the door and stepped in between the two women so he could gauge both of their facial expressions as this—whatever it was—went down. "Since Rick isn't coming back—" Meagan started.

"Rick isn't coming back?" Darla asked, her tone rippling with shock.

Meagan's gaze flicked Blake a "you didn't tell her?" look, before she replied, "No. He's not. He'll be recuperating for a while. As you know, Blake is filling in for Rick today, but I've thrown his name in the ring for a potential long-term replacement."

Darla gaped, her attention jerking to Blake's with accusation. "You're taking over for Rick?"

Could he get any more sideswiped? "I'm just rolling with the punches," he assured her, darting Meagan a warning glance. "I've agreed to nothing but helping out today. Maybe a few audition shows forward, if needed. Beyond that, nothing is even somewhat final."

"About your future with the show," Meagan said. "I just hung up from a conference call with your agent—who wants you to call him—and one of the studio executives." She glanced at Darla. "Right after I had a conversation with your agent and one of your studio executives."

Blake's spine stiffened and he could feel the tension emanating from Darla. He could almost hear her suck in a breath at the same time he did, waiting for what was about to come next, no doubt, thinking what he was thinking.

Was one or both of them about to be fired?

13

"I don't understand," Blake heard Darla say in a strained voice, her ivory skin pasty white. "Is there some sort of a problem with me being on the show because Blake is now potentially the host?"

"Because if there is," Blake said sternly, praying that he hadn't misjudged the situation. "Count me out of the show. I'll head home and stay there."

Meagan looked between the two of them, a keen expression on her face. "You'd walk away from a huge paycheck because it puts Darla in jeopardy?"

"Yes," he said at the same time Darla said, "No."

"No, you will not," Darla added, frowning at Blake. "This is your studio, not mine. You belong here."

"You both belong here," Meagan interrupted.

"I'm perfectly happy doing just my show." Blake focused on Darla. "The big Hollywood scene has never been my thing. *Stepping Up* works for me, not because of the big prime-time format, but because of the fans and the contestants. Those things hit the same hot buttons as my show."

"This is money and opportunity, as well," Darla said, being humble and generous, as he'd expect of her. But when she curled her fingers inside her palms, he could see she was shaking. She wanted this. She wanted it bad, and still she added fiercely, "You can't walk away from this."

"I'm not invested in this like you are," he reasoned. "I *can* walk away. And I will, if it has to be one or the other, you or me. It's the right thing to do."

"It's not," Meagan said firmly, drawing their attention. "This *is* a great opportunity. You're right about that, Darla. A great opportunity for *both* of you."

"What?" Darla asked. "I thought…so, wait. There's not a problem with Blake and I working together?"

"I never said there was," Meagan informed her. "You two just took a piece of what I was saying and ran with it. Nobody has a problem with the two of you working together. At least, not now that they've heard my plan. In fact, they're thrilled with the plan I've suggested. It's the two of you that I have to convince now."

Darla cast Blake a cautious look. "So," she said contemplatively, "let me just be sure I understand. My show being on a competing network, in a competing time slot with Blake, isn't an issue?"

"It's a bonus," Meagan asserted, "and the key to my team's plan to boost ratings this season."

"What are we missing here, Meagan?" Blake asked skeptically.

"Everyone at the bar last night noticed the combative chemistry the two of you have and they found it entertaining. Add to it the past history with the shoe incident, and people are interested to see how you might clash, or not clash, again."

"Oh, wow," Darla murmured. "Were we that obvious last night?"

"You say that like it's a problem," Meagan chided. "It's not. In fact, it's the opposite. It's magical, and a way to make this season unique. That's what we need— a way to keep the show from becoming repetitive and boring. Last season we had the curse. This season, two competing television personalities."

"Are we talking about some sort of format change for the show or a role change for myself or Darla?" Blake asked. "Because as it is, Darla and I won't be interacting much."

"The judges and the host have plenty of interaction during the live shows," she corrected. "Which is what we want to play up."

"Play up?" Darla asked. "I'm not following, Megan."

"The details will have to be fine-tuned based on your input. But what we know for certain is that we'll emphasize a rivalry between you two and tease the audience with the battle and/or sparks that might fly."

Blake's brow lifted. "Sparks?" His gaze flickered to Darla, who had turned paler still when he hadn't thought she could do so.

"Viewers love a good rivalry," Meagan explained. "They will either want you to clash or want you to fall into each other's arms. It will be a fun battle of the sexes theme we can use."

"I know you mean it when you say this is going to be good for the show and for us," Darla said. "And I believe you when you say that the studio is supportive of this idea, but I'm concerned this could backfire on me. I'm looking for longevity, not my fifteen minutes of fame. I'm the outsider, the one from a competing network. One misstep that makes them see me as having allegiances to this network over them could cost me my job."

"*One* of your jobs," Meagan said. "But you aren't going to leave either show on anyone's terms but your own. You're too good to have this end any differently."

"You don't know that," Darla argued. "This first season for me is more like an audition," she glanced at Blake, "and we all know it. If I get bad feedback from the audience, I'm gone."

"You won't," Blake said, unwilling to let her allow fear to affect her decision-making. He might not be a hot Hollywood star, but he knew opportunity when he saw it. "They'll love you just like your audience loves you."

"This is a different format from my show," Darla said. "I'll be openly critiquing people's performances, building and destroying dreams. Blake won't have that pressure, nor will he have the competing network issue."

"*Stepping Up* is going to be highly invested in you both," Meagan assured her. "We'll be doing a print and television campaign featuring the two of you. Any way you look at that, you two are the reasons both networks get this exposure—and Darla, your network gets it for free. *Because of you*. It's a sweet deal for them. Call your agent and your producer and talk it out at the next break."

"She's right, Darla," Blake said. "It's a sweet deal for your network—and even mine, for that matter. They win ratings and advertisers."

Darla shook her head, rejecting his encouragement. "Ultimately we're still competitors, Blake. The last one standing keeps their show and this one right along with it. You know that's how this ends."

"I don't know any such thing," Blake said. "And you could easily have this network pay you enough to make your show a nonissue."

She narrowed her gaze. "And you get rid of me as a competitor?"

"No," he objected. "Come on, Darla. You know better than that."

"How?" she asked. "How do I know better? I barely know you. And we both know our new variety-type shows could stay on the air for twenty years. Prime time rarely hits five seasons. Keeping our day jobs makes sense."

"Hey," Meagan sniped, "don't be numbering our days already. We are going to keep this show new and fresh, just like we're trying to do with you two injected into the season full-throttle now.

"Your daytime shows are your daytime shows," Megan assured her. "The idea is simply that this show gets your shows more exposure." She glanced at her watch. "Yikes! Okay. We don't have much time. You both have concerns. I understand fully, but I sincerely

think you will be glad you did this. So let me just arm
you both with information to think about and to talk
to your representation about." She glanced at Blake.
"Blake, we don't need you at every audition since we
don't shoot those segments live. We piece together random footage for audition segments. This gives us time
to finish planned shows in New York and pretape others
to give you breathing room. Vegas week is when we se-
lect the final twelve dancers, which will be crazy insanity, with emotions high and contestants sleep-deprived.
But it's also a perfect time to do some playful rival clash
stuff between the two of you. We'll talk through details.
I have ideas. Lots of ideas." She let out a breath. "That
brings me to the here and now. Blake, the studio wants
to see you at eight tomorrow morning to talk about contract terms and how you are going to juggle two shows.
That means you need to go catch a flight to NY now.
Your agent is working on finding you one."

"What?" Blake asked, taken off guard. "That's fast,
Meagan." The idea of leaving without the opportunity
to talk to Darla was really *not* a good one. "Surely, the
studio can wait until later tomorrow."

Meagan shook her head. "Darla is here to stay no
matter what. She's contracted. But if we can't work this
out with you, Blake, I have to find a new host. I need to
know where we are headed. If you manage to nail down
a contract, and Darla and her agent agree to everything
as well, then Darla and I will fly back to New York to
meet with everyone involved right after the next audition. We'll shoot promos and ad campaigns then."

A knock sounded on the door and Jimmy rushed inside, not waiting on an answer. "We need you and Darla back on set. And Blake, your agent called. You need to leave for the airport about fifteen minutes ago. I have a car waiting."

Damn it, Blake cursed silently.

"We're coming," Meagan called to Jimmy, then lowered her voice. "I'm thrilled about this. The possibilities the two of you represent for this season are endless."

Jimmy shouted again and Meagan nodded to Darla. "We better go." She started walking, and Darla cast Blake one long, meaningful look before she fell into step behind Meagan. She was creating reasons to make him the enemy. Blake stared after her, fighting the urge to grab her and pull her aside. Better yet, to grab her and kiss her, and remind her of what they'd shared. But then, like in the airplane, he held back. He was going to have to leave and wait to talk to Darla when he landed. That is, if she would take his calls.

DARLA FINALLY ENTERED her hotel room at eleven o'clock that evening after a very emotional day. She locked the door behind her and then froze instantly as her nostrils flared with a familiar scent. Blake's scent. She wasn't sure if she wanted to thank housekeeping for apparently not doing their job, or complain to management, considering the vivid images the smell provoked—delicious, naughty, wonderful images of her and Blake together. Images that were more proof of how conflicted she was over the man. It made her feel like she'd been naive, like he was using her. And yet, another image of the two of them against the wall, his hands on her breasts, his body pressed to hers, had her shoving away from the door and shaking her head. She was so very conflicted. Darla tossed her purse on the bed and dropped like a rock beside it onto her back, her legs dangling off the mattress. She had to be up early in the morning to fly to New Mexico with Meagan for the next round of auditions. They were going to talk more about the show then as well, and about Blake, although there wasn't much left to discuss at this point. Darla had spent a few short minutes on the phone with her agent, who had made it clear that not only did her contract allow for everything proposed, he had no idea why she wouldn't want to do it in the first place. This was exposure, money, all the perks. Her producer had been thrilled, as well. High ratings meant job stability for everyone involved in her daytime show. Neither her agent nor her producer seemed concerned about the things that concerned her, like the possibility that a short-term gain could lead to a crashing and burning. Everyone was so focused on the ratings now, now, now, that they weren't seeing the future. And money. It was always about money. It had never been that to her, but maybe that was wrong. Money allowed her to care for people she loved. To snub her nose at it would be crazy.

"The future, *your future,* could be *Stepping Up,*" she said to the empty room.

One door closes and another opens, her father's voice in her head added. The man had too many sayings and made too much sense. She wanted to call him, to tell him what she was feeling, to ask his advice. He'd make her feel better, but at what price? This time, it was her place to make him feel better. It was her role to make sure he knew everything was going to be okay.

Darla realized her phone was vibrating, still on silent from when she'd been filming. Shoot. It was probably her parents. She had to shake off her mood and be cheerful. She was going to have to resist the urge to do what she always did, and tell them everything.

Darla grabbed her purse and dug out her phone only to see a text come through. It's Blake was all the message read.

Darla stared at the text, waiting for him to say something more, but he didn't. She told herself not to respond, but the truth was, she was going to see him and see him plenty. Hiding from him wasn't an answer. Running from him wouldn't get her far. No. Blake was in her life to stay. Proof yet again that she was not only lousy at choosing her dates, she was lousy at choosing one-night stands.

She punched the pad of her phone and typed, It's Darla.

His reply was instant. The same Darla who won't answer her phone?

She punched the history on her phone and realized she'd missed four calls—all in the past hour. Her parents had called once. Blake owned the other three attempts.

Darla considered the situation, then typed I don't like to talk on the phone.

You're mean to me was his reply.

You're very perceptive, she typed back before she could stop herself.

I guess you don't want to know what I'm going to say in the meeting tomorrow, then.

She sat up and stared at the phone, then punched the call button. The instant he answered, she said, "That was manipulation, just like when you called me and told me to meet you by my room."

"Guilty," he agreed. "But both times were with good intentions."

"You knew about this hosting thing and didn't tell me," she accused, shifting the conversation to the thing that had bothered her all day long.

"Not guilty on that one," he said. "I—"

"*You didn't* tell me."

"I would have," he argued, "but once again you tucked tail and ran from me." She opened her mouth to deny it and he added, "And don't tell me you didn't, because we both know you did. That left me with two options. Tell you about the possible hosting job through the bathroom door so you had something to worry about besides Lana, or wait to tell you this evening, when you had put Lana behind you. I chose the latter and knowing what a worrier you are, I'd do it again. Unfortunately, Meagan's time line to deal with Rick's departure bit me in the ass. And speaking of being bitten in the proverbial ass, what was that about me trying to smash your show? That was a low blow."

Darla cringed inwardly. "You hadn't told me about the hosting thing."

"And that makes me a low-down dirty snake?"

"No."

"And?"

And what? "Okay. I tend to just react rather than think first when I feel trapped. I need to work on that. I'm sorry."

"Do you believe I want to destroy your show?"

"Before this conversation or after?"

"So you believed it when you said it?"

"I already admitted I reacted to being cornered," she admitted, and reluctantly added, because he deserved to have it said, "I know that you could have thrown me under the Lana bus, and you didn't."

He was silent a moment. "Did you talk to your agent?"

"Yes. You?"

"Yes."

"And?" she prodded.

"You first."

"Fine. He said a few good years on a prime-time show could equal more money and opportunity than twenty years on my daytime show."

"Why do I sense a *but?*"

"I just don't like the instability of being camera talent," she confessed, surprised at how easily she shared her feelings with him. "I liked casting because I knew I had a job—a stable job I could count on. This is like gambling all the time on the right step for this level of career or that level of career."

"I felt that same thing when I started out," he admitted. "But I invested well as soon as I had the money to do so, and I made sure I was secure even if I lose the show."

"Investing has never been my thing." But it was smart. She knew it was.

"Maybe you should watch my show," he teased, and then added, "And warning. If my father comes to any of these tapings, and he finds out you don't invest, he'll insist on it."

If his father came to any of the shows. "So. I guess that means you're taking the job?"

"My agent wants me to. We'll see how it goes with the studio. You really don't want me to take it, do you?"

No. Yes. She wanted him. That seemed a potential problem. "I'm conflicted."

"About me doing the show or about Meagan's plan or—"

"About all of it, but you in particular."

"I see," he drawled. "Well. Why don't we work on that when you come back to New York two days from now?" His voice was low, sensual.

Her body instantly reacted, heating up. His scent ever-present. "I'll only go back to New York if you take the job."

"That sounds like an incentive to me."

The way he said the words rushed over her and panic set in. She was going to wind up caring for this man, and either get hurt or ruin her career. "We can't see each other on a personal level. Not when we have to work so closely together. Had I known any of this was going to happen, I would never have started this."

More thick silence filled the air. "Okay," he agreed finally.

Okay? "Okay?" Her voice quivered and so did the muscles in her stomach. She didn't know why. She did know why. She didn't want to admit why.

"Isn't that what you wanted me to say?"

No, but it was the right answer, even if she didn't want it to be. "Yes."

"Fine then. I'll let you go. We both have big days tomorrow."

She inhaled. "Okay." She really hated that word.

"Good night, Darla," he said softly, and hung up.

She stared at the phone, emotion welling in her chest. And she didn't know how it happened, but she punched redial. "That's it?" she demanded when he answered. "Good night?" He laughed. "Don't laugh, Blake." He laughed again and she repeated, "I said—"

"Don't laugh. I know. I already told you that I'm crazy about you, Darla. That hasn't changed. But I've yet to hear you make one statement that says you feel the same about me. I'm no glutton for punishment. You want this to be all business, we'll make it all business."

She didn't know what to say. She liked him. She wanted him. She was just so damn…conflicted. "Okay." She hung up before she defined what she was saying *okay* to. Hung up! She pressed her hand to her face. Could she make more of a fool of herself with this man?

14

BLAKE HAD TAKEN THE HOSTING job. Now, three days after hanging up on her new coworker rival former lover, Darla was back in New York and about to see him for the first time since then. With a garment bag thrown over her shoulder, she stood outside the twentieth-floor studio of renowned photographer to the stars, Frankie Masse. He was shooting the promos for *Stepping Up*.

She reached for the door but pulled back, nervous not because Frankie had been an intimidating and bossy man during her solo shoot at his studio the day before, but because of Blake. Yes. She was, without question, ridiculously nervous about seeing Blake again.

"Is the door locked?"

Darla jumped at the unexpected sound of his voice. "Blake." Her hand balled on her chest at his presence, suddenly finding him so close she could reach up and touch him. And she wanted to. "I didn't hear the elevator. You scared me."

His blue eyes swept over the ivory suit that Frankie

had requested her to wear. He wore a black suit himself, the dark color a dramatic contrast to her lighter one. The expression on his face was both intimate and familiar, perhaps mimicking her own. He was remembering— just as she was, she had no doubt—how intimate and familiar they'd been together. She had been thinking a lot about Blake, and not just about the pleasure-filled moments in that hotel room. But also about their banter on the plane and the way he'd come to her rescue with Lana. The way his eyes danced with mischief at times when someone else's would burn with anger.

"You must have had something pretty intense on your mind," he suggested, his voice a gentle caress—a *knowing* caress. "Because the elevator creaks like an old man with arthritis."

"I guess I did," she admitted, realizing exactly what was bothering her and what she had to do. "About the phone call the other night—"

"When you hung up on me?"

Her lips thinned. "You hung up on me first."

"I said, 'Good night.' You just said 'Okay.'"

"Because *you* said, 'Okay.'"

His eyes narrowed. "Isn't that what you wanted me to say?"

She wet her lips, his eyes following the movement. Heat pooled low in her belly. No. No, it wasn't what she'd wanted him to say and that was the problem. Or maybe it wasn't really a problem. Maybe she was needlessly making it a problem. She wanted to just say that to him, to talk to him. That brought her clarity. She trusted

Blake enough to tell him how vulnerable she felt and that meant something. It meant he was worth taking a risk on.

She drew in a breath and let it out. "What I wanted, or rather, what I want—" she started to say, but the elevator creaked open as loudly as he had claimed.

"Is the door locked?" Meagan said from behind Blake.

"Saved by the proverbial bell," Blake said softly, before stepping to the side to greet Meagan. "We just arrived. We were about to go inside."

"Excellent, then," Meagan replied, waving them forward. "Let's get snapping those photos. I'd like to actually give myself and Darla a chance to relax before we head to Chicago at the crack of dawn tomorrow morning."

"Of course," Blake said, expecting Darla to step away from him. Instead, she leaned in, looking him in the eyes.

"You keep assuming I need, or want, to be saved." She threw open the door to the photography room, just as she had opened the door to the possibilities between herself and Blake.

TIME TICKED BY SLOWLY WHILE Blake waited on Darla to be out of hair and makeup for the photo shoot. He was thinking about their exchange in the hallway. Thinking about how much he wanted it to be enough. Enough to take her home with him tonight. Enough to hold her again—if not now, sometime soon. Enough to take the risk to get to know her better.

He shifted from foot to foot and leaned against the

wall framing a massive window overlooking the city. He'd seen the heat in Darla's stare, the desire glinting in the depths of her beautiful green eyes. Desire. Lust. An attraction that they seemed to generate when they were anywhere near each other. But he'd also seen her hesitation to answer his question about their phone call. She didn't need saving. She wasn't any more certain about him than she had been before. And the thing was, he was on uncertain ground of his own. Blake had never felt this way about a woman and he didn't know if that made it important that he press her now, or just the opposite. Maybe he needed to back off, to let her run. A few of his father's words echoed in his mind. *Son. You never want anything that doesn't come honest.*

Blake scrubbed his jaw. Damn it. He didn't want anything that wasn't honest from Darla—anything not genuine. He couldn't push Darla. He *wouldn't* push her. It had to come honest. *They* had to come honest.

"Let's get started," Frankie shouted. "Blake and Darla, I need you in the center of the room."

Blake shoved off the wall to find three of Frankie's staff members gathering nearby, while Meagan stepped away to take a call on her cell. Frankie waved Blake to a twelve-by-twelve squared-off area floored with white tiles and enclosed by hardwood, umbrellas and cameras. Darla appeared at the opposite edge of the set.

Her gaze swept over him and came to rest on his face. She actually managed to scald him with a look of pure lust in the same instant that she damned him for apparently making her do so. Would she ever figure out her feelings for him?

"Okay, Blake and Darla," Meagan said, shoving her slim phone back into snug, faded jeans. "One of the studio bigwigs is in town, and he and several of the show's top sponsors want to meet us all for dinner." She eyed her watch. "They made reservations for seven, which is going to make it tight for me to get home and change. If either of you have a reason to get us out of this that they'll buy, speak up now, please."

"Ten years in this business has taught me to say 'yes' as often as possible," Blake commented. "There will be more important times when you'll have to say 'no.'"

"Considering I'm with a competing network," Darla said, "I don't think it would get me brownie points to miss this."

"You work for both networks," Meagan corrected. "I wish you'd start feeling like you belong here." She grinned. "Blake, I really don't like how right you are, but okay. Dinner it is." She cast Darla a wistful look. "We'll have time to sleep on the plane."

"Have you flown with Darla?" Blake asked, disbelievingly. "Because she won't be sleeping—and neither will you if you're sitting next to her."

"Right," Meagan said drily. "Yes, I have, and you make another good point. Sorry, Darla. I might need to get my seat changed."

Darla sighed. "I understand. Send a new victim, I mean passenger, my way. I'll torture them so you can sleep."

Blake and Meagan started laughing, but so did Darla, just as she had in the hallway when she'd tripped, even in front of Lana. He liked her lack of airs, her willingness to be herself and to not take herself so seriously.

"Are we ready to get this moving?" Frankie asked testily.

Meagan stepped out of the way. "They're all yours."

"Both of you cross your arms in front of your chests," Frankie ordered immediately, "and stare each other down in challenge."

"That shouldn't be a problem for us," Blake said, refocusing on Darla and doing as Frankie directed.

"Not a problem at all," Darla agreed, mimicking his stance by folding her arms in front of her chest, her slim jacket defining her petite waist and flaring out to accent her womanly curves.

Frankie started snapping photos. "Good," he shouted, showing more excitement than Blake thought the man had in him. "Good. Darla. Step closer to Blake."

Darla didn't move. Blake arched a brow. "Thought you didn't need to be saved?"

A look of surprise flashed on her face, as if her hesitation had been instinctive and she hadn't realized what she'd done. She stepped forward. "I don't. In fact, I'd venture to say that if anyone needs to be saved, it's you."

"Love the anger, Darla!" Frankie shouted, as if she intended her attitude for the camera.

"Anger?" Darla repeated, still looking at Blake.

"You do sound pretty angry."

"I'm not angry," she insisted. "I'm not. I'm—"

"Conflicted," Blake supplied.

"Not anymore," she corrected.

"You seem conflicted to me."

"I'm not."

"Closer to each other," Frankie yelled. "I want you almost toe-to-toe, and Darla, give him another prickly stare."

"Prickly," Darla repeated, turning toward the camera. "I was not prickly and I'm not angry."

"Look at Blake!" Frankie ordered.

Darla jerked her gaze back to Blake, looking like a scolded child. He laughed. She glared.

"That's the anger I want," Frankie approved. "Closer, though. Closer."

"You laugh at the most inappropriate times," Darla scolded. She inched forward, leaving no room for Frankie to complain now that the tips of her high heel shoes were touching the tips of Blake's shoes.

He could smell her perfume, floral and soft. "Says who?"

"I imagine everyone who's experienced it."

"Is that right?"

"It is. Maybe that's your way of hiding from whatever it is that's being said."

"Hiding?" he said. "You're accusing *me* of hiding?"

"That's right. Hiding."

"Back to back," Frankie directed. "Backs touching, arms folded in front of your bodies again."

Darla turned. Blake laughed and rotated, then stepped backward, bringing them into direct contact. The connection delivered a jolt of awareness he'd foolishly been unprepared for. Heat sizzled a path through every nerve ending he had.

"Still laughing?" she challenged with a soft taunt for his ears only. She was feeling it, too—the sizzle. The heat.

Blake lowered his voice, ready to taunt in reply. "I didn't run into the bathroom and lock the door." He expected a quick jab back. He didn't get it.

There was a moment of silence, a thickening of the air, before she said, all signs of taunting gone, "I regret doing that. I regret it a lot."

The emotion he heard in her confession and radiating from her body language caught him off guard. "Don't," he started. "Do—"

"Lean back farther. Both of you," Frankie interrupted, and the instant they complied, a slew of pictures followed. Another pose, then another. Frankie kept the camera snapping until he sent them to opposite sides of the set to allow his crew to set up props.

A minute or two later, Blake was sitting in an office chair, while she sat on top of a desk, her legs crossed. Her long, gorgeous legs, he noted. "Roll the chair closer to Darla," Frankie directed Blake. "Darla, I want you to spike that high heel into his chest."

"No!" Meagan said, laughing. "They have a history with shoes and I've already lost one host to an injury."

"I'll be gentle," Darla promised, grinning at Meagan before fixing Blake with a mischievous look. "Though, it's awfully tempting to give him a little roughing up."

"Hurts so good," Blake assured her, motioning to her foot. "Bring it on." He rolled a little closer to her.

"Wait." Frankie motioned to several crew members, before giving Blake and Darla his back to huddle with the others. Blake seriously doubted that they were talking about a camera lens, but he knew an opportunity when he saw it.

Blake rolled the chair around so that only Darla could see his face. "About the bathroom—" he started.

"I ran," she finished for him quietly, glancing toward the others to make sure they still weren't paying them any mind. "I started freaking out about my job and—"

"And that's okay," he said, meaning it. He could barely contain the urge to touch her, but he was all too experienced with the camera to know it too easily captured what you didn't want captured. "It was an honest reaction to an honest emotion." Their eyes locked and held for several silent moments. "Honest is what I'm looking for. And I promise you, no matter how much this business defies you believing it, you won't get anything less from me."

Surprise lit her expression, her eyes softened from bright to light green. "I believe you."

Blake felt the warmth of her growing confidence. He'd never wanted a woman like he did this one, and it was all he could do to remind himself that this was a tiny step forward, not more. Not enough. Not yet.

"Let's go," Frankie said. "Darla. Spike that heel onto his chest. Gently, please. Save the rough stuff for later."

Darla's tongue darted over her red lips. "Later it is." She pressed her heel to his chest.

Instinctively, Blake's hand went to her calf.

Darla shivered, and he was pretty sure he shook on the inside. And only from a small, simple touch. Darla's claim of "it's complicated" came to his mind and he amended his thoughts. There was nothing simple about what this woman did to him.

"No touching!" Frankie ordered. "You aren't supposed to like each other."

"We don't," Darla assured Frankie, staring intently into Blake's eyes.

Blake took his hand away. "Not at all," he agreed.

Blake had promised himself when he'd ended that phone call with Darla back in Denver that he would take things slow with her from here on out, that he would backtrack and make up for rushing too fast out of the gate and into bed. But as he sat there, her skirt riding high on her toned thighs, her delicate knees opened just wide enough to tease him, his cock mercilessly stretched against his zipper and he knew he was in for a rough ride. Oh, yeah. He was definitely in for the rough stuff later, when he might be the one to walk away from a chance to use those five condoms. Because he would, because he had to, if he wanted more than sex with Darla. And he did, he realized with certainty. He did.

Tonight would be a test of his willpower, which he'd always considered solid. Until Darla.

15

EVEN THREE HOURS AFTER the sexually charged photo session, Blake's body still hummed with awareness, with desire, for Darla. It didn't seem to matter that she sat across but several seats down from him at the rectangular table of the happening uptown Italian eatery. She was nowhere near close enough for him to accidentally touch her or to draw in that delicate floral scent of hers.

"Excuse me," the stuffed studio shirt he'd been talking ratings with said when his phone rang. "I've been expecting this call." The man pushed to his feet and headed in search of privacy.

For the millionth time since arriving at the restaurant, Blake's gaze gravitated toward Darla, where she chatted stiffly with Mark Mercer, another studio exec whom Blake both knew and disliked. Mark was also enjoying Darla's time far too much for comfort. Blake wasn't sure who he was more irritated with, though. Mark, for managing to sit next to Darla. Or Darla, for clearly enjoying his company.

"Well, thank you, gentlemen, but it's time for me to head back to the hotel." Meagan rose to her feet as various members of the group followed. Finally, this little piece of hell was over, Blake thought, as he stood up with the rest of their party.

"Can I share a taxi with you?" Mark asked Darla. "I think we're going in the same direction." His tone was friendly and casual, but the look in his eyes was the opposite. Blake found himself sucking in a quiet breath and holding it, waiting for Darla's reply. Darla would say no. He knew she would say no. *If,* he added silently, he hadn't misjudged her ambition.

"Sorry to have to decline," Darla replied, sounding as if she meant it in a tight, forced kind of way. "I actually have a friend from out of town meeting me here for drinks in a few minutes."

Air escaped from Blake's lips and his muscles relaxed, telling him just how important her response had really been to him. Only then did he allow himself to admit the truth. In the back of his mind, worry had been alive and well. Worry that Darla's need to please everyone associated with *Stepping Up* would spell trouble.

Blake curled his fingers into his palms as he watched Mark slide his hand around her waist and whisper something in her ear. Darla gave a forced laugh in response before the man turned away from her. Darla's gaze found Blake's, and he felt the impact immediately. She affected him so easily—too easily. For just an instant,

he wasn't overly comfortable with that. But then her expression softened and he could feel her reaching out to
him. She wasn't meeting anyone. Neither was she leaving with the group. She didn't want him to, either. And
though he knew he should, knew that distance would
provide the willpower he needed to slow things down
between them, there wasn't a chance in hell that he
wasn't leaving here without her. He also wasn't about
to make that obvious.

Blake wished her a casual good-night and followed
the group to the front of the restaurant. Like the gentleman his parents raised, he hit the corner to flag the
needed cabs, starting with one for Meagan.

She stepped forward, but stopped at the cab door to
say, "There's still something going on with Darla." It
was a warning rather than a question. "You two have
chemistry. I like you together. But if the public figures
out you're together, like I have, then the advertising tease
we're doing—the daytime enemies come together in
prime time—it won't work. The tease will be gone. Stay
low-key. Don't let this affect the show. You know how
studios are. On top one day and kicked to the curb the
next. There are too many jobs on the line, too many lives
changed, to blow this."

"We'll be careful," Blake promised. "You have my
word."

She studied him for a moment longer and started to
slide into the car. "Meagan." She paused in midmotion,
giving him a questioning look. "I appreciate the way

you shoot straight," he said. "It's a rare quality in this business. With you, I'll do the same."

She smiled warmly. "You better."

ONCE BLAKE WAS THE ONLY ONE left standing on the sidewalk, he could feel the charge of anticipation of what was to come—of him and Darla being alone, even if it was in a public place.

He turned to go back inside the restaurant, only to find Darla standing behind him, her garment bag swung over her shoulder. Somehow she appeared a few inches shorter than he remembered. His gaze dropped to her feet, where her heels had been replaced with flats.

She glanced down and then back up. "A girl learns practicality when she lives in this city. My apartment's only a few blocks from here. I'm going to walk it."

"What about your friend that's meeting you?"

Her lips lifted slightly. That amazing awareness between them was back, and he wondered if the people milling on the sidewalk were feeling the charge. "His name is Blake," she finally said. "So glad you made it." Her voice was a caress, a promise.

He knew this could be a big mistake, but still, he found himself smiling and moving toward her. "I'll walk with you. What do you have in that bag, anyway?"

"Frankie had me bring three changes of clothes in case he hated one or more of my options, which he was sure he would," she said, handing him the bag. "He's a very cranky man."

"Artistic types that are too talented for their own good can be that way," he said.

"Very true," she agreed. She pointed to her right. "I'm this way." She wet her lips. Damn, every time she did that his body reacted. He really was ridiculously, insanely, affected by this woman.

He nodded, and they started walking. "What time do you fly out in the morning?" he asked, trying to get his mind back on the present and not on the bedroom that could be in their future.

"Eight. Which means leaving my apartment by six."

"Ouch. That stings."

"I'm not complaining," she said. "I feel blessed to have this opportunity. It's just a little challenging to film my morning show in between auditions. It'll be easier once I'm filming from the L.A. studios. And now that I put Lana in her place, I'm enjoying the auditions. I don't want to worry that I'm going to deliver poor quality content and disappoint my audience."

"I'm glad to hear you feel things are settled down with Lana, and you have a loyal audience so I don't think you have to worry. They watch because of your reactions to situations and your personality, not because of the setting you're in." He cast her a sideways glance and watched as a slight breeze dusted blond wisps of her hair across her pale cheek. Everything male inside him stirred, but there was more. There was emotion—unfamiliar and potent. Emotion that drove him to the burning questions that demanded to be answered. "You've conquered the Lana problem. What about flying? Are you handling that any better than you did that studio guy hitting on you tonight?"

She stopped and turned to him, her eyes flashing with rebuttal. "I handled him just fine."

"So you admit he was hitting on you?"

"I know what he was doing."

"You could have shut down his nonsense but you didn't."

"I was polite and standoffish. It's what girls do in that type of situation."

Right. "I guess."

"You guess? What did you want me to do? Make a fool of him so he hates me? Make everyone think he's an idiot? And because I'm reading an underlying meaning here, it had nothing to do with his position at the studio. I would never blatantly make someone feel bad."

"He was using your eagerness to please the studio to corner you."

"He's a jerk," she agreed. "But that doesn't mean I have to be. I was brought up better and smarter than that. It's a small industry, one that breeds enemies without having to look for them."

Damn. "You're right," he said, suddenly relaxing. He hadn't even realized until that moment just how tense he'd felt. "I'm sorry. I just get irritated at the entire casting couch mentality in this business. I wanted to belt him one."

Her expression softened. "I appreciate that, but I'm a big girl. I can handle myself. I tried to do exactly as you suggested earlier. Choose my battles smartly."

He shook his head. "I'm sorry. I shouldn't have put you on the defensive like that."

"Then why did you?" she asked, narrowing her gaze at him.

He didn't offer some fancy talking-in-circles reply. He wanted honesty; he had to give honesty. "I just want to know who you are, Darla. I want to know the real you. Not the public persona."

"There's no difference for me, Blake," she declared without so much as a blink of an eye. "I am all I know how to be."

An old, suppressed memory surfaced, and with it more raw emotions. A memory of a time when he had been young and naive, riding a wave of early success.

"Who burned you, Blake?" Darla asked softly, drawing his gaze, which had drifted to the pavement.

The question stopped him cold. How easily she had read him, read what he was denying even to himself. A name ran through his mind, a name he hadn't allowed himself to say, even silently, in years.

He shoved away the memory. He wasn't ready to talk about this. Hell, he hadn't even wanted to *think* about it. He hadn't even realized just how easily *he could* think about it. It—*she*—happened ten flipping years ago. He hadn't really loved her. He'd…

Suddenly, Darla held his hand. "Tell me when you're ready." She motioned them forward. "Let's walk."

He wasn't sure she could have done anything more perfect in that moment, giving him a pass but also giving him an open door, not to mention her understanding.

A few seconds passed and he gave a quick nod. They started walking again, both staring up at the dark sky, dotted with stars. And with each step, he felt himself relax. It was a comfortable night, no longer humid and not yet cold and all the more enjoyable because of Darla.

"Are you keeping your morning show focused on *Stepping Up* throughout the auditions?"

"Only a short segment for each show," she said. "I'm afraid to overdo it and drive away viewers who crave the usual things on the show. What about you?" She pointed and they turned down a tree-lined street with rows of condolike housing.

"I'm going to incorporate the travel destinations as much as I can. For instance, my dad's coming to Vegas Week. We're doing a mechanical-bull-riding competition with a group of ex-rodeo stars. Unfortunately, we couldn't get it booked at the same hotel as the show, so it's at a property owned by the company. The winner takes ten thousand dollars to their charity of choice, provided by the studio."

"That's an awesome idea, Blake. I love it. And you know, that's right up my alley. I am a rancher's daughter."

"I can see the down-home country girl in you," he said. "An accident-prone down-home country girl who must have driven her parents crazy."

"My father tried to keep me away from the ranch action," she admitted. "It never worked. Proven by the six times that I had to get stitches."

"You'll have to show me the scars."

She held up her elbow. "That's the only one you can see." She grinned. "Well, when I have my clothes on."

"Like I said, you'll have to show me the scars."

"I'll think about it," she teased playfully. "Did you inherit any of your dad's bull-riding skill?"

"I have an ex-rodeo champion for a father. If I couldn't ride, he'd have had me hung up by my toes for the bulls."

"I've ridden a mechanical bull a time or two," she declared.

"No way."

She nodded. "Way."

"Prove it. If you come to the event and ride, I'll personally donate to the charity of your choice myself."

She laughed. "I'm in. Well, as long as it's not a conflict with filming."

"It's the day after Vegas Week ends."

"Then get your checkbook ready. I'll be there."

"Good," he said, more than prepared to plan six weeks ahead with her. "We can fly out to L.A. together when it's over. Which brings me back to my earlier question. How *are* you handling the flying you're doing?"

She snorted. "Who said I'm handling it?"

"That good, huh?"

"That good." She stopped in front of a building. "This is me. How far away are you?"

"A cab ride," he said, not really wanting to tell her the high-end area he lived in, because it had taken him years of doing his show and investing well to get there. She would get there, too, probably sooner than he had.

"I see," she said, biting her bottom lip and gesturing toward the door. "You want to come up?"

He wanted to come up, all right, and that was a problem. Up meant he was one step away from being inside her apartment. Once he was there, it was all over. He'd forget all the reasons why he shouldn't strip her naked and make wild, passionate love to her. He'd have to survive a kiss. But not down here in the open.

"I'll walk you to your door."

DARLA WAS INCREDIBLY NERVOUS as she walked the narrow tenth-floor hallway with Blake on her heels. It wasn't as if this was the first time she'd been with Blake, but this time felt different. This time not only had she decided to take a chance on Blake, she knew he had taken a chance on her, as well. She'd seen the look on his face when she'd asked who had burned him. And now she knew he was diving into territory he wasn't comfortable in, but that he was doing it for her. She didn't have to know the details. She just wanted to know him. She wanted to understand him. She wanted to wipe away the pain she'd seen in his eyes before he'd looked away.

Her stomach fluttered as she reached her loft's tiny entryway. She reached for her purse, only to realize it was in the bag Blake was carrying. She turned. The space was small. He was big. He was good-looking. He was sexy. She was suddenly burning up, her cheeks flaming right along with the rest of her body.

"My keys are in my purse." She motioned to the bag. "In there."

He shifted the bag from his shoulder to hold it in front of him. She unzipped it and dug in her purse and somehow her shaking hand found her keys. She dropped them and immediately bent down to get them. So did Blake. Their hands touched and they both abandoned the keys.

"Blake," she whispered. "I—"

He snatched the keys and helped her to her feet. "I'll unlock the door for you."

"Okay." Though neither of them moved. A second later he abruptly tossed the bag and the keys to the floor.

His hand slid into her hair at the same instant his mouth came down on hers. She stood on her toes and leaned into him, meeting his kiss with her own. His breath was warm, his body hard. Sandwiched between Blake and the door, she couldn't think of a better place to be in that moment.

The first stroke of his tongue sent a sizzle down her spine. The second turned the sizzle to fire. She was burning up all over again, and he was the only way to cool down. She pressed herself against him, seeking that cool heat. He answered by deepening the kiss and running his hands in all kinds of places she wanted them, needed them. There was a wildness in her she'd never experienced, a hunger only this man gave her.

His free hand skimmed her waist, her breast, her nipple, sending a rush of sensation between her thighs— where she wanted him so very bad right now. Actually, she wanted to get lost in him. Her palms pulled him closer, caressing his powerfully muscled back. Yes. Lost. Please.

Voices suddenly echoed in the building, followed by the sound of keys jiggling in a lock. Blake pulled back, holding himself away from her. His breath was thick, his eyes dark. "I'm sorry, Darla. I didn't mean—"

She leaned in and kissed him. "I did." She bent down and snatched up the keys, then stood again. "Let's go inside." She turned and unlocked the door. Blake stepped in close to her, his hand sliding to her stomach, his lips lowering to her ear.

"I'm not coming in," he said, his voice low and gravelly. "I—"

"You are," she said. "You're coming in." She reached to the ground by his feet and grabbed her bag and shoved it inside, behind the door.

He rested a hand on the door frame above the ringer. "I promised myself I wouldn't do this again until I knew you couldn't write this off as just sex."

Instinct told her that he wanted to know she was taking this risk with him. "There's two of us in this relationship, Blake. And I should tell you right now, you don't get to set all the rules."

He went completely still. "Relationship?"

"Yes. Relationship. You were right, back in Denver. This was never a one-night stand."

"What about the competition thing?"

"You've proven to me that you'll look out for my best interests," she said, thinking of his expression again when she'd asked him who'd burned him. "I hope you believe I'll do the same for you, because I will." She reached out and drew his hand with hers. "I want you to come inside and not for one night. I want you to come inside my life. We'll figure out how to make that work together."

Still, he didn't move, and she started to feel sick, to anticipate rejection. Maybe she'd misjudged this—him, them. Maybe he had simply wanted the challenge of pursuit. The chase. Men liked the chase. He was going to walk away. He was going to leave. She retreated a step, feeling foolish and exposed. And that's when he took a step forward.

16

"BLAKE—" DARLA GASPED as he kicked the door shut and took her in his arms, his mouth soon on hers. She moaned against his lips and desperately tried to resist him, to reason with herself. But when his tongue stroked hers and his hand caressed down her hair, she did what she always did with Blake. She surrendered to what he made her feel, to that unnamed, ever-important something he always made her *need*.

"Whatever you were thinking when you started to back up," he breathed against her lips, "was wrong."

"You—"

"I what?" He kissed her, a deep passionate kiss that must have distracted Darla because she realized they were next to the couch. Again he asked, "I what, Darla?"

The heady masculine scent of him enveloped her, engulfing her in need. "You have this bad habit of having too many clothes on," she answered, shoving his jacket over his shoulders and caressing his powerful shoulders.

Blake caught the jacket at his elbows and reached up to frame her face with hands too big to be so gentle.

"What were you thinking when you backed away from me?" he demanded gently. "I want to know."

Her heart stilled a moment during which she considered avoidance or denial, but she quickly decided against any strategy at all. She didn't want secrets with Blake. She wanted what he had claimed he wanted: honesty.

"I thought," she admitted, "that you only wanted me when you thought I was a challenge. That when I invited you into my life freely, you would no longer want me."

He drew back, slightly surprised. His gorgeous, heavy-lidded eyes probed hers. "No," he said, shrugging his half-removed jacket off and letting it fall to the floor. His fingers framed her neck. "No. That's not the case, Darla. We are so much more than that. You do things to me that I can't even try to understand. I just want to keep feeling them. I want…I need to know I make you feel them, too."

Emotion swelled in her chest. Her hand went to one of his. "You do, Blake. I've just been freaked out because of our jobs and because I… My…" She stopped herself before she confessed her family struggles, her gaze dropping to his chest. There was a difference between being honest and revealing your most personal private secrets. She didn't want him to feel obligated to help or support her because she was struggling. No. Honest was what honest was, but he didn't deserve to carry her family's burden. Still, he just felt so big and strong, such an easily created hero, and it would be equally easy to just let him take care of her. And wrong and weak and…

He drew her fingers to his lips. "Tell me, Darla."

She blinked him back into view. She was tempted by the gentle prod he'd spoken once before back in the hotel, as well, and comforted by the fact that she was certain he wouldn't push her to reply, as she hadn't pushed him earlier on the street. She liked that. She liked that he'd wait on her to be ready, just as he was willing to wait before making love. Not that she wanted to wait. But he would wait—*for her.*

She touched his jaw, letting the light stubble rasp against her fingertips. "I'm just glad you're here, Blake. Right here, where you can be all mine." Her hand traveled the wall of his chest, then she pulled his shirt from his pants. She smoothed her hands underneath, over taut skin and flexing muscle. "Thank you for what you tried to do, but no thank you. Stay. I want you to stay." She nibbled his bottom lip, felt her core clench with anticipation. "I promise to make you as sleep-deprived as I'll be tomorrow."

"I'm not going anywhere," he said, molding her closer with a spray of longer fingers at the base of her back. "Not unless you make me." He leaned in and brushed his lips over hers, a soft caress and a flicker of tongue just past her teeth, a delicious tease as he murmured, "You taste too good." He pushed her jacket over her shoulders as she had his. Darla shrugged out of it and Blake was already pulling her to him again, claiming her mouth with his, making love to her with his tongue, his hands bringing her closer and driving her wild. Need charged every nerve ending in her body.

Darla fumbled with his shirt buttons, eager to touch him, to explore every last inch of his hard, hot body. He seemed to feel the same. He fumbled with her blouse, his anxious touch sent buttons flying. She didn't care. She just wanted skin against skin. He shoved down her bra on one side and palmed her breast, squeezed her nipple, rough but right. Oh, *so* right. Darla moaned with pleasure, covering his hand with hers.

He slipped a hand beneath her skirt, over her lacy thigh-high stockings and then over her bare backside. He moaned at the same time she did, nipping her bottom lip with his teeth. "Darla, do you have any idea how badly I wanted to do this when you were sitting on that desk during the photo shoot today?" His fingers dipped lower, teasing her with how close he was to the wet heat of her core. He lowered his head and she felt warm breath on her neck before his lips brushed her sensitive skin. "All I could think about was how easily I could have just pulled you close and tasted you again. How much I wanted to lick you and tease you until you called my name." He squeezed her nipple, flicked it. "Did you think of me touching you, Darla? Of me tasting you?"

"Yes," she whispered, shocked that she was admitting such a thing, that she had indeed thought those things in the middle of a public place. But she had. Yes, she had. She'd thought of everything, from him tasting her with his mouth on her in the most intimate of ways, to Blake, in all his naked glory, riding her, buried inside her. It had driven her wild. He was driving her wild now. He made her feel free and uninhibited.

"I've waited hours for this," Blake growled huskily. "Hours that I told myself I couldn't have you. Not tonight."

She leaned into him. He was strong and solid, and perfect in ways she couldn't begin to name or understand. He just…was. "I bet you say that to all the women."

His hands framed her face, his eyes finding hers. "Just you, Darla. You get that, right? There's just you."

Emotion expanded in her chest at the unexpected confession. "Good," she whispered, because it was all she could manage to get out before she could even think about perhaps holding back, being guarded.

"I like that answer," he said a moment before his mouth slanted over hers, his tongue caressing hers with sensual strokes that she felt from head to toe. There was something more happening between them than a few wild nights, something that had no place in the midst of their jobs, but she couldn't seem to care.

She lost herself in the sensation of him touching her, barely aware of how her skirt, his as well, even her bra, had disappeared, just as her inhibitions had the instant this man came into her life. There was only a momentary return to reality in which she realized she was giving him total control. That she trusted him enough to allow him to have it. To enjoy his hands on her bare breasts, to cover them with her own and silently beg him not to stop. His lips brushed her ear, his warm breath sending a shiver down her spine, as he repeated, "Are you going to show me what's under that skirt, or leave me in painful anticipation?" He slid her side zipper down.

"I'd say I'd tease you a little but I think that might have to wait until later," she confessed, letting him inch it down her hips. She kicked it away the instant it hit the floor.

He set her at arm's length, his hands resting on her hips. The heat of his sizzling inspection was as arousing as his touch. Her skin flushed and she still felt sexy, and with Blake, it felt good. *Trust.* She felt trust and freedom with him that defied their short relationship. It was the second time she'd had such a thought and it spurred her into action, piercing the protective walls she maintained, making her want to please him. To show him how good he made her feel.

She approached him, her lips parting at the hungry expression she'd captured on his face. Hunger that bled into her, fed her desire, her passion to show him just how much she wanted him. Darla scraped her teeth over her bottom lip.

"Show *me,*" she whispered. Then in a louder voice, "Undress." She leaned against the couch with her hands behind her, comfortable in her nakedness with him. She liked that. She didn't remember ever feeling as playful or comfortable with any man before. Not that there had been many, but then, maybe that was why—they hadn't ever made her feel this way.

His gaze raked over her body and he took a step toward her. She pointed, the corners of her mouth lifting.

"Not until you have undressed. Halfway wasn't good enough the first time, and it still isn't."

He didn't laugh. In fact, he looked like he was going to combust with the effort to control himself, but he stopped and reached for his pants and toed off his shoes. Her hands immediately went to his waist, then slid over his broad chest, and lower still to his cock.

He made a rough, primal sound and reached for her. But she instantly went down on her knees. His erection jutted forward, thick and pulsing, and she wrapped her hand around it, forming a tight grip. She licked the head. "I'm going to show you how glad I am you stayed tonight."

"You did that when you told me to stay."

"Not as thoroughly as I wanted to." She lapped at the head of his cock, swirling her tongue around it. "You like that?" she asked, playing coy.

"Hell, yeah, I like it," he replied, his voice laden with desire.

Now, she felt in control. She licked him up and down. His expression darkened and he let out a long breath. She licked him some more, drawing him in her mouth and swirling. She was teasing him and he knew it. She wanted him to want her so bad that he couldn't hold back.

"You know you're killing me," he ground out, "don't you?"

"How?" she asked innocently, sucking only a few inches of him into her mouth and drawing back.

"You know how."

She drew him into the wet heat of her mouth until she could take no more.

"Yes," he groaned, his hand going to her head, urging her to keep going. "That's good, baby."

The endearment spoken so naturally made her heart flutter. The desperate need in his voice drove her crazy. She suckled him, her mouth and hand pumping him. Her other hand wrapped around him, using that rock-hard ass of his to steady herself. She wanted him to come, she wanted to know she'd taken this man to the brink.

Suddenly though, he pulled away from her.

"Enough," he said. "Enough." He was completely aroused, set on what he wanted. Before Darla could protest, he had lifted her and was carrying her to her bed. He placed her down on the navy blue-and-gray comforter and was on top of her in an instant, settling between her legs.

He rested his forehead against hers. "You smell good."

She laughed. "You suddenly realize I smell good?"

"I always notice you smell good." He smiled. "Now I know you taste good, too."

Her fingers curled on his cheek, heat pooling low in her belly at the intimate words. "I'm not sure I know how to respond to that."

"And that honest answer makes me want to ask you a very serious question."

Her breath hitched and she tried to pull back to see his face. "What?"

"Please tell me you have condoms and they are nearby."

Again, she found herself laughing. "Dresser drawer."

He didn't waste any time rolling off her to open the drawer. She scooted across the mattress, sliding up to his back as he held up the package. "Four," he said, his tone suddenly gruff. "Why are there only four left?"

Darla barely contained her laughter as she reached over and snatched the condom packages from him, nibbling his shoulders in the process. "One is in my purse, silly man. I wanted to be prepared. I was seeing you, after all."

He rolled over and pulled her on top of him. "Is that right?"

There was a possessive quality to his voice, and she liked it. "That," she assured him, "is absolutely right."

"So you thought we might—"

"Yes," she admitted, tearing one of the condoms from the rest and opening it. "I told myself we wouldn't do this tonight, that I should leave them all at home to be sure we didn't." She reached behind her and stroked his shaft, then raised and shifted her body so that she had better access. Wasting no time, she rolled the condom down the length of him—but not without sneaking in one last teasing lick.

"You'll pay for that," he promised, dragging her up his body, the V of her pelvis flattening on his hard length. He claimed her mouth, his tongue catching hers. His fingers glided over her clit, entering the ultrasensitive core of her body.

She couldn't take it. "Blake, please." She reached between them, fisted his shaft and pressed him inside her.

Relief rushed from her lips as he sunk deep within her. "Finally."

"Finally," he agreed.

They stared at each other, both unmoving and breathing together almost as one. Emotion swelled her heart. That something she'd felt earlier was back, stronger than ever.

"I don't know what you're doing to me," he said, repeating what he'd said before, what he'd said in the hotel in Denver. "But don't stop. I like it, and us, way too much."

"Me, too," she agreed, a moment before his mouth closed down on hers. He shifted his hips and she felt him beginning a slow sway that sent sensations exploding inside her. Their rhythmic grind turned into a fierce, wicked passion, like nothing she'd ever experienced. Until they were not just moving together, but practically trying to crawl under each other's skin. She didn't want it to end, but it had to end. Nothing this good could last forever.

Too soon, she cried out as her body clenched around his cock, the spasms shaking her with such intense bliss it almost hurt. He thrust one last time with his fists pressed to the mattress beside her, his head thrown back and his face etched with pleasure.

She smiled, clinging to him, her teeth nibbling her bottom lip. Taking a risk, letting go of a little control, might not be so bad after all.

17

Darla woke in a dark room, noting that she was alone. She felt across the bed, searching for Blake and not finding him. Her heart twisted in her chest, memories flooding her mind. This wasn't how she thought the morning would turn out. Not after she and Blake had spent hours talking, exchanging stories about their families, their jobs, their likes and dislikes. And making love. There had been lots of wonderful lovemaking that had eventually led to raiding her empty fridge. Twinkies and Starbursts had been their only hope of nourishment, considering she'd been home so rarely and hadn't bothered to stock up. It had been wonderful. She'd taken that risk with him, she'd dared to let herself be free with him. She'd fallen asleep, thinking that it had paid off with something special—that she and Blake had been special. Instead, he was gone without so much as a goodbye. Suddenly angry, Darla sat up, wearing nothing more than a T-shirt she'd put on when she'd gotten cold. It smelled of spicy cologne, of Blake. She'd trusted him, she'd—

"You're up. I didn't mean to wake you." She blinked into the darkness at him, his silhouette starting to take shape. He was dressed, about to leave, apparently.

"Why are you skulking around in the dark?"

He crossed the small space to sit beside her, leaning in and kissing her, a warm caress of his mouth over hers. His hand smoothed her rumpled hair. "Because you have exactly fifteen minutes until your alarm goes off, cranky, and I wasn't going to wake you for another seven so we could talk. I'd planned to have coffee in hand when I woke you, but it's not quite ready."

Her stomach rolled. "Talk?"

"Can I turn on the light?"

"If you don't mind seeing me look like I just stuck my finger in the light socket, then go for it."

He reached over and flipped the switch on the brown crystal lamp that had been her grandmother's. A dim glow lit the room. Self-consciously, she brushed at her hair, not sure why she cared. If this talk was what she suspected, it didn't matter how she looked anyway.

"You're beautiful," he said, settling down fully beside her. *He* was beautiful, she thought, with all that dark stubble shadowing his jaw, his hair tousled. This was a different Blake than the Mr. *GQ* the cameras saw. This was the Blake she'd come to know last night, the casual, sexy, wonderful man who loved his family, loved his life.

"I'm a wreck," she blurted, and it wasn't a counter to his compliment. She wasn't talking about her looks. He was in his thirties, a bachelor who'd never been engaged, per his prior night's confession. She had a feeling she was about to find out that was because he had a commitment phobia that matched her phobia of flying.

"You're not a wreck," he assured her, curling his hand around hers. "I wanted to talk to you about this before now, but time got away from me. Last night—"

"Was a mistake," she supplied, the words exploding from her lips. "I get that. I understand. You don't owe me—"

"Whoa!" he said, leaning back as if slapped. "What just happened? How did last night become a mistake? Because it sure as hell wasn't for me."

"It wasn't?" she asked, confused, a tiny light of hope forming in her. "But I thought you…"

He arched a brow. "You thought I what?"

"That you were about to say that."

He was still, his jaw set, hard. "Is that what you hoped I'd say?"

"No," she said honestly, unwilling to talk in circles. She wanted to know where they stood. She couldn't take any more uncertainty in her life right now. "You were just up and dressed and—"

He bent his head and kissed her, a tender swipe of his tongue against hers that sent a shiver of desire down her spine. "Do I seem like I think last night, or this morning, or anytime in the future for us, is a mistake?"

No. He didn't. "I'm sorry," she whispered, brushing her hand over his jaw. "Last night happened and now I fly out of town and it's just confusing."

He inched back to look into her eyes. "*Relationship,*

Darla. We talked about us being at that place before I even decided to stay the night."

He's worth taking a risk for, the voice in her head reminded her. "Yes," she agreed. "Relationship."

"Good," he said, pressing his lips to her forehead, his fingers brushing a wild strand of her hair behind her ear. "Which brings me back to where I was a few seconds ago. Last night, when I was hailing cabs for the group to leave the restaurant, Meagan told me that she knows we have something going on, and she's fine with it, with one condition."

"A condition," Darla repeated, her stomach knotting up all over again. She had conditions left and right, and conditions from Meagan were big, because, friend or not, Meagan was her boss.

"This new advertising campaign is being built on the two of us being ratings enemies. The studio is spending a fortune on it and they expect people to be intrigued by our dynamics. Some will watch to see us do battle. Others will hope we end up right where we have. The good news is that us being seen together isn't an issue. It feeds speculation. Being seen together in a way that makes our real relationship obvious is trouble, though, for the show—and trouble for us. We can't let the cast or crew know we're together. It's too risky. People sell things to the tabloids."

Darla wasn't surprised that Meagan supported their relationship after their talk in Denver, nor was she surprised about the concerns. "She's trying to protect the show. I understand that."

"I understand, as well, because she really did dive

in headfirst into making us a ratings grabber for the season. Ultimately, it's exposure for us both. We have to show gratitude for it by making it work. When this season ends, however, we'll have to make it clear we're going public with our feelings."

"Next season?" she asked, shocked that he was planning so far in advance.

He wrapped her in his arms. "Next season," he repeated. "Because I'm pretty sure you're going to make me fall in love with you long before that."

"Love?" she murmured, her heart pounding in her chest. Blake thought he was falling in love with her. "Did you say—"

"Love," he said. "Yes. Do you have a problem with that?"

"No," she replied hoarsely, "I don't have a problem with it at all, actually. But isn't it early to say that?"

"I'm thirty-two years old," he said, "and I've never once used that word with a woman. I don't think I'd call it rushing."

"Never?" she asked. "Not with anyone?"

"Never."

"Not even close?"

He hesitated. "Once. I was young and it's a long story for another time."

"The person who burned you," she said softly, trying not to push. She saw the tension shudder through him and she laid her hand on his leg. "You don't have to answer."

"It's not that I don't want to tell you. It's just not for here and now. I should leave before you do to avoid any prying eyes. That's why I got dressed while you were sleeping."

She shook her head. "I'm not pressuring you."

"I know," he said, cupping her face. "And I appreciate that." He studied her. "What about you? Ever say 'I love you' to a man?"

"There was a college boyfriend I thought I might be headed there with, but it turned out he was headed there with several women who thought the same thing." That was when she'd really learned just how bad a judge of men she really was. But she didn't want regrets or fears to make her lose Blake. If she got hurt, she got hurt. "No one since then. I quickly learned this business is full of men with agendas and I didn't want to be with anyone like that." She pressed her lips to his, knowing the truth—she was falling in love for the first time in her life. "No one until you."

His eyes darkened, his fingers tangled in her hair as he reclaimed her mouth, his tongue brushing hers with tender, passionate strokes that had Darla sighing with the goodness of it—of them, of this new relationship. She was even beginning to think that maybe, just maybe, she and Blake could find that something special that lucky couples, like both her parents and his, shared. And all they had to do to claim their prize was survive the rest of the season.

TWO HOURS LATER, Darla had showered and dressed in a cotton peasant blouse and soft faded jeans for travel to a series of audition stops that would include Boston and Dallas, then on to Houston. Lugging her carry-on bag in front of her, Darla rushed down the center aisle of the plane to find Meagan, looking panicked, leaning over her armrest to watch for fellow passengers. "I thought you were going to miss the flight," she said, standing up to let Darla slide into the seat by the window.

"Sorry," Darla said. "I couldn't get a cab." She shoved her bag under the seat. "But never fear, I'm here, ready to make your travel experience a memorable one." And tired. So very tired.

"Long night?" Meagan asked, resnapping her seat belt into place.

Darla's cell phone buzzed and she dug it out of her purse before snapping her own seat belt into place. "I could have used a little more sleep, but then, who couldn't, right?" She glanced down at the text from Blake on her phone. Did you make it? Darla replied with Barely. He replied with Pull the shade down. She replied with No. He answered Yes. She smiled.

"Blake?"

Darla's head jerked up at the question. "What?"

"Are you texting with Blake?" Meagan asked, a smile playing on her lips. "Come on. I know you two have a thing going on."

Darla let out a breath. "I don't know how this happened."

"I didn't with Sam, either," she said. "Actually," she lowered her voice. "I thought I'd just have a hot night and get him out of my system. That didn't go as planned."

"Oh, my God," Darla said. "Me, too."

Meagan's lips curved. "I could have guessed that from miles away. So, you're pretty into him, huh?"

She nodded. "I don't know how that happened, either." Her chest tightened. "Meagan, I know how important this show is to you. I won't jeopardize its success. You have my word."

"Honey, I know that. I trust you. That was one of the reasons I so needed you as a judge. I know I can count on you. I know you will do what's right. It's a little piece of sanity for me. It's why I felt so secure focusing on you for this promotional campaign. You're rock-solid. And I don't know Blake as well as you do, but his reputation indicates he's the same."

Her phone buzzed again. Meagan's buzzed at the same time and she laughed as she looked at the screen. "Sam."

Darla looked at her phone, warming inside as she shared this moment with Meagan, as they both returned messages to the men in their lives.

Darla read Blake's text. Trust me. Put the shade down and close your eyes. You're exhausted. You'll fall asleep. Hello? Are you there?

I can't, Blake, she typed.

You can. Do it now before takeoff. You will barely feel takeoff then. Then close your eyes and think about last night. I am.

Darla glanced out of the window and drew a breath before deciding to take another risk, to believe in Blake. She pulled her shade down. She just had to believe she wouldn't crash and burn—with Blake and without.

18

TWO WEEKS AFTER DARLA and Blake's New York encounter, which had been followed by daily texting and phone calls, Darla sat at the judges' table in San Diego with morning auditions well underway.

"I do not understand why we let that girl have a Vegas pass," Lana complained of the contestant who'd just left. "She was a moth, not a butterfly."

"A moth?" Darla laughed, not about to let Lana get to her today. She had too many reasons to be in a good mood. Like finally seeing Blake again when he arrived later in the day. Not only that, she'd bought time on her parents' ranch by negotiating ridiculously high payments she'd sworn to her parents she could handle. "Hmm, well then," Darla continued, "I guess I should rebut by saying she's a caterpillar who will become a beautiful butterfly."

"I'm with Darla on this one," Ellie agreed, flipping her ever-changing hair—it was pink and blue today, yesterday it was some form of purple—over her shoulders.

"Butterfly in the making all the way. That girl is going to spread her wings and fly."

"You're always with Darla," Lana sneered. "One might think you have a crush on her."

Ellie grinned and wrapped an arm around Darla. "A *girl* crush," she joked. "I *lurve* her so much." She dropped her arm from Darla. "Sorry, Lana. I just agree with her choices and not yours."

"I guess I have a crush on her, too, then," Jason said, grabbing his cell phone to check his email, as he often did. "I thought that young woman had talent. Where the heck is the next audition?"

"Technical difficulties, guys," Meagan said over a speaker. "Three minutes and we're taping again."

Lana and Ellie started to argue over what made a butterfly. Darla tuned them out as her cell vibrated with a text. She snatched it from the table, expecting a message from her New York producer about a special guest for one of her shows. The text was from Blake instead. I have a crush on you, too.

She blinked at the text. How had he known what had been said? He wasn't supposed to be in until late afternoon. Her gaze jerked toward the door, half expecting him to walk in any second. Blake was here. He had to be here. Was he here?

Her phone vibrated with another message that read Yes. I'm here, as if he'd read her mind. She smiled, liking the way he really understood. This long-distance thing had been good. Instead of heating up the sheets, they'd spent hours just talking, getting to know each other. It was all Darla could do not to push to her feet to leave the room. She was nervous. She was excited. Wait, suddenly, she was *very* nervous. What if their chemistry had been a temporary illusion? What if the magic was gone? What if they'd imagined it in the first place?

The lights in the room flickered and then went dark. "Now *that's* what I call a technical difficulty," Jason commented.

One of the crew announced, "The entire hotel is dark. Meagan says to take fifteen minutes and not a second longer. We have a line of contestants to get through and a plane to catch to Washington for tomorrow's auditions."

Washington. That was where she and Blake were going to stay overnight together, before he went back to New York and she had to go to Nashville. The thought sent her to her feet, eager to freshen up before she saw Blake. She grabbed her purse and excused herself, heading toward the judges' private exit.

She'd never been this excited, and this nervous, over a man before. That had to be a good sign. Please let it be a good sign.

THE INSTANT DARLA REACHED the hallway where Blake was waiting, he reached for her.

"Darla," he whispered, trying not to scare her. He gently pulled her through the door and then behind it, before someone else entered.

She gasped and stiffened, only to sink into him. "Blake—"

He kissed his name from her lips, drinking in her

sweetness and absorbing her soft, warm body into his. His hand caressed her backside over her snug black jeans. She whimpered into his mouth—a sexy, feminine sound that had him wishing they could escape and be alone, where he could hold her, touch her, be with her without fear of observation.

"You feel so good," he murmured. "I missed you."

"I missed you, too." Her hands curled on his chest. "I can't believe you're here. You weren't supposed to be here until much later."

"I finished filming last night and I grabbed an early flight," he explained. "God. You have no idea how much I was looking forward to this, how much I needed to know it still felt this good."

"Me, too," she said quickly. "Oh, me, too." Her hands laced around his neck. "I can't believe you were thinking the same thing. I was afraid it wouldn't feel the same in person as before—as if I'd imagined it."

He wrapped his arm around her waist and pressed his forehead to hers. "It feels better than before. Every time I think I can't get more crazy about you, I do. I cannot wait to get you alone. I'm not sure I can wait until tomorrow night when we're in Washington."

Her hand flattened on his chest. "We agreed to be careful. The judges are always on the same floor."

"I know," he said. "But—"

"No buts." She kissed him. "We wait until tomorrow."

He sighed and leaned against the wall. "I don't suppose this means you'll reconsider the webcam?"

"No," she said tightly. "I'm not—"

"Going to have webcam sex," he finished for her, laughing. "So you told me three times before. But a guy has to try. So phone sex it is, then."

"We aren't—"

"Oh, yeah, we are," he said, holding her close. "And that's just for starters. There are so many things I want to do with you, Darla. You have no idea." And one thing he realized right then and there, he'd already done. He'd fallen in love.

IT WAS NEAR TEN O'CLOCK that night when Blake joined the rest of the cast and crew—a good twenty-five people—in a large room for the big unveiling. Meagan stood at the front of the group beside what looked like a sheet covering a large piece of art on a stand.

"Blake and Darla," Meagan called. "Can you both come up here, please?"

Blake moved to the front of the room, his gaze connecting with Darla's as they both took center stage, so to speak. He could feel the room fill with silent questions and curiosity, as he took a spot on the opposite side of the sheet-covered stand from Meagan. Darla crossed to stand beside him.

"I'm sorry to do this so late," Meagan said to the room. "I'd planned a little party, with cake and champagne, which will now be served on the flight to Washington, if you're awake enough to enjoy it. I have some exciting announcements about this season. Last season we had the curse that haunted the set and boosted ratings."

"And a tornado," someone shouted.

"Yes," Meagan agreed. "And a tornado. It almost makes you believe we really did have a curse. Except that the 'curse' turned into a ratings blessing. I have to admit that I hated that curse at first, and I wanted the show to stay about the dancers. But the truth is that because of that extra enticement, it brought viewers to tune in and gave the dancers the attention they deserved. So. That brings me to this season. Reality shows have become more common now, and the competition is steep. We have to have that extra something that makes each season unique. This season we have Blake and Darla who, as we all know, are competitors in daytime television. So we are going to use that as our gimmick. 'Will they kiss each other or kill each other?' is the concept that will be promoted on billboards and in television spots. Also, the big news that I'm sharing for the first time with Blake and Darla right here and now is that the studio rented Times Square ad space." She pulled the sheet off the display and the room broke into one huge gasp.

Blake and Darla both moved to get a better view of the mock billboard that read The Competition Is Turning Up The Heat On This Season of *Stepping Up*. And there was no question—the picture was hot. It was one of Blake's favorite shots of Darla on top of the desk with her long, gorgeous leg extended, her skirt hiked well above her knee, and her heel pressed to his chest.

Meagan slid between them and slipped her arms around their shoulders. "What do you both think? Pretty cool, right? Times Square, here we come."

"I think I'm blushing," Darla murmured.

"I think *I'm* blushing," Blake said, scrubbing his jaw.

"I know I am," Meagan agreed. "You look hot, honey. Hot!" Meagan darted away and called out to the rowdy, excited room. "Okay, folks. Quickly, so we can get to the airport. We want the press and the viewer to speculate about Darla and Blake. Friends, enemies—"

"Lovers!" someone shouted.

"Oh, yeah," someone else said. "The look on Blake's face in that picture says it all."

Darla's blush had turned to beet-red, and Blake decided he'd take matters into his own hands. "You know how you can find out the truth?" he called out to the room. "Tune in at eight central standard time on Wednesday nights. That's the idea, folks. Job security and ratings. Let's shoot for number one in our time slot!" The room filled with roars of excitement.

"Shuttle leaves in twenty minutes for the airport, folks!" The room started to clear and Meagan rushed toward Blake and Darla. "Even our cast is dying to know what's between you two. I have a good feeling about this." She glanced between them. "They all have confidentiality agreements but that doesn't mean they won't blab. Stay mysterious." She grinned and leaned in, lowering her voice. "You're the only two on your floor in Washington. You can thank me later." She turned and hurried away.

Blake looked at Darla. "I'm never going to stay away from you tonight now, you do know that, right?"

She blinked up at him. "Promise?"

He glanced at the mock billboard, feeling his blood run wicked-hot, and then glanced back at her. "That would be a solid yes on that promise."

DARLA AND BLAKE BURST INTO HER Washington hotel room in a clatter of luggage, bags and laptops being thrown aside. Locked in an embrace, they were against the wall, then the other wall. Then tearing off each other's clothes. Her shirt, her bra—his mouth on her breasts. She shoved at his shirt. "Take it off. Take it off. Take it all off."

"You, too," he said, nipping her lip.

She backed into the room without really seeing it. A bed. That was all she cared about. She unzipped her jeans and tossed a boot aside. Then tried to tug the next one free, only to somehow tumble to the floor, laughing. A shirtless, shoeless Blake came down on top of her, his long, hard body framing hers. "I feel like I've waited a lifetime for this," he murmured, his lips near hers. His breath was a warm, seductive promise of the hot, perfect kisses she'd been dreaming of for weeks now.

"I do, too," she whispered breathlessly.

His mouth captured hers, devouring her with long strokes of his tongue that had her meeting each one with equal hunger. Her hips arched into him. Even through his jeans, he was hard and thick. She craved the feeling of him inside her. *Finally,* inside her again.

He must have felt the same way, because his hand went to her hips, he started to shove her jeans down without success. He cursed softly out of frustration, which made her smile at his impatience. She knew what he felt. She felt it, too.

He lifted to his knees and half growled, "Raise up, baby." His voice and the endearment were a sexy combination that had Darla smiling. His gaze went to hers.

"Go faster," she said, letting him slip off her pants and her tiny G-string. "My boot is still on." He tossed it and her clothes aside then he stood up, immediately discarding his own pants and underwear. He had a hungry edge to him that she liked more than just a little.

Darla rose up on her elbows, intending to push to her feet, too, but she didn't make it. He was already sliding a condom over his thick erection, his firm body so damn stunning that she couldn't move.

Her throat went dry and she licked her lips. Blake whispered her name and started moving toward her. He bent and swept her up in his arms.

The bed was like lying on a cloud, she thought, as he smiled at her warmly, spreading her legs and settling his thick erection between them. She moaned at the feel of him there, at how much she wanted him inside her. He inhaled and stared down at her. His gaze raked over her breasts.

Darla forgot to breathe for a moment at what she felt with that connection and what she saw in his face—the desire and tenderness she'd never thought could exist in one look. She loved him. She loved this man. "Yes. I like this."

"Good," he said, touching her gently before sliding inside her. She sucked in a breath at the feel of him stretching her, taking him deeper until they were one. His hand went to her cheek, bringing her face to his. "Because I'm glad we're here, too. And I like you in my life, Darla."

A tremor of panic overcame her and she slid her hands to his face. "I like me in your life, too. I like you in mine. So please, don't be the wrong guy."

"I'm *not* the wrong guy," he promised, and then sealed it with a kiss.

It was a long, drugging kiss that took the wildness of their need for each other to another place. To a softer, more sensual place. And when he pulled back to look at her, his eyes smoldering with so much more than heat, she could feel him everywhere, inside and out. She could feel this connection they had growing and shifting.

She reached up and traced his lips. "Blake," she whispered, unable to find any other words to describe what she was feeling right then.

He covered her hand with his and kissed her fingers, before slipping his hand behind her neck and bringing her mouth to his. "This is where I want to be every night."

She smiled against his lips. "Really?"

He brushed hair from her face. "If it's with you."

"Yes," she said, her chest tightening again. "Yes. I want that."

She wasn't sure who moved first, but suddenly they were kissing, their bodies entwined in a seductive, mind-numbing dance, her body tingling and warm all over. Slow turned to fast and wild as their need expanded and took control. They clung together, pressing into each other, trying to get closer.

Release came on Darla without warning, and she tried to fight it, tried to make this last, but it was impossible. She gasped with the sudden spasm of her body, dropping her head to his chest. He moaned near her ear, and she felt him shake against her, felt the intensity of his release. Time stood still until she brought the room back into focus. For what felt like minutes she didn't want to end, they lay there, breathing together, just being together, until he affectionately stroked her hair.

"I have an important question for you," he announced.

She leaned back to look at him. "You say that at the worst times."

"What's bad about me asking you if you want to shower before or after we order pizza?"

She smiled. "While we wait for it to be delivered."

He kissed her nose. "I like the way you think. And once you feed me we can give the bed another whirl."

"Once you feed me," she said, "I might need to give sleep a whirl."

"As long as you let me try and talk you out of that, I'm a happy man." And she was most definitely a happy woman.

19

FOUR WEEKS LATER, WHEN DARLA stepped into the cabin of the Vegas-bound private jet in Dallas, Texas, she found Blake in the second row aisle seat. His brilliant blue eyes fixed her in one of his searing stares that always set her pulse racing and her body flaming. That it did so now, and that she was thinking of the naughty things they had done the night before, was a testament to just how hot and heavy their relationship had become, because she was sick and getting sicker by the second. "There are no other seats open," Ellie said from the front row next to Jason. "You're stuck with Lana."

Darla jerked her gaze from Blake's and centered her attention on the empty seat next to Lana opposite Ellie and Jason. A new wave of nausea overcame Darla, and she sunk into the aisle seat beside Lana, not even caring that Lana would leave the shade up and niggle at her nerves. It was nine o'clock and dark outside and she just needed to sit before she fell.

"I don't know why you and Blake don't just sit together," Lana commented. "We all know you two are an item."

"Sorry, Lana, but you're stuck with me," Darla said in the perpetual avoidance mode she'd been in since the first television commercial had run last week. The feedback from the television blogs, as well as the cast and crew, was buzzing about her and Blake. She kicked her bag under her seat, feeling like she was about to end up there, too, if she wasn't careful, and wishing the bathroom wasn't at the back of the plane.

"You okay, Darla?" Ellie asked, touching her arm from across the row. "You've gotten paler by the minute today and you didn't even try and change seats with me. In fact, you didn't even argue with Lana one time today. I'm worried about you."

"Thanks, sweetie, but I'm just tired," Darla said appreciatively. She liked Ellie, who was truly a nice person.

"You really do look as white as a ghost," Lana said, giving her a keen eye. "Are you sick?"

A ghost. Great. Just what she wanted to look like for Vegas Week. Darla turned to look at Lana. "Why? Are you afraid I'm going to throw up on you?"

Lana grimaced. "Don't be silly. I'm not heartless. I only give you a hard time because you're just so easy to rile up and, let's face it, because I knew the television viewers would love our dynamic—and they do. This thing with you and Blake will be a one-season mystery that can't last. The audience's desire to see us squabble will carry over beyond the season."

"Just remember you said that when we disagree in Vegas."

"I'll show you no mercy," Lana assured her. "For the good of the ratings and job security, of course."

Darla managed a small smile, suddenly liking Lana more than she thought possible. "Of course."

"We'll call a truce for now, though. It's not fun baiting you when you don't respond with appropriate rebellion."

"Truce," Darla agreed, shutting her eyes as they began to taxi, pretty sure the fact that she didn't care when the plane lifted off wasn't a good sign about just how sick she was. This couldn't happen at a worse time. Things were looking positive, but she'd seen enough in this business to know anything could go wrong, and sometimes nothing went wrong and the studio heads still made unexplainable decisions. Having a good audience response to her performance during Vegas Week, and then as she sat at the judges' table for the first four live shows, were critical to assuring her bonus.

BLAKE KNEW SOMETHING WAS WRONG with Darla and it was killing him to sit in his seat and not go to her. He'd tired of this game of hiding their relationship pretty much right out of the gate, but they were bound by their word to Meagan and by the show's ad campaign, and he'd live with it for now.

Darla pushed to her feet abruptly and rushed past him so quickly, he couldn't see her face. He sat there, telling himself not to get up and follow her. Fifteen minutes later, he was too concerned to stay seated. He stood up and Lana turned around, talking to him over the seat. "Yes. Check on her. She's more than a little sick."

Blake didn't reply. He headed toward the bathroom and knocked. "Darla?" No reply. He knocked again. "Darla." He yanked on the door and it opened, unlocked. She was sitting on the tiny space in front of the sink, her knees to her chest and her head on top of them. His heart lurched and he knew she was in trouble.

He didn't even consider how it looked. This was the woman he loved. To hell with charades and ratings. He bent down next to her. "Darla, honey," he whispered urgently, gently pulling her head back.

"Blake," she mouthed in a barely audible voice, her face was sheet-white with black makeup smudges marking her cheeks. "I…"

"It's okay. Don't try and talk. I'm going to find a place for you to lie down."

"No, I can't…move. Too…sick."

"What's happening?" Meagan asked, pushing in beside Blake. "Oh, God."

"Clear the back seats so she can lie down, will you?"

"Yes. Of course."

Blake started to lift Darla. "No. Sick. I'm sick."

"We'll get you a bag," he promised, "but you can't stay on the floor. It's not safe. I can't pick you up in this small space but I'll hold on to you, okay?" He was already pulling her to her feet and she all but collapsed into him, moaning as though she hurt.

Meagan stood in the aisle, her expression worried, as

she indicated the open row. "She needs a bag." Blake managed to maneuver Darla and himself into the seats.

"Bag," she said in a panicked voice. "Bag. Hurry."

The flight attendant rushed up the aisle and handed it to Meagan, who opened it just in time. Blake held her as her body shook. "I can't believe this is happening."

He ran his hand over her hair, hating that the seats were too small for her to lie down. "I know. I'm sorry, honey, but I'm here. We'll get you to a doc when we land."

Meagan bent down next to her. "Is it just your stomach?"

She wet her lips. "My head, too."

Meagan glanced at Blake. "It's so sudden and violent it might be food poisoning."

"Started after lunch," Darla whispered without opening her eyes.

Meagan nodded. "Food poisoning. It has to be. This is too wicked to be anything else." She pushed to her feet and claimed the seat in front of them, so that she could stay near Darla.

Eventually, Darla blinked up at him and whispered, "Thank you for taking care of me."

"You don't ever have to thank me for that."

"Yes, I do." Her lashes fluttered and she fell asleep. He held her for a good forty-five minutes, thankful she was resting.

When they were near to landing, Meagan squatted beside him. "The doctor is waiting on her, but he says if he's even slightly worried about her when he sees her, he's sending her to the E.R."

"I think that's smart." He hesitated, all too aware that everyone on the plane now knew he and Darla were together. "Meagan—"

"If I was this sick, no one would ever keep Sam away from me," she said, before he could say anything else. "I'll talk to everyone about keeping quiet but if it gets out, it gets out. The public is enthralled with the two of you. I don't see that changing."

BLAKE ESCORTED THE DOCTOR OUT of Darla's room, having given his diagnosis of food poisoning and prescribed an antinausea injection that seemed to be helping. Blake returned to find Darla sitting up in bed.

"Hey," he said, surprised. "The medicine must really be working."

She nodded. "It is. I'm a lot better."

He gave her a probing look. "And you're worried about everyone knowing we're together."

"I don't want to be worried. I'm so tired of hiding."

"Agreed," he said, crossing to the bed to sit down next to her.

"I'm glad you were with me," she said. "I am. I just… is Meagan upset?"

"No. She seems to believe we are deep enough into the tease that a happy ending is acceptable."

"A happy ending?"

"Yeah," he said, drawing her hand in his. "If I have any say in it, we're going to have a happy ending." He scooted down onto the bed, and pulled her next to him, curling his body around hers and kissing her temple.

"Blake?"

"Yeah, honey?"

"I really want that happy ending."

"So do I, honey. So do I." Finding Darla had changed him, torn down the walls of distrust this business had created in him, and made him happy. He was going shopping for a ring.

DARLA WOKE IN THE HOTEL BED to realize that not only was she fully dressed, Blake was wrapped around her, also fully dressed. Her chest tightened with emotion. There was something more intimate about this moment than any other she'd had with this man. She was so in love with him. A knock sounded on the door, and he stirred, then called out, "We don't need housekeeping!"

"Good," Meagan called. "Because I don't do windows."

"Whoops," Darla said.

"You're awake," Blake commented with unwarranted surprise.

"You just yelled in my ear," she teased. "Of course, I'm awake."

"And feeling better," he commented, kissing her temple. "Good."

"Hello!" Meagan called.

Blake got to his feet. "Boss lady calls," he murmured, heading to the door.

Darla sat up, pretty sure something had died in her

mouth. She needed a toothbrush urgently and she didn't even want to think about how she looked. If Blake still wanted her after this, he moved way up her ladder to the "keeper" shelf.

"Morning, sunshine," Meagan said, stopping at the end of the bed. "Don't you just look like flowers blooming on a spring day? Or not."

"Watch yourself," Blake warned, stepping by Meagan's side, his hands on his lean hips, his hair rumpled. "She's feeling feisty again already."

"I'd call myself about fifty percent," Darla said, glancing at the 7:00 a.m. time. There was a cast and crew meeting at eight-thirty, and the contestants would all be arriving through the day. "I'll be fine after I shower."

Megan dropped onto the mattress and leaned on one arm. "Today is the least important day. Rest if you need to."

"No," Darla said quickly. "No. I'm fine. I have footage for my daytime show to film anyway."

Blake leaned on the dresser directly in front of Darla. "She's too stubborn to rest. You might as well save your breath."

Meagan glanced between the two of them, and then settled her attention back on Darla. "So then, are you up to a conversation about the show?"

"Actually," Darla said flatly, "maybe I feel sick again."

"Don't start fretting on me," Meagan said. "What's done is done. If your relationship goes public, it goes public."

"But the studio—" Darla started.

"Will be happy if the ratings are good. So far, they are terrific. Which, admittedly, makes me want to string out this tease about you two a bit longer. We're not even into the live shows yet, which is where the dancers get the real exposure and, ultimately, this is about them. So that said, I'm going to warn the cast and crew to stay quiet. They're professionals with confidentiality contracts, and these types of secrets with reality shows are not uncommon."

"Why do I sense a 'but'?" Blake asked.

"The 'but' is this week, contestants are in the same hotel we're at," Meagan answered without pause. "We can't control them like our own people, especially those that Darla doesn't send through to the finals, who might lash out at her. So I think that you two need to stay low-key this week, and then we'll be fine. I want these kids who are dancing their hearts out to have viewers and opportunities, which means big ratings. Last season, the footage in the contestant house was a big ratings grabber." She patted Darla's leg. "So do your casting magic and we'll be set."

Right, Darla thought. Casting magic. She knew she was good at picking talent, but she'd never done it with this much pressure, with the world—including her parents' banker—watching. She glanced at Blake and saw him staring at her. She knew from the look on his face that something was wrong. Meagan rose to her feet. "I'll let you get showered and dressed and see you in a few."

Blake didn't move as Meagan departed. He just sat

there staring at her, and he wasn't happy. In fact, she was pretty sure he was downright unhappy.

"What's wrong?"

"What aren't you telling me, Darla?"

20

"WHAT AREN'T YOU TELLING ME, Darla?" Blake repeated.

Darla swallowed the dryness in her throat. "I don't know what you mean."

"Yes, you do. You're too desperate to keep this job."

"Blake," she reasoned, "this is a big opportunity."

"Yet you say you only wanted to be in casting, that you never wanted to be a star. You know, I've beat my head against the wall, wondering what's kept me from confessing my love for you, but I know now. Something doesn't add up, Darla."

He didn't love her. Or he did. She didn't know, but she was pretty sure that if he did, he was about to talk himself out of it. She moved to the edge of the bed. "Blake. I—"

"Do you remember when you asked me who burned me?"

Her throat was dry again. "Yes."

"Lara Wright."

"Lara," she repeated, feeling stunned. "Wright, as in the movie star?"

"Only, she wasn't a movie star when we were seeing each other."

Darla's stomach tightened. "She used you."

"Right."

She sat there, unable to speak, her mind racing. If she told him about the ranch, would he think she wanted his help? God. Had she told him before, would he have thought she was after his money?

Blake made a sound of frustration at her silence and pushed off the dresser, starting toward the door. "You're not being fair," she shouted, confused. "You're judging me because of her. I'm not her. I'm not."

He didn't turn. "I just need to think, Darla."

His back to her felt like a slap and her eyes started to burn. "*What* is wrong with me wanting this to work out? What is wrong with me wanting to work in casting, which I love, but instead of earning pennies, I get to give my family a better life?"

He turned to her. "Darla—"

"They aren't rich, Blake. They struggle. I have great parents. The best. I want to give back to them everything they've given to me." Tears started to stream down her face. She didn't mean to cry, but she was still sick and she was worried and overwhelmed by everything that had happened. "I'm not Lara, and if you think—"

Suddenly, he was on the bed, on his knees with her, pulling her close. "I'm sorry." He wiped away her tears with his thumbs. "I'm so sorry, Darla. I'm not too much of a man to admit I got scared."

"I'm not her."

"I know."

"No," she said, her heart twisting. "You don't." She pushed out of his arms. She was damned if she did and damned if she didn't with him, and she knew it. He would think she wanted his money if she told him about the ranch. He would think she was about fame if she didn't. In the end, he would turn his back on her and she wasn't turning her back on her family. "I think…we have to get through this season and see where we stand."

"Are you saying we shouldn't see each other?"

"Yes."

How Blake had stayed away from Darla for a full week, he didn't know. But when he walked into the Vegas wrap party on the top floor of the hotel, he had one thing in his mind. He scanned the room bustling with cast, crew and finalists, with tables of food and drink and a busy dance floor, looking for Darla. Ready to end the week of hell that was his life without Darla. A week of regretting he'd allowed the past to taint the present. A week of regretting the moment he'd walked out of her room without fighting for her. When he'd let pride and stubbornness convince him that she'd pushed him away because she didn't think he was worth fighting for, when the truth was, he'd been an ass and he knew it.

He found her standing at a table, talking with Lana and Jason. She was wearing a shimmery silver dress that hugged the curves he'd so intimately admired, her pale, silky hair a mass of silk spraying over her bare shoulders.

Her gaze lifted, sliding over his dark suit before connecting with his, as if she had sensed his presence. And like every other time this week when they found each other in a crowd, which had been often, he felt her tension, her pain and her reserve. It was that feeling, those emotions he felt in her, which had both convinced him she really cared about him, and convinced him how royally he'd screwed up by losing her. The only thing that had made him wait this long to pursue her was his fear that if he pushed her while she was under pressure for Vegas Week, he would end up pushing her away.

He took a step toward her, only to find one of the corporate bigwigs in his path and he was forced to make small talk. By the time he pried himself from the man's grip, Darla was gone. Blake silently cursed, and headed to the table where Lana and Jason were still talking.

Lana looked up immediately. "Oh, please tell me you two are going to make up. The rest of us are miserable with you."

"For once I have to agree with Lana," Jason said, clinking his beer with Lana's and taking a swig.

"Where is she?"

"Hiding in the bathroom," Lana said.

Blake was walking before she even finished her sentence. Blake arrived at the bathroom as one of the camera ladies came out. She nodded at him, as if he'd asked a question, clearly one of the many cast and crew rooting for him and Darla to make up. "She's alone," the woman said. "I'll watch the door."

Blake didn't need any further encouragement. He shoved open the door and went inside, rounding a long hall to find Darla sitting in a lounge chair with her elbows on her knees and her face in her hands. Her head jerked up a moment before she came to her feet.

"What are you doing in here?" she demanded.

"I love you more than you can possibly imagine."

"What?" she gasped.

"I love you, Darla. I've loved you since the moment you fell off of your shoe and into my arms and I'm miserable without you."

Her eyes clouded over and she hugged herself. "It took you a week to decide this?"

"No, honey," he said. "I waited a week to tell you because I want us to get the hell out of here so I can finally spend some private time proving it to you."

She squeezed her eyes shut. "I can't do this, Blake. The timing is wrong." Her eyes were dark, etched with shadows. "I have reasons to need this job and you have reasons to resent that I do."

"Darla, no. I was an idiot. I—"

"Blake," the camera lady yelled from the door. "We have a line out here. Hurry."

"Coming," he called over his shoulder. He searched Darla's face and he saw the decision there, the stubborn decision that said he wasn't getting past no, not without a fight. "You're on for tomorrow's charity bull-riding event. Nine o'clock at the Wind Walker Hotel. Don't be late."

Her eyes went wide. "I'm what? We never confirmed I was doing that. We haven't talked about it for weeks."

He pulled her close and kissed her, slid his tongue past her teeth for a deep, sweet taste. "We just did." He brushed his fingers down her cheek and turned away, promising himself it would be the last time he left her like this.

Blake exited the bathroom to find five women waiting in a line, one of whom was Meagan, who smiled as he walked by, but he barely saw her. He was thinking of Darla's words. *It took you a week to decide this?* Damn it to hell. He'd gambled on timing working in his favor, when instead, it might have been the final nail in his coffin, the fatal flaw that cost him the woman he loved.

RELIVING BLAKE'S WORDS—and his kiss—had kept Darla up all night. By seven, she couldn't take it anymore, so she showered and dressed in her best Wranglers, cowboy boots and pink Western shirt. She told herself she was early to the Wind Walker Hotel because she needed to know what her day consisted of, so she could be prepared, when she knew deep down she wanted to see Blake. She was miserable without him but she couldn't see how they could get past his betrayal, and what she still hadn't confided in him.

She checked into the hotel and soon entered the typical high-end Vegas room, which had a large plush bed and some sort of floral design theme going on with pictures and drapes. In the middle of the mattress was an envelope with her name on it, and she knew the writing was Blake's. Beside it was an event T-shirt she assumed she was supposed to wear. Her heart thundered in her chest as she sat down and opened the envelope.

Inside was a printed formal event agenda and a folded card. She opened the card and a room key fell out. "Room 1212. That's where I'm at and where I want you to be. With me." Darla pressed the key to her forehead and squeezed her eyes shut. He was letting her choose, as he always had. And she had more than a room choice to make. She'd thought long and hard about this. She had two options. Choose to weather this storm with the bank on her own, without Blake in her life. Or choose to tell Blake what was going on and risk being hurt again. There was no in between. Until now, it had never seemed the right time. But now, it was time.

If he loved her, if she loved him, he should be a part of what she had going on. She wanted to tell him everything, to believe he really could see beyond his past, beyond Lara Wright, to *her*. She thought of being on that plane, so sick she thought she'd been dying, and how Blake had held her, how he'd whispered she was beautiful when she'd been a wreck, how amazing she was when she'd felt things were out of control.

Darla scanned the agenda, trying to figure out where Blake would be right now, and it looked like he was doing an opening ceremony at eight. That meant he'd be downstairs, already working. Damn. She was going to go all day with this need to talk to him burning inside her.

Hoping to get lucky, she dialed room 1212. Blake

didn't answer. She found her cell phone and called him. He answered on the second ring. "Darla—"

"Blake."

"Where are you?"

"I'm here. In my room."

"I'm glad you're here."

"Listen, I really need to talk to you and I know you're busy and I can't, we can't, but—"

"We will. I promise. My father is with me. Come meet him." Someone said something in the background. "He says he'll take care of you during the opening ceremonies while I film, and tell you all my dirty little secrets."

Secrets. She swallowed hard. "I'll be right down."

He told her the location and then softened his voice. "I mean it, Darla. I'm really glad you're here." And then the line went dead.

DARLA EXITED THE ELEVATOR and headed toward the busy entrance to the Mountainscape Entertainment Center, which was basically an indoor amusement park and the place where today's rodeo events were being held.

Her heart pounded in her chest as Blake and his father, Nick Nelson, came into view. Their resemblance to one another was obvious. In fact, they were so remarkably alike—both tall, lean and good-looking, both in jeans and their event T-shirts—that it was quite something. And if Blake's father was a testament to how Blake was going to age, Darla wasn't complaining. The man was in great physical shape and wore his gray hair and wrinkles with charm and appeal one couldn't help but admire. But it was Blake she focused on, Blake who stole her breath with his dark good looks. Blake who made her heart squeeze and her body ache. Blake who she loved with all of her heart.

In an instant, the two men spotted her. She opened her mouth to greet Blake's father, when Blake pulled her close and kissed her solidly on the lips. He released her and said, "Good morning!"

Her hand sizzled where it rested on his chest. "Good morning."

Nick cleared his throat. "That's certainly a good way to wake up if I ever saw one."

Darla blushed and Blake slid his arm over her shoulder so she could face his father. "Darla, meet my father, Nick Nelson."

Darla smiled and accepted his hand. "Any woman who can wrangle this bullheaded man here is someone I want to spend some time with. And I hear you can ride a mechanical bull."

Darla's cheeks heated at the innuendo—by Blake's father, of all people. "I have a feeling this is going to be an interesting day."

Blake snorted. "You have no idea." Someone called his name from behind. "Gotta run." He pointed at his father. "Behave." He glanced at Darla. "And don't believe anything he says."

DARLA SAT IN THE BLEACHERS while clowns entertained the crowd and Blake's father entertained her with truly hilarious Blake stories.

"He can't ride the mechanical bull, you know."

"Really? He told me he could."

"You don't see him on the agenda to ride today, now, do you?"

"Actually, I don't," she said. "I just assumed he was busy."

Nick snorted. "His mother rides better than him, though that isn't really a good comparison. His mother is pretty damn good. I wish she could have been here today, but her and her sister are doing a girls' weekend. She does a lot of charity work."

"What kind of charities?"

"She's big into animal rescue."

"My parents are, as well. They have a shelter at their ranch in Colorado. That's actually the charity I want to ride for today."

"Well, isn't that something," he said. "You know, we're looking for a place big enough to house some retired rodeo animals until I can find a permanent location. Your parents have any room at their place? There would be a generous donation to the charity, of course."

Darla swallowed hard. "They have the ranch up for sale right now. So yes, they have room, but I think it would be a month or so before they decide if they are staying or not."

He gave her a keen, way too intelligent look. "So it's for sale or it's not for sale?"

"Where's Darla?" Blake said over the microphone.

Darla jerked her attention to Blake and stood up,

happy for the escape. A few seconds later, she was on the stage with a microphone in hand.

"We hear you're going to ride this here cow today," Blake joked, patting the mechanical bull's backside.

Darla grinned. "I hear you're going to ride this here cow." She patted the metal as he had.

"Oh, no," he said. "You aren't using me to get out of this." He held a hand up to the audience. "Is she folks?" Shouts and cheers followed.

"I'm going to ride because I know how to ride. I hear from a reliable source—" she playfully lowered her voice and whispered into the microphone "—his father, that Blake can't ride."

"Thank you, father dearest," Blake said, waving at Nick in the crowd. "I can always count on you to make me look bad."

"What are good fathers for?" Nick shouted, to have a roar of laughter follow.

Darla walked up to Blake and gave him a challenging look. "So you can't ride?"

"Not a mechanical bull," he said playfully.

The crowd hooted and hollered at that one. Darla looked at the crowd. "Just like a man. Talk big when you can't deliver." She grabbed Blake's hand and slapped the microphone into it and then raised up on her toes to whisper in his ear. "I love you." Then, before he could respond, she sauntered over to the bull to hop on top.

21

DARLA FINISHED HER BULL RIDE to the cheers of the crowd. She'd been nervous and plenty rusty, but she'd done well enough to suit the audience. Blake was there when she finished, pulling her against him to help her down, and holding her just long enough to whisper into her ear, "I love you, too, and you are too damn sexy for my own good."

She laughed, enjoying the moment and not letting herself think about the conversation to come later between them. They felt too good, too right. It was going to work out.

Blake raised his microphone and spoke to the crowd. "Darla and I had a bet, ladies and gentlemen. If she got on that bull and conquered it, which I think we all agree she did, I vowed to personally donate to the charity of her choice. And I'm a man of my word. So, Darla, which charity do you want me to send a ten thousand dollar donation to?"

Darla gaped and spoke to him, not the crowd. "Blake. That's a huge figure. Are you sure?"

"I donate a certain amount of my earnings every year. This time you get to pick where." He spoke into the microphone again. "And your charity is?"

She covered the microphone with her hand. "My parents' animal shelter. Is that okay?"

"Sure it is. What's the name?"

She paused and then spoke into the microphone. "Colorado Angel Rescue."

"Ten thousand dollars to Colorado Angel Rescue," he agreed.

Darla reached for the microphone, her hand folding over his. She spoke to the entire room, but looked at him. "Thank you. Really. Thank you so much. It's a great place that does a lot of good for a lot of animals." She held back her tears. She tore her gaze from Blake's, needing to be out of the spotlight before she made a spectacle of herself—and him. She waved at the crowd and headed for the exit.

BLAKE WATCHED DARLA DASH AWAY from him and knew she was upset, though he had no idea why. The one thing he did know, though, was that he wasn't about to risk her taking off before he could get to her. He quickly announced the next bull rider and headed to the sidelines, where his father was waiting on him.

"I'll take over," his father said, leaning in close to add softly, "I'd gamble on her parents being in some kind of financial trouble and she must not have the means yet to take care of them. I think your donation hit a tender spot, son." His father patted him on the back and headed toward the center ring.

Blake stood there for an instant, shell-shocked as everything came together for him. Darla's desperation to make the show work. Her declaration about taking care of her parents. Her self-diagnosed irrational worry over losing both jobs. Damn it to hell, if he hadn't been so busy looking for Lara in Darla, maybe he would have seen Darla for the great person she truly was.

Blake sprinted through the lobby, heading toward the elevators, impatient to get to Darla's room before she could escape. By the time he was at her door knocking, his heart was in his throat. She either didn't answer or wouldn't answer. Or maybe she wasn't even in her room. She might have left or never really checked in. He pressed his hands and his head against the door, digging out his cell phone to call her.

"I'm here," she said from behind him.

He turned to find her standing there, the room key in her trembling hand. "I got on the wrong elevator and I…" She started to cry.

He was there in an instant, wrapping her in his arms and quickly ushering her inside to sit on the bed. Blake went down on his knees in front of her.

"What aren't you telling me, Darla?" he said gently, brushing tears from her eyes. "What is it that you think I can't handle?"

She inhaled and let it out. "It's not that you can't handle it. It's that you might think I need you to handle it, or that you might think I want something from you because of it. And I don't. I just need to tell you so it's not this grinding secret wearing on my nerves. I…I have it handled."

That one statement stabbed him in the heart all over again. "I made you feel like you couldn't come to me over this Lara thing, didn't I?"

"At first, no. At first, I just thought it was too soon to tell you," she said. "It's a lot of baggage. I didn't want that muddling up where we were—or weren't—headed together. Then, when I was close to telling you, there was the Lara thing, and I thought you might think I had an agenda of some sort. Sometimes I think I should have just told you from the beginning, it wouldn't have grown into such a big issue."

"Tell me now."

She gave a quick nod. "My parents got behind on their bank note for the ranch and they didn't tell me until it was pretty close to too late. I negotiated a ridiculous payment plan to catch them up and told them I was making enough money to cover it."

Another lightbulb went off for Blake. "You're not getting paid well for this show." She shook her head. "Being on a competing network and having the ability to keep my daytime show and film on set meant compromise. SAG minimum wage with a balloon payment bonus if the studio options me for season two. They have to make that decision before the fifth live show."

He leaned back on his heels. "Wait. What? SAG freaking minimum wage? Who the *hell* is your agent?"

"That's not common in this situation?"

"Ah, no." Blake was furious. "You have to do something about this. I'll help you."

Fifteen minutes later Darla had fired her agent and hired Blake's—a well-known industry profession.

Her new agent guaranteed her a better contract as soon as he could contact the studio.

He set the phone on the bed and settled his hands on Darla's knees. "Next problem," Blake said. "How much to catch your parents' note up completely?"

She shook her head. "No. No, I'm—"

He leaned in and kissed her, his lips pressing hers and lingering before he whispered, "Marry me. Then it's our money anyway."

"What?" she blurted, pulling back to stare at him. "Did you…do you…?"

"Yes and yes. And that's the same answer I hope you give me." He reached into his pocket and pulled out the silk pouch he'd hidden there for just the right moment. He removed the sapphire diamond ring and showed it to her. "Unique, just like the woman. This isn't spontaneous, Darla, brought on by some big new revelation. This is planned. This is thought out. *You* are the woman I want to spend the rest of my life with. Will you, Darla James, be my wife?"

"Yes. Yes." She threw her arms around him and hugged him. "Yes. Absolutely."

Blake held her tightly. His woman, his wife-to-be. "No more secrets. We're in this for whatever life throws our way, good or bad, okay?"

"No more secrets," she promised.

He leaned in and took her hand, staring into the beautiful green eyes he planned to get lost in for an eternity. "Shall we seal this deal officially?"

She laughed. "Oh, yes."

He slipped the ring onto her finger.

Epilogue

FOUR MONTHS LATER, on a beautiful sparkling fall day, Darla and Blake were married in her parents' Colorado ranch house. They'd been offered money to televise the event, and they'd declined. The media frenzy over their rumored engagement had not only created huge ratings for *Stepping Up,* it had created a media frenzy they didn't want at their wedding.

Now, with all the guests gone, Darla was still riding cloud nine as she and Blake loaded the SUV they'd rented for the short drive to Aspen for their honeymoon. Watching one of the contestants she'd fought for win the show had been exciting for Darla, especially since the young dancer had scored a role on a new television drama based around a dance team.

Blake slammed the trunk shut. "I think we're all set." His cell phone rang and he snatched it from his belt. "It's our agent."

Darla leaned against the truck, eager to hear what

Jack had to say about their contract negotiations with the studio.

"Hold on," Blake said to Jack, covering the receiver. "He says our contracts for the next season of *Stepping Up* are in and they look good, but he's not happy with the terms for the *Blake and Darla Nelson Show*, and he says he doesn't want to void our individual shows until he has what he wants. He wants to know that we both give him full authority to negotiate while we are gone."

"Go get 'em, Jack," Darla replied, settling her hands on her hips. After the man had not only gotten her back-pay but a raise to boot, she trusted him fully. She'd been learning that sometimes giving away control to the right person was just like having it yourself.

Blake uncovered the receiver. "'Go get 'em' were her words. I'll agree with that. But Jack, don't screw this up." Blake laughed and hung up.

"He told you he never screws up," Darla supplied.

"Exactly."

Darla glanced at the porch where her mother and Blake's sat talking, both with rescue cats in their laps. Blake slid his arms around her from behind. "Our parents really seem to get along."

The front door opened and their fathers appeared, their voices in a heated debate. It seemed to have something to do with how to deal with a fence one of the half dozen horses Nick had brought to the ranch kept jumping.

"Well, they do," Darla said with a chuckle. "I can see why you'd think that."

"That's manly love, honey."

She laughed and hugged him tightly. "How long do you think it will take them to notice that the newlyweds are gone if we leave without saying anything?"

"At least ten minutes." He glanced at his watch. "Starting now." They both took off for the truck and hopped in, laughing as they started just one of the many journeys ahead of them.

* * * * *

Winning Moves

1

KATHERINE "KAT" Moore stepped off the exit ramp into the Las Vegas International Airport with her long blond hair piled on top of her head, ready for a hot bath, cool sheets and her own bed, which she hadn't slept in for months. After globe-trotting with a couple of big-name pop stars' tours back-to-back, she'd found the escape she'd sought, but the lifestyle had taken a toll. She was done. This was it. She wanted roots, a pet, a fridge full of her favorite things. Stability.

Wearily, she headed toward the luggage area when her cell phone started to ring. Dang it, she knew she should have left the darn thing off. Kat sighed and dug the phone out of her purse to see her agent's number on the display. Of course. They'd been arguing when she'd had to turn off her phone in Italy to head to the States.

"Yes, I'm home, Michael," she said, without saying hello. "And no, I'm still not taking the new tour. I don't care if it's Derek Mercer or how many number-one hits he has. I don't need the money and you probably need it less." She needed a life. She needed… No. No, she didn't. She refused to think of what she really needed, what she'd run away from—apparently unsuccessfully.

"You're right," Michael answered. "You're not taking a tour. I have something just as big and you get to stay right here in Vegas."

She stopped walking. "I'm listening." Someone bumped into her and she quickly moved to the side of the walkway as clusters of people passed by.

"I got a call this morning from M&M Studios. They have a top secret project they're working on. They won't release details over the phone, but the pay is double your tour pay if you get the gig and you were requested by name."

"Double? You have to be freaking kidding me."

"Money isn't something I ever joke about."

"No kidding," she said, thinking that the house she'd planned to surprise her parents with for their retirement next year might just have gotten bigger. "And I'm not complaining."

"I need you at the Wind Walker Hotel in thirty minutes."

"Wait. No. I'm a mess. I'm grimy and tired. I've traveled halfway across the world. And who asked for me, anyway?"

"They want to make a decision today. They're waiting on you. I told them you'd be there. This is my reputation and yours. You're committed."

She was going to kill him. "Michael—"

"You said you wanted to stay home in Vegas. You said you wanted stability. I'm giving it to you. Get your skinny, pretty little backside over there—and do it now. Call me from a cab and I'll fill you in on whatever details I can." He hung up.

She gaped at the phone. He'd flipping hung up on her. She growled low in her throat and started walking. She'd been with Michael ten years, since she'd turned twenty and landed her first big dancing job. If she didn't like him so much, she'd fire *his* "pretty little backside." She wasn't going to an interview now.

Damn. Damn. Damn. She had to go. He told them she'd go, and her decision to put down some roots meant there would be less opportunities for work. She glanced down at herself as she stepped onto an escalator leading to baggage claim. She had on a PINK Victoria's Secret T-shirt and faded jeans with a rip down the leg. She looked more like she was hanging out at the house on a day off—not to mention that she felt like death warmed over, after a number of time changes.

She rushed onward to baggage claim to discover her bag was missing. Frustrated, she dialed Michael. She couldn't do this interview. Not now. She'd make a bad impression.

He didn't answer. She glanced at the time of their last call. She was never going to make it to the interview if she stayed and argued about her luggage. She hesitated and thought of her parents, of their dream retirement, of living close enough so she could actually see them. She hurried toward the exit and the cab line.

The interview was poorly scheduled, but it was a blessing, and if it worked out, she'd be thanking Michael for pushing her.

TWENTY MINUTES LATER, Kat still hadn't reached Michael and she was pretty sure he was avoiding her calls so she couldn't back out of the interview. By the time the cab pulled up to the front of the towering Wind Walker Hotel, one of the largest casinos on the strip, Kat had removed her hair clip, applied lipstick and unsuccessfully tried to cover her dark circles.

She paid the driver and dialed Michael again. She didn't even know where she was going at this point. *Finally* he answered, and before she could even speak, he demanded, "Are you there?"

"Yes, and—"

"I have my contact on my cell so hold on," he said, and she heard him say, "She's there." He came back to Kat. "Where are you?"

"I'm at the front door, but—"

"Front door," he told whoever he was talking to, then back to Kat, "Go to the bellman and give him your name. You'll be escorted."

"Okay, but—"

"Hurry," he said. "Kat. This is bigger than I thought. This is huge. Call me after. Go get 'em, tiger." He hung up.

Kat let out a breath and just gave up. She found the bellman and gave him her name. She resolved to do what she did in the middle of a tour when something went wrong—she just needed to roll with the punches. An employee led her to the hotel theater ticket booth and a row of offices behind it.

The woman knocked on a door. A few seconds later, to Kat's surprise, Ellie Campbell, an old friend and top-notch choreographer, rushed from the room, pulling the door shut behind her. "Kat!" Ellie's arms were outstretched, her long hair that, at least for today, was a pale shade of light blue, floating behind her.

Kat hugged Ellie, whom she'd met on a television project a good seven or eight years before.

"I can't believe you're here," Ellie said, leaning back to inspect her friend. "I wanted you for this project so badly. I couldn't believe the timing of you coming home today!"

"I can't wait to hear the details, but what happened to *Stepping Up?* I thought you were judging?"

"Oh, I am," she said. "I love it. Absolutely love it."

Kat's stomach twisted with the connection the show held to the very past she was avoiding. "I'm confused. Then why am I here? Why are you here? Surely you don't have time to work on a Vegas show?"

"The studio came up with this idea that we should organize a multi-state tour in between seasons and a Vegas show to run for a full year here at the hotel. The show will open a month before auditions start for season three of *Stepping Up.* The catch? They gave us a whole six weeks to make this happen. Thankfully though, the tour will be after season three ends. It's fun and exciting, but—" she grinned and rubbed her stomach "—I have a bun in the oven. I just dropped the bombshell on the studio. I can't travel to judge and do the Vegas show. It's too much."

Kat gaped. "A bun in the oven. How?"

They both laughed.

"Okay," Kat said. "I know how."

Ellie raised her finger. "Last season we had a new production manager for *Stepping Up.* Needless to say, we sort of hit it off."

"Sort of?" Kat teased, staring at the gorgeous white diamond on her friend's finger.

"I'll tell you the story later. But right now, we need a replacement for me on the live show and the tour. I saw your name on a prospect list and knew you were the one, but I called and got your service."

"I've been out of the country for months."

"So they told me, but I was determined to reach you. I contacted your agent. It has to be fate, honey, because you arrived today, and we really need to wrap up interviews today. Good, bad or ugly, we need to nail this down. You can make this end with good, and leave the bad and the ugly behind. I just know it."

The door behind them opened, and a sixty-something woman whose hair was dyed a dark chestnut color appeared. Ellie turned to her. "Dawn. Thanks for coming. How did it go?"

"Excellent. I agreed to take the job. I'm thrilled."

"Wonderful. I am, too." Ellie hugged Dawn before she departed, then whispered to Kat. "You'd never know from looking at her, but that woman is the hottest new costume designer in this city. I'm talking smoking-hot designs. And we aren't in prime time like *Stepping Up* is. We have to dirty up this show to make it work for Vegas."

Kat laughed, but it didn't sound completely genuine and she knew it. All she could think of was the TV show and its connection to her past. "I've learned to never judge a book by its cover in this business. I'd love to see Dawn's designs."

Ellie motioned to the door. "Let's go meet everyone. I'm excited. This is going to be so good."

He wasn't here, she decided. He wasn't a part of this. If he had heard her name, he would have said no. This was going to be okay. It was going to be good. They wouldn't see each other. "Me, too," Kat said decisively. This *was* exciting. It was a great opportunity.

Ellie rushed into the room. "I have a surprise. I made a phone call and got lucky. The perfect choreographer I've been telling you guys about is here. She's the one."

Kat felt her cheeks heat and her stomach twist. Ellie was giving her some big shoes to fill. She drew a calming breath and then followed Ellie into the room. A group of six people sat around a conference table, but she only saw one—the one sitting at the head of the table. She only saw *him*. Jason Alright, with his light brown tousled hair, his square jaw shadowed with stubble and his deep green eyes, intense as they met hers. Those eyes reached inside her and warmed her in all kinds of wickedly wonderful, and yet painful, ways, as they always did. Those soulfully sexy eyes had landed her in bed with him two years before, just before she'd left the country. And ten years before, those same eyes had spoken to her heart, her soul, the day they'd stood at the altar and gotten married.

This wasn't going to work. She had to leave now.

Jason's eyes narrowed and he shook his head ever-so-slightly, telling her not to leave, and reading her like he always did. Did he know she was coming? Surely, he hadn't known.

"This is Kat Moore," Ellie said to the group, touching Kat's arm and announcing, "Kat is the best choreographer in this business." She elbowed Kat. "After me, of course."

Kat laughed. "Of course."

Ellie grinned and continued, "She just got back from

a world tour with the pop star Marcus Knight today, which was pure luck for us." She glanced at Kat, explaining, "We're basically trying to bring *Stepping Up* to life in a musical, and the best people to make that happen are those who are a part of the television show, who understand what that means. So we're important to the creative process, though most of us won't stay involved beyond that. We just can't swing the time for both the Vegas production and the TV show."

Kat let out a discreet breath. Maybe Jason wasn't going to be involved long-term. Maybe that's why he didn't want her to leave. Maybe.

Ellie began her introductions, going around the table quickly. Kat greeted two women and a man before Ellie said, "Meet Lana Taylor and Darla Nelson, both judges for the show, as I'm sure you know. We trust them, so their help enables us to work under such a tight time crunch."

"We're arguing over casting," said Lana, a pretty brunette known for her diva attitude on the show. "Nothing new there, though, if you watch the show."

Kat didn't watch. Ever. But it wasn't like she could say, *Sorry. I don't watch because my ex-husband that I've never stopped loving, who's ripped my heart out a few too many times, is one of the stars.*

"No, indeed," Darla chimed in, shoving a long lock of blond hair behind her ear. "There's nothing new about Lana and I disagreeing." She smiled at Kat. "You'll get used to us fighting, though. Even I have. It's very nice to meet you, Kat. I'm excited to meet someone Ellie is so excited about."

"Oh, please," Lana said. "Enough with the excitement."

Darla laughed and wrapped an arm around Lana. "You'd never know she likes me."

"I don't," Lana said tightly and then sighed. "Oh, okay, I do, but that's a big secret, Kat. The audience loves our bickering."

The mention of a secret echoed in Kat's mind, and her gaze discreetly slid to Jason's, the connection tingling down her spine with shared understanding. They had a secret, too. A past they'd never hidden, but it had been so long ago, before either of them were established in the industry.

"And last but not least," Ellie announced. "Meet Jason Alright. He's—"

"Hello, Kat."

"Jason," she said softly.

"You look good. Your hair's longer now."

"And you forgot how to shave."

He ran his hand behind his neck and laughed, a soft, warm sexy sound that sizzled along her nerve endings. She loved the man's laugh. "I guess I did," he agreed, glancing around the room and announcing, "Yes. We know each other." They knew each other all right, and a few people understood how, but then, they'd been unknowns, barely getting started, always apart. He patted the table beside him. "Come sit down, Kat."

By him. She wanted to be by him. That was dangerous. She'd be so close to touching him—way, way too close. Touching him was bad and oh-so-good. She'd proven, over and over again, that not only was she putty in Jason's hands, she enjoyed every second of it.

Jason rose and, pulling the chair out for her, she moved toward him. It was official. Not only was he still tall, lean and muscular, he still made black jeans, a Harley T-shirt and biker boots look like the definition of sin in the city. And she would bet her left arm that somewhere nearby he had a leather jacket, despite the heat of Vegas in July.

"Oh, good grief," Lana grumbled. "The man doesn't hold a chair for me and I sit next to him at the judges' table for months of every year. Do tell, Kat. How exactly do you and Jason know each other?"

Jason glanced at Lana. "If I held your chair for you, you'd just roll it over my foot. I've learned to keep my distance."

Darla nodded in agreement. "Smart man."

Kat cut her gaze from Jason's to sit down and gain composure before facing the group, but it didn't help. He was close, so close, and his all-too-familiar spicy masculine scent flared in her nostrils. He still wore the same cologne, and she remembered burying her nose in his chest to inhale that amazing scent.

He helped her scoot her chair forward and his fingers brushed her shoulders, sending a shock wave of sensations rushing over her, heating her skin.

A knock sounded on the door and a woman walked in. "Ms. Moore's agent sent over her demo reel."

"Oh, excellent," Ellie exclaimed. "Please load it for us." The woman moved to the end of the table where a pedestal held a television and various electronic equipment. Ellie looked at Kat. "You're okay with that, right? I know your work, but not everyone else does."

"Of course," Kat assured her. "That's expected."

The lights went out and the demo began to play, but Jason wasn't watching it. He was watching her. She could feel his stare, hot and heavy, *impossibly* hot and heavy. It was all she could do not to turn to him, not to tell him to stop, not to reach out and touch him. She was as conflicted about the man as she'd always been.

The demo ended in seven minutes, though it felt like an hour, and the lights came back on.

"That was fantastic," Darla commented, and several of the other people in attendance murmured similar comments. "I knew you'd worked with some big names, but you've worked with a lot more than I thought."

"I've been blessed with opportunities," Kat said.

"And some big egos," Darla said. "How do you manage to teach a routine to a famous pop star who thinks they have nothing to learn?"

"I've been lucky enough to have worked with stars who want to stay stars and want to deserve their hype," Kat answered.

"Lucky is right," Ellie said. "I haven't been that lucky."

"I've had more of the power-trip ego issues with dancers who resent a new choreographer getting the job they wanted," Kat added.

"And how do you handle that?" Darla asked.

Ellie snorted. "Out-dance them and shut them up."

Kat reluctantly agreed. "I've been forced into that position but I don't like it. I try to enlist their help and stroke their egos."

Darla studied her a long moment. "You've been all over the world. Are you going to be happy here in one place? We really need someone who will stick it out at least a year. And even when we do travel, right now it's all in the States."

"Vegas is my home," Kat explained. "I grew up here. My parents are here. I really am ready to be here as well. I want to put down roots and sleep in my own bed every night."

"I told you this was perfect timing," Ellie added, and to Kat, "And girlfriend, I don't know how you did back-to-back concert tours. I did one and it almost killed me."

"You have to be at the right place in your life to do it," Kat said. "I was young and free and I saw the world. Now I'm *home*."

"So that's it?" Jason asked, his question forcing her to look at him. "No more traveling?"

"Not for me," she said, unintentionally referencing the past history between them, of demanding careers that had separated them, then tore them apart. Kat could have kicked herself for the slip, watching his eyes narrow with understanding. He couldn't have known she was coming today because he knew, just as she did, that the past was never the past. She just had to survive this interview and get out of here and let Jason deal with how he told everyone she wasn't the right choice.

"Kat," Darla said, drawing Kat's attention back to the present. Darla then led her into the first of a series of questions that seemed to come from everyone but Jason. As a former casting director, Darla was tough and detailed, but Kat liked her quite a lot and they hit if off quickly.

A good forty-five minutes later, Darla leaned back in her chair and said, "You have my vote, honey. You rock."

"For once we agree," Lana said. "I'm sold. We obviously need to talk amongst ourselves but I'm going on record as a 'yes.'" Murmurs of agreement followed around the table.

"Thank you, ladies," Kat said, feeling her stomach twist with regret. She liked these people. She could get excited about this job.

Ellie clapped, always youthful by nature. "Now we just need our director to give the okay."

"Who's the director?" Kat asked, mostly out of curiosity. She wasn't taking this job.

"I am," Jason said softly, drawing her shocked gaze. "And I know what Kat is capable of. She'd be perfect."

Kat sucked in a breath at Jason's double meaning, and the very idea that Jason was suggesting they work together. She turned her head so the others couldn't see her, giving him an "are you crazy?" look before deciding she was missing something. "How can you direct this show and do *Stepping Up?* You have auditions and filming in L.A."

"We're filming the entire season here in the hotel this year," he said, leaning back in his seat. In other words, he'd be here, with her, far more than he'd be gone. No. Not with her. She wasn't with him. She wouldn't be with him. His lips curved. "As far as I'm concerned, you have the job. We'll contact your agent with an offer right away."

She couldn't seem to form any words. Her and Jason, both in Vegas, both working on the same show. She tore her gaze from his and pushed to her feet. "Thanks, everyone, for your time and consideration. I sincerely enjoyed meeting you all. Darla—" she offered her hand to Darla, who stood up to shake it "—let's have lunch sometime soon."

Darla gave her a keen look. "Because we aren't going to be working together, are we?"

"I hope we will work together, yes," she said.

"But not now," Darla pushed.

"I have some conflicts I need to talk to my agent about," she said honestly, refusing to look at Jason, who was still seated. She maneuvered around the chair and waved at the group, telling them goodbye, and finally darted for the exit.

She shut the door behind her and raced down the hall, her heart in her throat, choking her. She made it to the ticket booth when Jason's hand gently shackled her arm. Suddenly, she was in a small hallway behind the booth, back against the wall, his hand on the surface above her head. She could smell his damnable cologne, feel the heat of his body, and it made her mad.

"Did you know I was coming?" she asked.

"Yes."

"And you didn't warn me?"

"Would you have come?"

"You wanted me to come?"

"Yes."

"Yes? That's all you're going to say? Just 'yes'?"

"It's not complicated. It doesn't require a long explanation. Yes. Yes, I wanted you to come."

"You know we can't work together."

"We work great together. No one gets my creative vision more than you."

"No," she said. "No. This won't work." She leaned away from the wall.

"Come on, KandyKat," he said sincerely. His hand closed on her shoulder, sending a rush of heat all the way to her toes. "We're good together. You know we are. We'll rock this show in a big way."

"Don't call me that," she snapped, referring to the old nick-name that only he used. "And 'good together' doesn't make us good for each other."

"The show needs you. *I need you.*"

I need you. His words shuddered through her, and she knew she was in trouble. In trouble, because she wanted him to mean something beyond the show.

"No." She stepped around him. "I'm not doing this with you again." She took off walking, and this time he let her. Just like he had two years before. Just like he always did.

JASON KNEW THE minute he'd said he needed her, he'd screwed up and sent her running for the hills like she always did. But not this time. He'd let her go before, and regretted it every day since.

He rounded the corner and entered the hallway, then walked back into the interview room. The room went silent, everyone was staring at him. He went to his seat and grabbed his notebook.

"We're done," he said. "And Kat's in. I'll get her."

"Do you need her agent's number?" Ellie asked.

"I know Michael," he said. "I'll talk to him."

He headed to the door. The minute he'd been told about this project, he knew it was meant to be. That it had come to him—to him and Kat—at the right time. They were both home, where they belonged. *Together*.

2

TWO DAYS LATER, on a Friday afternoon, Kat sat on her overstuffed brown couch with her feet bare, wearing blue jeans, a tank and minus a bra or makeup. The idea was to indulge in a leisurely afternoon in her cozy, too-often-unoccupied home, and to stop the constant replay of her encounter with Jason in her mind. Her current effort to distract herself had her with a book in her hand and a movie playing on her flat-screen television.

Her cell phone rang and she ignored it. She knew who it was. Her agent. Michael had called her ten times today, begging her to take the job with Jason, which wasn't making her efforts to forget her ex any easier.

The doorbell rang and she hit the mute button on the remote control. She grabbed the forty bucks she'd put on the glossy maple coffee table for the teenage sisters who lived next-door who had hit her up for their school chocolate sale. She'd made them squeal when she'd told them she'd take forty bars. Kat's mom and dad loved candy and she loved seeing the kids get excited. The bell rang again and she smiled. Eager teenage girls. Gotta love 'em.

Kat padded across the marble tiled floor to open the door, and before she even opened the screen, she flashed the money. "I have the cash."

Jason grinned and leaned on the door frame, muscles flexing under a plain black T-shirt that didn't look plain on him at all. "That's not enough to make me go away," he said, eying the two twenties in her hand. His gaze slid over her pink tank top and then lifted. "Not even close."

She growled and shoved the money into her pocket, then crossed her arms in front of her chest as she inadvertently noted his clean-shaven jaw, all smooth and ready…for her skin. That little bad girl thought made her as angry as she was eternally hot for the man. "I'm going to kill Michael for giving you my address."

"Your parents," Jason supplied.

She rolled her eyes and dropped her arms in frustration. "Oh, good grief."

"They always liked me."

Oh, didn't she know it. They loved the man almost as much as she did. "Why are you here?"

"You know why."

"Save your breath."

"Not a chance. Invite me in."

"Not happening."

"Why?"

"You know why."

He stared at her, his green eyes cutting through the screen like a diamond on glass. "Kat," he said softly, pressing his hand on the screen. "Let me in." The words vibrated with a plea, and she knew he wasn't talking about the door anymore.

"I can't," she whispered, unable to stop herself from flattening her hand against his. Warmth spread up her arm and over her chest. His head dropped to the screen and so did hers. She could feel him everywhere he wasn't touching, everywhere he wasn't—*shouldn't*—be. She wanted to rip the screen away, to hold him and to feel him hold her—to get lost in him just one last time. It was always *just one last time*.

"I can't do this again. This is what happens. The door is the only thing keeping it from happening now."

"I'm not going to tell you we won't end up in bed together," he said after a long pause.

"That's not helping your case if you want me to take this job," she said, wondering why his assurance that they might end up between the sheets was comforting rather than the opposite.

"I've never lied to you, Kat," he said, his voice thickening. "I'm not going to start now. I want you. I never stopped wanting you. And I want you involved in the show. Enough that I used my pull to double the salary offer originally sent to your agent's office."

She pulled back to gape. "What? That's an insane amount of money." She shook her head. "This isn't about money to me. You know money isn't why I do what I do."

"You love spoiling your parents rotten, and you know it. This will let you do it in a big way. This is security for them and for you."

"I spoil them because we spent a lot of years struggling when I was growing up."

"You don't have to justify it to me of all people. You know I love your parents, I know how they struggled. I was there when they were helping you through college, remember?"

Yes, oh yes, she remembered. Love, marriage and his career that started two years before hers and tore them apart.

"I admire you for what you do for them," he continued. "You know I spoil mine as well. Look, Kat, I have to get you in or out by Monday. We have open call tomorrow and Sunday and with seventy spots to fill. Ellie can handle it, but if you're in, I know you. You'll want to cherry-pick the dancers. At least come to the set and observe. See how you feel being there with me. And if it's still a 'no,' I'll let this go. Just give me one day."

"Why are you pushing so hard to make this happen?"

"Do you remember when we went to San Francisco and we got down to the pier and we couldn't get a cab back to the hotel, and the trams were shut down?"

The weekend he'd proposed. "You know I remember that weekend." She thought of that panicked moment on the pier and found herself smiling in spite of everything. "My feet were killing me and we just had to keep walking."

"I carried you."

"And fell down."

"And you pulled me back to my feet, spotted a midnight movie joint, where we ate too much popcorn, and then the cabs were free. We worked it out together, just like we'll work this out. We're older, wiser and more mature. We're both professionals." He touched the screen again. "Tomorrow, Kat. 6:00 a.m. Please. Be there." He backed up, his eyes holding hers. Her cell phone began to ring. "And take your agent's calls. He might have something to say worth listening to." He turned and started walking away.

Kat stared after him, watching his sexy, loose-legged swagger as he headed to his motorcycle, fighting the urge to go drag him back and rip off his clothes and have her wicked way with him.

With a frustrated sound, she rushed back to the living room, away from the door and the hot man on the bike. Her phone had stopped ringing, but Jason's words played in her mind. *Take your agent's calls. He might have something to say worth listening to.* She frowned and reached over the couch to snap up her cell. Jason didn't say anything without a purpose. Kat hit her voice mail button and listened to the most recent message from Michael.

"I know you're a perfectionist even when it comes to being stubborn, but listen up." Kat ground her teeth. Michael had been with her through her painful split from Jason. He knew good, darn well she was trying to be smart and keep her personal and professional lives separate. That wasn't stubborn, it was smart. *"I don't know what's going on with you and Jason, but he wants you on this job in a big way. He gave the studio an ultimatum, Kat. He insisted they do whatever it takes to get you—including doubling your offer—or he'll pay back his signing bonus and walk. I know Jason's involvement is messing with your head, but if you won't call me back, call him. Call one of us."*

Kat dropped the phone and stared at it like it was a snake about to bite her. A second later, she launched herself into action and ran for the door, yanking it and the screen open, just in time to see Jason's motorcycle turn the corner.

"What are you doing, Jason?" she whispered, at the same moment her eyes caught on something sitting on top of the porch stairs. Her heart skipped a beat as she forced her bare feet to cross the porch and pick up the KandyKat bar, all too aware of the memory it was meant to stir. *You're sweeter than candy,* Jason used to say, right before he proceeded to prove he meant it. He had no intention of keeping his hands off of her. That was the message now. He wanted her to show up tomorrow with her eyes wide open.

Kat turned and went back inside, shutting the door behind her, trying to shut out temptation, the memories, to shut out *him.* She fumbled to find her phone to call Jason, and then stopped. If she called, he'd know years hadn't erased his number from her memory any more than they had erased him from her heart. Not that he didn't know that. He knew. She didn't hide how affected she was by him. She couldn't if she tried, so she just didn't try. Still, she hesitated. Jason had threatened to quit over her. She glanced down at the Kit Kat bar. She didn't understand what was going on with him, only that she had to talk to him. She had to understand. Kat dropped her face into her hands. She was going to the auditions tomorrow.

IT WAS SIX O'CLOCK on the dot the next morning and Jason sat at a long table beneath the stage with Darla and Lana to his left, when the odd sixth sense he'd always had for Kat shot through him. He turned on the pretense of surveying the rows of stadium seating filled with hopeful dancers waiting to audition. He scanned and found her inside the entrance, off to the right of the doors, leaning against the wall. Jason smiled to himself and turned back around. He picked up his coffee and took a sip, savoring more than the caffeine. She was here, that was what counted. And he knew his Kat. She wouldn't be against that back wall for long, especially considering Ellie and her assistant choreographer for the day were calling the first group of dancers to the stage. No, she would stand back there, adrenaline pumping with the desire to be in the mix of things. He gave her an hour, tops, before she was on the stage.

He relaxed into his seat, watching Ellie take the dancers through steps. He glanced at the scorecard he and the other judges would use to rank the dancers, then compare them to Ellie's notes. Those with the top scores at the end of the day would be called back for another audition. Darla wouldn't need her scorecard. She'd know every dancer and their strengths with incredible exactness.

Ellie was about to dismiss the third group forty-five minutes later, when Kat called out, "Wait! Wait! Ellie, hold on a minute."

Jason smiled, not even needing to turn around to know she was running down the aisle. "It's Kat," Darla said, glancing behind her and then at him, narrowing her gaze. "You knew she was here."

"Yeah," he said.

"Kat!" Ellie yelled into her mic. "Well, yeehaw!" Ellie stepped to the edge of the stage right as Kat stopped beside the judges' table. She reached over him, the sweet scent of woman—his woman, or she would be again if he had anything to say about it—teased his nostrils. Damn, he wanted her.

"Can you have this group run the routine once more, please?" Kat asked.

Ellie grinned. "If it gets you one step closer to getting your backside up here, then sure thing."

Darla and Lana waved at Kat. "We're so glad you're here."

"Does this mean we get to keep you?" Darla asked.

"Yeah," Jason said. "Does it mean we—" translate *he* "—get to keep you?"

Kat gave him an incredulous look. "You didn't tell them?"

"No," Darla said. "He didn't tell us. Did you take the job?"

"No," Kat said. "I appreciate your eagerness but I'm observing while I try to figure out a bit of a conflict before the Monday deadline for me to make a decision." Her gaze touched Jason's. She still had her backpack over her shoulder, as if she was ready to bolt. "This *doesn't* mean I'm in."

"You're just a very hands-on observer," he teased, glancing at her skintight leggings and tank top, and the long braid down her back that she wore when she worked. All of which said that she'd come to dance.

She grimaced and motioned between her and him. "You and I need to talk."

He leaned into the microphone. "Give us ten, Ellie." He stood up and faced her, lowering his voice for her ears only. "At your beck and call. I always am. You should know that by now." He was all about talking, and he'd like to start with what had happened the last time they were together, but he knew better. Not only was there no time now, but she ran then, and if he pushed too hard she'd run now. He wasn't going to let that happen.

"I didn't mean this second," she said. "Later."

God, she was beautiful with her hair pulled back, her blue eyes luminous against her pale, perfect skin. "Fine, then," he said softly. "We'll talk later."

She opened her mouth and shut it, then shoved her backpack at him. "Tell Ellie to go ahead," she said, and turned away, but not before he saw the panic in her face.

She was afraid of getting hurt, and so was he. But they couldn't go on like this either. They were together, and before he let her get away, they were either saying goodbye for good, or she was putting his ring back on her finger forever. And if he had to kiss every last inch of her a couple dozen times over to get her to let down her walls—well, it was a tough job, but he was the man to do it, and do it right.

3

JASON SAT BACK down and settled Kat's bag in the empty seat next to him before he spoke into the microphone. "We're a go, Ellie."

"Do you want to sit down, Kat?" Darla asked, leaning forward. "I can get you a score sheet."

"I'll stand," Kat said, "but thank you." The music started and Kat's full attention was riveted on the stage she'd soon be on, he was certain.

The dancers began their performance, but Jason watched Kat, her expression focused on the dancers. He could see her mentally pacing the routine, analyzing, thinking and rethinking. The music stopped and Ellie turned to see what Kat wanted her to do now.

Kat squatted down next to Jason, losing her balance and grabbing his leg, scorching it with her hand. The woman had far too much control over him, but he didn't care. Not anymore. He'd done his own share of running, but it had been over for a long time.

Their eyes met and he saw her swallow hard. The touch, the connection, shook her, and it damn sure shook him. She moved her hand to the empty seat next to him.

"How did you rate number seven?" she asked.

He didn't have to look at the scorecard. He hadn't rated many in this group well. "Poorly." He leaned back so that he could talk to Darla with Kat involved. "What did you do on number seven?"

"I marked her as a no," Darla said, after glancing at her clipboard. "Cute little blonde thing that screams of sugar and spice, but she doesn't know it yet. She's just not ready for this."

"Ditto," Lana said, leaning forward to join the conversation. "I love how she looks angelic and still has tattoos. It's that sugar and spice thing, but she doesn't deliver the promise of her first impression." She sighed. "And I'm agreeing with Darla way too much. I'll have to fix that before the show starts."

Jason studied Kat a moment. "I know you. You see something in her. Go do your thing. Save her."

She hesitated only an instant. "This doesn't mean I'm in." And then she was up, heading to the stage.

He laughed. She was so "in" and they both knew it.

"Just what exactly is your relationship with Kat?" Lana asked, ever the nosy one.

Jason had no intention of hiding his relationship with Kat, but he wanted everyone to see she was so special before he explained. He already knew. "My relationship with Kat isn't what matters," he said, motioning toward the stage. "Her skill is. Watch her and you'll agree."

Jason turned his attention to Kat, watching her put on a headset.

"Okay," she said the instant she had sound, to the

group of twenty dancers, ten male and ten female. "One more time and make it good. Number seven, front row." The young girl gaped, looking stunned and frightened rather than excited by the notice. Jason didn't see what Kat saw in the girl, but he trusted her judgment.

The music started and Kat watched a minute, focused on number seven, and he smiled as she started to sway, slowly easing into the routine. Suddenly, she turned and stepped into the row of females, just slightly behind number seven. And his little KandyKat danced like she'd practiced the routine a million times. She was nothing shy of spectacular.

Darla and Lana both leaned forward to look at Jason. "What have I missed?" Darla asked.

"Yeah," Lana agreed. "Has Kat been working with Ellie the past few days and we weren't told?"

"Nope," Jason said, his words laced with the pride he'd always felt for Kat's skill. "Kat has this unreal, almost freaky ability to watch a routine and then perform it perfectly." Yet, she couldn't remember their hotel name, he added silently with a private smile. Of course, neither had he.

"Wow," Darla said. "She is just…wow."

"I'm officially impressed," Lana said. "And I don't impress easily."

Ellie stood on the sidelines and gave a thumbs-up sign to Jason.

Jason settled back in his seat to enjoy the show. "You ladies haven't seen half of what she's about yet."

"Stop!" Kat yelled into her headset and walked to number seven, flipping her mic away from her mouth and settling her hands on the girl's shoulders. The girl listened in earnest and then Kat flipped her mic back and said, "Everyone stand aside except for me and number seven." She glanced at the girl and smiled. "I mean Shannon." The dancers split half to one side of the stage and half to the other. Kat signaled and the music started again. She gave Shannon a nod.

Shannon started dancing and Kat watched all of twenty seconds. "Face me," she ordered, taking Shannon by the shoulders again, but she didn't turn off the mic this time. "If you stop now you're going home. Is that what you want?" The girl shook her head. "You're letting fear beat you. I know skill when I see it but I can't do this for you. You have to deliver." Kat stepped back and started dancing. The girl joined her and Kat shouted, "Attitude. Give me attitude."

Jason smiled as suddenly Kat *and* that young girl owned the stage, and with every step Shannon transformed. Kat was gorgeous, a goddess on that stage. No one who ever met her and worked with her understood why she wanted to be behind the camera, not in front of it. But he did. Kat loved to dance, but ultimately saving number seven defined who she was as a person. She loved mentoring. She loved helping people achieve their dreams.

Darla leaned close to Jason. "Ah, Jason?" She pointed to the male dancer making a lewd gesture to another male dancer that seemed to have something to do with Kat's stellar backside. And it was stellar. "You want to go kick that kid's ass or do you want me to?"

"Neither," Jason said, knowing his Kat all too well. "Kat can handle herself." And she'd be ticked if he didn't let her anyway. He'd barely made the confident declaration when Kat did exactly what he'd expected. She handled it. Taking the kid off guard, and proving she was ever-aware of her dancers, she stopped dancing and turned suddenly, walking up to the male dancer. She got up close, toe to toe with him.

Jason laughed, "And here comes the fun. Kat runs a tight ship. She's fair but tough."

"You see something you like?" Kat demanded of the kid with her microphone loud and clear for all to hear.

"Ah, yeah," the kid said. And he was a kid. Maybe eighteen or nineteen with dark curly hair and dark skin tones.

"Try again," Kat said.

"Ah, no?" he asked.

"That sounded like a question. I'm looking for an answer. The *right* answer."

"No, ma'am!" he shouted so even the judges heard loud and clear. "No, I do not."

Lana and Darla burst out laughing. "Oh, she *so* has to take this job," Darla insisted. "You have to sign her, Jason."

"That's what I thought," Kat said to the kid. "Because, you see, this is a professional stage. My girls have to put on skimpy costumes and trust the male dancers who have their hands all over them. This isn't a night club."

"She said 'my girls,'" Darla whispered.

"Yeah," Jason said with satisfaction. "I heard."

"Yes, ma'am," the boy shouted. "I'm sorry. It won't ever happen again."

"You're going to have to dance like Michael Jackson

at this point not to get sent home. In fact…" Kat glanced over her shoulder. "Ellie?"

"Coming right up," Ellie said, choking on laughter with her mic still on.

A few seconds later, Michael Jackson's "Thriller" started to play and Kat motioned the boy forward. He hesitated for a tenth of a second and then moved to center stage, where he proceeded to dance his backside off. The kid was good—very good.

Kat and Ellie let him dance for a solid two minutes before she held up a hand and stopped the music. She and Ellie whispered to each other, careful to cover their mouth pieces, before Kat said, "That was Michael in diapers. Give us grown-up Michael tomorrow or you're out."

"I'm returning?" he asked, looking stunned.

"Yes," Kat said. "And don't make us sorry."

The kid slid on his knees to Kat's feet and bowed. "Thank you. Thank you. I won't make you sorry. I promise."

"Get out of here before I change my mind," she teased with a smile and then turned to Shannon. "And you go home and practice being a diva in the mirror."

"I'm coming back?" Shannon asked, and yelped with joy when Kat confirmed. She raced forward and hugged Kat.

"Everyone else will get your fate at the end of the day," Ellie announced, and sent everyone, Shannon included, on their way.

Kat and Ellie both flipped their microphones aside and put their heads together in a short conversation before Kat headed toward the stairs.

Jason's cell buzzed with a text. He quickly replied to Kat's agent, telling Michael that yes, she was here, and he was working on making that permanent.

"Uh-oh." Darla laughed from beside him. "I think you're in trouble, Jason."

"You two so have a past," Lana said. "I can smell it a mile away."

Jason jerked his gaze upward at the comments to find Kat headed their way, or rather *his* way, with her gaze fixed intently on him. Oh yeah, he was in trouble. She'd apparently been thinking about more than dancing on that stage, because she was fired up. He could almost feel the heat of flames crackling off her. That kid wasn't the only one leaving here busted. Jason had to hope this ended as well for him as it had for the kid: with a second chance. Okay, in his case, maybe more like a third or fourth. But this was going to be the one he made count.

4

KAT WAS FURIOUS—at herself and at Jason. They both knew what would happen if she came here today, yet he'd baited her and she'd let him. Now it was done. She was attached to the show and she was going to get hurt again. *He* was going to hurt her again. And she'd lose him and the show in one short season. Why would he want to put either of them through that?

Jason stood up as she neared. "I'm guessing it's time for that talk?"

She gave a nod and he motioned her toward the back-stage exit. "Should we keep going?" Darla asked.

Jason arched a brow at Kat. "Yes," she said. "Go ahead. I don't want to back things up." Her gaze returned to Jason. "I need to deal with my conflict once and for all."

"My exact thoughts," he agreed, motioning her to the right, to a path that led behind the stage.

Her chest tightened and she clung to her anger. If she was angry, she wasn't turning to melted chocolate in the man's hands. *No,* a voice in her head reminded.

That always came after the anger. But she always, always turned to melted chocolate.

Side by side, they walked past the stage and around it, then down to a sunken hallway that had doors. "This way," he said, indicating the rows of doors and opening one of them, letting her enter first.

Kat found herself in a small costume room. Racks of clothes pressed in on either side of her. No, it wasn't even a small room. It was a closet, and the tiny space set her on edge. Maybe this had been a bad idea. A small room, alone with Jason and a closed door.

She whirled on him the minute he shut the door. "You knew what would happen if I came here today and I told you I can't do this thing with us again. I can't. If I take this job then it has to be work only."

He leaned against the wall. "If that's what you want."

She swallowed hard and leaned against the opposite wall, still so close that only a few steps separated them. "That was too easy." She studied him. "Damn it, Jason. I know you. 'If that's what you want' translates to you planning to change what I want but not until I've signed a contract." He didn't say anything. He just stared at her with those gorgeous, intense eyes, and she pushed, "No reply?"

"I think I was pretty clear. As long as that's what you want, that's how it will be. The fact that I'm leaning against this door, when I want to be over there with you, kissing you like there's no tomorrow, should prove I mean it. This job has your name written all over it. And since we're in Vegas, I'm going to say that you coming home right when we were casting and looking for a choreographer says it's in the cards. You were meant to be here. We were meant to be here. I believe that so strongly that if I have to agree to keep this all business to get you to take the job, I will. But don't think for one minute that I won't be hoping you'll give me the opportunity to change your mind."

Her skin prickled with awareness and a part of her screamed—convince me now—while another wanted to dart for the door he was blocking.

"You think that's the answer I'm looking for? You think that makes this an easy decision for me?"

"It's the only answer I have. You know me. I'm straight up. Take the job, Kat. Do this one last thing for me, for us, and I swear I will never ask you to do anything for me ever again."

For him. His plea shouldn't matter, but it did. God, she still loved this man. And she knew he loved her. She did. Where they were concerned, love always hurt, and she didn't know if she could live through it again. But then, she never seemed to move on from it, or from him, either.

"What do we tell the cast and crew?"

"That you took the job."

"About us, Jason."

"Why do we have to tell them anything?"

"Someone will find out."

"Do you really care?" he asked. "Because I don't, Kat."

"I don't want anyone thinking I slept my way into this job. I have six weeks to get a show audience-ready. I need respect."

"One hour with you, and you'll have their respect," he assured her, "but I understand. You know I'll respect your wishes. We've known each other since college. Old friends, both from Vegas."

"The tour," she said. "I'm not thrilled with being on the road again. I need a home, a solid foundation."

"Three months and that's it," he said. "And if *Stepping Up* continues to a fourth season, we can negotiate the tour out of your contract."

"And if the show is cancelled?"

"My hope is that the Vegas show outlasts the television show," he said. "We have to make sure it's good enough to become a Vegas fixture."

She liked that idea. A steady job. A home. Stability. And how ironic that Jason, of all people, would deliver her the opportunity. "This is only work."

"Whatever you want," he said smoothly, knowing all too well, she wanted him. "I sent Michael a copy of the contract. He's already reviewing them."

"Because you knew if I showed up here today, I'd take the job."

His far-too-sexy lips curved. "It was a good bet." He pushed off the door to let her pass. "I know you're eager to get back to the auditions."

She knew darn well she was about to be too close to him for comfort, but she also knew she couldn't run from him, or them, if she took this job. Kat walked toward him and as she suspected, he didn't let her pass.

They stood there toe-to-toe, their gazes locked, until he let his hand settle on her arm, the touch warming her skin, her entire body. Her will to push him away evaporated. Slowly, he let his fingers trail downward until he laced them with hers and then brought her knuckles to his lips.

"You're going to be great," he said, the intimate tone of his voice familiar, seductive. "We're going to be great. You watch and see." And then, just like that, he released her hand and opened the door, leaving her aching with the need to touch him again, and swearing she wouldn't. Knowing her willpower to keep her hands off of him was one bet she'd never take in Vegas, if she was a betting woman, and she wasn't.

AUDITIONS FINALLY CLEARED out at six that night and Kat and Ellie immediately headed to a break area behind the stage. Making good use of the rectangular steel table sitting in the middle of the room, with the fridge and some cabinets behind them, they spread out head shots, comparing notes.

"We aren't going to be able to feature more than a couple of these dancers," Ellie said of the hundred they had for call backs. "We need sixty total dancers, and the twenty-four finalists and winners from the first two seasons of *Stepping Up* have to be your stars."

"But we're talking a long-running show, or so we hope," Kat said, the idea of a permanent gig starting to excite her. "We need people who can fill in for anyone who gets sick, hurt or drops out. They have to be just as good as the stars."

Ellie rubbed her stomach. "Or knocked up."

Kat laughed. "Yes. Or knocked up."

"Speaking of knocked up," she said. "What's up with you and Jason? Jason was quick to approve you for an interview but I had no idea you two knew each other as well as you do."

"Why does your pregnancy somehow create a connection to me and Jason?" She glanced down. "Are you trying to tell me I've packed on some pounds or what?"

"No, silly," she said. "And you know it. You're tiny. The electricity between you two is intense, sweets. That's what I'm talking about. And electricity is what got me in trouble." She smiled. "The good kind of trouble."

"I don't know what you're talking about," Kat fibbed, sliding paperwork into her folder. "Jason and I were hardly even around each other this afternoon."

"Not much," she agreed. "And that's how combustible you two are. It's how you look at each other, even from across the auditorium, especially when neither of you know the other is looking. So, what's the scoop? Exes? Almost lovers?"

"I think we are both just shocked that our paths have crossed," she said. "We went to college together. And don't go spreading the word that I'm involved with Jason. I'm not. If I'm going to take over this show, I need respect, not casting couch gossip."

"Anything you say to me, stays with me," Ellie assured her. "And I understand why you want it that way."

Kat glanced at her watch and grabbed the excuse to leave, which wasn't made up. "Gotta go. I'm late. I'm meeting my agent in the restaurant." She pointed at Ellie and then stuffed files into her bag. "You go to your room and rest. I'm glad that husband of yours is coming in next week. Someone has to slow you down."

"I'm pretty sure the baby on board is going to force that issue. I'm exhausted and I'm not even showing yet." She motioned her away. "Scoot. Go get to it."

Kat took off toward the typical twenty-four-hour

basic restaurant every Vegas hotel sported for all-nighters, complete with gambling cards on the table. A quick scan didn't produce Michael, so she flagged a hostess who immediately led her to the back section behind a wall, and that was when her heart fluttered in her chest. Jason sat in a booth across from Michael. It was not only unexpected, it was a bit awkward.

"Why couldn't you get a table?" she murmured under her breath, before inhaling and sitting down at the booth. She tried to steel herself for the moment Jason's gaze lifted. She failed. The instant those clear, knowing eyes met hers, she felt weak in the knees.

She dropped her bag on the floor next to Michael, who, as usual, looked his best, his blond hair neatly groomed, and his suit perfectly pressed.

"You were right," Michael grumbled, and slid a hundred dollar bill across the table toward Jason.

Kat grimaced. "Right about what?"

"Who you'd sit next to," Jason explained, his eyes twinkling with mischief. "He said you'd sit next to me. I said you'd sit next to him."

"You bet on where I'd sit?" she asked, gaping at both of them.

"Yeah, we bet all right," Michael admitted, pulling out a folder from his briefcase resting between them. "You know me. I bet on people, not games of chance. I thought you'd want to prove you weren't intimidated by your past."

"I thought you'd want to avoid me enough not to care," Jason added.

A waitress stopped at the table. "Coffee for me," Kat said, glad for the diversion. She didn't know what to say to his perceptive comment. Jason was right. She was avoiding being close to him.

"Make that two coffees," Michael said.

Jason held up three fingers and turned back to the conversation, his eyes dancing with amusement, seeing too much, and answering the question she had yet to speak. "I'm here because Michael invited me."

"And I didn't tell you because you didn't answer your phone," Michael said. "Which has become a very bad habit, by the way. I've drawn up the amendment you and I talked about on the phone, Kat, before you stopped answering, but Jason has been our go-to person on this. He's negotiated with the studio, in my place. I thought we should do him the courtesy of explaining what we've added. So to start…"

The waitress returned with a pot of coffee and filled their cups as Michael began ticking down a list of minor contractual changes. "The main concern," Michael said, "is travel. The contract was written in a way that could send Kat on the road to promote *Stepping Up*. She's not doing it without added compensation, and a separate contract, period. The end."

Kat poured two creamers in her cup. "It's not about money. I just don't want to think I'm here to stay, and suddenly I'm contractually obligated to hit the road again." She reached for the sweetener.

Jason handed her three packets, the exact three she always used, and her gaze went to his face, only to realize he wasn't even looking at her.

"I've discussed this with Kat," Jason assured Michael. "I can't do anything about the travel for this season. After that, we can negotiate it out."

"That's not the issue," Michael said. "The contract is written in vague language that could make her a slave to the studio beyond the Vegas production. I marked it out and added our wording to an amendment." He flipped the paper around for Jason to read.

He read the marked-out text and then the new version. "Good catch," Jason said. "I'd never have signed it as it was myself." He glanced at Kat. "I see why you keep him around."

"He's convenient," she teased, glancing at Michael.

"I look out for your money," he said. "Which you sometimes forget to make as important as it is."

"Sometimes it's hard to believe I get paid this well for something I love to do."

"Point made," Michael said. "You need me."

Kat's eyes met Jason's, the memory of him saying "I need you" settling between them.

Nearly an hour later, Michael stuffed his paperwork back into his briefcase, leaving Jason his copies. "I have to get out of here. I have a meeting with the Ricco family attorney."

"Ricco?" Kat asked, sliding out of her seat. "As in the famous designer?"

"That's right," Michael said, standing up. "They're buying up properties and negotiating with some of my talent." He turned and glanced between them. "It's good to see you two together again." He walked away.

Kat stood there staring at Jason, not sure what to do.

"Sit down, Kat," he said. "I can't bite you here. Not in public. No matter how much I might want to. I have something I want you to know."

Kat shook her head. "I really need to go."

He considered her, then stood up, tossing money onto the table. "You're in the garage?"

"Yes."

"Me, too," he said. "So I'll walk with you. I'm ready to get home myself."

"Home? Aren't you staying in the hotel like the rest of the cast?"

"Nope," he said. "As soon as I signed on for the show, I bought a house a few miles from yours."

"But…you're always traveling."

"My contract with the show is up this season," he said. "I've already told them I'm not renewing."

"Jason, there you are," a female voice called out, drawing their attention.

Heather Wright, the twenty-something, red-headed bombshell of a script manager Kat had met earlier, stopped beside them. Her hand went to Jason's arm, sliding down it as if she enjoyed the opportunity to touch him, and she quickly said, "Hi, Kat," before turning her full attention and the deep V of her red top in his direction.

Kat cut her gaze to the floor, feeling the familiar punch in her gut that she'd come to associate with Jason. It wasn't jealousy. She knew he didn't want this woman. She knew he'd never cheated on her. It was more about the separateness of their lives that became more apparent in every passing second.

She inhaled, calming her nerves, and her gaze lifted to find Jason staring at her as Heather continued talking.

"You promised we could review the script changes with you before morning. I know there aren't a lot of lines, but I was handed new contractual requirements for the number of lines per person for several of the *Stepping Up* stars that don't fit anything I have set up."

"I need to head out anyway," she said and started walking toward the exit of the restaurant and quickly cutting through the crowd to head to the garage.

JASON DEALT WITH Heather and went after Kat, only to watch her disappear into the elevator a second before he could get to her. He took the stairs, determined to catch her and hit the bottom level at the same moment she exited the sliding doors to the garage.

"Kat," he called, falling into step with her, thankful the garage had plenty of cars, but no people. "Why'd you take off like that?"

"You had work to do and I've changed time zones so many times that I need sleep desperately."

She didn't look at him and he followed her down an incline to the same rental car he'd seen at her house. She clicked the locks and opened the door to toss her bag inside before she turned to face him, leaning against the back door.

"You need to buy a car," he commented. "A rental will get expensive. I can go with you if you want."

She crossed her arms in front of her. "I expected to have time to shop."

"I'll get the car paid for by the studio until you can get to a dealership."

"I don't care about the car."

He pressed his hand to the roof beside her head, and studied her, trying to understand her. "You know there is absolutely nothing going on between me and Heather, right? I want you, Kat."

"I know. And I want you, too, and that's the problem."

"You're going to have to explain to me exactly why that's a problem, because it sounds like exactly what I want to hear."

"I don't want to want you. I don't want to feel the pinch in my chest I felt when you were talking to Heather—and I'm not talking about jealousy, Jason. I'm talking about the sense of being in a world that's yours, and I'm a visitor with a temporary pass. Another hot bedroom romp and another goodbye sure to follow. And that's what's coming. Before this is over, that's what will happen. A part of me says let's just go get a damn room and work this out of our systems now so we can focus on work."

"Let's go, Kat. I'm happy to take that challenge and prove to you that just won't happen."

"You don't know that," she said. "We haven't had more than one night together in years."

"I'm all for fixing that, starting now."

She stared at him for a long moment. "I'm leaving," she announced and then tried to duck under his arm.

He stopped her from getting past him. "If you're so confident you can work me out of your system, then why leave now?"

"I didn't say we could do it in one night and I haven't slept anyway. If I'm going to do something crazy like hop in bed with you again, I'm going to be awake for it."

He laughed. "All right then. I'll let you go—*for tonight*." He moved off the car. "And for the record, Kat. You have had a place in my life since I first met you. I'm hoping I can convince you I deserve one in yours."

He turned and headed back to the hotel, not giving her a chance to tell him all the reasons it wasn't possible. He knew he was wasting his breath telling Kat they could make things work. He was going to show her, which meant doing far more than getting her into bed, though he was looking forward to that moment. It had to be the right moment though, and it had to be her decision.

He stopped inside the building and watched her pull away, swearing to himself that he wasn't going to watch her walk away again. Promising himself no matter how much he wanted to push, no matter how much he'd happily get that room and prove she couldn't work him out of her system, he was going to take this at her pace. He was going to prove to her he was here to stay.

5

It was Friday night, a week after Kat had stood in the parking garage and forced herself to get into the car, rather than wrap her arms around Jason and kiss him. A long week too, filled with confusing emotions, with wanting, needing and…rehearsals.

Kat stood in a private studio inside the Wind Walker Hotel overseeing fifteen dancers, six of whom were performing. While she was happy with the execution of the routine, she was unhappy with the sideline action. Tabitha, a pretty blonde and one of the stars from season one of *Stepping Up,* was leaning against the wall, watching her understudy, Marissa, perform. There was hatred on Tabitha's face, and her general nasty attitude throughout the several hours of rehearsals toward Marissa wasn't sitting well with Kat. It was a behavior she'd come to know over the years, a signal that the dancer delivering such nastiness saw his or her target as a threat.

Tabitha leaned in close to Jensen, her boyfriend and the dancer who'd taken home the grand prize from season one of the show, and whispered something in his ear that made him look Marissa up and down. They laughed, and Kat ground her teeth. She wasn't going to handle this in front of the group for Marissa's sake. Kat could already tell how the situation intimidated the young dancer. Kat didn't care how secure Tabitha and Jensen felt, based on their contracts. She was going to take action.

"That's a wrap for tonight," Kat said, turning off the music. "This group will be with Heather in the script room tomorrow morning. Six o'clock sharp." Everyone seemed to relax all at once and murmurs filled the room as they did a mass exodus.

Kat quickly grabbed a pink sweatshirt and tugged it down over her leggings, and stuffed various items into an oversized bag. The one remaining dancer in the room, a twentyish brunette named Carrie, approached her.

"It's déjà vu from season one," Carrie said. "Only I'm not the one getting the brunt of Tabitha's ugliness. I was hoping I wouldn't be working this closely with her when I accepted this job, but now I think maybe it's good that I am so I can help Marissa blow them off."

"That's very thoughtful of you, Carrie," Kat said, making a mental note to stop being stubborn and watch the old episodes of the TV show, sooner rather than later. "But don't you worry. I'm pretty proactive. I'm going to get everyone playing nice and quickly."

"I had a feeling you would," Carrie said, "but I plan to offer Marissa my friendship and support tomorrow. Aside from Marissa, I wanted to ask you about interning—volunteer, of course—to do some choreographing with you. I did some for season two of the show, as well as some production work, and I'd really like to keep expanding my resume."

Kat smiled. "That's exactly how I started out. I volunteered to help out on a couple shows and proved I had a knack for this work. I'd be happy to have you do the same but let's get you through these grueling weeks of rehearsals before the show opens first. Once it does, and we have things settled, come see me again, and you can help me prepare for the tour."

Her eyes lit. "Really? Oh my God. That would be a dream come true. Thank you, Kat. Thank you so much. My fiancé just got a job here at the hotel, thanks to the studio. He transferred from Los Angeles. He's made so many sacrifices for me and my career, I really want to make every second count that I'm here."

Kat felt a twinge of regret that she and Jason couldn't have made it work for the same reason. She chatted with Carrie for several more minutes before they parted ways.

Kat smiled to herself as she headed down the hallway, seeking Jason and the DVDs of the television show to take home with her. Carrie had called choreographing her "dream come true" when most of the dancers would call the show their dream. Kat related to that feeling and liked Carrie. It was going to be fun to work with her and watch her grow.

After a quick search of all the places Jason tended to dwell at this time of the day, Kat headed to the break area to grab a drink and call him. She was about to enter when she heard Jason and one of the production assistants.

"I'm trying to line up lunch for tomorrow's production meeting," she said. "We're ordering from Joe's Sub Machine. I need yours and Kat's orders but I can't seem to find her."

"Steak and cheese for me," he said. "Veggie with avocado and Swiss for Kat. No onion and no mayo or mustard."

"You know Kat's sandwich order," came another familiar voice that made Kat cringe. Lana was in the break room and Kat had already figured out she was the Queen of Nosiness. "How very interesting."

"Yes," he said. "I know her sandwich order. Just like I know that you not only drink your coffee black, but that you're a royal witch until you drink it. And you chew cherry gum that you smack in my ear all the time."

"And now that I know that gum bothers you," Lana declared, "I'll never stop chewing it."

Kat smiled at the exchange, and not just because Jason was quick witted and he'd covered her backside. It didn't surprise her that he respected her desire to earn everyone's respect and to keep their past quiet for a while. But the realization that he still knew her so well was what got to her and created a strange flutter in her chest.

The production assistant headed out and stopped beside Kat to confirm her sandwich order, which Kat gave a thumbs-up to before entering the break room. "I have a sudden urge for a piece of gum," she announced, finding Jason and Lana sitting at the the table, paperwork spread out. "And this burning desire to smack it very loudly."

Lana started laughing. "Oh, I do believe I'll stock up and pass it out before I head to Los Angeles tomorrow."

Jason grimaced, his strong, square jaw once again sporting a sexy light brown shadow. "I have no doubt you will." He glanced at Kat, those deep green eyes stirring her inside, as they did all too easily, as he added, "Just remember payback is a promise when you choose to participate in Lana's little games."

"I'm scared," Kat assured him with a laugh, trying not to seem too knowing about just how delicious she knew his payback to be. She sat down across from Jason and beside Lana. "So, you're leaving us?"

"I have something scheduled before the TV show auditions get going and my work here is done. Casting is complete and any minor things I could help with are finished." She pushed to her feet, slashing long blonde hair behind her ear. "And on that note I should go to my room. I have an early flight." She pointed at Kat. "Keep him in line. I have to deal with him in a month when we start the crazy travel for the television show auditions."

"I will," Kat assured her, but the jest in her voice was strained, gone with Lana's reminder that Jason would soon be leaving. "Have a safe trip."

Lana hurried from the room, leaving a strong wave of powerful perfume behind her. "One last traveling job," Jason said. "One more and I'm done."

He'd read her discomfort, responded to what she'd not spoken aloud. He knew her like no one else did. He had been her best friend, never replaced by another, and that reality made it hard to call what was between them just sex. But it was just sex, because people who loved each other, really loved each other, found a way to be together.

Kat slowly let her gaze slide back to his, and she felt

the connection in every pore of her body. *It's sex,* she told herself. *Chemistry. You want him. He wants you. It means nothing.* "I said my last tour was it for me, too," she finally managed. "No more travel, yet in a few months I'll be traveling with this show."

"Kat—"

"Whatever you're going to say, this isn't the time or place."

"Then let's go somewhere else."

"That would be good," she said. "I have a challenge with a couple of the dancers I need to talk to you about."

"There's a bar on the top level of the hotel. It's quiet there and I could sure use a drink. It's been a hell of a couple of weeks."

Heat pooled low in her tummy. "We both know how well I handle my alcohol," she said, cringing at her reference to their past, the past she couldn't seem to avoid. "I still have to drive home."

"Stay at the hotel," he said. "I know you prefer home. Living on the road is rough, but so are the late nights and early mornings right now. Exactly why the studio provides you a room."

She wanted to go have a drink with him, she wanted to talk to him, to touch him, to just be with him. And a part of her said to just do it, do him. Get this damnable need for him out of her system once and for all. Another part of her said he was a drug, and she had an addiction she had to break, or she'd never really live her life. And you didn't beat an addiction by doing more of the drug. You broke it by just saying "no."

Thanks to this show, their paths were going to cross. She couldn't start down a path of hopping in and out of bed with him when he was around, and really expect to move on with her life. Right. Exactly. That made perfect, logical sense. Damn it.

Kat inhaled and bound herself to mature logic, and reached to ensure temptation did not become indulgence. "How about the diner again?" she finally said. "I haven't eaten and we can talk there."

WITH KAT BY his side, Jason stopped at the doorway of the very public, very unromantic, diner. He didn't love her location preference, but after spending an eternally long week of wanting her, he'd take what he could get. And no matter how challenging it might be to give her time to digest that not only was he here, he was here to stay, he was committed to taking things on her time line. Well, with a little nudging to hurry things, he thought.

"Two?" the hostess asked.

"Two," Jason agreed, and then leaned in and whispered to her, before slipping her a large bill.

She smiled and motioned for them to follow her. "This way."

Kat frowned at him as they fell into step behind the woman. "What did you just do?"

"Moi?" he asked innocently, hoping the little French reference would remind her of their honeymoon in Paris.

"Oui, vous," she replied quickly.

He laughed at the "yes, you" in French, pleased with both her reply, and the fact that the hostess had just led them past double glass doors to a private, empty seating area.

He and Kat slid into the booth across from each other

and when they were alone he wiggled an eyebrow. "Just how much of your French do you remember?"

"If you're asking if I can still talk dirty, I'm pretty sure it would come back to me, *if* I tried. I'm also quite certain I can remember how to curse you out in French." She grimaced. "You paid the hostess to put us back here alone."

"That's right," he said. "We needed alone time. Now reward me and talk dirty to me in French." She complied with a graphic rant that was meant to be far more "curse him out" than "turn him on," but it did the job anyway.

"Naughty little thing, aren't you?" he asked, feeling his cock thicken at the sexy way she'd rolled her tongue on the words.

"Hello there," a white-haired waitress greeted, stuffing a pencil in the poof of her hair above her ear. "What can I get you two?"

"Two frozen margaritas and chips and salsa to start," Jason said. "And we'll give you the rest when you return."

"I told you I can't drink and drive," Kat argued, the instant the woman departed.

"If I don't get a drink down you," he countered, "you're going to spend this entire time we're here worried about what happens after dinner."

"I…" She started to object and then quirked her lips. "Okay, maybe you're right. And I suppose I'm safe. As you said the other day, it's not like you can bite me right here in public."

"No matter how much we both might want me to," he said, reminding her of the rest of his previous statement, his blood running hot at a vivid, mental image of just the spot he'd like to nip and tease first.

"Jason," she warned, her voice raspy, her lips parting in an alluring, come kiss me, kind of way.

"Distract me, baby, before I forget I promised myself to give you space to come around. Talk to me about work. What's going on with the dancers?"

She swallowed hard, and brushed her teeth over her delectable full bottom lip. "Right. The dancers. I need to know what latitude I have to deal with the finalists from *Stepping Up* considering they're supposed to be the stars of the live show."

"As much as you need," he said. "No one is going to hold you, me or anyone on this show, captive. If you can't get someone to do what you need them to do, there are provisions in the contracts to get rid of them."

"You don't even want to know who I'm talking about before you stand by that statement?"

"If this wasn't you asking," he said, "then yes, but I know you and I know you wouldn't do something that wasn't necessary."

"You trust me that much after all these years?"

"Yes. Do you trust me?"

Her expression slowly softening, she said, "Yes. Of course I do."

He leaned in closer. "Then trust me when I tell you I'm going to fight for you, and for us, Kat. I'm not going to let this time end like every other before it."

"Here you go," the waitress said, setting the drinks before them and then the chips and salsa. She tugged a pad from her napkin. "Now what can I get you?"

Kat glanced up at her. "Grilled chicken sandwich and salad with Italian rather than fries."

"Greasy cheeseburger and fries for me," Jason said.

Kat sipped her drink and the waitress disappeared. "You eat like crap."

"I know," he agreed, all too aware that she had just dodged a response to his vow. "I plan to fix that in the next few years."

"In the next few years," she repeated. "Well, at least you have goals." Her smiled faded, and suddenly they weren't talking about food anymore, even before she declared, "I have a confession to make."

He arched a brow. "You can't stop thinking about getting me naked and having your way with me."

She laughed and shook her head. "I doubt you need me to confess that to know it's true, which is why I won't deny it."

Interesting. He was beginning to think his assumption that she was trying to make this all about sex was still on target. "Feel free to confess whatever you need to."

"I hate to even admit this considering I've taken this job, but," she hesitated, and then blurted, "I've never watched one single episode of *Stepping Up*."

"Really?" he said, surprised by just how much her admission bothered him.

"I'm finding out that there are some conflicts that occurred between contestants that I probably should know about. Do you happen to have copies of the first two seasons?"

"At home," he said tightly, certain there wasn't a

show of hers he'd have ever missed. "I can bring them into work tomorrow."

"You don't like that I didn't watch your show."

"No," he said. "I don't."

"I don't do well on the outside looking in."

Emotion settled in his chest, as understanding took hold, and warmed the cold spot that had formed there. "Then don't stand on the outside."

"I didn't."

"You ran from me after Denver."

"I had a tour to go on."

"You didn't say that."

"You didn't ask, Jason."

"Oh, no, sweetheart," he said, laughing but not with humor. "Don't put that one on me. It killed me to leave you that morning and you knew it. We agreed to talk through a plan the next day, but that never happened because *you ran.*"

"I didn't run."

"You're running now."

"I am not!"

"The other night you claimed this was all sex between us and that a few bedroom romps would get it out of our systems." He whispered, "But you backed off when I called your bluff, didn't you? I'm guessing that's because you're afraid that no matter how many 'romps' we have, your plan won't work. And then, KandyKat, you'll have to face what's really between us, be it good or bad, once and for all."

She stared at him, unmoving, her expression intense, before she stood up. "Let's go."

He followed her to her feet. "Where exactly are we going?"

"Your place," she announced. "And I'll follow you in my car."

"I can live with that."

He tossed money on the table, finding her choice interesting, and knowing her well enough to know why she'd made it. She actually thought that keeping him outside her world, her personal space and home, would let her hide from the truth. That home was with him.

"I get a head start," she added. "I'll leave first and meet you at…the burger joint on the corner that everyone orders lunch from all the time. In the parking lot."

He reached for her and pulled her close, pressing his lips to her ear. "As long as you remember that I'm the cat and you're the mouse, and I will catch up to you. Even if it means showing up at your doorstep."

Kat had already made the decision to cave to desire. She wasn't holding back. She flattened her hand on his chest, pressed to her toes, and brought her mouth to his ear. "I'm counting on it."

6

KAT FOLLOWED JASON as he turned his motorcycle into the long driveway of his gorgeous stucco home and then into a garage, shocked that he lived only a few miles from her. Maybe she shouldn't have been shocked. They both gravitated toward the same things, as much as they did to each other.

She killed the engine on her rental. She couldn't believe she was about to have her wicked way with Jason. She watched him swing a powerful thigh over the bike to dismount and edited that thought. She couldn't believe she'd ever kidded herself into thinking she could resist this man. Seriously, that had been certifiably nuts. The man did it for her in every possible way.

She grabbed her bag and shut her car door. He'd removed his helmet and was there when she stood up. He reached for her bag, his fingers brushing her shoulder and sending chills down her spine. Her gaze collided with his and her body reacted instantly to the sizzle in the depths of his stare. They stood there, not touching, but yet her skin tingled as if they were. She resisted reaching for him when it was all she wanted and everything she needed. He didn't reach for her either, and she was pretty sure he knew what she did. If they caved in to the burn right here, right this instant, they'd end up on the hood of the car, rather than on a soft bed.

They moved at the same time, in tune even without words. Kat inched out of the way from the door, and Jason shoved it closed. She followed him to the house, and let him motion for her to enter first. The anticipation of touching him tingled deep in her nerve endings. She entered the house, the air conditioning chilling her ultra-sensitized skin in a way it might not otherwise have done if she wasn't so aware of Jason on every level. Of how tall and broad, how raw and male, he was. How easily he read her needs, her pleasure, how long she'd ached for him, for this.

Kat immediately walked up a flight of carpet-covered steps to a second level with a tiled foyer, and she continued up the next set of stairs. The lights came on behind and in front of her and she stepped to the room above, taking in a massive living area with an open kitchen and dining area to its left. More expensive tile covered the entire floor, and a brown and cream rug sat under a sleek brown leather couch and love seat.

Kat softly inhaled against the pain pinching her chest. What had she been thinking by coming here, taunting herself with the life he had without her? No. No. No. She wasn't going to think about things like that. Not now, not anymore. And maybe, just maybe, sex *would* cure all. Maybe distance and random good sexual encounters had built her and Jason up to more than they were. Tonight, a few nights, and they both could see that there was a reason they had divorced.

Kat turned at the same moment Jason cleared the top step, and she shoved him against wall, desperate to focus on him, not the house. To touch him, to feel him, to forget everything but pleasure.

He dropped her bag and wrapped his strong arms around her and, God, it felt good to have him touch her. Heat radiated from him, warming her palm where it rested, her skin where he touched, where he didn't touch but she wanted him to. Suddenly, they were kissing, drinking each other in, and Kat felt like she'd die if she didn't have more of him. Her tongue stroked his, her hands pushed under his T-shirt, feeling the flex of his strong muscles.

He twined his fingers into her hair, tugging away the band holding it at her nape, and angling her mouth to his, taking more of her, and still not enough. Kat leaned into him, the thick ridge of his erection melding to her hips, and she moaned with the need expanding inside her.

"You feel good," he murmured. "So damn good."

So did he. Too good. Scary, wonderful good. "This is sex," she panted. "Just sex."

"If you say so." His palms caressed her ribs, then cupped her breasts, and he slanted his mouth over hers, tasting her, before adding, "I'm fine with anything that means you take your clothes off and we keep doing what we're doing."

On some level, his refusal to say this was just sex pleased her, on another it scared her, but remembering why it scared her was becoming a challenge. Kat nipped his lip and shoved his shirt upward. He yanked it over his head and tossed it away, giving no resistance at all. She explored his broad, hard chest, absorbing the feel of him with near desperation.

"Sex," she reminded him.

"Great sex," he countered.

"Just sex," she said. "Say it."

"Whatever you want, KandyKat."

She stared at him, knowing he wasn't going to say it. And she was glad, which made her pretty messed up where he was concerned. Or maybe insane to think she could get over him by being with him.

"Then you won't mind if I do this," she replied, dropping to her knees, as she tugged at his belt.

He held his hands out to his sides. "Feel free to use me all you like, sweetheart."

She tugged his pants down, freeing his shaft and wrapping her hand around the width. "I intend to."

THIS WASN'T JUST sex, but Jason didn't figure he'd convince Kat of that when she was on her knees with his cock in her hand. Besides, he was pretty sure she was trying to convince herself, not him, anyway. Though when she licked the tip of his shaft and set every damn nerve ending he owned to prickling, he was pretty open to her trying to convince him, too. She wouldn't change his mind, but when she ran her tongue over the sexy curve of her bottom lip, as if she didn't dare waste one little taste of him, she damn near brought him to his knees in front of her.

She ran her tongue around the head of his cock, casting a sexy look up at him that said she knew she was in control, and she knew what he liked. Which was exactly why they were here. Because she did know him, and he knew her, in a way only two people who shared a special bond could. He'd never had this with any other woman, and he'd tried. He'd dated. And he'd remained unsatisfied in every possible way.

She sucked him deeper, and it felt good, but somehow his mind cleared when he'd have thought the opposite would occur. He replayed his thoughts from moments before, reason invading escape and pleasure. He would never convince her this was more than sex while her hand was around his cock, while *her mouth* was around his cock. He had to make her stop. Ah. Yeah. Stop. She drew him deeper, took all of him, and then started to pump her hand and her mouth at the same time.

He balled his fists by his side, resisting the urge to slide his fingers into her hair, to encourage her to keep going. Jason inhaled and then forced the air out, reaching down and pulling Kat from his body, wanting far more from her than a few minutes of bliss.

Jason wrapped his arms around her and pulled her close, twining his fingers in her silky blonde hair again. He inhaled the familiar scent of roses that was so Kat, so his woman, then lowered his lips a breath from hers.

"What are you doing?" she whispered, her hands on his chest. "You like when I do that. *I* like when I do that."

"I've waited way too long to have you like this again, to waste any of it, with your clothes on."

"Is that right?" she asked, sounding as breathless as he felt.

"Oh yeah," he assured her, "that's right." He slanted

his mouth over hers, his tongue caressing hers in a long, languid stroke that had them both moaning with the contact, with the connection, the need burning between them.

The air shifted with that kiss, swelled with past and present, pain and passion, love and loss. Until their lips parted, the air hung heavy with so many unspoken words.

Seconds ticked by, and then something seemed to snap between them, and they were kissing again—hot and wild—their hands exploring all over each other.

Jason barely remembered how his pants and boots came off, but he remembered everything about undressing Kat. He shoved her shirt upward and unhooked her bra. She tossed it aside and he filled his hands with her high, full breasts, and stroked her plump pink nipples.

He switched places with her, pressing her back to the wall, caressing a path down her arms, his gaze devouring her naked body. "I specifically remember saying 'whatever you want,' KandyKat." He trailed a finger over a stiff peak, flicking it. "And I don't think you'd argue that I'm a man of my word."

"I wanted to do what I was doing."

"Not as much as you want this." He went down on one knee, his hands framing her slender hips, his lips brushing her stomach, pleased to discover her shoes were gone, though he couldn't for the life of him say how. His gaze lifted to hers as he inched down her leggings and the barely there slip of black panties. At another time he'd have enjoyed admiring the scrap of fabric. Right now, he just wanted to taste her, lick her and hear her cry out his name. Those three things and he could die a happy man.

She kicked aside her leggings with his urging and his hands went back to her hips, his lips back to her sexy tummy. "Finally," he breathed out. "I haven't had you like this in far, far too long."

She blinked down at him and then nodded. "Yes," she agreed, her voice raspy. "Too long."

His lips lifted at her admission, and he slid his hands around her delicious backside. "Remember you said that," he insisted before he bent his head, brushing his lips over her hip, trailing kisses over her midsection, widening her thighs as he did, opening her for his touch. He explored the intimate vee of her body, his fingers teasing the slick wet heat of her sex.

She arched toward the touch, a soft sound of pleasure playing like music in the air, delicate and sensual, teasing his cock. He lifted her leg over his shoulder, lapping gently at her clit. She rewarded him with a whimper that had his cock jerking and left him craving another taste, more of her pleasure. Jason licked her, teased her, then spread the sensitive folds to press one finger and then another inside her, stretching her, caressing her. He knew just where and how to touch her to deliver her to release and he took his time, kept her on the edge, waited until she begged for more.

Her fingers laced into his hair, her breathing shallow, urgent. "Jason…I—oh…" She tensed and then spasms wrapped his fingers, intense, hard.

He licked her, suckled her, led her all the way to the height of pleasure, until he felt her muscles begin to relax. He softened his touch, bringing her back down, catching her around the waist when her knees buckled. He kissed her stomach before he stood up, scooping her off of her feet and into his arms, heading up a flight of stairs to the place she belonged for far longer than one night—in his bed.

7

MOONLIGHT SPILLED INTO the large master bedroom as Jason carried Kat to his king-sized sleigh bed. He settled her on her feet beside the nightstand and sat down on the bed, pulling her close.

She leaned into him, urging him farther onto the bed, and he didn't argue. He turned and rested his back against the headboard. Kat followed him, straddling him, his shaft pressing to her backside, thick and hard, and pulsing with his need to bury himself inside her and feel the wet, tight heat of her sex.

Jason slid his hand into her hair and pulled her mouth to his. "I missed this, Kat. I missed us. I missed *you*."

"Me, too," she whispered against his lips. "Me, too."

"Then stop saying this is just sex. We both know it isn't." He trailed his fingers down her cheek. "I love you, Kat. I always have and I always will."

Kat pressed her lips to his, slid her tongue into his mouth, the sweetness of her filling his senses, and he tasted her reply—her fear and yes, her love.

Jason wrapped his arms around her, molding her

closer, deepening their kiss, reassuring her he meant his words, understanding she needed to feel them, not just hear them. He told himself to go slow, not to push her, but she moaned, her tongue testing his, tangling with him, pushing him to give her more. More and slow didn't compute, not to a man starving for her. His hands traveled her body, and she shivered with pleasure, the way she always had in the past. It drove him wild. He palmed her breast, teased her nipple, plucking it into a tight peak. She covered his hand, molding it over her, and broke their kiss. For an instant, their gazes collided, and he swore the connection sent a rush of heat straight to his cock.

"I need—" she started. "Jason, I—"

"Me, too," he said. "Me, too, baby." He lifted her, and shifted his throbbing erection between them, the idea of finally being inside her consumed him.

Kat wrapped her hand around the base of his erection, and he could feel himself thicken with the touch, with the anticipation of what was to come. She guided him to the blessed wet, slick heat of her body and he was breathing hard, shaking inside with need, trying to resist pushing inside her, rather than waiting for her to take him there. When she reached down and parted the V of her body, touching herself, he just about snapped. He'd been hard a long time, an impossibly long time.

For the sake of his sanity, Kat noted. She pressed his throbbing shaft inside her, biting her bottom lip on a sound of pleasure when she did, her lashes fluttering as she slid down his length taking him all in.

The torture of the wait was so worth this moment.

Kat was hot and tight, and oh so wet for him, and she felt so good.

He had no idea how, but a little piece of unwanted reality slipped inside the pleasure. Damn this reality thing that kept intruding in the middle of the best and worst of moments. They weren't using birth control.

"Kat—"

"The pill," she whispered, reading his mind as she often did, and lacing her fingers behind his neck, her nipples teasing his chest.

The pill. For a second, he didn't move, feeling the blunt edge of yet another bite of reality in the part of Kat's life that he'd tried to never think about. Of course she'd had other lovers, and he had no right to even go there anyway. He'd lost her, and he'd deserved to lose her, too. Taken jobs she'd asked him not to take. Asked her to give up work she wanted to accommodate his career. He'd taken her for granted and he had to prove himself to earn her back. Worse, he had no doubt she'd seen him as unchanged, a selfish ass, when he'd left her in Denver, expecting she'd wait on him. It really had killed him to leave her and meet his obligation to *Stepping Up.*

Jason slid his hands up her back, bringing her mouth to his, planning to confess just how wrong he'd been, how much he regretted the past. "Kat—"

She brushed her lips over his. "Don't do this now. Please. I just want to be with you. I want to pretend nothing else exists for just right now." She didn't give him time to object. She kissed him, took his mouth and drugged him into a spell of her taste, her tongue and her body slowly rocking against his.

Raw hunger rose inside him, the past fading into the present. He moaned into her mouth, pressing her down against him, and lifting his hips to thrust. Her sex tightened on him, clamped down and took him hard and deep. Her fingers were in his hair, soft little touches that sent shivers down his spine. And her kisses, those delicate, sweet lips that could be so wild and wicked, and everything he wanted them to be. He was hungry for her, and she was hungry for him. It was in the air, in their every touch, taste and moan. If they could melt into each other, become one, they would have.

Kat leaned back, her hands behind her on his thighs. Jason's hand settled on her flat stomach, pumping into her even as she rode him in an erotic dance, her beautiful breasts swaying with the rhythm, her tight little nipples begging for his mouth. He wrapped his arm around her slender waist, his hand palming her breast, kneading it before he suckled one nipple, alternately licking and flicking it with his tongue, and then sucking it deep into his mouth.

She spiked her fingers through his hair, her moans turning to sexy little purrs of pleasure that were driving him wild. Jason pushed her hard against his hips, thrusting into her. "Yes," she moaned, burying her face in his neck. "So…good. I…Jaso…n."

His name on her lips, asking for pleasure and for release, drove him over the edge. Jason couldn't get close enough to Kat, couldn't pump hard enough or go deep enough inside her. Harder, faster. The room disappeared, the past faded. There was only this moment, there was only Kat, being with her, holding her, loving her and pleasing her.

He could feel the tension stiffening her body, and the tightening of her arms around him. The sweet sound of her gasp came an instant before her sex reacted, rippling with release, with her pleasure that became his.

Sensations spiraled through Jason. He pressed Kat down and lifted into her, shaking with the intensity of his completion. Burying his face in her hair, the scent of it—so soft and feminine, so her—relaxing him.

For long seconds, they clung to one another, skin damp, breathing heavy, and he felt her tense, sensed an emotional struggle in her and braced for it. Would it be regret? Anger? Something completely different?

"I love you, too," she whispered next to his ear.

So softly spoken were those words that Jason didn't dare believe he'd heard them, until she leaned back and met his stare, repeating the golden words. "I love you, too. I do. You know I do."

Tenderness and hope filled him. "We'll make it work out this time."

"You really think that's possible? That this time is really different?"

"I don't think. I *know*." But she didn't. He could see the doubt in her eyes. He had to give her time, had to convince her that the only place he'd ever felt at home was when he was with her. He just hoped he wasn't too late, that she could still find home with him.

It was nine o'clock, hours after Kat had arrived at Jason's house and she rested on his bed, on her stomach, and wearing his T-shirt. She watched him disappear into the hall, on his way to meet the pizza delivery man at the door, sighing with the pure satisfaction of being with him again. She blocked out any argument that it might be a mistake. She didn't care. It was too late. She'd done exactly what she'd promised herself she wouldn't do. Kat had fallen for Jason all over again. It was too late to run, too late to hide, because she simply didn't want to.

Kat turned her attention back to the huge flat-screen TV. She and Jason had been watching the first season of *Stepping Up.* The screen flashed from the dancers to the judges' table.

Kat sucked in a breath and sat up, her spine stiff, watching Jason interact with the other judges. It was the first time she'd seen him on television, aside from a commercial for the show, and she was hit hard with a good dose of reality. He looked good, natural and right on the screen, in the spotlight instead of behind the camera. He belonged on that screen, in the public eye, on that show. He was never going to stay here in Vegas. He would be pulled to bigger and better things, and he deserved those things.

That realization washed away her good mood, and stole the joy of minutes before when she'd been happily watching the program with Jason, pretending fairy tales did come true. She wanted those minutes back, and the hours before them. She liked here and now.

"I grabbed your bag," Jason said, sauntering into the room with it and a pizza box in hand, his hair rumpled, his broad chest deliciously bare, his jeans slung low on his waist. He set the bag at the foot of the bed. "I think your phone is inside. I heard it ringing."

"Why would you leave *Stepping Up?*" she asked, the question exploding from her lips, her urgency for the answer far more important than her growling stomach. "It's the number-one show on television. That's a dream come true. It's security. It's opportunity. It's stability going into a fourth season is hard to find in this business. You can't walk away. Even for a Vegas production."

He looked surprised by her sudden outburst. Her phone started to ring again, but she ignored it. She didn't want to pretend everything was roses without thorns, and she almost had. That wasn't good for him or her. She wanted everything out now, before those thorns tore them apart again.

Jason let out a breath and scrubbed his hand over the light stubble on his jaw before setting the pizza on the bed and out of the way.

"Kat." He settled onto the mattress in front of her. "It's a job and it's money. I don't need either of those things."

"It's a huge show, Jason," she said. "They're going to offer you big money to stay. You can't walk away from that."

"Why?"

"I told you why. Because you'll regret it later. What if nothing like this ever comes around again?"

"That's what we both said every single time one of us had an opportunity. We're both older and wiser now. We have money and we have work if we want it. We don't have to walk around in fear that there will never be another 'big' opportunity."

"Tell me you aren't doing this for me."

"For us."

She shook her head, her chest tightened. "No. No. I won't let you do this. You'll resent me, and you'll resent us, later." Her phone started to ring again and she ground her teeth, silently cursing the interruption. "Good grief, who keeps calling?" She reached into the side pocket of the bag, meaning to turn off her ringer, but hesitating when she noted her mother's number. Her mother was a former E.R. nurse who, after five years of retirement, still went to bed at eight and got up at five in the morning.

Kat answered the phone. "Mom? Is something wrong?" No reply. She had been too slow to answer. She punched the recall button and it went to voice mail, her gaze finding Jason's. He arched a brow and she shook her head. "She's not answering."

Kat stood up and grabbed her bag. "I have to go over there." She took off for the hall, dialing her mom's number again. Voice mail again. Her heart was in her throat. She could feel it in her bones that something was wrong in a very bad way.

She dropped her bag at the bottom of the stairs and searched for her pants, racing around the room, to no avail. She dialed the phone again and heard Jason charging down the stairs.

"Did you reach her?" he asked, and the urgency in his voice did her heart good. He was worried with her, he cared. She wasn't alone.

"No," Kat said, turning to him as she reached the bottom step. "I don't know what to do and I can't find my damn pants."

He handed her pants to her. Gratefully, she accepted them and started to pull them on. "Thank you."

Jason tugged a shirt on over his head. "Have you

tried your father?" he asked, grabbing his boots to put them on.

Kat started dialing, not sure why she hadn't thought of that, knowing she needed to calm down and invite a little reason into her thoughts. She tucked the phone between her shoulder and ear to shove her feet into her socks and tennis shoes. The phone went to voice mail two times in a row. She ended the call and redialed.

"Nothing," she said grimly.

"Keep trying," he said, standing up. "It's probably nothing. You're overreacting, but we'll go check to be safe."

"We'll?"

"You drive bad enough when you aren't worried," he reminded her

"I do not," she said, grabbing her bag, where her keys were stuffed. "I don't need a chauffeur."

"Good," he said, taking her bag from her, his eyes dark as they collided with hers. "Because there are a lot of things I want to be to you, Kat, and chauffeur isn't one of them."

She opened her mouth to argue, scared to count on him, to lean on him, only to have him leave again. He *was* going to leave again. But the voice of reason she'd been looking for reminded her that he was here now and she needed him.

Kat reached for the bag on his shoulder and pulled out the keys before dangling them in front of him.

8

THE RIDE TO her parents' house was ten minutes that felt like forever. "Why aren't they answering?" Kat asked Jason from the passenger seat of her rental car.

"Maybe they were fighting and now they're making up," he suggested, "in which case we could really embarrass everyone, including ourselves, by showing up unannounced."

"Please do not suggest my parents are having makeup sex," she said. "That isn't something I like to think about."

"Makeup sex is a logical answer," he pressed. "If there was something wrong when she called, then I'm sure your mother would have left a message. Better yet, she would have taken your calls. Think about it. What's the one time when you wouldn't answer your mother's call? While working or while having sex."

"Again, Jason," Kat chided. "I know you're trying to distract me, but it's not working. I have this bad feeling in my gut I can't ignore. Maybe they aren't taking my calls because one of them is rushing the other one to the hospital and doesn't want to scare me."

"Yet they tried to call you earlier?" he asked, and then gentled his tone. "Kat, baby, you're working yourself up for what is probably nothing. This isn't like you at all." He turned the corner to her parents' house. "See? No firetrucks and no police cars."

Kat let out a relieved breath before quickly fretting again. "Unless they're already gone."

"What is up with you?" Jason queried. "Do you really have that bad of a feeling or is it something else? You're supposed to be more calm now that you're home and close to them, not less."

"I know," she agreed. "I know. I do, but they don't tell me things, Jason. I found out six months after the fact that my mother had a cancer scare last year. She must have been terrified and I wasn't even aware it was going on. They're older now. I need to be here if they need me. I need them to know I'm here for them."

"They know," he promised. "And they're proud of you for all you've achieved. You know they are." He pulled the car into her parents' driveway, and put the gear in Park. "Let's go put your mind at ease that all is well."

Kat was already shoving open her door before he finished the sentence, but Jason was fast and met her at the hood of the car, falling into pace with her as she headed up the drive. It had been so long since she'd had him by her side, she was surprised by just how right he felt there. But then, maybe she shouldn't have been surprised at all. Their breakup wasn't created by cheating and lies, or even love lost, between them. It was distance that always destroyed them.

"The porch light is on," Kat commented as they neared the blue-and-white cottage-style home she'd grown up in. "They aren't in bed or they'd turn it off."

"Kitchen light, too," Jason commented, taking the first of five wooden steps to the porch in unison with Kat.

"But they won't answer their phones," Kat said, taking the final step to the porch. "I don't get it."

Jason laughed and wiggled a brow. "I told you why they won't answer."

Kat was about to knock when the door flew open, and Sheila Moore, Kat's mother, appeared before them. "Kat. Jason. I didn't expect you to come over."

Kat's brows dipped at her mother's rather stiff, uncomfortable reply, that was far from the normal, eager welcome she was used to.

"Please tell me you two aren't here because you worried over my calls," her mother exclaimed. "Because I'm really going to feel horrible I did that to you. I just wanted to chitchat and when you didn't answer I called a friend. You know how I am. Every time I click over to a call, I hang up on the other person."

"Of course we were worried," Kat said quickly, glancing at her mother's attire, which wasn't at all the robe she'd expected. No, not at all. Her mother was fully dressed, looking stylish, and as usual, a good ten years younger than her age of sixty-five, in a pair of jeans and a floral shirt, her shoulder-length light brown hair sleek and straight. "Were you and Dad on your way out?"

"I was bored and tried to talk your father into a

movie. Clearly that didn't work out. I'm sure I ruined whatever plans you two had in the process. I hate that I scared you into driving over here."

"We were about to eat pizza," Jason put in quickly. "So if you happen to have some of that home cooking of yours you love to test on visitors, I'll be happy to volunteer for the job."

"Certainly," her mother said, motioning them forward. "The least I can do after scaring you is to feed you." She disappeared inside the house, clearly expecting them to follow.

Kat faced Jason, puzzled by a number of things. "Why isn't my mother surprised you're with me?"

"I told you I got your new address from your parents," he said. "So I stopped by and had a long chat with them."

"You stopped by and had a long chat with them?" she repeated. "What the heck did you say to them?"

Her mother popped her head back out of the door. "You two want coffee or iced tea?" she asked, as if she didn't notice they hadn't come inside yet.

"Both," Kat said at the same time Jason did.

Her mother smiled, but it didn't quite reach her light green eyes and Kat could feel the tension radiating from her.

Kat turned to Jason the instant her mother disappeared again. "I want that answer. Just not now. Something is up with my mother, no matter how much she is trying to act like there isn't."

"I agree, something is up," he said, his hands settling on her shoulders before he gave her a quick kiss. "But the answer to your question is that I told them I want you back. The same thing I told you. Fortunately, they're 'Team Jason.'" He drew her hands into his and kissed her knuckles. "Now, if I could just get you on board."

Her heart skipped a beat. "I've always been 'Team Jason.'"

"Correction then," he said, his voice gentle, even tender. "I need you on 'Team Jason and Kat.'"

Oh, how Kat wished it were as easy as just jumping on board that request, but she wasn't sure she could be on "Team Jason" and still be on "Team Jason and Kat." If she held him back, if she'd held him back in the past, would there even be a "Team Jason and Kat" to talk about?

He motioned toward the door with his head. "Your mother wants to feed us. Let's not stop her. She'll be happy and so will my stomach."

"Mine, too," Kat agreed, her shoulders relaxing as she dodged the difficult topic of what the future held. "I was beyond starving when we ordered the pizza."

They entered the house, turning to their immediate left where her mother busied herself with the coffee pot in the pale blue-and-white rectangular-shaped oversized kitchen. The whole house had the same color scheme, which her parents both loved.

"Tell me you have some of that famous cheesecake of yours stashed away for dessert," Jason pleaded, making a beeline for the fridge, as comfortable here as if he had never left the family. "I love that stuff."

"You'll have to settle for chocolate cake," her mother informed him, walking toward Jason and pointing at something inside the fridge. "Hand me that tray. It's lasagna. I just made it a few hours ago."

"Thank goodness you didn't answer your phone," Jason said, handing the requested container to Kat's mother and elbowing the door shut. "Do you know how long it's been since I had home-cooked anything?"

"I'd have thought your mom would keep you well fed since you moved your folks to California," Kat's mother replied.

Kat digested that with a twist in her gut, her gaze dropping to the floor in an effort to hide her immediate reaction. How had she forgotten that Jason had moved his parents to L.A. a few years back? Sure, he'd bought a house here, a convenience and tax write-off, while filming this season's show, but he had one there as well. He was no more rooted here than he'd been before. Not really.

"My parents have minds of their own," Jason replied. "They hated L.A. and they hated being retired. They both took jobs teaching English in Thailand two years ago."

"They're in Thailand?" Kat asked, her eyes lifting, seeking Jason, and finding him propped against the counter, arms and legs crossed, his gaze on her.

"Yes," he said, the look on his face telling her that he knew what she'd been thinking. "They're in Thailand."

So he wasn't bound to L.A. by anything but the work he might choose to take, but hadn't.

She swallowed hard. "Aren't you worried about them?"

"I was until the first time I went to visit them and saw how happy they are," he said, "though I admit the visit was meant to beg, bargain and plead for their return."

"Oh!" Kat's mother exclaimed. "I would love to do something like that. I've been volunteering at the children's hospital and Hank has been helping out at a free legal service since selling his firm. We are both going nuts with nothing to do. I've been trying to talk him into travel." Her gaze settled on Jason. "Maybe I could talk to Isabel about it?"

"My mother would be thrilled to hear from you," Jason assured her. "Call her on Skype by using her first and last name. She's always online."

"Skype?" Kat's mother asked, looking confused. "Is that the same thing as Twitter? Because I don't want to tell the world my life story in ten words or less. I just want to talk to Isabel."

Kat and Jason exchanged a look and laughed. "Twitter is one hundred and forty characters or less," Kat informed her mother. "Skype is a private chat without long-distance fees, a lot like instant message. I'll show you how to do it."

"Is it forty characters or less? That seems very limiting."

"No limit," Kat assured her. "Just type as you like and you can even do video if you want."

"Perfect," her mom replied, putting the food in the oven and rubbing her hands together. "Dinner in about fifteen minutes."

"*That's* perfect," Jason agreed. "I have to admit the one thing I'd change about your daughter is her hatred of cooking."

Kat's mother laughed, but that forced and tense

quality to her demeanor had returned, and abruptly, at that. Even her tone was tight as she jokingly replied, "Kat prefers eating to cooking." She winked at Kat and turned away to the stainless steel stove, opening the door and checking the lasagna, as if she hadn't just put the tray inside.

Kat and Jason exchanged a concerned look. "Where's Dad?" Kat asked, determined to find out what the heck was going on.

"Yeah, where is ol' Hank?" Jason asked. "He and I haven't gotten in a good game of chess in years."

"Oh, he went out for a while," Sheila said, using a pot holder to adjust the foil on the tray before fiddling with the temperature only to change it right back to what it had been a second before.

Kat walked to her mother, resting her hand on her back. "Talk to me, Mom. What's wrong?"

Her mother inhaled heavily and stood up. "I don't know. I just…don't know."

"What does that mean, Sheila?" Jason asked, sounding as concerned as Kat felt.

"It means that Hank says that he's out drinking and that every man deserves to go drinking now and then. And when I told him I was calling Kat, he got mad, and now he won't answer his phone."

"Dad is out drinking?" Kat asked, glancing at Jason and confirming he was as baffled as she was.

"Since when does Hank drink?" Jason asked. "I could barely get the man to have a beer with me during the holiday football games."

"He started today, apparently," Sheila said. "Which is why I know something is wrong. He doesn't want me

to know about whatever it is." She shook her head. "I…
What if it's another woman?"

Kat gasped and grabbed her mother's hand. "Oh,
God, Mother. It's not another woman." She hoped.

"It's bad, whatever it is," she said. "And I'd rather
him be cheating than hiding some medical condition
from me. What other two things can you think of that
he would want to hide from me?"

"Hey, Hank," Jason said, and Kat and her mother
turned their gazes to find the phone to his ear as he
continued talking. "What's this about you having a
drink and not inviting me?" He listened a minute and
then added, "Yeah. I know the exact spot. I'll see you
in about half an hour." He hung up and dialed another
number. "Yeah, I need a cab." He quickly spouted off
Kat's parents' address and ended the call.

"Where is he?" Sheila asked. "And why did he answer your calls and not mine?"

"Or mine? And why did you call a cab?" Kat asked.

"In the order asked," Jason replied, "I'll try to answer. He's downtown at a casino. He answered because
I check in with him every now and then, and he knows
my number. And finally, I called a cab because sometimes a man has to dump back a few drinks to get another man whose already drinking to talk."

"I'm going with you," Kat said at the same time as
her mother .

Jason smiled. "No, you both are not."

"Yes—" Kat and her mother said again at the same
time.

"No," Jason finished for them. "If you want to know
what's going on with Hank, then give the man some

space to talk to me. I'll get us both back here alive. Maybe not sober, but alive."

Kat and her mother looked at each other and then reluctantly nodded. "Call us when you know what's going on though," Sheila insisted.

"I will," Jason said, and gestured to the door at Kat. "Wait for the cab with me outside?"

She nodded and they headed outside, with Jason calling over his shoulder, "Don't eat all the cake while I'm gone, Sheila. I'll be back."

Kat smiled at his comment, his natural way with people, that made him a great leader on a set. They stepped onto the porch, pulling the door shut behind them.

"Do you have any clue what's going on?" Kat asked.

Jason twined the fingers of one of his hands with hers, and pulled her close to him. "Only that he was quick to invite me to join him, and he told me to come alone. That tells me he needs to talk."

"It really could be either of those things my mom said, couldn't it?"

"Let's not jump to conclusions," he said, settling down on the top step of the porch and pulling her down beside him. He slid his hand over her knee, aligning their legs. "Maybe he's simply experiencing the same thing your mother is, lost in retirement."

The feel of Jason's hand possessively on her leg, his hip joined with hers, warmed her well beyond the physical desire he so easily stirred within her. She was worried about her parents, and he was here for her.

"Why not just tell her that?" Kat asked.

He faced her more fully. "Maybe he's afraid she'll

think this is something to do with her, when it's about him."

"What if they've grown apart? What if—"

He kissed her, his fingers curling on her cheek. "They haven't," he said. "There are a lucky few people in this world that have a special bond, Kat, like they do. Like we do. Space and time doesn't divide those people. It hasn't divided us."

Kat's lashes fluttered, the warmth of his breath teasing her lips. "Jason," she whispered, because there were no other words ample enough to explain what she felt. She didn't even know what she felt.

A horn honked and Kat jumped at the sound. The cab had parked in front of the house.

"My limo has arrived," Jason joked, brushing his thumb over the corner of her mouth. He stood and helped Kat to her feet. "I'll text you when I get to your father's side."

"That would be great," she said. She trusted Jason. He was very much a part of her life again. When she'd told him she didn't know what she felt, she was wrong. She felt scared of getting hurt, scared of what might be going on with her parents, but she could say that to Jason and he would listen, he'd care. And that made her feel lucky.

"Jason!" Kat yelled, running down the steps to catch him.

He paused, halfway inside the cab, and stood up, turning to her. Kat rushed up and leaned into him, pressing to her tip-toes to kiss him, and then whispered, "I missed you."

His arms closed around her, his tongue pressing past her lips, caressing hers. "I missed you, too. Later, I'll show you how much."

9

JASON WAS INSIDE the busy downtown Blue Moon Casino, searching the blackjack tables for Kat's father, Hank, within fifteen minutes of sliding into the cab. To say that he was eager to get back to Kat after that "I missed you" proclamation she'd made by the cab was an understatement. But because he loved Kat, he was also eager to find out what was going on with her parents, especially her father.

Jason easily spotted Hank at a busy table, with a drink in his hand and a sexy red-haired woman twenty years his junior batting her eyes at him. Jason grimaced, and moved in Hank's direction, cursing that Sean Connery appeal Hank had with women, hoping this wasn't a sign that he was cheating and this was his mistress.

He slid into the only seat across the table from Hank and dropped a hundred dollar bill on the table. "Hello, Hank."

"Jason, my boy," he said as the dealer swept away the chips that Hank had just lost.

"Oh my God," the woman said, blinking at Jason.

"You're… Oh my God. You're the judge from that dance show." The dealer and the three other people at the table immediately looked at Jason.

Jason grimaced quickly and said, "No. No, but I get that all the time. It's the name. He's older and shorter. I swear." He loved the judges' table, helping dreams come true and helping new stars develop. He didn't like being recognized, or becoming the star himself. It just wasn't him.

The woman smiled. "Well, you'll do just fine by me."

"Shuffle," the dealer said, and one of the people at the table got up.

Hank elbowed the redhead. "That's my son-in-law," he explained to her. "Would you mind if he switched places with you?"

"I'll share my chair," she purred.

"Son-in-law," Hank repeated. "As in married to *my daughter.* If he shares a chair with you, I'll be kicking him in his seat."

"Oh." She pouted and grabbed her chips. "In that case, I'll leave. All you married guys are no fun."

Relief washed over Jason. Hank wasn't flirting with the woman, that was clear. Jason grabbed his hundred since the dealer had yet to touch it, and moved to the stool next to Hank.

"*Was* married to your daughter," Jason said softly.

"I'm counting on you to fix that," Hank told him. "The power of positive thinking. She's happy when she's with you. Just stop running off and leaving her behind."

"I plan to," Jason said, feeling the reprimand like

a slap in the face and a reminder of the past he had to overcome with Kat.

The dealer called for bets and slid chips in front of Jason. Hank slid two twenty-five dollar chips to the table.

"Since when do you gamble?" Jason asked, sliding his own bet forward.

"Since today," Hank said, downing his drink and flagging the waitress to say, "Two shots of tequila."

No food and alcohol. Not a winning plan, Jason thought, catching the waitress to add, "And something to eat. Pretzels, nuts, whatever you can get me that's allowed in the gaming area." He turned back to the table as the dealer looked to Hank to make decisions on his cards. Hank hit sixteen when the dealer had a three. You never hit a sixteen when the dealer had a three, because you knew the dealer's best hand was thirteen while your chances of going out were high.

The dealer threw down a face card and Hank now had more than twenty-one. He was busted. He cursed. Jason had a three and a five. He took a hit and was dealt another three. He hit again. The dealer gave him a face card and a solid winning hand of twenty-one. Hank's screw-up worked out okay for him. The rest of the table—not so much. Everyone else lost their hand. Someone grumbled about bad players and got up. Jason didn't blame him. He might not make a habit of gambling, but he knew his game when he did and he didn't play with people who didn't.

Jason cocked his head at Hank. "Why are we here, Hank? You know Sheila and Kat are worried sick."

The waitress stopped beside them and Hank tossed

down a few gambling chips for a tip, then grabbed his shot off the tray, downed it, and gave the waitress the empty glass. "We're here because I'm trying to make back mine and Sheila's stock portfolio she has no idea I lost."

Jason sat there in stunned silence before emptying his shot glass as well, and giving it to the waitress. He ignored the bowl of nuts and his phone vibrating at his hip. "How much?"

"Two hundred and fifty thousand," Hank said, and then to the waitress. "Another round."

"Scratch that," Jason said to the woman. "We're going to the bar where they have larger glasses."

"I'm all for that," Hank agreed, and shoved his chips toward the dealer. "Cash me out."

"And me," Jason said, pushing his forward, but he suddenly realized the waitress was still standing there.

She thrust her empty tray at him with a pen and a napkin on top. "Can I have your autograph?"

"Why does everyone think you are that guy on that show?" Hank asked in an impressively convincing voice. "You're not near as good-looking even if you think you are." He eyed the waitress. "You want my autograph, too? I'll sign Sean Connery if you want. You can tell them all I have a lot more hair than you thought I did."

The girl was young, not more than twenty-one, and she blushed, her cheeks flushing a bright red. "I'm so sorry. I really thought you were him. You just look so much like him and I heard he was in Vegas for a show."

Her embarrassment sent a rush of guilt through Jason. His fame was a blessing, even if it didn't feel like it at times. He knew that. It let him do things for his family. It would let him help Kat's. He just couldn't get used to living under a microscope. He enjoyed creating stars, not being one himself.

Jason grabbed the he napkin and signed it, then snatched the hundred dollar chip the dealer had given him to cash out and tossed it on her tray. "Please make sure anyone you told I was here believes you were mistaken. At least, until I'm not here anymore."

"It *is* you," she whispered. "It is."

"Yes. It is."

She smiled brightly. "My lips are sealed. You are not *you*. Thank you so much." She rushed away.

Jason and Hank quickly headed for a dimly lit bar area with leather armchairs and round glowing blue tables. Hank flagged a waitress and ordered drinks while Jason quickly typed a message to Kat. Bad phone reception in casino. No other woman. No one sick or dying. Try to sleep. I know you won't but try.

She immediately replied, What is going on?

At least he knew she got the message. He typed, I'll explain later, and then knew Kat wouldn't take that answer, and quickly added, retirement jitters, now go to bed. Trust me, Kat. Everything is going to be fine.

"Must be hell to be famous," Hank said. "I mean, it has to be tough to have all them girls pawing all over you, and movie stars hanging on your arms."

Jason tensed, more than a little surprised by the accusation in Hank's words when he'd sensed nothing of this before now. They did say that alcohol made people say what was on their minds, and there was no missing the undertone. Nor did Jason doubt the fragility of it coming from a protective father with too much tequila and a really bad day under his belt.

Jason returned his phone to his belt without answering Kat's next message and focused on her father, looking Hank straight in the eye. "The life I want is with Kat."

"Now that you got the starlets out of your system?"

"Kat and I were split up," he said. "I tried to move on. It didn't work."

"It took you too long to figure that out."

That wasn't true, but that was a conversation for Jason and Kat. "Things between Kat and I have always been complicated."

"Then it won't work out now any more than in the past. You should walk away before you tear her apart right when I'm about to destroy her mother."

Destroy? Whoa. That was a strong word and Jason was officially concerned that there was more going on here than he'd first imagined. Jason leaned forward, resting his elbows on his knees. "Talk to me, Hank. What happened? What the hell is going on?"

A muscle in Hank's jaw clenched. "You hear about the Smith-Wright investment company?"

"Yeah," Jason said, seeing where this was headed. "It's been all over the news. All of the key executives were arrested for fraud."

"That's the one," he said. "They had our retirement portfolio for ten years, though Sheila never knew. I take care of our finances and I always have. Those guys gave me reports, showed I'd doubled our money and kept me investing. According to them I'd turned two hundred thousand dollars into five hundred thousand dollars

over that decade. Sheila and I were set for retirement."
He scrubbed his hand over his lightly stubbled jaw and
when the waitress appeared by his side he paid her and
downed his shot before handing Jason his.

"Don't make me drink alone, son," Hank said when
Jason went to set the glass on the table. "Not tonight."

Jason didn't enjoy being drunk or out of control, not
even a little bit. And even if he did, like it or not, he
was famous, and he had to guard his public behavior.
He also needed Hank to keep talking.

Jason braced himself for the bite of the liquor and
poured the shot into his mouth. "That's it for me until I
eat," he announced when the burn let him speak again.
"I'm done."

"It's gone now," Hank said, and he wasn't talking
about the tequila. "All of the money is gone. Every
dime Sheila and I had saved. Every dime Kat insisted
we take when I didn't want to take it. I figured I was
just investing it for her. I'd give it back with a little
extra in return."

"And you thought coming here was the way to get
the money back?" Jason asked, trying to ignore the
angry churn of his stomach and hating the slight buzz
in his head.

"Why the hell not?" Hank demanded defensively.
"I see people get lucky all the time, living on the edge
and doing things wrong. I've spent a lifetime doing everything right, planning and preparing, and where did
that get me? Sheila wants to travel. She's waited that
lifetime with me, and worked her backside off to see
the world. Now I have to tell her she waited with the
wrong man. I destroyed her dream."

Jason and Kat had spent years apart, chasing opportunities he'd naively called dreams that were supposed to make them happy. For him that idea had been a big failure. "You two have something special, Hank. Whatever goes right or wrong, you have each other, and that's what matters."

"I know that," he said. "I do. But Sheila has always dreamed and I swore I'd make those dreams come true."

"You still can," Jason said. "I'll give you the money you lost including the return you were promised."

Hank stared at him blankly, as if he didn't compute what he'd said. "You're telling me that you'd give me five hundred thousand dollars," he snapped his fingers, "just like that."

"Without a second of hesitation."

Hank blinked at him and then scrubbed his jaw. "Holy hell." He mumbled something to himself and then refocused on Jason. "I'm not taking your money, son, but the fact that you just offered it to me tells me that you love my daughter even more than I thought you did. You do what you have to do to make her see that. You win her back."

"I'm going to give it a try," Jason assured him. "Look, Hank, you and Sheila have always been family to me. Besides, the studio pays me an insane amount of money for sitting at the judging table. Millions of dollars which I invest and turn into more. I won't miss this money, but you will. You and Sheila go live your dreams together, the way Kat and I should have lived ours."

"If you were me, would *you* take the money?"

No, Jason thought. He'd have too much pride. "This will be our secret with no strings attached. If Kat kicks me to the curb, it changes nothing. This is my gift to you."

"I'm not taking your money, Jason."

There was such absoluteness to the tone that Jason knew he had to change strategies. "How much do you have left in your retirement fund?"

"Ten thousand."

Of the five *hundred thousand* he'd thought he had. Jason knew that had to sting. "You say you want to gamble tonight? To throw caution to the wind?"

"That was the idea."

"Then bet with me. Give me the ten thousand dollars to play, because let's be honest here, you don't know what you are doing at those tables. If I can turn that money into a hundred thousand, then you let me take it to my investment guy to work some magic. Your money turned into more money. No borrowing and no gift. No need to be prideful. You can forget any of this ever happened and book your first trip to wherever you want to go."

"How are you going to turn ten thousand into a hundred thousand?"

"I'm really good at craps," Jason said, pushing to his feet. "Which I'm going to play at the high stakes tables. You have to bet big to win big."

Hank stood up, his eyes clouded over, his pupils dilated. "And if you lose?"

Jason patted his back. "We'll be needing a lot more tequila."

The waitress approached but Jason waved her away before Hank saw her. The last thing Jason needed right now was more of a buzz going on in his own head.

They left the lounge area with Jason fully intending to get Hank to take his money one way or another. Jason was taking care of Kat's parents. The craps tables were confusing to newbies, and though Jason really was good at the game, Hank would never know if Jason won or lost. Not if he tipped the right people enough money, which he intended to do. He had this under control despite the tequila. *Everything was going to be fine.* And Jason believed that right up until the moment he and Hank walked around a corner and straight into the path of two men in suits. Hank and the two men stopped dead in their tracks.

Hank—calm, collected, normally reserved Hank— was apparently hanging by a thread that snapped. "These two buzzards work at Smith-Wright," Hank growled and shoved one of them.

Before Jason could even react, the cameras began to flash and people gathered around them. Trouble was here and it wasn't going to go away without dragging him and Hank into a whole lot of that spotlight Jason didn't enjoy. And he knew the press. They'd investigate Hank, and they'd figure out the connection. He and Kat were about to be outed as exes and if he didn't calm Hank down, that might be the best of the worst to come.

An hour after Jason's last text, Kat snuggled into the oversized blue chair in her parents' living room, with her mother resting on the matching couch, and flipped on the ten o'clock news.

"I wish they'd call," her mother murmured, clearly not watching the television. She leaned up on her elbow. "What if it's not retirement jitters? What if Hank is having a full-fledged midlife crisis and we're not as happy as I thought we were?"

"Stop doing this to yourself, Mom. I read you Jason's text. If there was something to worry about, he would have told me."

"You're sure?"

"Yes, I'm sure."

"What if Hank hadn't told Jason everything yet? And my God, what did he tell him?"

"Mom," Kat said softly, understanding how she must feel. How Kat herself would feel if this were Jason acting strangely. "Jason is with him. Dad knows he will tell me what is going on. If he didn't want you to know do you think he would have been that quick to invite Jason to join him?"

"…Jason Alright from *Stepping Up*…"

Kat's attention whipped to the television and her mother sat up and increased the volume.

"…was involved in a disturbance at the Blue Moon Casino…"

Kat and her mother were both standing now, both dialing their phones, trying to reach Jason and Hank.

"…a section of the casino was shut down but has now reopened. No more details are available."

"No answer," Kat said.

Sheila shook her head. "Let's get over there. I'll call the hotel while you drive."

"And the police station," Kat said grimly. "And let's hope they aren't there."

10

JASON AND HER father weren't answering their phones, but they weren't in jail, per her mother's call to the police station. That was the one good thing Kat had to cling to as she and her mother rushed to the front desk of the Blue Moon Casino.

"I need to locate Jason Alright," Kat said to the tall, thin twenty-something male attendant behind the counter.

"Jason Alright?" the man asked, looking down on her from beneath his dark rimmed glasses.

Her brows dipped. "I know you know who I'm talking about."

"No, ma'am," he said primly. "I'm afraid I do not."

"Listen up," her mother said, letting the tough E.R. nurse who took charge in the center of disaster shine through for the first time tonight. "You can't tell me you don't know the judge from *Stepping Up* when he was the center of attention right here in this hotel only a short while ago. Jason is her husband. Find him, find someone who knows how to find him or just plain go get him yourself."

The man stared at her for several terse seconds and then eyed Kat, inspecting her T-shirt and messy hair with a bit of disdain. Thank goodness her leggings were hidden below the counter. His lips tightened. "I'll return momentarily." He turned away and left them to wait.

Kat glanced around the crowded lobby, and it was clear that her mother's loudly spoken words had garnered unwanted attention as pointing and whispering had begun. Kat cringed as numerous cell phone pictures were taken. She was officially outed as Jason's wife, and she wasn't even his wife anymore. Nevertheless, they had a history, and the connection between them was bound to come out. She'd simply hoped to get a little farther into the show than the first week of rehearsals.

"Mom," Kat said. "Jason and I—"

"Love each other," she finished. "So don't let him go. This time is it, Kat. I feel it in my gut. He's going all the way or he's going away and it has to be that way. You both have to get on with life, one way or the other."

Kat sucked in a breath at the blunt reality etched so precisely into those words. Deep down Kat knew that if Jason exited her life again, he was gone for good, but hearing it from her mother was a blow. Her stomach knotted because history said he would leave again, and while part of her said this time together was something, they needed to be able to move on. Another part of her though could still feel his touch and smell him on her skin, could still hear his deep voice, see his smile, and that part of her hoped for a future with Jason.

"Ms. Moore?"

Kat turned to find a big burly giant who wore one of those concrete expressions that screamed "security" even more so than his black jacket and the ear piece.

"Yes?" her mother asked the man.

Kat raised her hand. "And yes. Same name."

"Your party is waiting for you, and I'd send you without an escort but it appears you've drawn a bit of attention." A camera flashed and he glanced at a group of three women, studying them. "We don't need any more excitement here tonight."

"I guess I shouldn't have told the world we were here to see Jason," her mother admitted with a sigh. "I forget he's a big star now."

"Not a problem," the man assured them. "I'll just get you out of the crush here and I'm sure everything will be fine." He motioned them forward and indicated a path, before falling into step behind them.

Kat replayed her mother's words in her head. Jason was a star—no—*big star,* she'd said. Boy, oh boy, was her mother throwing bombs tonight.

"Sorry I got a little loud and out of control," her mother said. "I didn't mean to get us an escort."

"Let's talk later," Kat told her, having some experience with this kind of thing after traveling with Marcus, whose fans were downright rabid. "There are cameras everywhere, and believe me, everything and anything could end up in the tabloids, especially given what happened earlier tonight."

"We don't know what happened," her mother exclaimed. "That's the point."

"We know it ended up on the news." And they knew that Jason was that big of a name now to draw that kind of attention, which drove home how much *Stepping Up* had changed his life. Yet he seemed like the same Jason she'd always known, virtually unchanged, and that was special, unique even.

She'd seen plenty of people changed by stardom. He'd helped her parents tonight without question, and not just because of her. He was just that kind of guy, and always had been. If anyone deserved fame, he did. Her stomach sunk at what that meant. To hold him back would be selfish and she loved him too much to do that. She had to get a grip.

Emotion tightened her chest, but she didn't have time to analyze her feelings as they had arrived at an elevator corridor. From there, the three of them—Kat, her mother, and the stone-faced guard—traveled to the twenty-seventh floor.

When the doors opened, their security escort placed his hand on the button to keep them from shutting again. "Room 2711," he instructed, evidently not joining them beyond this point.

"Thank you," Kat said, and she and her mother exited the car.

The instant the elevator shut behind them, her mother asked, "Do you think this is some kind of security screening room we're going to?"

"We're about to find out," Kat said, pointing in the direction they needed to go.

"I'm guessing the code isn't a good sign," her mother said as they passed several doors, and appeared to be heading to the far end of a long hallway.

"VIP floors are reserved for big money, government officials and celebrities," Kat explained. "Extra security isn't a sign of anything being wrong." She lifted her chin to indicate the final door. "This is us."

"Finally," her mother said, rushing forward and knocking three times.

Kat caught up to her right as the door flew open to reveal Jason standing there, looking so sexy that Kat could have sworn her legs wobbled. His hair was rumpled, his jaw shadowed, his body long and lean, and yes, hard. Every bit of this man was hard and made her soft and yet hot for him. She couldn't resist him. She was weak. She was selfish. So very selfish because she didn't want to let him go.

"Where's Hank, Jason?" her mother asked. "Is he okay?"

"He's fine considering he's hanging over the toilet with tequila fever," he said, stepping back to let her mother pass. "Other than that, everything is fine."

Kat knew Jason well enough to know that he wouldn't make any declaration lightly and relief washed over her.

Her mother didn't seem to agree, exclaiming, "Oh, God!" and hurried into the room.

Kat hesitated, also knowing herself. One touch from Jason and she'd forget why selfishly wanting him was wrong. Jason reached for her and tugged her inside the room, shutting the door behind them. His touch sizzled through Kat like an electric charge, the spicy male scent of him she knew and loved so much, tickling her nostrils. And when his eyes met hers, for the briefest, most intimate of moments, and he bent down to brush his lips over hers, she might as well have been chocolate melting in the hot sun.

"What happened?" Kat's mom asked, drawing their

attention to where she'd stopped at the edge of the room, her focus on Jason. "Why were you on the news? Why are you in this room?"

"He drank too much and almost got into a fight," Jason explained without an instant's hesitation. "Fortunately, the powers-that-be here want our show here next season. They eagerly comped us a room so we could hide until the media calms down and we can get out of here."

"Why didn't you call us?" Sheila demanded. "Why didn't Hank call me?"

"He's not capable of conversation right now," Jason said. "And we'd just made it to the room when I heard you two were up front."

Kat watched her mother curl her arms in front of her chest, the distress and tension rolling off of her as she asked, "Why was he here drinking, Jason? Why was he here at all?"

"He needs to explain that to you, Sheila," he said, trailing his hand down Kat's arm to rest his hand on the small of her back. "I doubt he's capable of that right now, but know this. He's not cheating, he's not dying and he's still very much in love with you. In fact, tonight was more about how much he wants to make you happy than anything else. Let him get the tequila out of his system though. He drank a lot for a man who doesn't drink. Hell, he drank a lot for a man who does drink."

Kat's mother studied him a moment and then turned away, disappearing down the hall.

Jason immediately pulled Kat into the box-like kitchen immediately to Kat's left, pressing her against the counter, his muscular thighs framing hers, the warmth of his body heating her skin. His gaze searched her expression. "What's wrong?"

"You were on the news. I was worried sick."

"That's not what's wrong."

"I just… I…" She drew a breath and let it out, her hand settling on his chest. "Yesterday I was telling myself 'I don't want to want him again' and already today it's changed to 'I don't want to lose him again.'"

His fingers slid around her neck, his eyes darkened. "I don't want to lose you again either." He kissed her, a deep, sexy kiss, and she could taste the tequila and desire on his mouth.

Kat moaned and wrapped her arms around his neck, unable to fight the sweet, hot, warmth of his tongue against her, the feel of his hands running over her back, molding her closer.

"God, I missed you," he murmured. "Your parents need time alone and so do we. Let's get out of here."

She swallowed hard, fighting through her need for Jason, to focus on her love for her parents. "What happened with my father?"

"He made a bad investment," he said grimly. "Really bad. Enough so that he's worried he can't take your mother traveling like they'd planned."

"Oh, no," Kat said. "He's so cautious. How did this happen?"

"Fraud by the investment firm," he said, "but it's handled, Kat. I'm getting my investment guy involved to make back the money they lost. In the meantime, I figure we can give them a trip for their wedding anniversary next month to start them off."

Kat leaned back to study him more closely. "We?"

"We," he repeated softly.

Kat studied him, her heart squeezing with the reference, with the "we" she wanted to be with him again. And while she might not have him forever, she knew one thing for certain, with all of her heart. She was so done fighting Jason. If this was truly their last hurrah, she didn't want to waste a moment of it.

"Let's get out of here, Jason," she said, and pressed her lips to his.

AN HOUR LATER, after they'd been discreetly ushered out of the hotel by security, Jason followed Kat up the stairs from his garage again, on the phone with Calvin Newport, his long-time agent.

"I wasn't drunk," Jason said grumpily. "I wasn't fighting."

"You have a moral clause," Calvin said.

Jason scrubbed a hand through his hair and stomped up the last step to his living room. "I know I have a moral clause. And like I said, I wasn't drinking and I wasn't fighting."

"They want to talk to us in the morning," Calvin said. "A conference call."

"This is ridiculous," Jason said, rubbing the ball of tension at his neck. He was concerned. He might not want another season with *Stepping Up,* but he did want this Vegas show to go well for him and Kat. "What time?"

"Nine," Calvin said. "I'll get them on the line and then dial your office."

"Fine," he said, his gaze lifting to find Kat watching him, her expression etched with more than a little worry.

"Fine what?" Calvin pressed.

Kat turned and walked toward the kitchen and he heard the balcony door open and Jason quickly tried to end the conversation. "I'll expect your call, Calvin."

"Try to get some rest so you won't be this foul."

"Goodnight, Calvin," he said, snapping his phone shut to follow Kat.

He found the door cracked open and Kat standing at the wooden railing with her back to him. He stepped outside but she didn't turn.

He walked up behind her, wrapped his arms around her, and held her close.

The stars were bright, the sky clear, the moon full and high in the night sky. It was warm, but there was a breeze off the mountains, lifting the silky blond strands of her hair off her slender shoulders. His gut, and his groin, tightened at the sight of her, and the soft feminine scent of her.

"Don't turn this into an excuse to push me away, Kat."

She turned in his arms to face him. "The studio's all over you, Jason. Do you have any idea how much I regret letting you go to that casino tonight?"

"You didn't *let me* do anything. You didn't even ask me. I did it because I wanted to and I'd do it again if I knew the outcome."

"The press is going to figure out our past, Jason, and then the studio will, too."

"The studio knows about our past, Kat."

"What?" Her eyes went wide. "How? When? Because of tonight? Jason, I'll leave before I let this affect your career. I'll—"

He kissed her, slanting his mouth over hers, his tongue stealing a quick, sweet taste of her. "Before you signed the contract. I had no intention of hiding our relationship past, present or future, for any reason but your request."

"Oh," she breathed out. "I'm pretty sure after tonight everyone is going to know anyway."

He stroked her hair. "How do you feel about that?"

"I would have liked to have it come out once I was more established, but honestly, Jason, all I care about right now is you. I don't want this to hurt you with the studio."

"Ah, my little KandyKat," he murmured. "How am I going to get you to understand that the only thing I care about is *you*. Hmm. I think I'll start with you in my bed again."

"I thought we were going to my place?"

"We were," he said. "But your clothes are never going to stay on that long." He bent down and picked her up, as he had done earlier.

Kat clung to his neck and laughed, a sexy, lilting sound that heated his limbs and stirred his emotions. If he heard that laugh every day of his life, it wouldn't be enough.

11

KAT WOKE UP in Jason's bed to him nuzzling her neck, and with the scent of him, the feel of him, all around her. "It's time to get up, KandyKat."

"Hmmm." She sank deeper under the blankets. "Hit snooze, please."

"You said that seven minutes ago."

"Just once more," she murmured, pressing her backside against his hips, and pulling his arm around her. Oh, how she missed waking up to this man.

He laughed, low and rough in her ear, nipping it gently. "You've said that twice now."

She groaned and rolled to her back, blinking into the dim light of the lamp he'd turned on. "What time is it?" she asked, running her hand over the sexy stubble on his jaw.

"Four-thirty."

Her eyes went wide and she sat up, the sheet falling down her naked body. She had to get to rehearsals. Jason's eyes raked her breasts and he reached for her. She darted off the bed, dodging him. "We can't do that right now. I have to shower." She rushed away from him, grabbing her bag on the way to his massive white tiled master bathroom.

"I'll guess this means you don't want me to join you?"

Kat peeked around the door frame. "I'll be late if you do that." She closed the door and headed to the shower. When done, she dressed in clean leggings and a light blue T-shirt she'd had in her bag. By the time she was blow drying her hair, she had officially begun to worry about the day before her.

She and Jason agreed that secrets fed gossip. They would tell their story before the press did it for them. They used to be married and they were seeing each other again. It had seemed like a good plan when they'd talked about it, but now, with it about to be put into play, she had doubts. What if the studio felt Kat was a bad influence on Jason? What if they wanted her fired and he didn't want to do it? What if…? There were so many what ifs.

Kat followed the blessed scent of coffee and found Jason leaning against the kitchen cabinet with a cup in his hand. His hair was damp and rumpled, his jaw clean shaven, his jeans low on his hips, and his Black Sabbath T-shirt pulled snug on his impressive chest.

"I'll quit the show before I let what happened last night hurt your job, Jason," she blurted. "I need you to know that."

He frowned and set his cup on the counter before reaching for her. "Come here," he murmured, wrapping her in his powerful arms, and stroking her hair. "If last night puts your job or mine on the line, then I have no desire to keep working for this studio."

"You—"

His lips brushed hers. "Want you very badly, so unless you want me to strip you naked and set you on this counter, I suggest you go now."

"Jason—"

He slanted his mouth over hers, his tongue stroking, hot with demand, and anything she might have said faded. Kat's arms slid around his neck, the spicy taste of him warming her, calming her. When they were together like this she felt like they could face anything and survive. They could even survive being late to work, but when he tore his mouth from hers, and warned, "Last chance," Kat took off for the door, laughing.

This was their last chance, she thought, sliding into her car. Right now, despite the media drama, it felt like their best chance, too.

NEAR NOON, KAT stood on the stage next to Ellie and watched a group of dancers perform. She'd spoken to her mother during a short break, just long enough to hear that her father was too sick to head home yet, and to tell them that Jason had taken care of the room for them for the day and even the rest of the night if they wanted. Both she and Kat had expected her father wouldn't want to move too quickly. Drinking tequila like a fish when you didn't regularly swim equaled drowning in pain.

She hadn't mentioned the investment loss that had brought on the drinking binge. She wanted to give them time to talk that out on their own and she wasn't sure her father would be up for that yet.

Kat's gaze slid to the distant doors of the auditorium, willing Jason to walk through them. She hadn't heard from him and no one had seen him all day, which only made people more curious about what was going on. The buzz about the night before was loud and steady, but the connection between Kat and Jason had yet to be made. It wouldn't take long. Kat had been around the tabloid mess more than a few times, most recently with Marcus, who was a total media magnet.

Another half hour passed, and another set of dancers were running through a routine when Kat's skin tingled with the awareness she always felt when Jason was watching her. Her gaze lifted to find him sauntering down the center aisle with a loose-legged sexy swagger that had her conjuring up images of the night before: of him naked, of her naked and in his arms. No man but Jason had ever affected her so easily, so completely, though she'd tried to find one. She'd tried to forget Jason and always failed.

He held a thumb up to Kat, silently telling her everything was okay, and relief washed over her. Whatever had tied him up today, the results were good, and ultimately that was all that mattered.

"Bossman sure stirred up trouble last night," Ellie commented quietly. "Any idea what happened?"

Kat wasn't a fool. Ellie had seen her thumbs-up exchange with Jason, and she was digging to find out just how close Kat and Jason really were.

"My father had a retirement crisis and dragged Jason along for the ride," Kat explained.

"What?" Ellie asked, shock hissing through her whisper. "Your father knows Jason?"

Kat glanced at her. "Well, he *was* at our wedding."

"What?" she asked again, facing Kat now, and ignoring the dancers. "Whose wedding?"

"Jason and I were married a very long time ago," Kat said. "It's not a secret."

"You said you were old friends. You didn't say you were *married*."

Kat shrugged. "Now I am."

"I knew something was up with you two," Ellie replied. "I knew it."

Kat's gaze veered over Ellie's shoulder, her attention caught on the opposite side of the stage. There, Carrie and Tabitha were clearly arguing. Kat could see Carrie's face pinched in anger before she turned away, exiting behind the curtain. Tabitha immediately followed her.

"Are you and Jason—"

"Hold that question," Kat said. "I think we have trouble with that situation I told you about this morning. Tabitha and Carrie just headed off stage in the midst of an argument. Call for lunch if I'm not back in fifteen minutes."

Kat darted behind the curtain and rushed toward the other side of the stage, arriving just in time to see Tabitha disappear out of a door leading to the dressing rooms.

Kat hurried after her, covering the distance in a near run. She really didn't need this turning nasty and she'd seen the way Tabitha and Carrie had interacted on the DVD the night before. It wasn't pretty. Right now, Kat and Jason had enough trouble brewing without a fight on set.

Kat shoved open the door Tabitha had used and quickly headed down a long, narrow hallway. She was almost to the end, where there was a section of twelve dressing rooms, when she heard Tabitha's raised voice.

"I put up with you in the contestant house," Tabitha said, "because I knew you weren't good enough to stay around long. If you think I'm going to tolerate you here, you'd better think again."

Kat stopped at the end of the hall, listening to get a true picture of what was happening.

"Are you threatening me?" Carrie asked, her voice soft but surprisingly confrontational for what Kat had observed of her personality.

"No," Tabitha said. "I'm making you a promise. If you interfere with my work, which includes how I handle my understudy, I'll make sure you get fired and we'll be better off as a show for it. You weren't good enough for the competition, you weren't good enough for Jensen and you aren't good enough for Vegas."

"She's not only good enough for me," came a male voice, "I feel lucky she thinks I'm good enough for her."

Kat checked around the corner to see a tall hunk of a guy with a military haircut and a broad chest wrap his arm around Carrie. He had to be her fiancé. Go, Carrie! And go, fiancé for coming to the rescue!

"Who are *you?*" Tabitha asked snidely but there was a crack in her voice, a chink in her armor.

"The new head of security here at the hotel and Carrie's very protective fiancé." He glanced at Carrie. "Are you out for lunch?"

"Yes she is," Kat said as she stepped into the large room. "Take her to eat. I need to have a word with

Tabitha alone anyway." Kat glanced at Carrie. "And I look forward to being properly introduced to your fiancé soon. After all, Carrie, we will be working on some choreography together."

Carrie beamed. "Thank you, Kat. I can't wait." She and her fiancé left the dressing room.

"So, Tabitha," Kat said, "let's find Ellie and have a chat." Kat knew having a witness to any reprimand was smart with someone like Tabitha. It kept details from being twisted.

"She started this," Tabitha blurted. "She involved herself in my work with my understudy. Why would you send Carrie to lunch and then talk to me?"

Kat sighed. "Okay, Tabitha. I'm going to make this quick. I've observed how you treat Marissa and it's simply not acceptable. I saw how you treated Carrie tonight, as well, when Carrie is simply trying to protect Marissa. Marissa is your understudy and you have to be nice to her. You make snide comments and sneer at her. This is not appropriate and it undermines our opportunity to be a team that succeeds together. I'm going to draw up a warning for you to sign. If you continue such actions then you simply won't be here any longer."

"I have a contract," Tabitha stated. "I can't be fired by the choreographer."

"Read the contract," Kat said. "It specifically requires your professional behavior on the set."

"I will not be threatened," Tabitha spat.

"It's not a threat," Kat said, repeating Tabitha's words. "It's a promise. Be respectful to the cast and crew or you won't be here."

"I'll go to my agent. He'll take care of this and you."

"I would, too, if I were you," Kat said. "Have your agent help you understand the terms of the contract."

"This is crazy. I'm going to talk to Jason."

"I'm right here." Jason stepped to Kat's side, his brand of cool confidence and casual authority expanding around them. "And I heard part of the conversation. Kat is far from just a choreographer. She has my permission to make any casting changes needed and I didn't sign on to this show with my hands tied. No one is here without an exit plan in place if needed. We have a small window to make this show perfect. Either you want to be a part of that or you don't."

"I do," Tabitha said, sounding sweeter than Kat had ever heard her sound. "That's why I don't want to be silent when someone isn't giving their all."

"Then don't," Jason said flatly. "Tell Kat. She's your boss. One of the reasons Kat does such a good job is that her dancers know she'll take the fall for a problem rather than place blame, but she deserves loyalty in return." He glanced at Kat, those wintery green eyes of his warm in a way that made her hot. "You got a few minutes?"

Yes. Yes. Yes. She desperately wanted to know how his meeting went with the studio. "We're about to call lunch so it's perfect timing." Kat's gaze returned to Tabitha's. "Let's skip that second meeting with Ellie, Tabitha. You're talented, and I look forward to helping you shine, but as one of the stars of the show, I need you to be a positive leader."

Tabitha crossed her arms in front of her. "I will be."

The statement was wrapped in barely contained resentment and Kat mentally sighed. No. She wouldn't. But with any luck Tabitha now hated her more than

Marissa, and would focus her anger Kat's way. At least then poor Marissa could catch a break.

"You should go eat, Tabitha," Kat said. "We have a long afternoon ahead."

Tabitha gave a little lift of her chin and headed back toward the stage entrance.

Jason let out a soft whistle the instant Tabitha was out of view. "You weren't joking about that one. She's a problem."

"She and Carrie had a spat on stage. It wasn't pretty but most importantly—" she lowered her voice though they were alone "—I've been worried sick all morning."

"Everything is fine, baby," he said gently. "I told you not to worry."

"What's your definition of 'fine'?"

He grinned. "I convinced them I'm not a lush."

"Oh, God, Jason, tell me they didn't actually call you that?"

"Might as well have," he said, "but in the end, surprise surprise, they're pleased to report that website hits for the *Stepping Up* site tripled last night. Free advertising at our expense. Which reminds me, we need to get your parents on a vacation and out of town before the bloodhounds find them."

Kat nodded. She wasn't eager for them to take off when she'd only just arrived, but she'd already figured out how much traveling meant to her mother. "I think that's a good idea."

"I was hoping you'd say that. I bought them tickets to visit my parents in Thailand this morning but I didn't want to send them over until you gave me the okay. I didn't think they'd take the gift if it wasn't framed as a job. Not with the pride thing your dad has going on right now."

Her lips parted with her surprise. "Jason, you didn't have to do that."

"Yes, I did. I made public the one time in your father's life he ever had a meltdown. I got together with my investment guy as well and he'll meet with them tomorrow, before they head to the airport."

Kat blinked at him, speechless for a moment. Without her father's craziness in that casino, Jason would never had ended up in the news, but he didn't blame her father. He blamed himself. "Fame hasn't changed you. I don't know why, but it hasn't."

"I'm still the same guy who can't stand this close to you without wanting to kiss you."

Her knees felt weak again. He had a way of doing that to her. "And I'm apparently the same ol' Kat who likes that about you." Her lips curved. "Except, of course, when I'm trying to resist you."

"And are you?" he asked. "Trying to resist me?"

"If I knew what was good for both of us, I would be," she said. "But no. I'm not. Whatever is going to be, is going to be."

The door burst open from the stage area and voices filled the hallway as the dancers rushed forward. Ellie had clearly called for a lunch break.

"Let's make a run for lunch before some other crisis stops us." He motioned toward the direction Carrie and her man had headed out.

"I'm all for that," Kat said, rushing down the hall with him.

They were in the hotel and almost at the diner when

they heard Ellie calling after them. "Kat! Jason! Wait. Wait. I need you two."

"So close to escaping," Jason whispered.

Kat laughed and turned with him to greet Ellie. "What's going on?"

Ellie jerked to a halt in front of them. "That tabloid website 'Truth' just posted a story about the two of you being married. The minute we broke for lunch and the cast and crew cranked up their smartphones, the news was out. We have to figure out what to say about it."

Jason glanced at Kat. "I don't know about you, but I'm starving. I say we go eat. I need to talk to both of you about a nightclub promotion the hotel wants us to do anyway."

"I'm all for lunch," Kat agreed. "How about you, Ellie?"

Ellie gaped at them. "That's it? You two want to eat lunch? Aren't you worried about this?"

Jason shrugged. "The studio knows we're exes. It's not a secret. And it's certainly not taboo. You married one of our producers. Darla married the host of *Stepping Up*."

"So, do nothing?" Ellie asked, looking distressed by that idea.

"Besides tell anyone who asks that it's true and to focus on a rapidly approaching opening night?" Jason said. "Yes. Nothing. This only has the wings we give it."

Ellie's gaze flickered between them. "You're positive?"

Kat glanced at Jason, who gave a firm, "Yes. Positive."

Kat couldn't help but hope he was right.

12

SEVERAL HOURS LATER, Jason was finally through with the studio heads and media damage control, and could get to work on his real job of directing. He sauntered into the theater and headed to the front row seating where a table was set up for staff. Kat and Ellie stood center stage, talking with the script manager, while dancers prepared to work through the opening scene of the show. Seeing Kat up there, doing what she loved, back in his life, felt right like nothing else had in a very long time.

He settled into the chair on the end of the row, next to his assistant director Ronnie Wilks, a young film school graduate that was quickly building an impressive resume.

"How's it going, Bossman?" Ronnie asked, turning his Texas Longhorns hat backward and running his hand down his jeans-clad leg.

"As fine as any day in the tabloids can go," Jason replied dryly.

"That's what you get for being famous," Ronnie joked.

Only it wasn't a joke to Jason. It was reality, and one he was ready to leave behind. "Let's make this show the star," Jason commented. "Not me." He motioned to the computer on the desk. "Do we have the schedule drafted for tomorrow? We need to be fully blocked and on to polishing by next week."

Jason and Ronnie talked through their plans briefly before the entire cast of more than a hundred filed into the theater and filled the seating across the aisle from Jason and his crew. The energy in the room changed almost immediately, the glances between Jason and Kat impossible to miss.

Ronnie called out a list of names to ensure everyone who was supposed to be on stage was, and then leaned in close to Jason. "You and Kat sure know how to shake things up. Talk about an armadillo in the room."

"An armadillo?" Jason asked, arching a brow.

"That's the Texas version of an elephant in the room."

"I get it," Jason said, and he knew Kat felt it. She was stiff on the stage, and tension radiated from her. "It'll pass."

Apparently Kat didn't think so. She grabbed a microphone. "I need everyone's attention, please. We have a show to get ready and everyone appears to be distracted. So let's just cut to the chase and get focused. The answer to all the whispered questions is that yes, Jason is my ex-husband, and yes, we're dating. And finally, yes, Jason was with my father last night when a group of reporters did some creative story building. Any questions?"

Jason saw his producer choke on a drink and silence zipped through the room as if she'd hit the mute on a remote control. Ah, his KandyKat. She had a way of making a point. Jason scrubbed his jaw and laughed— because really, what else could he do?—and then he leaned across the table and grabbed a microphone of his own. "I have a question…"

IT WAS LATE that evening and Jason and Kat sat with her parents at their kitchen table. Dinner was darn good lasagna that Hank was finally well enough to enjoy, and the past twenty-four hours had given them plenty to laugh at.

"So we're standing at the diner and I told Ellie that we weren't going to make any announcement," Jason said, recounting the moment when they'd discovered the tabloids had found out he and Kat were exes. "And we all agreed and went to eat lunch. The next thing I know, I'm sitting in a theater with the entire cast and crew, with the whispers and gossip buzzing around the room. So what does Kat do? She finds a microphone and says, 'I need everyone's attention, please.'"

Hank laughed and Sheila went, "Uh-oh."

Jason laughed and speared a tomato. "Exactly what I said. Uh-oh."

"What was I supposed to do, Jason?" Kat asked. "The dancers kept whispering to themselves. Nothing was getting done. We needed focus."

"What'd you do, Kitten?" Hank asked Kat.

Kat motioned to Jason. "Oh, let him tell you. He started this story."

"Don't mind if I do," Jason agreed. "Kat proceeded

to make her version of a public service announcement that went something like this. 'Yes, Jason is my ex-husband, and yes, we're dating. And yes, he was with my father last night when a group of reporters did their creative story building. Any questions?'"

Sheila gasped and covered her mouth and Hank chuckled. "Were there any questions?"

"Surely no one had the nerve to ask a question," Sheila replied, dropping her hand from her mouth.

Kat's eyes flashed at Jason. "Oh, yes. Someone did." She pointed at Jason.

"Oh, God," Sheila murmured. "What did you ask?"

Jason shrugged. "I asked if anyone had an aspirin or maybe ten."

Hank and Sheila both laughed. "Then what?" Sheila asked, laughing now herself, and wiping tears from her eyes.

"Everyone laughed but me," Jason said. "I was serious. I had a damn tequila headache, no thanks to you, Hank."

"Did you get your aspirin?" Sheila asked.

"I didn't even get a Tic Tac," he complained. "But everyone seemed to get focused and do their job after that."

"Oh, good," Sheila said. "I hope that means last night is behind you two."

Kat's questioning eyes found Jason's, and he answered with a quick nod. She grabbed her purse and removed the plane tickets. "Jason and I were talking and we think the press is going to keep coming at us, and you."

"So I called my parents today," Jason added. "They

invited you both to come visit them and see what they do in Thailand."

Kat placed the tickets on the table, hopeful her father wouldn't let his pride over the bad investments get in the way of this trip. "You leave tomorrow and we bought a non-refundable package deal. The money is spent. You might as well enjoy the trip."

"We can't take those tickets," Hank said quickly. "No. We can't. It's too much money."

"The money is spent, Dad," Kat said. "So either you take the trip or the money goes to waste."

"I know why you're doing this," Hank said, his gaze meeting Jason's. "And no. I told Sheila everything. We'll meet your investment expert, but we won't take charity."

Jason slid his plate aside and leaned forward. "Nick— that's my investment expert—is expecting you at ten in the morning. Your flight is at two. The trip is a gift from myself and Kat, for all the love and support you showed us both while we worked to build our careers. A gift that pleases us both very much to give you."

Jason watched Sheila and Hank look at each other. He took Kat's hand under the table as they waited for a response. "You think we can get teaching jobs there?"

Jason hesitated and glanced at Kat. He knew she was excited to be back with her parents, but she gave a nod of her head, her approval. "I know you can."

Sheila glanced at Hank, who said, "You really want to do this, don't you?"

She nodded. "I do."

He hesitated, seeming to struggle with his pride before letting out a breath. "Okay then. We'll go."

Sheila clapped and hugged him before rushing to

Jason and Kat for hugs as well. "My parents want us to call them on Skype," Jason announced when things finally settled down.

A few minutes later, after dialing up his parents, Kat and Jason left Sheila and Hank in front of the computer, talking excitedly about their trip.

Jason followed Kat to the wooden deck off the back of her parents' house. "Our families have always gotten along as well as we did," Jason commented, sitting down on the wooden swing next to Kat. The sky was clear, the moon full, the stars bright, and the cool breeze off the mountain a perfect temperature on what could have been a hot night.

"They did," Kat said, glancing at him. "They do. I'm excited they're going on this trip." She angled her body toward him, lacing her fingers in his. "Thank you for making this happen for them."

"There's a lot of things we can do for them, Kat," he said. "For both of our families. It's what we always wanted. What we talked about."

She drew a deep breath, shadows dancing in her eyes. "We did. Yes."

He drew their joined hands to his mouth and kissed her knuckles. "We didn't get here the way we wanted to, but we're here, nonetheless."

"Yes," she said, shifting away from him, her gaze lifting to the sky. "We're here now."

His gut clenched. She didn't have to say more for him to read the subtext that said, "But for how long?", before she added, "I believed we'd really make all of those things happen, too."

"So did I."

She turned back to him, her soft fingers trailing over his jaw. "I know you did."

"We let distance exist where it shouldn't have."

"There wasn't a way around it," she said. "One of us would get a job offer when the other was already committed and we both would know it was too good to pass up. And if one of us missed an opportunity and never got another that good, or big, it would have fed resentment." She shook her head. "We couldn't have done anything but what we did."

Guilt twisted inside Jason because he knew he'd had opportunities to put Kat first, to turn down work that in hindsight hadn't moved his dreams along. Not only had they not been the best career moves, he'd lost the person he wanted to share his dreams with. He'd lost her.

"We did a lot of things wrong, Kat—I did a lot of things wrong—but they molded me, and us, into the people we are now. We can't change those things but we can use them to make a better future."

"I don't want to think about the future. When I do that, I think about a time limit, because we always have one. I want to think about right now. I just want to enjoy what time we have."

Jason fought the urge to argue, to demand she see his sincerity, his regret, his love. They had years of pain and separation, years of built-up emotions.

"Kat—" he started.

"Jason!" Sheila called. "Your mother wants to talk to you."

Jason silently cursed the bad timing, needing to tell Kat how much he loved her.

"They're all excited and that's because of you," Kat

said, and leaned in to kiss him. "Now is good, Jason. Now is what I want to live." She got to her feet and pulled him up with her, motioning to the door.

Two hours later, Jason parked Kat's rental car in his garage and got out. He would have rounded the car to get Kat's door, but she was out before he could make it. He met her at the hood of the car.

"I should have gone to my place and picked up some clothes."

Jason kept his expression unchanged and said, "Why would you do that?"

"Well I...I thought I was staying here."

He shook his head and wrapped her in his arms. "I'm packing a bag to stay with you, if you'll have me."

"What? Why? We're here."

"Because I've made you believe my world is more important than yours and it's not."

"No," she said, her fingers curling in his shirt. "I don't think that."

"Well," he said, "I'm just going to make sure you don't feel that now and I know I can't expect to prove that to you overnight. So I'm going to make a deal with you, or I hope I am, if you'll agree." He brushed the hair from her eyes. "I'll stay with you until I leave for the auditions. We'll live in the present. Then, Kat, when I'm back next month, when you know I'm really back, I'm going to ask you to marry me again."

Shock slid over her face. "Jason—"

He kissed her, and her moment of resistance melted into a soft, sensual joining of tongues.

"Don't respond," he said. "I'll take the living in the 'now' if that's what you want. But know this. I hope the 'now' is still going on in fifty years."

13

WEEKS LATER, KAT stood inside a busy, oversized dressing room, where a group of twenty dancers, as well as makeup, hair and costume people, were preparing for a live television special inside the hotel's Blue Moon nightclub, with Jason and a list of special superstar guests hosting. Kat knew the guest list, but few of the others did, for security reasons.

Nicole Smith, a rising star who'd been an opening act for Marcus on Kat's last tour, would be there. The idea was to promote the stage show and the new season of *Stepping Up*. The TV show would begin auditions in a week, and Jason would leave with it.

Kat's fingers tightened on the clipboard she held. She told herself to stop thinking about "the end" when it came to her and Jason. Over and over, she had to remind herself to enjoy what time they had together, not to regret living outside the present.

"I need my female understudies now," Kat shouted into the room. Three excited dancers rushed forward.

Kat felt they'd earned their own special moment on stage, and choreographed a unique performance for them.

Kat frowned as her fourth dancer failed to appear. "Where's Marissa?"

The room turned to a murmur with shouts for Marissa randomly being heard, but Marissa simply wasn't present.

"She's been gone a good half an hour," one of the hairdressers commented. "She got a phone call and left."

"Kat!"

Kat turned at the sound of Ellie's voice behind her. "We have a problem," Ellie said, entering the room.

"What problem?" Aside from Marissa being nowhere to be found, Kat thought grimly.

"Marissa says she's too sick to dance," Ellie said, as if replying to Kat's unspoken concerns.

"I can fill in for her," Tabitha said, stepping into the room, dressed in sweats and a tee. "Kate taught me the routine."

Why would Tabitha have one of the understudies teach her this routine? Warning bells went off in Kat's head, and her gaze brushed Ellie's. The look on the other choreographer's face told her that Ellie heard those bells as well.

"Where's Marissa?" Kat asked Ellie, repeating her earlier question to someone who hopefully could give her an answer.

"In the bathroom right off the stage," Ellie said. "She says she can't come out without throwing up." She laughed without humor. "I asked her if she was pregnant." She held up a hand. "Don't worry. She said she isn't." Her gaze brushed the three dancers' skimpy outfits. "And a good thing in those outfits. Yowza, they're sexy." She sighed and rubbed her stomach. "I better cut back on the chocolate or I'll never be able to wear anything but a clown costume again."

Tabitha snorted. "That doesn't stop a few dancers I know from indulging."

Kat's gaze flicked to Tabitha, who'd just barely contained her nastiness to Marissa since their talk a month before. Kat had heard a few too loudly spoken remarks from Tabitha and her slender frame compared to Marissa's more Kim Kardashian-type figure, not to know who she was talking about. "How did you know to be here, Tabitha? You were off tonight."

"Marissa called me and told me she needed me to fill in for her."

"Marissa called you," Kat said flatly, her gaze boring into Tabitha's. She didn't believe her, not for a New York minute. She watched the young dancer, waiting for her to break under scrutiny, but quickly surmised that wasn't going to happen. Tabitha was an ice witch, after fame at all costs. Kat was pretty sure Marissa was the one paying, or she would be, if Kat let it happen. Kat glanced at Ellie. "Jason wants the featured dancers on stage to meet Nicole before we go live."

"Should I get into costume?" Tabitha called from behind Kat.

Kat turned at the door, grinding her teeth at that question because her gut said that Tabitha was up to no good. "Yes," she said, pausing. "As a precautionary measure."

Kat headed out of the dressing room and double-timed it down the narrow hallway, pausing to the shout of her name at least four times in a short distance. Finally, Kat managed to make it to a small private bathroom just off the stage door, and she knocked on the wooden door.

"Marissa?"

"Yes," she said immediately and Kat could hear the stuffy nose and gravely voice that could be from sickness, as easily as they could be a product of tears. "I'm here."

"Can you open the door?" Kat asked.

"No. No. I'm sick and I don't want to make you get sick. Opening night is coming."

Kat frowned. "Marissa, what's going on? You weren't sick an hour ago."

"I was," she said. "I was hiding it. I tried so hard to hide it."

Kat didn't believe her. She just didn't. "If you're sick then let's get you to your room. Open up, Marissa. I can't go deal with the show knowing you might pass out in there and be seriously ill."

"Kat, I'm fine. I am. Please go do the show."

"I can't do that, Marissa," Kat said, testing the theory bouncing around in her head. "I know Tabitha has something to do with this."

There was a telling silence before Marissa said, "I'm sick. I really am sick."

Oh, man, Kat thought. Marissa wasn't sick. Kat had been right. Tabitha was up to no good. "Let me in and let's talk."

"You have to go do the show."

"So do you," Kat said. "This is your dream, Marissa." Silence. "Open up, honey. We need to talk." More silence and then the lock on the door popped. Marissa appeared in the doorway with mascara dripping down her pale cheeks, her eyes red, her hair a dark, rumpled mess of curls.

Kat stepped into the bathroom and urged Marissa back inside. "Talk to me, Marissa."

Marissa hugged herself. "This just isn't for me, Kat," she said, bypassing the sick excuse.

"Funny," Kat said. "It sure looks like it's for you when you're dancing."

"I…" She hesitated, her lip quivering. "No. I…don't think so."

"You do know that Tabitha wouldn't waste her time taunting you if she wasn't intimidated, right?"

Marissa cut her gaze away.

"Marissa," Kat said softly. "Talk to me."

She looked at Kat. "I don't like the nastiness," she said. "It's not who I am or what I'm made of."

"You're talking about Tabitha," Kat said, and it wasn't a question.

"It's not just Tabitha," Marissa said. "It's a lot of people in this business."

"That's true," Kat said. "I've dealt with my share of egos, but I've met big stars who were humble, and who did good things for others with the rewards of their success, too. I focus on those people."

"I just want to dance, Kat," she said. "I don't want to play the popularity contest. I don't want to be threatened and bullied."

"Wait. Who threatened you?"

"It doesn't matter."

"It does matter. Who threatened you?"

"It wasn't really a threat. Not directly." She bent down and pulled something from a bag on the floor, a newspaper clipping, and held it out to Kat.

Kat took it and read the headline, about a robbery ten years before, and glanced up at Tabitha. "What does this have to do with you?"

"My father," she said. "My mother had a heart condition and we didn't have the money for her medical care. He tried to rob a bank. He's out now and rebuilding his life. It would destroy him to have this all over the paper and it would be a scandal for the show."

Kat's heart squeezed. "Your mother?"

"Died six months after he went to prison." Her voice cracked. "So you see why I can't go on."

"No," Kat said, knowing now why she liked Marissa, and even felt protective of her. Marissa was a sweet girl and a good person. "I see a reason for you to do this show and rise to the top. Tonight comes with a big paycheck and a whole lot of exposure."

"I know but—"

"Did you call Tabitha to take your spot?"

"Yes."

"Because she gave you this clipping, didn't she?" Kat asked, holding up the paper.

Marissa looked to the ground.

"That means yes," Kat said, furious now. "Are you willing to write a statement about what happened tonight?"

Her eyes went wide. "No. Kat, no. If I do that she'll call the tabloids and turn this into a nightmare."

"She's not dancing tonight in your place," Kat said, "so I suggest you get to hair and makeup and then meet me on stage in fifteen minutes. We'll head to the club from there."

"I can't do this, Kat."

"You can," she said. "And by doing so you'll make a better life for you and your father. There will always be a bully in everything you do. That's life. Face this down and fight for your dream. No one else can do it for you." Kat hugged her. "Fix your face so no one knows you were crying and head to the dressing room. I'll see you on stage for some last-minute instructions before we head to the club."

Kat didn't give her time to say no. She exited the bathroom, quickly heading out onto the stage. She was already walking toward the group standing in the center when she stopped dead in her tracks.

"Marcus," Kat croaked at the sight of the tall, dark and good-looking, incredibly famous pop singer—the ex she hadn't told Jason about.

"There's my tigress," Marcus said and then rolled his tongue. "Surprise, baby. Somebody had the flu so I'm filling in. I came to help give you a grand opening."

The old saying "you could hear a pin drop" had never been so true. The room had just learned what she'd failed to tell Jason and what Marcus clearly assumed everyone already knew—that she and Marcus had dated. Everyone but Marcus understood the implications of Jason and Marcus standing there side by side. Kat's gaze went to Jason's and she saw the hurt in his face.

Someone called his name from below the stage. "Jason! We need you at the club. We have a problem."

"Kat," Jason said, and there was no mistaking the tightness in his voice. "Marcus is going to perform for us tonight. He says you know the number and he only needs one dancer. *You.* I'll leave you all to talk this out." He turned away without another word.

Kat's gaze went to Marcus's dark brown stare, the rest of the room fading away. "That, Marcus, would be my ex-husband I told you about."

His eyes went wide. "Jason is your ex? Oh damn, Kat. You never told me his name. I'm sorry."

"I know," she said, already in motion to follow Jason. Marcus wasn't the type of person to start trouble. In fact, he hated people who were. This was her fault for not telling Jason. It was past history, and it just hadn't seemed important.

Kat caught up to him. "Jason, wait. Please."

"Now is not a good time for this, Kat," he said without looking at her.

"I love you, Jason."

"Just not enough," he said. "That's the part I never seem to get."

She grabbed his arm forcing him to stop walking. "That's not true."

He turned to her. "I get the math, Kat. You left Denver and went to him."

"No," she said, shaking her head. "I hadn't even met Marcus when we were in Denver."

"Jason," Kevin, one of the production assistants, shouted running down the hall toward them. "Camera one blew. I'm trying to move in another one but I'm having trouble with the club manager."

Desperation expanded inside of Kat, tightening her throat. "I know now isn't the time for this, but please tell me you'll give me a chance to explain."

He stared at her a hard two seconds and turned away without an answer. A vise tightened on her chest. Kat couldn't watch him leave. Taking action was the only way to fix this.

She made a beeline to the bathroom and knocked. "Marissa, if you're in there, open up now."

Marissa appeared almost instantly. "Come with me," Kat said. "You're going to dance with Marcus tonight and I need you to learn the routine."

"Marcus? As in the amazingly hot pop star Marcus?"

"I wouldn't say amazingly hot," came Marcus's voice from behind Kat and she would have laughed if not for the fact that she wanted to cry. Marcus wasn't conceited. In fact, he was as perfect a guy as anyone could want, minus one important detail. He wasn't Jason.

14

AFTER SENDING MARISSA to the costume department and getting Marcus to the right person to fit him with a microphone, Kat headed to the stage where Ellie, Tabitha and the three other featured dancers were still congregating.

"Tabitha," Kat said, already with a plan in mind. "You're dancing for Marissa." She glanced at Ellie. "Marissa will be dancing with Marcus, so I'm going to be working with them to get ready. Can you please make sure they have Marcus performing last?"

"Done," Ellie said, her eyes alight with interest at the announcement. "He's already set up to be the final guest so we can tease the audience with a surprise coming at the end of the show. So, you're not dancing with Marcus?"

"No," Kat confirmed. "I'm not dancing with Marcus."

"Why is Marissa dancing with Marcus?" Tabitha demanded, her hands on her hips. "I'm the one the audience already knows."

"Marcus is the one the audience already knows," Kat corrected, hoping she was teaching Tabitha a lesson about how doing things wrong wasn't going to get her to the top. "And why are you not in your costume yet?" Tabitha looked like she might argue, but decided against it and hightailed it off the stage.

Ellie motioned to the remaining dancers. "You three, go get on your Egyptian robes and make sure the others are lined up at the exit door." The robes fit into the theme of their first pop star's performance. It was the beginning of a big show with a grand entry. So big and intensive to put together that Kat was thankful Jason had given everyone the next day off. She glanced at her watch. "We have ten minutes until we do the dramatic walk across the hotel to the club in the west wing."

The dancers scurried away, whispering with nerves and excitement about being in throne-like chairs carried by other dancers.

"Try not to fall out of those chairs," Ellie yelled after them. "I'm too pregnant to catch you." They laughed and disappeared.

Kat and Ellie stepped closer to one another. "You're taking a risk with Marissa." Ellie sounded concerned. "All eyes will be on Marcus's performance. Are you sure she's ready for this?"

"All eyes will be on Marcus," Kat repeated, "not Marissa. And Marcus won't let her look bad. He's a nice guy. He'll take care of her."

"A nice guy, but not the *right* guy," Ellie said, reading between the lines.

"Exactly," Kat agreed, and in a rare moment of spilling her personal baggage, she added, "It's killing me that Jason thinks there's something going on with me and Marcus."

"It sure seemed that way," she pointed out grimly. "Marcus greeted you like his girlfriend. And let's face it, Marcus is one of the few men that could make someone as confident and sexy as Jason feel insecure. It's not a good combination."

"Thank you for the words of encouragement," Kat said, feeling as if a knife had just torn through her chest. Jason was confident, and jealousy had never been a problem for them, but this wasn't exactly a normal situation.

Ellie squeezed Kat's arm. "I'm just being honest. But honey, dancing with Marcus would have been the kiss of death with Jason if I'm reading him right. You're doing what you have to and not only does it show you love him, you sure as heck have my respect for this. Not many people would pass up the spotlight for a relationship."

She didn't want the spotlight. She never had. She wanted Jason. "I just hope it matters to Jason."

"It will," Ellie said with a firm nod. "I'm sure it will. How can it not?" The door to the stage burst open and dancers filed in. A rush of activity took over the room. Ellie's eyes lit up. "Here we go. The beginning of something grand, I hope."

Fifteen minutes later, the dancers were gone, and only Kat, Marcus and Marissa were left on the stage. Forty-five minutes after that, Kat was feeling pretty darn good about Marissa's performance and she knew Marcus well enough to know he approved as well.

"You learn fast," Marcus complimented Marissa.

"Consider yourself invited to join my next tour." Marcus winked at Kat. "That is, if I can steal you away from your boss here."

Marissa didn't jump up and down, and didn't scream with the excitement others would have. She paled instantly, as if she had just received bad news. "I hope you still feel that way after the show."

Marcus arched a brow in Kat's direction, seemingly surprised at the nervous gulp. She gave him a quick nod, her look meant to tell him that she thought a lot of Marissa. He returned the nod, and his gaze settled back on Marissa, his expression softening. Kat knew how Marcus struggled with the insincerity of the people around him, and how everyone wanted a piece of him. And she knew right then that he saw what she did in Marissa.

"I need to check on the rest of show," Kat said, wondering if Marissa might be just the woman Marcus needed. "You two keep working."

Kat exited the stage area and smiled at the romantic door she'd just opened, if not for the door Jason had shut on her tonight. She regretted not telling him about Marcus, but the truth was that it hadn't seemed important. Marcus had been more a friend than a lover. They'd both been riding the bumpy path of heartache, trying to fill a hole in their lives. She'd simply been a little more ready to admit it than he had been that their relationship hadn't filled the hole.

Jason's words replayed in her mind. *Not enough,* he'd said about her loving him. She'd said those exact words to herself about him before she'd left Denver for Marcus's tour. She knew what they meant, and she knew they came with great pain. Her stomach knotted with fear that he might have sealed the door shut forever.

Kat had just reached the cluster of empty dressing rooms when the door from the main hotel was shoved open. Tabitha hobbled inside with Joe, one of the production assistants, holding her up, one knee bent to keep her foot off the ground.

"What happened?" Kat asked, rushing toward them.

Tabitha sobbed, but there were no tears, which struck Kat as odd. "I fell off the podium."

"There's a doctor on the way," Joe said as the three of them made their way into the closest dressing room.

Tabitha sat down in a chair and buried her face in her hands. "I can't believe this is happening."

"Ellie said she has to have her replaced and quickly," Joe said. "The empty podium is obvious to the cameras."

Right, of course it was, and when Marcus performed, the four dancers would do a lead-in routine and then freeze frame, like mannequins. That would leave the podium obviously open if Marissa tried to do both dances.

Kat studied Tabitha, pretty darn certain that Tabitha was up to no good. "You're sure your ankle is too bad to dance on?"

Tabitha let her hands drop to her lap for a moment and her eyes met Kat's. "Positive." Kat saw an instant of hatred in the other woman's expression that was quickly replaced by a sob and crinkled-up expression. "Yessssss." A whimper followed and she buried her face in her hands again.

Kat ground her teeth and stood up. She had no doubt

Tabitha intended for Marissa to miss her moment in the spotlight with Marcus, and she was done trying. She'd have to proceed cautiously so Tabitha couldn't say she was being fired for getting hurt on the job, but nevertheless, Tabitha had just sealed her exit from the show. No one here had time for these kinds of manipulative games. Kat pushed to her feet, her mind racing with options, searching for an answer that didn't leave her dancing with Marcus again.

"HI, BOSS."

Jason heard Kat's voice in his earpiece through the mic system he used with his crew. Nearby, music blasted through the speakers as a pop singer named Stacey P performed. He stood by the stage, and despite the rowdy crowd that was more sardines in a can than an audience, he knew without looking the instant she was beside him. He could feel her there, as he always could feel her.

He cut her a sideways look, taking in the skimpy outfit she wore that matched that of the other three featured dancers, cursing the tightening of his body at the sight. He wasn't surprised at how hot she looked, but he was surprised she'd chosen an outfit to match the other dancers, rather than something special for Marcus's performance.

That thought had him grinding his teeth, and about breaking his jaw from the force. It was eating him alive to think about Kat rehearsing with Marcus, about her performing with Marcus, about her kissing him.

"I need Tabitha or Marissa on that podium at commercial," he said into his mic.

"You got me instead," she said, "and I'm on my way. I'll be where you need me to be."

"How are you going to cover your spot on the podium and be where Marcus needs you?"

"Marissa is dancing with Marcus," she said. "Not me, Jason." She cut around him, her hand discreetly brushing his back, until she was on the opposite side of him, and staring up at him to repeat. "Not me." Their eyes held a moment, and more than music thrummed through his body. Every emotion he'd ever felt for Kat was there, too, twisting him into knots.

"Thirty seconds to commercial," one of his people said into their ears.

Kat turned away immediately, darting through the crowd, and when the song ended, he wasn't watching the famous singer on stage. He was watching Kat, who had taken the podium in a skimpy outfit that was getting plenty of male attention. But not Marcus's.

She wasn't dancing with him now. It should have made Jason feel better. So why did he still feel as if he'd lost something valuable?

Jason didn't have time to analyze it. He had to be on stage himself, acting as if nothing bothered him. He didn't like the on-camera work, and he wasn't a host. This judging stuff had spun out of control, as had this night. But he'd agreed to all of this for a reason. To make this show work, and to create an opportunity where he and Kat could stay in one place together.

Jason headed to the stage, greeting the singer, and exchanging some banter with her for the audience and the cameras. And when he and Stacey P, a pretty blond singer most men would kill to be with, stepped off the stage to allow Marcus to claim it, she stayed by his side.

"So, Jason," she said, leaning in close, her hand settling on his arm. "I'm in town through tomorrow if you want to get together later tonight."

Jason knew just about every man watching this show would say yes to the offer, but he'd been there, done that, and didn't give a damn about the shirt. Nothing, and no one, replaced Kat. Jason politely declined and fortunately had directorial duties to attend that made escape easy. From Stacey that was. There was no escaping Kat, and after what he'd learned tonight, that was about as hard to swallow as it got. One way or the other, tonight, this was it for his relationship with Kat. He was in or he was out for good.

KAT HAD STOOD on the podium, after striking her mannequin-like pose, while Marcus and Marissa performed brilliantly. She felt like a proud mama watching Marissa coming out of her shell, showing her talent to the world.

When the number ended, Jason stepped onto the stage with Marcus and Kat felt her hopes fall and land hard. She knew how awkward this moment was for Jason, and she feared what Marcus, even with good intentions, might say.

But the moment came and went quickly. Jason said goodnight to television land and shook Marcus's hand. The crowd shouted and chanted for Marcus to sing another song and he agreed.

"Cut," Jason said into the microphone feed. "We are

off air. Dancers, hold your positions for Marcus's final number. Kat, Marissa is headed up there to replace you."

It wasn't long before Kat was giving Marissa a quick hug and stepping to the top level of the club, only to find Jason standing there waiting for her. He took her hand and pulled her down a hallway, around a corner and against a wall. His hand rested by her head.

"Do you have any idea how I'm feeling right now?"

Kat wanted to wrap her arms around him and tell him how sorry she was, but she knew Jason. She knew he needed words, he needed understanding. "He is a friend."

"Don't patronize me, Kat. I saw how he looked at you, and more so, I saw your face when you saw him."

"You saw dread," she said, her heart beating so fast it was making it hard to talk. "Not happiness."

"And why exactly would you feel dread if a friend was here to help, Kat? You went from my bed to his."

"It wasn't like that," Kat said. "I told you. I barely knew Marcus before I started the tour. And yes, I dated him. I was trying to get over you, Jason."

"I wasn't trying to get over you, Kat," he said. "I was trying to reach you. I was trying to get you back in my life."

"I dated him, Jason. It meant nothing. Come on. You dated that one Hollywood actress for months and there was talk of marriage. How do you think that made me feel?"

"I never once talked marriage with her," he said. "I never even thought about it. I didn't marry her. I married you."

"And I didn't marry Marcus," she said, knowing the statement had been a mistake before it even left her lips.

"He asked you to marry him?"

She'd never lied to Jason, never wanted to, until this moment, but she wouldn't. She couldn't. "I didn't marry him, Jason. I married you."

"Did he ask you to marry him?"

"Yes, but—"

He cursed and shoved off the wall, giving her his back.

"Jason, he wasn't you—"

He whirled around and leaned in close again, his hand back on the wall. "Let me guess. You convinced him to keep it all about sex."

"No—"

"We're done, Kat. I'm done. You've had a decade of my life in some way, shape or form. That's enough."

He left her standing there, gone before she could say a word, and it was all she could do to not chase him. Making a scene wouldn't help anything. Worse though, she didn't think anything would help. He'd never before said he was done with her.

Truthfully, they'd never had a fight like this. A spat, a disagreement, a little thing, yes. But nothing like this and that alone said everything.

He meant what he'd said. He was done.

15

MARCUS'S NEW SONG broke through the haze of Kat's shock and she came back to the present. Jason's words had devastated her. How long had she been paralyzed against the wall? She didn't know. She just knew it hurt, she hurt. Her heart raced wildly and she drew a deep breath and let it out slowly, forcing herself to calm down.

"Pull yourself together," she whispered. She had to be professional, and deal with the cast and crew. She was supposed to relieve Ellie fully so she could rest. Ellie, who was pushing herself too hard. Ellie. Right. She marched back into the main bar, and wove through the crowd. She focused on her purpose, on taking care of Ellie.

"Ellie," Kat said, tapping the button that would allow the crew to hear her through the microphone. "Can you meet me in the dressing rooms?"

"On my way," Ellie said immediately.

A few minutes later Kat and Ellie were in a private dressing room, while Kat changed back into her clothes.

Ellie rubbed her increasingly large stomach. "So how are things with you and Jason?" she asked before grimacing. "Oh, wow. Not feeling so good. I need to sit."

Kat pulled her T-shirt over her head and grabbed a chair for Ellie. "Are you okay?"

Ellie sunk into the seat the instant it was behind her. "I've been feeling sick all day. I think it was the pressure of the show. Tonight's ratings will be looked at hard by the studio, and not just as a feeler for how the stage show will be received. They'll see tonight as a preview of interest for the third season of *Stepping Up.* Jason should have gotten a call about the ratings by now. I really—" She stiffened and made a funny face.

"Ellie, honey, what are you feeling? Was that pain?"

"It's nothing," she said dismissively. "The doctor said it's from ligaments stretching. It's normal."

"All the same, let's get you up to your room so you can lie down."

"Really, I'm fine," Ellie insisted. "I want to find out about tonight's ratings before I go upstairs."

"We'll call Jason from your room," Kat suggested. "Will that work?"

"You don't need to walk with me," Ellie said. "You stay and close things down here."

"I'm coming with you," Kat said, not pleased with how pale Ellie looked. She was worried. "And you don't know me well enough yet to understand this, so let me save us both some time. I'm stubborn as a mule and proud of it. You're going upstairs to rest."

Ellie laughed and then grimaced again. "Maybe I do need to rest." She stood up and swayed. Kat grabbed her arm and Ellie laughed without humor. "When was the last time I ate?"

"Too long ago if you have to ask," Kat chided. "Room service it is."

"Room service for sure," Ellie agreed, as she and Kat stepped into the hallway and directly into the path of Jason, his assistant director Ronnie, and several of his crew members.

Kat's eyes met his and awareness rushed over her, along with a huge dose of emotion. She cut her gaze away before she could see the rejection, the anger, and maybe something worse, that might be in Jason's expression. She'd have to manage this quickly to be professional on the job, but not tonight, not when this change between them had just happened. The hurt was too raw.

"Oh, good," Ellie said at the sight of Jason. "Talk to us, Jason. What's the ratings news?"

"Fifteen million viewers," he said. "A couple million over expectations."

It was an announcement Kat would normally have celebrated with Jason, but instead, she turned to Ellie. "See? Now can you rest?"

Ellie let out a breath. "Now I can rest."

Kat flicked a fleeting look in Jason's direction. "She's feeling sick. I'm taking her to her room and feeding her."

"We can finish up here," Jason said. "Ellie, you should slow down. Consider taking off the entire weekend like I told you to."

"I'm fine," Ellie insisted. "I just need food and bed."

One of the cameramen shouted Jason's name from behind them, and Jason turned to address the man. Kat took that opportunity to hustle Ellie toward the stage. "Let's exit through the theater to avoid running into anyone who might convince you something is going on you need to be involved with."

She laughed. "I guess you know me pretty darn well."

It wasn't until they were alone in the elevator that Ellie studied Kat. "What happened?"

Kat didn't pretend she didn't know what she was talking about. "We fought."

"Everyone fights, Kat."

She shook her head. "Not us, not like this."

"You want to talk about it?"

"I can't," Kat said. "Not without really losing it and I don't cry often, but when I do, I do it right. I'll be swollen up like a blowfish and I'll never get out of here without everyone knowing."

"You can stay with me tonight," she said. "Or you can have your own room a few doors down."

"Thank you, Ellie, but I need to be home tonight more than ever." Home was a place she hadn't felt she'd had in a long time, a place where she could retreat and deal with this.

The elevator dinged open. "I understand," Ellie said.

It didn't take long for Kat to get Ellie settled onto her bed and order room service. Ellie still felt dizzy and Kat offered the kitchen staff a big tip if they rushed the food. By the time she hung up, Ellie's husband David called and Kat felt awkward listening to them talk.

"I have to chat with Kat," Ellie told him.

Kat shook her head. "No. No, it's—"

"I'm off tomorrow. I'll sleep all day. I'm fine. I'll call you when I'm done eating."

Kat sunk down onto the mattress with Ellie and did something she never did. She interfered in Ellie's personal life. "What if *Stepping Up* decided to film in Vegas every season?"

"I'm sure you and Jason would be happy."

"I'm not talking about me and Jason," Kat said. "I'm talking about you."

Her expression sobered. "We've talked about it," she said. "It's only a few months every year."

"And the audition travel."

"The baby can go with me," she said, "and by the time she's in school, it won't be likely that this show will still be around. We'll make it work. We both know this job is our chance to retire young and just be with our kids and each other."

"That's what Jason and I said every time a big job came up that separated us. And before you say, you're close, you won't fall apart like the rest of us, we did, too. Look. Ellie. I regret our choices. I regret saying there might not be another opportunity. What there might not be is another shot at each other. Just…think about it. Be cautious. None of this matters without the person you love with you to share it."

A knock sounded at the door. Kat quickly paid for the food and sat down with Ellie to eat. Kat rolled the tray to the bed so Ellie could stay and rest.

Ellie sat up and uncovered her sandwich, staring down at it as Kat pulled the desk chair opposite the cart. "It's all very confusing," Ellie finally said, her eyes lifting to Kat's. "I hate being pregnant without him here and I make plenty of money for him to quit. But how can I ask him to give up his career for me?"

What could Kat say? She knew this dilemma like she knew her own name. Far too well. "Find a solution," she said, and poured ketchup on her plate. She was starving, which surprised her considering how knotted up she was over Jason.

They ate in silence for a short while before Ellie asked, "What would you do?"

The answer was immediate for Kat. "I don't know. I just know what I did do before didn't work."

"That doesn't help me."

"I know," Kat said. "But it's the only answer I have."

"I need more than that," she said. "Because when I see how you and Jason look at each other, I know how much you love each other. Yet, still this business tore you apart."

"Not this business," Kat said. "We did. We made our choices and we have no one to blame but ourselves."

IT WAS NEARLY two in the morning when Kat left Ellie's room, having spent a solid hour with her. Ellie wasn't in pain and Kat had left her in her bed and talking to her husband. Kat, however, wasn't feeling better. Not at all. Talking about her fears of losing her relationship only drove home where she and Jason were, which was in no place good.

Kat tracked a path past the club. Everything was back to normal and Marcus was no longer around. She'd thanked him for his help tonight when they'd been rehearsing with Marissa, but she owed him another one.

She didn't want to hurt Marcus. He was, and she hoped he always would be, a friend.

She was almost back at the theater to check on things and grab her purse before she left, when she heard Marcus call her name. She turned to find him hurrying toward her and met him at the entry to the dressing rooms.

"I have to head out early tomorrow," he said. "I've got an interview."

She felt his departure like sandpaper roughing up an already raw wound, and she didn't know why. Her eyes prickled and she fought back tears.

"Hey," he said softly, lifting her chin to see her face. "What's wrong, baby?"

"I'm…okay."

"No," he said. "You're not. I really screwed this up for you, didn't I?"

"I did," she said, pressing two fingers to her forehead. "I didn't tell him about you and…it's a mess but you aren't to blame."

"You're shaking, Kat," he said, drawing her hand into his. "I've never seen you like this. I messed this up. I'll talk to him."

"No," Kat said, pressing her hand to his chest to still him. "Please. No. He will not respond well to that."

"Kat, I caused this," he said. "I'll fix it."

"You didn't cause this, Marcus. I did."

"Kat—"

"Please, Marcus. I'm fine. And you are a wonderful friend I don't intend to lose. You came here tonight because of that friendship and—"

"I came here tonight because I still love you," he said. "But I'm no fool. I see exactly what you told me now. You love Jason. And I care enough for you to want you to be happy."

"You don't love me, Marcus. You'll see that when you really fall in love."

"You keep saying that."

"Deep down you know it, too. You love me but you are not *in love* with me."

"Is there a difference?"

"Yes," Kat said. "And I love you enough to hope that you find that out very soon. You deserve it."

He kissed her hand. "You're sure I can't—"

"Positive," she said. "I'm good. You just take care of you, okay?"

"I'm going to get something to eat. You want to come with me?"

She shook her head. "I need to go home."

"I'll call you," he said and kissed her forehead.

"You better," she insisted as he walked away. She was about to head into the dressing rooms when she spotted Marissa waiting nearby. Marcus stopped by her side and she smiled as she caught a glimpse of his expression. Maybe, just maybe, Marcus was on his way to falling in love sooner than later.

That smile faded as she walked through the dark hallway and felt the emptiness. Everyone was gone. Jason was gone.

She made the walk to the parking area and the shaking started again. Or maybe it had never ended. She pulled out of the garage and rain pounded her window. She ignored a fleeting thought that it was dangerous to drive this tired, and this upset, in this bad of a storm.

She turned up her wipers to see through the fury of the storm, determined to get home before she fell apart.

JASON NEEDED TO ride, needed the wind and feel of the motorcycle humming beneath him, the escape it gave him. He pulled out into the storm, refusing to stay at the casino for the night. He had a helmet and he had proper riding gear to survive fairly damage free, at least from the rain. He'd seen Kat with her hand pressed to Marcus's chest and it had done a good job of shredding him to the core.

That Kat had walked to her car alone and departed only seconds before him should have eased some of his ache, but somehow it only made it worse. No, what made it worse was how much he wanted to ignore what Denver told him, what her actions said loud and clear. That she didn't want what he did or it would have happened long before now. He and Marcus were two of a kind, fools for the same woman.

He pulled onto the highway, the rain blinding him, but he didn't stop. He pressed onward, following Kat's taillights, his mind following the path of their relationship over the past few weeks. He wanted to see Kat not dancing with Marcus as a sign of her love, but he knew Kat. She wouldn't do anything to intentionally hurt anyone. She'd skip the dance to keep from hurting him. And it would have hurt.

Thunder roared and lightning blasted through the darkness, followed by a loud pop. Holy crap, Kat's tire had just blown. His heart stopped beating as he watched her struggle for control and skid toward the ditch. Jason came to a halt, ripping off his helmet and leaving his bike at the side of the road. He could barely breathe with the fear of Kat being injured as he took off running.

16

THE CAR SLID down a slope and stopped halfway into a ditch. Kat sat there, frozen in place, afraid it wasn't really over. She didn't breathe, didn't blink. Suddenly, she was years in the past, back in the day that she and Jason had decided to divorce.

"Of course you have to take the job," Kat said, her chest tight with emotion, her voice strained as she tried to hide her disappointment that he wasn't joining her on her movie set at the end of the week as planned. "It's a huge opportunity. You'll be directing one of the biggest stars in Hollywood."

"It's filming in Paris, KandyKat," he said. "We've wanted to go there. I'll arrange to have you flown out. Just tell me the exact day and I'll arrange everything."

"No," she said. "No. I can't. I have the Ms. America Pageant to choreograph in a week. You know that. I took it because you were going to be free by then and we could be together. By the time I'd get there I'd have to leave."

"Kat—"

"It's just how it is, Jason. It's how it always is. I think... I think it's time we face reality."

"What are you talking about?"

"We just can't make marriage and our careers work."

"That's crazy," he said. "Yes, we can. I won't take the job. I'm coming there."

"I'm leaving early," she said. "The movie I've been working on wrapped."

"Kat—"

"It's time, Jason," she said. "We've battled this for years and spent more time apart than together. I just can't stand the idea that I hold you back."

"You don't hold me back. Stop this. Please. I love you. None of this matters without you. We planned this out. We'll take the hits now and retire early. We'll travel, then have kids."

"I love you, too," she whispered. "Too much to hold on to you like this no matter how much I want to."

"I'm holding on," he said. "I'll hold on tight enough for us both if I have to."

The car door jerked open.

"Kat!" Jason shouted, bending down beside her. "Kat, are you okay?"

"Yes." Kat could barely pry her vise-like grip from the steering wheel. "Yes, I'm okay. Just shaken up."

She turned toward him, letting her legs slide over the seat. Jason pulled her to her feet and into the rain before wrapping his powerful arms around her.

He brushed her hair from her face, inspecting her carefully. "You're sure? You don't hurt anywhere?"

She stared up at him, not caring about the storm,

the car, or the deserted highway. "Yes," she said. "My heart," she said. "My heart hurts because you—"

The next thing she knew, Jason's mouth came down on hers. She moaned and clung to him, the taste of him pouring through her, the rain pouring over her. There was a desperateness to the kiss she recognized as hers, as his, a hunger for each other that washed over Kat, filled her and gave her hope. No two people who felt this passionately for each other belonged apart. They had to make it work, they could make it work.

He tore his mouth from hers. "Let's get out of here," he said, taking her hand to help her up the slope to the highway, and she was far from complaining. She wanted to be alone with him, to talk to him, to be in his arms.

They ran to the motorcycle, where he wrapped his jacket around her. When he started to put his helmet on her as well she stopped him. "Wait," she said. "To your house. I want to go to your house." The idea of being somewhere he could walk away again was too much right now. She couldn't deal with that tonight.

He stared at her, unaffected by what seemed like gallons of water pouring over him before he raised the helmet again. She let him put it on her this time, wishing he would have replied, wishing she could say more, but the blasted rain stifled the conversation.

Kat watched him climb onto the Harley, and then took her spot behind him. *Her spot.* The place she'd ridden many times before. She leaned into him and wrapped her arms around him, the warmth of his body seeping through his now wet shirt, and right through to her soul. She held on, not for safety, but on to him, to the years that had led them here, to the past few weeks that had brought them back together. She'd known when they'd begun this project together that this was it, a new beginning or the end of their path together. And those years, those weeks, had come down to now. Whatever happened tonight really was it. But he was here with her, and he'd kissed her.

She clung to those things, telling her they meant something, right up until the second when she realized that Jason wasn't taking her to his house. He was taking her to her own home, where he would leave her and go to his. He'd meant his words back in that bar, when he'd told her he was done. She knew him and he'd never said anything like that to her.

When the bike stopped in her driveway, Jason shouted over his shoulder, "Garage door opener?"

No, she realized, with yet another kick in the teeth when she'd had too many already tonight. In the midst of the mess created by her raging emotions, she'd left her purse in the car. That meant her keys and her phone were also on the side of the road.

Kat pushed off of the bike and shoved Jason's jacket at him, then tugged off the helmet. "Thanks for the ride," she shouted over the engine and another loud roll of thunder from directly above them. "I'm fine from here." She took off running.

The backyard was Kat's target destination, and she prayed she'd left the sliding glass door open. But she didn't leave things unlocked any more than she normally left them in places they didn't belong, like the side of the road, so the chances of getting inside were slim.

"Kat!" Jason shouted, but she didn't turn. She pulled open the gate and would have closed it behind her but it hung on mud and grass. She struggled with it, and seeing Jason running in her direction, she abandoned the door.

She was up the concrete stairs and under the covered patio that spanned most of the back of the house, when Jason shackled her hand. "Kat, damn it," he growled. "What are you doing?"

She whirled on him, pulling out of his loose hold. He'd left his jacket and his T-shirt was soaked, outlining his perfect torso. "I'll call the rental place. They'll take care of this from here."

Water ran over his face. "Let's go inside and talk."

"No," she said, hugging herself. "We have nothing to talk about."

"We have years of things to talk about."

"You said you were done," she said. "And I get that, Jason. I know you and I know you meant it. And I know why you brought me here. So you could leave when you were ready. Well, leave then. You're really good at leaving."

He stepped back as if she'd hit him and Kat couldn't believe she'd said those words. She'd never, ever thrown his past choices in his face, but she'd felt those choices with a whole heck of a lot of pain.

"I never wanted to leave you," he reminded her, "and I know you have to know that."

"But yet you excel at it," she said, unable to hold back. "I didn't leave you for Marcus, Jason. You left me in yet another hotel room, alone."

"I had no choice," he said. "The auditions were the next day. I was contracted. We talked about this before I left."

"We did, and like always, I knew you had to go. Denver was just a repeat of history, a look into the same future. You feel good when I'm with you but you feel really bad when I'm not. And when I sat there in that hotel room, I swore it was the last time."

"You had a tour you didn't even tell me about," he argued.

"I would have," she countered. "But you told me you were leaving long before I had the chance."

"And I foolishly didn't ask," he supplied.

"You didn't ask," she agreed. "That night, I swore you would never leave me in a damnable hotel room alone again. I swore that I was done. And still you haunted me, Jason. Still, I couldn't forget you. Marcus's one of the good guys fame hasn't corrupted. He was good to me, but he wasn't you, and I couldn't make him you no matter how I tried. But Jason, I did try. For the first time since we divorced, I really did try. And still, I failed. I couldn't get past you, and I wanted to."

Long seconds ticked by, the silence filled with nothing but a steady, slow tapping of rain on the ground.

"Let's go inside, Kat," he finally said, his voice softer now, his eyes as dark and turbulent as the weather.

"I don't have my keys," she admitted. "I left them in my purse in the car."

"Damn. I should have thought about your purse. I'll go get it, and then we have to talk, Kat. Really talk about all of this, not talk around it." He turned to leave.

Kat grabbed his arm. "No. I don't want you to help me. If you're done, you're done. Be done and go home."

Before she knew his intent, he pulled her close and

she wanted to push him away. Again, she failed. She couldn't push Jason away. She just didn't have it in her.

"I'm never done with you, Kat," his voice raspy with evident emotion. "Even when you hurt me like you did tonight with Marcus, I can't say it's over and mean it."

"I didn't know he was coming."

"And you didn't tell me about him, either."

"Because he changed nothing between us," she said. "Or so I thought."

He studied her intensely, then said, "Let me go get your purse and—"

"I can't stand here and wait for you to get back," she said. "I'll go crazy. I'll end up breaking the window to get off this porch."

"Then come with me."

She shook her head and backed away from him. "No. Then you'll take me to your place to prove something when it's too late. You brought me here. This is where you wanted me and where I belong. I don't have my phone either. Just please call me a cab and I'll take care of this."

"I can be there and back before the cab ever gets here," he said. "And I brought you here because I swore to you, and myself, that I wouldn't force you into my world."

"You never forced me into your world, Jason. You forced me out."

"I'm the one who pursued you, Kat," he said. "I tried to hold on to you. I tried to get you back." He ran his hand over his wet hair. "Look. There's plenty more I'd say right now, but your purse is important. I'm going to get it and I'll be back." He turned away again.

"Marcus didn't know who you were or he wouldn't have come."

He kept his back to her, his spine just a little stiffer. "So you never even told him about me either."

"I never told him your name. Our relationship was, and is, ours alone. I simply told him I had an ex-husband I was still in love with."

He was perfectly still, the sound of the rain pattering on the roof filling the silence, before he finally said, "Wait for me." And then he was gone. How many times had she said those words in her head? *And then he was gone.*

THE EX-HUSBAND I was still in love with. Kat's words replayed in Jason's mind as he rode through the rain, keeping his Harley on slow and easy. There was nothing slow and easy about his thoughts, that was for sure.

He loved Kat. He wanted Kat. He needed her. But she was tearing him apart. In his heart, he yearned to believe that Marcus meant nothing, to her or about them. *Leave. You're good at it.* Those had been her words, in various rephrased ways tonight. Marcus wasn't the problem. The past was the problem.

Jason pulled to a halt behind Kat's car when a police vehicle pulled up behind him. He headed toward the officer who was wearing a yellow rain jacket and met him halfway.

"Not a good night to be out," the officer shouted. "Anyone hurt here?"

"We're fine," he said. "My wife had a blowout, and we forgot her purse inside the vehicle." Wife. He'd said wife, just like Kat's father had in the casino. How easily that had come out of his mouth, too.

"You call for roadside assistance, I assume?" the cop asked.

"Not yet," he said. "The rain was pounding on us too hard. It's a rental."

"I'll call for you," the officer said. "Who's the agency?"

Jason told him, having seen the bumper sticker on Kat's car. "I'll stay here and make sure you get off all right," the officer offered.

Jason gave him a salute and took off down the muddy incline. He slid inside the vehicle, the water pouring off him.

"Glad it's a rental and not the BMW you've always wanted," he murmured. His hands tightened on the steering wheel with the thought. They were supposed to car shop tomorrow and he'd been looking forward to it. He wanted to buy that car with her, he wanted to be there for her, share her excitement at finally getting "the" car she'd always pined for.

He grabbed her purse and had a terrifying flash of the rental sliding off the road. Too easily, things could have ended up differently. She could have flipped. She could have died. He pounded the steering wheel. Life was too short for them to screw around like this, pussyfooting around issues. He could have lost her tonight forever. He grabbed her purse, shoved it under his jacket and ran up the hill. He and Kat were going to do something they should have done a long time ago. They were going to really clear the air, they were going to fight and yell, and get everything out in the open. And then, if he was lucky, they'd make love and they'd stay in love. He refused to consider any other option.

17

JASON PULLED INTO Kat's driveway, putting the garage door opener he'd fished from Kat's purse, along with her keys, to good use. Finally, he was out of the downpour and off his bike and he had plenty he wanted to talk to Kat about. He shrugged out of his jacket and left his bag behind, making a beeline inside the house and to the sliding glass door off the kitchen. The instant he was outside, Kat rounded the wall to face him, her hair beginning to dry and forming wispy strands around her face.

"Jason—" she started, sounding surprised.

He didn't give her a chance to finish. He closed his arms around her and slanted his mouth over hers, the sweet taste of her like an addictive drug filling his senses. When he was certain he'd kissed her thoroughly, he said, "I love you, Kat. I want to marry you again. I want you to be my wife. Just remember that before, and when, we're fighting."

"I love you, too," she said breathlessly and leaned back. "Wait. What? Fighting?"

Jason led her inside and shut the door, then put the table between them. When he was touching her, he couldn't think. He just wanted to forget everything, to touch her and to love her.

"It's time we have it out, Kat. We need to say everything we have ever thought and see if we can survive it."

She sucked in a breath, and looked terrified at the idea. "I can't," she said, shaking her head. "If you say anything that hurts I...I can't take anymore, Jason."

"What hurts is goodbye, Kat," he argued. "I took jobs because you encouraged me to take them."

"What kind of selfish person would I have been to do anything but encourage you?"

"But yet you blame me for taking the jobs?"

"No," she said. "I don't blame you."

"But?"

"No but."

"Kat, damn it—"

"Don't curse at me, Jason."

"If that's what it takes to get you to be honest with me—"

"I knew your career was the most important thing to you."

"*You* were the most important thing to me."

She made a frustrated sound and took off toward the other room. Jason caught up with her quickly. "We talked about this, Kat. Build up our careers and retire young, raise a family, travel. Whatever we wanted to do."

"That's what Ellie and her husband are doing," she said. "And he's missing her pregnancy."

"We aren't them, Kat."

"No. They're still together."

A knot formed in his chest. "I'd turn back time if I could. I'd do it right because I clearly didn't do it right the first time. But I will this time if you give me the chance."

"Tonight, you said you were done with me. I let you back in and in a snap of your fingers, you broke me like a twig."

"I found out about you and Marcus in front of a group of people who knew we were in a relationship," he said. "Not only did it feel like a ten-ton boulder had been dropped on my chest, I had to pretend that boulder didn't exist. For the first time in my life, Kat, I wanted to walk out of the show and just say I'm done with everything. You have no idea how hard it was for me to get on national television and act like I was okay. Because I wasn't. I *wasn't* okay." Suddenly, he needed space. He left the kitchen, walking down a small flight of stairs that led to her living room.

"Jason," she said, catching his arm as he reached the landing. "I'm so very sorry that happened. I'd never, ever, put you in a position like that. I'd never intentionally hurt you, either."

"I know," he said. "But I don't think you know how important you are to me, or how important you always have been to me. We can't fix this, can we, Kat?"

"Don't say that," she whispered. "Don't say we can't fix things." She held his hands. "I want to and that's one of the reasons you saying you were done hurt so much. I'm really trying. I really want this time to work."

Jason picked her up and Kat laughed. "You're always picking me up. I don't remember you doing that in the past."

He sat down on her couch, with her back against the arm of the sofa, and her legs draped over his.

"I just realized that I am soaking wet and now your floor and your couch are, too."

"I don't care," she said. "You're here. That's all that matters." She leaned forward and pressed her lips to his, before whispering, "On second thought, I think you should take those wet clothes off."

He cupped the back of her head and kissed her, a quick, passionate kiss. "Do you know why I keep picking you up?"

"Why?"

"Because I'm always afraid you're going to run away again."

She shifted, climbing on top of him, straddling him, and then pulled his wet shirt off and tossed it behind him.

"I'm not going anywhere."

She tossed her shirt with his, but when she tried to remove her bra, he tugged her against him.

"Don't do that. I can't think when you're naked and we haven't solved anything yet."

"I'm not going anywhere, Jason," she promised.

"But you think I am."

"I don't want to hold you back, Jason. If you feel like you can never take another job that requires you to travel, that isn't any more healthy than me always feeling like you will. I don't want that for you or for us."

He let his head drop back, staring at the ceiling. He

felt defeated in a battle he'd given everything he was in order to win it. She kissed his throat.

"What did I say wrong? What is wrong with me wanting the best for you?"

"I'm not taking any more jobs that require I travel unless you can go with me," he said, bringing her back into view. "Not after I get past these auditions. If I don't do them, I break my contract, and the studio will either kill the stage show or replace me. I did this for us."

"I know," she said. "I know you did and that scares me. Jason, I feel the same fear I always did. What if you get bored with the show and resent me because you're tied to it?"

He rolled her to her back and came down on top of her. "I have traveled the world. I've worked with some of the biggest names in show business. I have more money than I can ever spend. And I'm not happy. You are what makes me happy. You, Kat."

"Until you have to miss something big because of me."

"I already missed the only thing that mattered, and that was us. I want you to believe that right here and now, but I know you won't. I know it's about time and actions and all I can say is, I'm up for the challenge. And by the way, about me bringing you here tonight. I already told you I was staying here. I'm not leaving unless you kick me out." His lips quirked. "Besides, I have a personal goal of making love to you in every room and then doing it all over again." He glanced around. "Starting with the living room."

She slid her arms around his neck. "We do have all day tomorrow."

"I like how you think." He reached underneath her and unhooked her bra before tossing it away and melding her chest to his. "And I love how you feel. I love you, Kat."

Jason took his time showing her—one lick, one kiss, one pleasurable moment after another. If he had the chance, he'd spend a lifetime showing her. But he wasn't there yet—to the place when she'd give him a lifetime. He knew that, no matter how much she told him she was. He felt it, sensed it. He knew his KandyKat. He was going to have to do just what he'd vowed: be patient and prove to her just how well he really could love her.

IT WAS NEARLY dawn and Kat wasn't sure how long she and Jason had been talking, but she didn't want to stop. It felt like forever since she'd had her best friend to talk to.

"We should sleep," Jason said, absently stroking her shoulder. "We have to go find you a car tomorrow and then Sunday we're back in the whirlwind of preparation for next week's opening."

Kat propped herself up on her elbows. "You didn't comment on how well Marissa worked with Marcus last night."

"No, I didn't," he said. "That was risky, by the way."

"I had a feeling she and Marcus would hit it off," she replied with a smile.

He laughed. "I didn't even notice."

"I paired them up because I believe in Marissa," she said. "And because I thought throwing her into the spotlight with someone I knew would keep her from stumbling, both literally and proverbially."

"And you thought they'd make a good couple," he said, showing just how well he knew her.

"Yeah." She grinned. "I knew. And you should have seen how they were looking at each other."

"I saw you with him," he said, suddenly solemn. "He had you cornered by the door, and…"

"He was saying goodbye," she said, climbing on top of Jason, naked and determined to get him to focus on her, not Marcus. "And Marissa was waiting on him a few feet away." She reached behind her and stroked his cock. "I'm waiting for you, right here in bed."

He rolled her onto her back, spread her legs and settled between them.

"Always playing director, aren't you?" she teased.

"I'll let you direct later," he promised, lowering his head to kiss her.

"Oh. Wait. I forgot to tell you something I'm afraid you'll be upset about."

He stiffened. "What? Tell me."

"I have to fire Tabitha. She pulled something—"

He kissed her, a deep, passionate kiss that left her breathless for more. "It does nothing for my confidence," he half growled, "when you talk about Tabitha when I'm on top of you."

She laughed and held on to him tightly. "Well, you are my director. If you want me to be silent I'll be silent."

"Unless you're talking dirty to me, or telling me how much you love me, yes. Silence right about now would be ideal."

He pressed inside her, filled her, and Kat moaned rather loudly. "I'm not sure I can follow that direction."

"You never follow my direction," he said, "but somehow you always get it right."

"So do you—"

Jason drove slowly, deeply inside her.

She moaned again.

COME MORNING, OR rather mid-morning, Kat was in her favorite short Minnie Mouse robe, making coffee with a smile on her face. That smile grew when she heard Jason whistling his way down the stairs. It had been too long since she'd heard that whistle. He cursed as he passed the living room, and she knew why. She leaned on the counter and waited for him to enter.

Wearing nothing but a pair of blue-checkered pajama pants, he strolled into the kitchen. "Holy crap, Kat," he said. "We need to make a little deal."

She arched a brow. "Which would be what?"

"Don't go into the living room until I have time to get someone to clean your carpet and your couch." He glanced down at the muddy floor by the sliding glass door. "And to mop."

"I already looked," she said. "And I'm not freaked out. It'll clean."

"If it won't, we'll buy a new whatever we have to buy."

"I really am not worried about it." Material items weren't her thing.

He sauntered over to her. "You aren't. I know you aren't. You don't get all worked up over stuff and I've always loved that about you." He stopped in front of her and eyed the counter, grabbing the whipped cream. "You still use whipped cream in your coffee."

"Yes, I still do."

He picked her up and set her on the counter and she laughed, knowing where this was headed. "You are not putting whipped cream on me. I just took a shower."

"We'll take another together." He toyed with the can of whipped cream.

"No, Jason," she warned. "Don't you dare."

He tugged at her robe. The phone on the wall rang. Kat frowned. "Only my parents have that number. That can't be good. They'd call my cell, which is—"

"In the garage in my backpack, with mine," Jason said. "Make sure nothing is wrong and I'll go get them." He set her down on the ground and she rushed to the wall by the fridge and answered.

"Hello."

"Is everything okay?" her mother asked. "You aren't answering and I was worried."

"I'm fine, Mom. I had the day off and slept late. Are *you* fine?"

"I'm more than fine. I'm wonderful. Thailand is wonderful. We are loving life here."

"Good," Kat said, and nodded to Jason that everything was okay. He visibly relaxed and pointed to the garage before heading that way.

Her mother murmured something to someone else that ended with, "I'm going to ask. Just hold your horses." She spoke into the phone again. "So, Kat honey, big plans for your day off?"

"Isn't it the middle of the night there, Mom?"

"Well, yes. Yes, it is. We couldn't reach you, so we all just stayed up chatting. So…big plans or what?" She murmured something to someone else again.

Kat frowned. "Are you talking to Dad?"

"Yes," her mother confirmed. "And Jason's parents."

Jason walked back into the room and set his backpack on the table, which he unzipped.

"Is Jason there with you?" her mother asked.

"Yes," Kat answered. "Do his parents want to talk to him?"

"He's there," her mother said, sounding excited. Laughter erupted before Kat heard Jason's mother say, "I told you so." Next, Kat specifically heard her father say "you owe me fifty bucks."

Kat gaped. "Mother! Are they betting on whether or not Jason and I would be together?"

Jason laughed, a deep, sexy sound that always did funny, wonderful things to Kat. He joined her by the fridge and kissed her on the nose. "Let me talk to my father."

"We bet because we all want you back together," her mother said indignantly.

"Jason wants to talk to his father," Kat informed her mother. She handed the receiver to Jason.

He covered the receiver with his palm. "Why shouldn't they bet on us? I am." He winked and kissed her. "I think our phones are beeping with messages. Can you check my voice mail and make sure there isn't anything urgent? Thanks."

Her gaze touched his with understanding. It was a small request but it meant a lot. He was offering her an invitation back into his life in every possible way and it was surprisingly scary. Why? Why was it scary?

"Yes," she said. "Of course." She tried to move away,

but he caught her, a question on his too-handsome face. She loved this man. Why was she scared?

She rose onto her toes and kissed him. "Talk to my father. That's an expensive call you're just sitting on."

He hesitated and let her go, but she could see and feel the reluctance in him. "What's this about a bet, *Father?*" he asked in a playfully authoritative voice, as if he was the father, not the son.

Kat gave Jason her back as she grappled with, and tried to identify, whatever this was that she was feeling. She removed her purse from the bag and grabbed her phone from where Jason had set it down. She knew Jason's calls were probably more urgent than hers but she wasn't sure she was ready to listen to his.

She had a number of text message alerts from different people. First was Ellie, who'd let her know that Tabitha had come to her early this morning, claiming her innocence for whatever Kat had accused her of. I suggested strongly that she smarten up and start respecting you. Kat snorted.

"Like that is going to happen," she murmured and went on to the next message, which was from Marissa.

Kat glanced up, giving in to the urge to look at Jason, bringing his profile into view. She could tell that he was now talking to her father about some big investment return they'd both gotten. He leaned on the counter, handsome and shirtless, with his hair rumpled and sexy. But it wasn't his looks that made her heart beat a little faster. It was the way he was chatting with their families. The way he was truly a son to her parents. He fit her so well.

Kat inhaled and forced her attention to her phone, and read Marissa's message.

Marcus is the most amazing humble, sexy person. I like him too much. It's kind of scary. Need girl talk, please? Oh, and Tabitha called to apologize. Please don't fire her, Kat. I don't want to ruin anyone's career.

Kat smiled at that final part of the message. Marissa was a special person and Tabitha had no idea how lucky she was she'd picked Marissa as her target. Kat would give Tabitha another shot because of Marissa. Hopefully, Tabitha would finally see the light, and value her second—correction—her third, chance. Kat checked her call log and found four attempts from her parents to reach her. She set her phone down and picked up Jason's, an unmistakable flutter in her stomach. His call log also showed four missed calls from his parents. She could just imagine the four of them all sitting together, talking, laughing, and betting that their children were together in the same house. Then urging each other to try the calls again. They hadn't been worried. They'd been curious and hopeful.

The final call on Jason's phone was a number that Kat didn't recognize and it had gone to voice mail. She punched the button and listened to a studio executive telling Jason how impressive the show's television ratings had been. The studio wanted to talk contract renewal with Jason.

"I'm working on that," Jason said behind her. "Yes.

I am. I promise. I'll let you know when I've properly convinced her."

She squeezed her eyes shut, certain she knew what he was talking about, because she knew him so very well. *Marriage.* She wanted to marry Jason again. She wanted it very badly, but it had taken them years to get here, to a place where they were together again.

She wasn't going to rush things now. She needed to know they could find a way to make their careers and love mix. No matter what he'd claimed about his career not being important, it was. It mattered and it had to matter to make this work. He'd worked hard and he'd earned a call like that from the studio. She wasn't going to take that away from him.

Suddenly, Jason was behind her, having ended the call much sooner than she expected, but then it was the middle of the night in Thailand. "You okay, baby?" he asked, his breath warm on her ear.

Kat turned around, letting her hands settle on his chest, knowing now what was bothering her. "I need you to know that I don't blame you for us breaking up. We were young. We made mistakes. I probably didn't deal with what bothered me the way I should have, and certainly not like I would now."

"It wasn't your fault either, Kat," he said. "I would have done a million things differently myself. And believe me, I've replayed far too many of those things over and over in my head."

"That's just it," she said. "The past is the past. And Jason, I'm proud of your accomplishments. I'm so very proud. You of all people deserve success. You're the same humble person you always have been when I've seen plenty of others in your type of role get carried away with arrogance and ego. If you get a great opportunity, you have to take it, and I'll be excited with you, I promise."

"Kat—"

She kissed him. "It won't destroy us. We're both at different places in our careers and our lives. If you turn down something wonderful to make me happy, you won't make me happy at all. We'll work this out. We will. I know we can."

He studied her, his gaze keen. "What was on my voice mail that brought this on?"

"It wasn't the voice mail," she said, and then reluctantly admitted, "Not entirely. You had a call from a studio executive named Sabrina something. She complimented you on the show's ratings last night and wants to talk about your contract renewal for the television show."

He wrapped his arm around her waist. "I'm done with television, Kat. I've meant that every time I've said it. I want out of the spotlight. But yes, I want to direct. It's my second passion and you're my first." He brushed the hair from her eyes, his expression turning grim. "I'm dreading the day I have to get on a plane for auditions. I have the gut-wrenching fear that it will be the end of us."

"It won't," she promised. "I won't lie to you and say I'm not nervous about it, but it's necessary for all kinds of reasons. I think…I think we both need to know we can survive a separation and be okay. I need to know you'll be back. You need to know I won't be gone when you get here."

It would be the ultimate test of their relationship.

LATE THAT EVENING, Jason was in the passenger seat when Kat pulled her shiny new black BMW into her garage. They'd been all over the city, and he'd found her many excuses to keep driving more than a little adorable. Ending the night at their favorite Chinese restaurant had been a walk down memory lane in a good way, but then, that wasn't unexpected. He and Kat had far more good memories than they did bad.

Kat killed the engine and ran her hands up and down the steering wheel. "I can't believe I finally bought this car. I think I might have to sleep out here."

"Oh, no," he said, shaking his head. "I'm not sleeping in here, and you're sleeping with me." He tried to open his door. She locked it.

"Oh, no, you don't," she said, grinning. "You're my captive and I want to celebrate."

Jason arched a brow. "What have we been doing the rest of the day?"

"Celebrating," she said. "But not enough." She pushed her seat back and then climbed onto his lap, straddling him.

Jason laughed, and by the time she had that sweet backside of hers nestled against him, he was hard and more than willing to participate in her celebration.

She tugged his shirt up and pressed soft, cool hands against him with a scorching effect. He reached for her and she leaned back, a teasing glint in her eyes before she moved her finger back and forth.

"I'm the director of my celebration," she said. "You get kissed when I want to kiss you." She sighed and laughed. "Which would be now."

Jason chuckled, wrapping his arms around her, and

welcoming her mouth against his, her tongue's soft caress. She tasted like honey and tea, and like forbidden fruit no longer forbidden. He twined his fingers in her hair, deepened the kiss, hungry for more of that taste and more of her.

His cell phone rang and dang it, he knew who it was, and that he had to take it. He broke their kiss. "I have to answer."

"No, you don't," she said breathlessly, trying to kiss him again.

"I do," he said, struggling to remember why. "It's important."

Her hands were on his face, her lips a hairsbreadth from his. "You do know that you taking a call during my celebration is far worse than me talking about Tabitha while we were making love, don't you?"

"Oh, no," he said. "Not even close." He punched the answer key.

"It's Daniel," the man on the other line announced. Daniel worked with Jason's investment guy, Nick, and specialized in real estate.

"What do you have for me, Daniel?" Jason asked, trying to focus while Kat nibbled at his neck.

"The house has a good hundred-thousand in equity that we can invest smartly and turn into a larger sum. But the housing market is in the ground right now. Selling it will take a good six months to a year."

"I'll buy it," Jason said. "Then I get the tax write-off from two properties while you're re-selling it."

Kat drew back and gaped at him. "You took an investment call." She tried to wiggle off his lap and he laughed and held her, mouthing "I'll explain."

"Sure," Daniel continued, "We can buy it right away. You want me to contact the owner?"

"No," he said, trying not to laugh again as Kat crossed her arms in front of her, and glared at him. "I know the owners," Jason continued, "I'll handle contact. You guys just need to deal with the bank while I'm gone. And I'll give you the hundred grand in advance to go ahead and start investing."

Daniel whistled. "Your wish is most definitely my command."

Jason ended the call and Kat immediately blasted him. "We were…celebrating, and you took an investment call. Seriously, Jason? Maybe I don't know you because you never would have done that before."

He laughed hard. She glared harder. "Ask me why that investment was important," he ordered.

"I don't care about the investment."

"Not even if it was to help your parents."

She deflated instantly and then blushed and buried her face in his shirt. "Oh, no. I'm sorry."

He ran his hand down her hair. "I'm not." He pressed her against his lap, showing her what he meant. "You're sexy when you're mad."

She lifted her head. "While I might, ah, appreciate your method of complimenting me," she said, "I still feel like a jerk."

"I talked to your dad about selling their house and investing the money."

She leaned all the way back. "What? Why? You think they're staying in Thailand? Jason, I grew up in that house. I love that house."

"I'd pay it off and just give it to them, but they

wouldn't go for that. I had to be a little more creative to make this happen. I told them we weren't going to need two houses, but I needed a tax write-off so I'd keep my house and just let it sit. I explained that if they take it over, it saves me from paying a property management company to look out for it."

"And they didn't ask why you'd need a property management company when you were here in town?"

"Of course they did," he said. "I told them my schedule was too crazy to think about a second house."

"You really want to give up your house?"

"I'm home with you, Kat. Right here is fine by me." He grinned. "I do mean the house, not the car. I like the car, but it's a bit cramped."

Her fingers curled in his shirt, her gaze fixing on his chest. "I don't want a house that's mine. If we do this, Jason." Her lashes lifted. "If we really get back together—"

"We're already back together."

"I want something that's ours."

She couldn't have said anything that would make him happier. "Then we'll call my guy back and start looking."

"Not yet," she said. "Not until after the auditions, when we have solid time together."

Translation: not until she was sure he was really coming back to stay. "Kat—"

She kissed him. "I know you're coming back." She tugged his shirt upward, and he helped her pull it over his head. Then he watched her remove hers. Next came her bra. She sat there, looking gorgeously naked, with her full, high breasts and her pretty pink nipples begging for his mouth. He wanted her.

When she leaned in and pressed his hands to her breasts and her mouth to his, he wanted her even more. But he couldn't celebrate. Not until he was home to stay. No. Not until she believed he was home. And somehow he had to make that not about a place, but about them, about their relationship, about being anywhere in the world, and being home because they were together.

Together. That was the key, and one he couldn't turn, at least not until he was home for good, with the auditions behind them. The next seven weeks were going to feel like a lifetime.

18

THE WEDNESDAY NIGHT opening came with a full house and huge success. Despite Jason's departure the next day, and to of all places, Denver, Kat was happy. She stood backstage in the midst of a flurry of excitement with champagne and roses everywhere, and was not one bit surprised to find Marcus beside Marissa.

"Aren't you two a cute pair," Kat teased.

"Cute is really not what a guy wants to hear," Marcus said with a grimace.

"It works for me," Marissa said playfully, laughing up at him, and Kat didn't miss how the rather timid Marissa didn't seem timid with Marcus at all.

Jason joined them, not one bit of hesitation over Marcus's presence showing in his demeanor. "It's over. I feel like I just gave birth instead of Ellie."

"Great show, man," Marcus said. "You and Kat make a hell of a team."

Jason glanced at Kat. "Damn, he really is a nice guy. I'm gonna have to like him, aren't I?"

"Funny," Marcus replied. "I said the same thing

when Marissa was telling me about the way you treat the cast and crew."

Kat watched the two men shake hands and if it was possible to fall more in love with Jason, she did in that instant. So few people could be as accepting as Jason was about Marcus.

"And by the way, Marcus," Jason added. "We appreciate you helping us out the other night."

"I think me being here was in the cards," Marcus joked, and slipped his arm around Marissa to be clear about what he meant. Marissa blushed and Kat grinned at her.

"Kat!" someone yelled.

"Jason!" someone else shouted.

"Someone call 911!" came another cry.

Kat and Jason took off running toward the voices, which led them to the hallway outside the stage. Kat gasped as she found Ellie slumped over on the ground, with Tabitha of all people, kneeling beside her.

"She was dizzy and stumbled, and God, Kat," Tabitha said urgently, "I tried to catch her but I couldn't. She fell hard."

"I'm okay," Ellie said as Kat and Jason bent down beside her.

"No," Kat said firmly. "You are not okay. You've been working too much and you won't listen when I tell you to go home."

"You won't listen when I say I'm fine," Ellie said, trying to smile and failing. "Nag, nag, nag."

"Apparently, nagging is a skill I need to perfect," Kat said. "Or you wouldn't be on the floor."

"Get the hotel medic!" Jason shouted, standing up.

"Someone go find the medic and make sure 911 is on the way."

"I'll go find someone myself," Tabitha said, hurrying away.

"My husband can give you lessons," Ellie said, and then gasped with pain.

"What was that?" Kat asked, officially terrified for Ellie. She should have forced her to slow down.

"Same pains as last week," she said. "They're normal but… David, my husband. I need to call my husband."

And that alone told Kat that Ellie didn't think she was okay.

Jason squatted back down beside Ellie. "I'll call him, Ellie. What's the number?" He punched it in and then rubbed her arm. "Try to relax."

Ellie laughed in the midst of a frown. "Nothing like the floor for a good rest."

Kat drew Ellie's hand in her own, reading her fear through the humor. "You're not alone. You're not. I'm here and Jason is here." But Kat knew there was only one person that could possibly comfort Ellie right now, and that was her husband, who was in another state, and couldn't possibly get here tonight.

KAT AND JASON sat in the hospital room with Ellie, who was dehydrated and exhausted. She was also very lucky that she and her unborn baby were fine.

"I guess I won't be joining you for auditions tomorrow," Ellie said, trying to laugh but sounding like she might cry instead.

"The auditions don't matter," Jason replied. "What matters is you and your baby. The studio knows that."

"The studio is about money," Ellie insisted. "They can replace me for the season and work me out of the show. My contract is up this year."

"You have a contract though," Jason said. "They can't do that to you this year and you'll be on the live shows which are the ones that really matter."

"Read the fine print in your contract," she said. "I've read mine. They can replace me. They still have to pay me but it will be my final check."

"If they replace you over this," Jason asserted, "I'll be clear that I'm walking out."

"What?" Ellie gasped. "No, you will not. Kat, tell him that no, he is not."

"I'm not going back next season anyway," he said. "I think now would be a good time to tell them that. It will encourage them to hang on to you. They won't want to shake anything up too dramatically."

"Or it could make them think they have to make changes and so they might as well get it over with," Ellie said. "So that will do you no good. You can't quit. Do you know how much they will pay us for next season?"

"I don't care," he said firmly. "I'm done, Ellie." He shifted his attention to Kat and back to Ellie. "Not only is the spotlight not for me, I'm ready for roots and family. I'm ready to have my wife back."

Ellie's expression softened. "I understand that. I can see that in you. I don't want to care, either. I don't. The pressure feels too much sometimes. I want to have this baby and enjoy every second."

"Then have the baby and enjoy every second," Jason insisted. "This baby, this pregnancy, is an experience you can't relive."

"Choreographers do not earn the kind of paycheck I'm earning," she argued. "After another couple of years with this show, ratings be with us, my child, and my child's child, and that child's children, will be taken care of forever. How do I not make that happen, if I can?"

"You're not just a choreographer," Jason countered without missing a beat. "This show has let you demonstrate that. You, unlike me, are a television personality."

Ellie shook her head, utterly baffled. "How do you not see yourself as the star you are?" She glanced at Kat. "How does he not see it? Because I know he really doesn't."

Kat noticed Jason and she knew exactly why. She even went so far as to let herself, for the first time, believe it was true. "He knows what he wants and it's not the show," she said. Jason's eyes warmed with her obvious understanding, and she added, "He wants to direct. He doesn't want the spotlight." She refocused on Ellie. "But if you want to host, or judge, or whatever it is you want to do, you'll get to do it. There's always an opportunity for someone great and you *are* great, Ellie. I've worked with you. Many big-name stars have worked with you. Everyone sings your praises. The studio knows you're worth waiting for."

Ellie swallowed hard, looking pale and strained. "David wants to quit his job to be with me. I don't want him to quit. His career is important, too. What if he blames me for losing opportunities that may never come up again?"

Jason's cell phone rang and he glanced at it. "That's our producer checking on Ellie. I'll take it outside."

He headed out of the room and when the door was

shut, Ellie asked, "What do I do, Kat? I don't know how to make this work. What did you do when it was you and Jason?"

Everything wrong, Kat thought. She'd done everything wrong, and so how could she dare offer advice to Ellie, when she herself had failed in the same circumstances? But how did she sit back and watch Ellie make the same mistakes?

Kat let out a breath. "You go with your heart, not your ambition, and only you know where that is. But more than anything, you take care of yourself and you take care of your baby."

"I don't want to lose my baby or my husband, and I've worked so hard for my career. I thought I could have it all. Maybe that was overly ambitious."

"You can have it all," Kat assured her. "Just don't let yourself get wrapped up in the fear factor this business creates. You and your husband sit down and think about how to make your dreams come true, but don't forget that dreams are to be shared with the person, and people, you love. Don't make rash decisions. Talk to David. Really talk to him about your actions and how they impact both you and your family. Then listen to his thoughts, his feelings, his needs. Both of you have to voice your fears. Don't hold them inside. Don't assume the other one knows what they are."

The phone rang and Ellie answered it, and Kat quickly realized it was David. Kat stood up and headed to the hallway, exhausted to the bone, and didn't see Jason anywhere. It was three in the morning and Jason would be leaving that afternoon. She sank down into a chair. In only a few hours, he would get on a plane and fly to Denver.

Kat rested her elbows on her knees and dropped her face to her hands. This situation with Ellie was like reliving her past with Jason. She couldn't help but let her thoughts travel to the biggest regret of their relationship, and the one moment that had changed everything. To a hotel room and a phone call that had led to "the end."

Suddenly, Jason was there, kneeling in front of her. "We aren't them," he said, one hand stroking over her hair and the other resting on her leg, strong and comforting in a way only his touch could be.

She lifted her head, trailing her fingers over his cheek, feeling the anguish of her memories. "I should have come to Europe. We *wanted* to go to Europe."

He covered her hand with his and brought it to his lap. "We still can. We have the rest of our lives."

"I should have gone then."

"And I should have been confident enough in myself as a director to ask for a few days to think about the Europe project. I could have flown to you and talked to you in person. I should have made sure we decided our next move together."

"I guess we both have a lot of regrets. Ellie is going to have them, too, and I don't know how to help her."

"Be there for her. Give her someone to talk to who understands her situation. Not everyone does but you do. I'm not sure there's much else you, or I, can do for her."

"I'm scared that I'll tell her the wrong things and I'll be to blame for something else that goes wrong."

"Tell her that," he said. "Tell her you can share your

experiences, but she has to make her own choices." He gently cupped her face. "Just please remember that we aren't them. We've been there, yes, but we're here now, together, and we can choose to be better and stronger than our past. I need you to promise me that when I get on that plane, you won't forget that. It's the only way I'm going to be able to get on that flight."

"I'm okay," she said. "I'll be okay with this, Jason. *We're* okay."

"Kat!" came Ellie's shout from the room.

Jason and Kat were both on their feet in an instant. They rushed into the room and Kat brought a smiling Ellie into focus. "I have an idea!" Ellie declared.

Kat and Jason both let out a breath and joined Ellie by her bed. "Good gosh, woman," Kat chided. "Don't yell like that and scare me or I might need a bed rolled in here for me."

Ellie grinned. "Sorry about that. I just got really excited. I was talking to David and I was fretting that the studio would have guest judges fill in for me, and they'd all be pining for my job."

"You mean my job," Jason corrected. "I'm leaving the show."

She waved that off. "We'll see about that. Anyway. I said there was only one person that I not only thought would be a great judge, but that I knew didn't want my job. And that person is Kat."

"Me?" Kat repeated, stunned by the announcement. "I'm not a television personality."

"Welcome to my world," Jason said. "Neither am I, but I've made it work. I love the idea."

"We could change roles until the local filming begins for *Stepping Up,* Kat," Ellie added eagerly, sounding more excited by the second. "David is going to try to arrange to be here for the next six weeks, so he can help out, too."

Kat didn't know what to say. "I…no. That won't work."

"Why not?" Ellie asked as Jason arched a brow in question.

"Because…it won't work." Because she needed to know that she and Jason could survive this. He needed to know that, too. She needed to overcome this one last fear to say "I do" a second time. Distance had destroyed them once before. If it could do it again, it was best they found out now.

JASON PULLED KAT'S BMW into her garage right at four in the morning. He was bone tired and his flight left at three that afternoon, but sleep was the last thing on his mind. He glanced at Kat, who was curled on the seat with her eyes shut, only he wasn't sure she was sleeping. Or if she was, he was pretty sure it was to avoid talking. She hadn't made eye contact with him since Ellie had suggested she become a guest judge.

On their walk to the garage to get Kat's car, he'd gotten a call. By the time he got off the phone, Kat had snuggled into the seat, and was sleeping with her hand curled under her cheek. Later, he hit the remote to Kat's garage, watching the door rise, and thinking about car shopping with her a few days before.

She'd been adorably excited while they'd shopped. Even more excited when she'd been able to drive the new car off the lot. He pulled into the garage, a smile tugging at his lips as he thought of their celebration, and of her climbing into his lap in this very parking spot.

He put the car in Park and hit the remote to shut the garage. The door ground its way to a close, and still Kat didn't move. He sat there, not moving, just thinking. He'd paid for her car in cash, though she didn't know it. She thought it was financed. And it was, for all of a few hours.

He'd planned to make it a surprise engagement gift, but knew he had to get her to agree to put a ring on her finger before he could get her to really accept the car. He'd thought that was just a matter of getting past these auditions, but her complete rejection of the idea that she should judge in Ellie's place baffled him. He wasn't sure what to make of it. He was pretty darn sure though that it was somehow directly connected to his ability to get said ring on her finger.

Jason opened his door and rounded the vehicle to Kat's side of the car. She didn't twitch a muscle when he reached for her. He carried her inside and thought about her comment. *You're always picking me up.* Then his reply. *So you can't run from me.* Was she running from him? Was he fooling himself into thinking everything was going to work out?

He set Kat on her bed and went so far as to remove her shoes and cover her. Still she slept. She was exhausted, he knew. She'd been tireless for weeks and it had clearly all just hit her now.

Jason didn't lie down. He walked to the bathroom, cracked the door only slightly in case Kat called for him, and turned on the hot water. He pressed his hands on the sink and stared in the mirror. Directing had taught him that he could only do his best, and then what followed was what followed. Once something was on film, it was done, and he couldn't change it. He'd applied that rule to his life and it had served him well. Except with Kat. He replayed the past far too often. She was right. He had regrets.

He stripped down and stepped under the water, letting it pour over him, trying to relax, when suddenly the curtain was pulled back and Kat, naked and beautiful, joined him. She wrapped her arms around him.

"I don't want to go with you because I need you to know you can leave and I'll still be here. And I need you to know that I'm not the same person I was when we divorced. I'll understand. I'll go to Europe this time, Jason, or wherever life leads us."

"But you won't take the judge's job?"

"It hasn't even been offered."

"I can make it happen," he said. "I think you know that. I *want* to make it happen."

"Then how will you know that I'll be okay the next time you have to leave?"

"Don't you mean, how will *you* know?"

"No. Yes. I don't know."

"You're making this an obstacle course it doesn't have to be. You're scared, baby. I'm scared, too. Let's be scared together. Say you'll take the job."

She scraped her bottom lip, a fretful look on her face, but she nodded her acceptance. "Yes. Yes, I'll take it."

Jason wasn't sure if Kat had ever made him as happy as she did with those words. He held her in his arms and kissed her, having absolutely no intentions of sleeping, or allowing her to sleep, before he got on the plane later that day.

19

KAT WOKE CURLED at Jason's side, her head on his shoulder. She inhaled, drawing in the rich male scent that was so him, so perfect, so… Suddenly, she realized a cell phone was ringing and she blinked into sunlight. Sunlight. She sat straight up, ignoring her nudity. "What time is it?"

Jason pressed to his elbows, his hair a rumpled, sexy mess, his eyes heavy with slumber. "What's wrong? What's happening?"

The phone kept buzzing. Kat scrambled over Jason, and grabbed it from the nightstand, and in the process, she launched her bare backside in the air. Jason smacked it.

"Hey!" she yelled over her shoulder, noting the clock with a cringe.

"I will happily wake up this way every day of my life," he said, leaning up to kiss one cheek of her backside.

Kat snatched her phone and answered it. "Ellie. Hold

on a second." Kat covered the receiver and slid off Jason. "It's noon. We have three hours until you leave."

"Oh, crap," he ground out. "Say it isn't so."

"I wish I could." She didn't even remember how they'd ended up asleep when they'd vowed not to. They'd made love. They'd made love again. They'd… fallen asleep talking.

"Are you okay, Ellie?" Kat asked, watching Jason scramble off the bed to pull on a pair of boxers.

"I'm fine," she said. "David's here and I'm busting out of this place any minute now."

"You're not going to the auditions?" Kat asked.

Jason tossed his bag on the bed. "Surely not?"

"No," Ellie said and Kat shook her head to Jason's question as Ellie continued, "I'm released to work but the doctor here doesn't want me traveling and my regular doctor agrees. I'm supposed to limit my hours."

"You can't push it, Ellie," Kat chided. "We just talked about this."

"David got approval this morning to work here in Vegas from the production location for the live shows until we start filming. He'll be around if Ronnie needs him, too. He says he's happy to help if it will get me to slow down."

"Your own personal bodyguard," Kat said with approval. "I can see you enjoying that."

"Don't you know it," Ellie agreed.

"This is all good," Kat said. "It really is."

"I know," she chimed quickly. "And I do get carried away. It's better that I'll have David here to tie me down if needed." She laughed and Kat heard her add,

"I didn't mean that literally, David," before she spoke into the phone again. "I've told David that even if you aren't here, now that the show is together, I won't need to work around the clock. David's still waiting for a call back about you and I switching places."

"Jason talked to one of the studio executives at eight this morning," Kat said. "He thinks it's going to happen."

After a few more seconds of chatter, Kat said goodbye to Ellie and ended the call. Jason gave her an inquiring look. "This is all starting to sound too good to be true," Kat told him.

Jason zipped his bag and settled onto the bed, taking her with him. "Don't you think we deserve 'too good to be true' after everything we've been through?"

"Yeah," she said, running her fingers through his hair. "I do."

"The way I see it," he continued, the playfulness in his voice barely masking the rasp of desire in its depths. "I have an hour and thirty minutes to try my best to get enough of you to last through my Denver trip." He brushed his mouth over hers, slid his tongue past her lips and teased her with a quick taste of masculine spice before he added, "It's never going to be enough."

His kiss was passionate, deep, dragging her into escape. The last thing she remembered beyond pure bliss for at least an hour and twenty-nine minutes was thinking how hard it was going to be to watch him get on that plane.

KAT'S FEELINGS WERE in knots when she and Jason walked hand in hand through the airport and stopped in front of the security area. Thankfully though, due to the private, studio-owned plane that Jason was flying on, Kat was able to make it to this point in the airport. She'd take every extra second she could get with him. They had yet to receive studio approval for Kat to fill-in for Ellie and travel with Jason.

Jason dropped his baseball hat and sunglasses in a bin to be x-rayed. Both items were used as a disguise and meant to prevent unwanted attention. He'd grumbled the explanation when she'd inquired, and made his dislike of having to hide from the press evident. *I don't mind fans,* he'd said. *It's the paparazzi that drive me crazy.*

Kat watched Jason put his boots and belt back on, and tuck his glasses and hat into the bag he carried.

"Jason," she said. Anything else she might have added slid away, and they were lost in each other's eyes. Neither one of them made any attempt to move, and Kat felt like her chest was going to explode with the swell of emotion.

"I don't want to go," he said, his voice low, rough with his own dose of emotion. "I'm not going to go."

He meant it. She saw it in his face, heard it in his voice. He was going to do something crazy, like ruin his reputation with the studio. "I don't want you to go, but you have to." She took her hand in his, and tugged him along. "Let's go and get this over with so you can come home." A large clock hanging from above a desk at one of the gates caught Kat's attention. "You leave in ten minutes. We are really pushing it."

"Kat," he repeated, stopping near his gate and pulling her to face him, his hands on her shoulders. "I—"

"Sir," the attendant said. "We're ready to get you on board and prepare for takeoff. We have another stop on the way to Denver."

"I'll be right there," Jason said.

"You have to go," Kat urged. "They're waiting on you and we both know this is necessary. I'm fine, Jason. It's a few weeks that will protect your career. And in case you start thinking too hard on that plane, I don't think you're choosing your career over me, and I regret ever saying that to you. You're doing this for us. I know that."

A muscle in his jaw flexed. "I'm going to leave but I'm coming back."

"I know," she said, lacing her words with confidence, determined to be strong right up until the second he was on that plane and out of sight. Afterward, she was fairly certain that she was going to have her second meltdown, like the one when Marcus had shown up.

Jason kissed her, and it wasn't some proper public peck, either. He kissed her Hollywood style, with everything he had, wrapped her in his arms, and tasted her like a starving man who hungered for her and only her.

"I love you," he growled near her ear, and started walking away, as if he was afraid he wouldn't if he didn't go right then. Too quickly, he went out to the tarmac, and didn't look back.

Kat ran to the window to watch him walk toward the plane. Her eyes prickled. She could feel the tears burning to escape and she fought them. Jason stopped at the stairs and turned to her, waving when she knew he couldn't see her. But he knew she was there. She inhaled and she thought she was okay, but when he stepped onto that plane and disappeared again, the tears spilled down her cheeks. She backed up and sat down in a chair, burying her face in her hands to try and pull herself together.

JASON SET HIS bag on the leather seat of the luxury plane, but he remained standing, his hand on the overhead bin. He had his phone out, dialing the studio again. He got voice mail again.

Leaving Kat was crazy. In fact, why was he leaving her? Ellie would be here to look after things. Why the heck hadn't he thought of this several hours ago? There was no reason Kat couldn't come with him. They didn't need anyone's permission to be together. He hesitated, thinking of Kat's complicated obstacle course that required him to leave and come back, as if that proved they were going to make it.

He dialed his boss Sabrina again and left a message. "I'm chartering a plane to Denver," he said. "Don't worry, I'll make auditions. I'm taking Kat with me though, so whether you put her at the audition table or not, she's coming along for the trip. Ellie, her husband and Ronnie are covering the show." He hung up and grabbed his bag.

"Do you need me to put that somewhere for you?" a stewardess asked.

"No," Jason said. "I'm not staying. Feel free to depart without me." Jason was out of the plane and running toward the airport door in a flash.

He burst through the door, praying that Kat wasn't already gone. "Kat!"

"Jason!"

He spotted her in a seat with tears streaming down her face. "Baby," he said hurrying to her, tossing his bag on the ground, and dropping down on one knee in front of her. He wiped dampness from her cheeks. "Why are you crying? Don't cry. I don't ever want to make you cry like this."

"Because you're leaving," she said. "It's just hard. I... why aren't you on that plane?" She grabbed his arm, her eyes wide. "Go get on that plane." She tried to stand up.

Jason kept her in the seat. "I left, just like you said I had to. I didn't like it and you didn't seem to either. So, I came back. That exercise is done and over. We passed the test."

"Jason, you have to get on that plane. The studio—"

"I'm chartering a later flight," he said. "I'll make tomorrow's audition. And you're going to be on that plane with me if I have any influence at all. Ellie is here. There's no reason you can't come with me."

"But—"

He kissed her. "No 'buts' allowed. I want to show you something." He unzipped his bag and pulled out a velvet box, but kept it out of her sight. "I carried this with me to remind me of what waited on me at home, Kat. I planned to do this when the auditions were over, but I can't wait." He lifted the box and opened the lid to display a platinum ring that he'd had designed for her. It was shaped like a lily, the flower theme they'd had at their first wedding. "I need my wife back to share my life with. Marry me, Kat. You are, and have always been, the woman I love. Marry me in Europe. Marry me in the Elvis Chapel, or heck, let's find someone here in this airport who has the power vested in them, and let's get married now."

Kat hugged him tight.

"Please tell me that's a yes," he said, holding on to her, holding his breath at the same time as he waited for her reply.

"Yes, yes, yes," she quickly said, and leaned back, cupping his face and kissing him. "Of course, it's yes." She stared down at the ring and started crying again. "It's gorgeous. It's perfect. It's our flower."

Jason slipped the ring onto her finger. "I only have one other request," he said.

"Don't lose the ring?" she asked.

"That, too," he agreed. "But I was thinking more along the lines of don't divorce me again."

She laughed. "You're stuck with me this time. In fact, why don't we go find that airport preacher right now?"

He laughed and kissed her and they really did go look, but they had no luck. Instead, they spent the flight to Denver planning a wedding in Thailand, where they and their parents could bet on forever.

THREE MONTHS LATER, Kat stood in the empty house they'd purchased, having just returned from Thailand newlyweds yet again. Jason walked in the front door and set down a box. They were only a few miles from her old place, and close to his house that was now her parents'. Not that she thought they'd ever use it. They were in love with Thailand.

"The moving guys said they'd be here in half an hour," Jason announced.

Kat spun around in the center of the hardwood living room floor. "I love this place."

Jason laughed and wiggled an eyebrow. "You do know we'll have to test out every room in our own very special way?"

"Hmmm," she said. "I do like your way of breaking in a new house."

A car pulled into the driveway. "Is that the movers?" Kat asked, walking to the window, and then looking over her shoulder at Jason. "It's your agent, Jason. Oh. Wait. It's both our agents." With the ratings for season three of *Stepping Up* at an all-time high, the studio had been after both Jason, and unbelievably, Kat, to sign on as judges for the new season.

Jason joined her. "They're trying that ol' double team thing, I guess. This is Ellie's fault for leaving the show."

"She got her own reality show," Kat said. "I can't say I blame her for moving on."

"They're going to offer us ridiculous money," Jason said.

"Yeah," Kat agreed, glancing at him. "What do you want to do?"

"I want to make that independent film that I told you about. And I want you to try your hand at producing."

She wound her arms around his neck. "Then I say, let's make that movie."

Footsteps sounded on the porch and Jason grinned. "Want to teach them a lesson about surprising us like this?"

She shook her head. "Oh, yeah. What did you have in mind?"

He kissed her, a hot wild kiss that was sure to

make even a grown man blush, or in this case, two grown men.

Life really was too good to be true, Kat thought.

* * * * *

Sparkling Christmas kisses!

Bryony's daughter, Lizzie, wants was a *dad* for Christmas
and Bryony's determined to fulfil this Christmas wish.
But when every date ends in disaster, Bryony fears she'll
need a miracle. But she only needs a man for
Christmas, not for love…right?

Unlike Bryony, the last thing Helen needs is a man! In her
eyes, all men are *Trouble*! Of course, it doesn't help that as
soon as she arrives in the snow-covered mountains, she
meets Mr Tall, Dark and Handsome *Trouble*!

www.millsandboon.co.uk

1112/MB391

Come home to the magic of
Nora Roberts

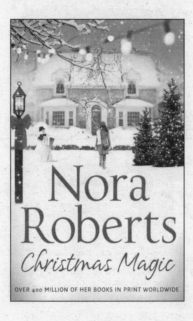

Nora
Roberts
Christmas Magic

OVER 400 MILLION OF HER BOOKS IN PRINT WORLDWIDE

Identical twin boys Zeke and Zach wished for
only one gift from Santa this year: a new mum!
But convincing their love-wary dad that their
music teacher, Miss Davis, is his destiny and
part of Santa's plan isn't as easy as
they'd hoped…

The World of Mills & Boon®

There's a Mills & Boon® series that's perfect for you. We publish ten series and, with new titles every month, you never have to wait long for your favourite to come along.

Blaze®

Scorching hot, sexy reads
4 new stories every month

By Request

Relive the romance with the best of the best
9 new stories every month

Cherish™

Romance to melt the heart every time
12 new stories every month

Desire™

Passionate and dramatic love stories
8 new stories every month

 *Have Your Say*

You've just finished your book.
So what did you think?

We'd love to hear your thoughts on our
'Have your say' online panel
www.millsandboon.co.uk/haveyoursay

- Easy to use
- Short questionnaire
- Chance to win Mills & Boon® goodies

Visit us Online | Tell us what you thought of this book now at
www.millsandboon.co.uk/haveyoursay

YOUR_SAY